Ghost in the Flames

Jonathan Moeller

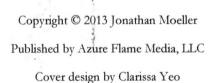

ISBN: 1489545344
ISBN-13: 978-1489545343

EPIGRAPH

'You are a god, and never have I heard anything more divine!' If this thought were to gain possession of you, it would change you as you are, or perhaps crush you.

-Friedrich Nietzsche

OTHER BOOKS BY THE AUTHOR

Child of the Ghosts

Ghost in the Flames

Ghost in the Blood

Ghost in the Storm

Ghost in the Stone

Ghost in the Forge

Demonsouled

Soul of Tyrants

Soul of Serpents

Soul of Dragons

Soul of Sorcery

Soul of Skulls

Soul of Swords

CHAPTER 1
PYRES IN THE NIGHT

Caina thought she might have to do some killing, so she dressed for business.

In many tales, the Emperor's Ghosts were always women of perilous beauty, clad in skin-tight black leather. Caina thought that ridiculous. Black leather made too much noise, and reflected too much light. Instead she wore loose black clothes, black gloves, and a black mask that concealed her face. Around her waist went a leather belt of throwing knives and other useful tools, and she secured a heavy dagger in each of her boots.

Next came the cloak.

Light as air and blacker than night, it was a wondrous thing. Halfdan had told her that only the Ghosts knew the making of these cloaks, fused together of spider silk and captured shadows. It mingled and blurred with the shadows around her, and when she pulled up the cowl, it made her face all but invisible.

Last, the ring.

It was a man's signet ring, heavy and thick; she wore it on the first finger of her left hand, beneath the glove. It was old and nicked, the sigil worn smooth with use. Unlike everything else Caina carried, it could not be used as a weapon, nor did it have a practical use.

But she wore it anyway.

###

Night lay over the city of Mors Crisius, and Caina glided from shadow to shadow.

Long ago, she had been told, the city had been prosperous, built

1

around the tomb and mortuary cult of some long-dead Emperor. But the city's harbor had worn away, bit by bit, and the merchant ships went instead to Rasadda. Mors Crisius had become a sleepy town of fishermen, farmers, and mortuary priests, and now only pirates and smugglers made use of its decaying harbor.

Along with worse people.

Caina stopped and stared at Vanio's townhouse.

It looked like the townhouse of a thousand other prosperous merchants. White walls, a roof of fired red tiles, a paved courtyard ringed within a low wall. It did not look at all like a home of a man who would kidnap fellow Imperial citizens and sell them as slaves.

But, then, appearances lied. Caina knew that well. She took a deep breath and went to it.

She sprang up, caught one of the ornamental metal spikes crowning the wall, pulled herself up, and waited. The courtyard lay quiet, its flagstones worn and smooth, a fountain bubbling by the gate. One of Vanio's watchmen strolled towards the house. He wore a studded leather jerkin, his belt heavy with sword and dagger. The watchman opened the main door and vanished into the house. No other guards emerged.

Beneath the cowl and the mask, Caina's lip curled. Vanio's security was barely adequate to keep out common thieves, let alone one of the Emperor's Ghosts. No doubt Vanio thought himself safe from the retribution his crimes had earned.

Well, that might change, tonight.

She counted to three hundred, but no other watchmen appeared, and she saw no signs of life from the house. Caina dropped into the courtyard, the black cloak pooling around her. A single light gleamed in one of the windows, no doubt where Vanio's guards sat earning their keep. She crossed the courtyard and tried the front door. It was locked, of course, and the lock was a fine one, but Caina had seen worse. She knelt, pulled some tools from her belt, and set to work.

Her skill made short work of the lock. Caina pushed the door open as slowly as she could. Within she saw a darkened atrium, the floor covered in an expensive mosaic, but heard nothing.

The smell hit her at once.

Caina slipped into the atrium, pulling the door closed behind her. The smell was stronger in here, thicker and heavier. For a moment Caina thought that the house had caught fire, but she saw no smoke, no signs of panic. She had never smelled anything quite like it. It was a burnt, greasy odor, almost like fat dripping upon a fire. Or like burnt pork.

Burnt pork? Were the watchmen trying to cook something?

Caina shook her head and crept into the townhouse, her boots making no sound against the floor. She glanced around, and noted that Vanio had done quite well for himself. Like so many of these provincial merchants, he had done his utmost to copy the High Nighmarian style. The mosaic beneath her feet showed the Emperor Crisius triumphing over Corazain the Ashbringer. Freestanding marble statues littered the halls, along with busts resting in niches, all copies of famous artworks in the capital. The statuary alone must cost twice what every fisherman in Mors Crisius earned in a year, and the rare woods in the doors had come from the forests of Varia Province on the other side of the Empire of Nighmar.

Someone like Vanio could not make that kind of money doing something honest.

Caina crept through a dining room, the gleaming table set with polished silver, and found the stairs. She had reached the landing when she heard the voices, saw the gleam of light. Caina sank into a corner, her cloak blending with the shadows, and waited. The voices came louder, and Caina realized that two men stood at the top of the stairs, one of them holding a lantern. The watchmen, most likely.

They were speaking in Saddaic. Fortunately, she knew the tongue.

"What in hell's name is that stink?"

"Damned if I know," said a second man. "You did the last walk. Are they cooking anything?"

"It's past midnight! All of Vanio's servants are lazy dogs. You'll not see any of them out of bed before dawn."

"Something must be burning."

"I told you," said the first man, irritated, "I already walked around the house. I didn't see any smoke. The house is not on fire."

"Then why is the smell getting worse?"

The first man spat. "Must be coming from one of the inns. Cooking a pig for tomorrow's stew or something. What of it? It's no concern of ours."

"The nearest inn's a half-mile away! Something's burning, I tell you. Maybe we should wake old Vanio."

"Are you mad? You know how that greedy bastard loves his sleep. Wake him now and we'll be out of work before dawn. Do you want to go back to work on a fishing boat? Or into the Legions? No, we'll do nothing, and that's that."

"I still think something's burning," said the second man. "What if something is on fire? Do you think Vanio'll keep us on if we let his house burn down?"

"Damn you, nothing's on fire," said the first man. "You worry worse than an old woman. But if it'll shut you up, we'll go look." Boots clicked against the stairs.

Caina flung herself backwards, rolled over the landing's railing, and ducked under the massive table. She slipped a throwing knife from her belt, the blade tucked against her gloved hand to hide its gleam. Two of them.

3

Not good. She adjusted her grip on the blade and braced herself.

The watchmen came down the stairs, and Caina saw that there were in fact three of them. The third man, older than the other two, hadn't opened his mouth. The first watchman carried a lantern, and all three wore studded leather jerkins and carried swords and daggers on their belts.

For a moment Caina thought they would see her. The watchman lifted his lantern, throwing shadows across the dining hall, and Caina remained motionless. They walked past her, and their eyes glanced over the table without alarm. Caina blinked in surprised relief. She heard them open the front door and walk into the courtyard. Apparently they hadn't noticed the opened lock.

Caina hurried up the stairs, cloak flowing behind her. The stairs opened into a narrow upstairs hallway, with two doors on the left and one on the right. She had spied out Vanio's townhouse yesterday, and knew that the left doors opened into the study and the solar, while the right door lead to Vanio's bedchamber.

The burnt smell was very strong up here, almost overpowering. The air almost tasted of it, even through her mask. No wonder the watchmen had complained. Caina crossed the hall, listened at the study door for a moment, and swung it open.

The study shared the townhouse's ostentatious opulence. The shelves held the sort of works an educated man was expected to own; histories of the Nighmarian Empire, lives of the Emperors, treatises on oratory and virtue. A thin layer of dust covered most of the books, except for a trio of weighty histories in the corner. She pushed aside the books, and saw the gleam of a safe built into the wall.

Caina grinned, produced her tools, and got to work. The safe, like the lock on the front door, was excellent work, but Caina had seen better. After a short time, she tugged and the door swung open. Only one thing lay in the safe, a battered merchant's ledger, worn with much use. Caina took the ledger, carried it to the window, and flipped through the pages.

Her mouth tightened into a hard line. The ledger detailed Vanio's inventory of slaves. It seemed that he specialized in buying children at cut-rate prices from impoverished peasant farmers, and selling them at an enormous profit to the Carthian and Alqaarin merchants who dealt in such things. He also turned a substantial profit dealing in artworks, old Saddai and Kyracian artifacts and the like, but the bulk of his money came from selling children. Caina closed the ledger, her hand twitching towards the knives in her belt. A short detour on her way out, a quick slash of her knife, and the villainous scum would die choking in his own blood...

No. Not yet. Halfdan had only wanted evidence, not blood. And the Emperor had declared slaving a crime against the Empire, and the penalty for a crime against the Empire was worse than anything Caina had time to inflict upon Vanio now. She closed the safe, replaced the books, tucked the ledger under her arm, and made for the door.

She stepped into the hallway just in time to see the watchmen come up the stairs.

Caina froze in the doorway. For a moment she thought the watchmen wouldn't see her. They were arguing about the smell again, and none of them even glanced towards the study door.

"I'm telling you," said the man in the lead, "that damned smell is worse! Where the hell is that coming from?" He looked around, glancing at the study door.

His eyes got wide.

"Gods!" he said, fumbling for his sword, "what the hell is…"

Caina stepped forward and flung a knife, her foot forward, her arm thrown back, her back arched. Her entire body snapped like a bowstring. The knife hurtled forward and buried itself in the man's throat. He fell to his knees, gagging. The other two watchmen leapt past the fallen man, yanking their swords from their scabbards. Caina threw the heavy ledger. It caught the older man in the face, and he stumbled back with a curse, bouncing off the door to Vanio's bedchamber.

The last man ran at her, his sword a silvery blur.

Caina stepped back and yanked the daggers from her boots. She did not want to take the man in a fair fight. She had trained with short blades for years, along with the open-handed fighting style favored by the Ghosts. She was quick and agile, but she was not a large woman, and she simply did not have the raw strength to fight toe-to-toe with most men.

No matter. She had learned long ago that to fight fair was to lose.

The sword came towards her head, and Caina caught it in a cross-parry between her daggers, her arms straining with the effort. Her left foot lashed out and slammed hard into the man's knee. He gasped with pain, leaning forward, and Caina disengaged and whirled to the side. The watchman stumbled forward, and as he did Caina slashed with her right hand. The blade opened the artery in his neck, and the watchman toppled, blood spurting between his fingers as he vainly tried to stem the flow.

Caina turned just in time to meet the older, silent watchman's attack. He came at her with both sword and dagger, and he knew how to use his weapons. Caina retreated before his advance, her blades working to beat aside his attacks. She sent a knife spinning for his face, but a flick of his sword sent the blade clattering to the floor. Sooner or later he would pin her against a wall, and that would be that.

In a fair fight.

Caina reached up and undid the black silver brooch that pinned her cloak. It came loose and dangled from her right hand, a drape of shadow billowing from her arm. The watchman stopped, frowning at her, and Caina

5

flung the cloak at his face. He sneered and slashed his dagger to knock the cloak aside.

But mundane steel passed through the shadow-spun cloak without touching it, and the black cloth fell over him. He snarled in fury and clawed at his face, his sword sweeping back and forth before him. Caina ducked below the waving sword and drove her dagger into his gut. The watchman screamed and fell to his knees, the cloak slipping from his face, and Caina dragged her blade across his throat.

He joined the others on the floor a few seconds later, his blood pooling across the tiles.

Caina retrieved her cloak and stood, breathing hard. She stared down at the bodies, and the blood staining the floor and walls. They would have killed her, and not thought twice about it. Yet her stomach still twisted with nausea. Suddenly she was eleven years old again, and she saw the men lying sprawled on the floor of her father's library, their glassy eyes staring at the ceiling...

Later. The noise might have woken the servants. And there was no way Vanio could have slept through the racket. She had to get out of here now. Caina retrieved her knives, picked up the dropped ledger, and started for their stairs.

And stopped.

The burnt smell was stronger. Much stronger. Almost overpowering. Caina turned, puzzled. She saw that the door to Vanio's bedchamber stood partway open. For a moment she thought Vanio himself had opened it, but the door must have been knocked ajar during the fight.

The burnt smell poured out through the open door.

Caina hesitated for a heartbeat. She ought to get out of the townhouse, now, before someone discovered the bodies. Yet that smell. Had Vanio taken to burning pork in his bedchamber? It made no sense, and Caina did not like things that made no sense.

She pushed the door open the rest of the way and glided into the bedchamber.

If the townhouse was opulent, the bedchamber was palatial. Her boots sank into a rich, thick carpet. Tapestries hung from the walls, and the wooden furniture gleamed. A massive double bed stood in the center of the room, draped in curtains. The smell was very bad in here, almost overpowering.

It was coming from the bed.

Again another memory from that awful day came to her, as she crossed her father's study, her heart pounding with terror, towards the chair at his desk...

Caina shook aside the memory. She crossed the room, flung open the curtains, and found the source of the awful stench.

Vanio himself lay sprawled across the silken sheets.

Or, rather, what was left of Vanio.

His corpulent body had been reduced to a twisted mass of black char, his fingers curled into shriveled claws, his mouth yawning in an eternal scream, his eyes and nose blackened pits. His teeth seemed shockingly white in the black ruin of his face. The smell rolled off his charred flesh in nauseating waves. Grease seeped from red cracks in his torso, staining into the silken sheets.

Impossible.

Caina stepped back, staring at the gruesome corpse. Vanio looked as if he had been roasted atop a pyre, or burned at the stake. Yet she saw no fire damage to the bed or the room, no smoke stains on the walls. Had he been burned elsewhere and carried here? That made no sense either. Caina had been able to sneak into the townhouse, but she doubted a pair of men carrying a charred corpse could have managed the same feat.

Her mouth tightened. That left only…

"Murder!" shrieked a woman's voice from the hallway. One of the maids, no doubt. "Murder! Murder! Master Vanio!"

Time to go.

Caina tore the curtain from the bed, wrapped her fist in it, and smashed the window. Leaded glass fell in a rain to the courtyard below. She threw the ledger out the window, and then went through herself, finding easy footholds in the townhouse's stonework. More lights came on in the windows, and Caina heard more shouts, followed by a shrill scream from the broken windows.

No doubt the poor maid had found Vanio's corpse.

Caina dropped into the courtyard, retrieved the ledger, and scrambled over the wall. More screams and panicked shouts came from the house, but it didn't sound as if anyone had spotted her. Caina had only wanted to get in and out with Vanio's ledger, and she hadn't wanted to kill anyone. How had things gone so wrong?

Well. She hadn't planned on finding a charred corpse, for one thing.

Caina broke into a full run, the cloak billowing out behind her like a living shadow.

CHAPTER 2
ARK

A run across Mors Crisius took Caina to the Caravaners' Inn.

It sat on one side of the city's dusty caravanserai, a rambling pile of whitewashed walls, squared timbers, and red clay roofing tiles. The place could have held two hundred men with ample room to spare. Of course, caravans rarely came through the city now, and hardly anyone stayed at the Caravaners' Inn.

Halfdan liked it that way. When they had come to the city a month past, he had bought the Inn from its previous owner, and it now served as the Ghosts' local headquarters.

Caina hurried across the dark, dusty square, passed the Inn's closed front doors, and came to a small door in the back. She rapped twice on the door with the handle of her knife, then thrice, and then twice more. Nothing happened for a few moments. Then an iron plate rattled aside. A thin shaft of firelight stabbed into the darkness.

It gleamed on the razor-edged tip of a crossbow quarrel.

"Sign?" rasped a man's voice, low and harsh.

"There are Ghosts in the shadows," said Caina, reciting the countersign in High Nighmarian, the formal language of the Imperial court, "and let the tyrants tremble in their beds, for the shadows are ever watchful."

The heavy door swung open.

A hulking man stood on the threshold, his face half-hidden beneath locks of greasy gray hair. His scarred arms were heavy with muscle, and he carried a massive crossbow drawn and ready. He stared at her for a moment, eyes glittering beneath his lank hair, and then jerked his head.

"Halfdan," said Caina, stepping inside.

"You're late, girl," said her circlemaster, closing the door and redoing the locks. He switched to the common Caerish tongue. "I expected you back an hour past."

"There were complications," said Caina in the same language.

"There are always complications," said Halfdan. "Did you get the evidence?"

Caina held up the ledger. Halfdan took it, flipped through the pages, and nodded to himself once. "Good. Very good. This is just what we need. When some anonymous fellow takes this evidence to the magistrate, Vanio will go to the sword for his crimes."

"That will be unnecessary," said Caina.

Halfdan stared at her for a moment. "I happened to hear the alarm bells in the mortuary temple ringing a short time ago. Murder, I would guess. Did you have something to do with that?"

Caina sighed, drew back her hood, and nodded.

"Is Vanio dead?"

"Yes."

Halfdan's breath rasped through his nostrils. "I told you not to kill Vanio. With proper inducement the magistrate would have made an example of him. Now the people will think that a business rival murdered him, or that the slavers turned on him. Where is the justice in that?"

"I didn't kill Vanio," said Caina, pulling off her mask.

"Who did you kill, then?" said Halfdan. "You killed someone. I can see it in your face."

"Some of the watchmen," said Caina. She shook her head. "I got sloppy. I should have just gone out the window, but I ran into them in the hallway."

Halfdan scowled. "So Vanio yet lives, then? And now he is warned to our presence! We cannot spy for the Emperor if we reveal ourselves."

"No," said Caina. "Vanio was dead when I found him."

"Dead?" said Halfdan, surprised. "How? I saw him walking the streets this very afternoon. Someone got to him before we did?" He scowled suddenly, and leaned towards to her. "You smell...burnt."

"He was burned to death," said Caina, voice soft.

Halfdan blinked, and then his face went very still. Caina had trained under him, had worked under him for years, and she knew that meant trouble.

"Burned?" he said.

"Burned," said Caina. "It looked as if he had been roasted over a fire for hours. I don't understand it. There was no fire damage to the room, no smoke damage. Yet it didn't look as if his corpse had been carried..."

"It looked as if he had been burned to death right there," said Halfdan, "but the room showed no damage. Is that it?"

"Yes," said Caina, "how did you know?"

Halfdan lifted a scarred hand. "Wait." A flicker of worry went through his face. "You will tell me everything. But with a clear head. I don't want you to forget any details." He beckoned, tucking the crossbow under one arm. "Come."

Caina followed him down the narrow hallway. They went down a flight of stairs to the Inn's common room, its ceiling supported by thick wooden pillars. Casks of wine rested against the stone walls, while wine bottles stood in neat racks, and a fire crackled in a cavernous stone hearth. Caina sank wearily into a wooden chair, while Halfdan picked up a pair of goblets and crossed to one of the casks.

"What will you have?"

"I don't care," said Caina. "So long as it's mixed." Halfdan opened one of the casks and began filling the goblets. Caina did not know what Halfdan had done before he had joined the Emperor's Ghosts, but she had a strong suspicion that he had been a vintner. He knew more about wine than any man she had ever met.

She did not know how his old life had ended and his new life as a circlemaster of the Ghosts had begun, but the scars on his arms suggested that experience had not been pleasant.

Nor had Caina's.

"Mixed?" said Halfdan, cutting into her thoughts. "That ruins the palate."

"Mixed," said Caina.

"You brood too much, girl."

"I cannot argue. And alcohol makes me brood. So mixed wine."

"Suit yourself," said Halfdan. He handed her a goblet. Caina took it and drank. It did feel cool and pleasant against her throat, and the aroma helped drown out the stench of burned flesh that still clung to her.

"Thank you."

"Now," said Halfdan, settling into another chair. "Tell me everything. Leave nothing out."

She told him. She described the townhouse, the watchmen, the safe and the ledger, and the sharp, vicious fight in the upstairs hallway. Halfdan listened without interrupting, and at last she came to Vanio's charred corpse.

"So you could smell it the entire time?" said Halfdan.

"Yes."

"Recent, then," said Halfdan. "And no damage to the room?"

"No," said Caina. "He was a big man. Three hundred pounds, at least. Yet he'd been burned down to a husk. A fire like that should have reduced that house to ashes. And yet there weren't even smoke stains on the walls."

"So his body was moved into the room, then."

"No," said Caina again. "No. There were no char marks on the floor." She frowned, watching the wine ripple within the goblet. "And he had been...cooked. There was grease pooling beneath him, staining the sheets. I did not see any grease on the floor."

Halfdan grunted, took a long swallow of wine. "Could it have been cleaned up?"

Caina scoffed. "That carpet he had on the floor? It would take a dozen maids all day to clean that carpet. I don't see how it could have been cleaned. Especially if Vanio had only been dead for a few hours."

"Very well," said Halfdan. He glanced at the door, then back at her. "Then we have a man burned to death in his bed, with no damage to the bed or the room, and no signs that the body was moved. How, then, was Vanio killed?"

Caina stared at the fire, rolling the goblet in her fingers.

"I don't know," she said at last.

"Think it through. Have I not always told you that the mind is sharper than any blade?"

Caina thought for a moment. "Sorcery." Her voice hardened with contempt. "A brother of the Imperial Magisterium."

"But have you ever seen a magus do something like this?" said Halfdan. "Or even heard of it?"

"No," said Caina. She had seen magi use their arts to dominate the minds of others, to lift boulders with a thought, to cloak themselves in illusion and ward themselves from all harm. And to do worse things, but nothing like what had happened to Vanio. "No. The magi are villains, cowards, liars, and murderers, but I've never heard of a magus using fire. Isn't that one of the arcane sciences forbidden to them?"

Not that such a restriction would ever stop them, of course. She kept her voice level, but her thumb rubbed the heavy signet ring through her glove.

"So if the magi didn't kill Vanio, who did?" said Halfdan.

"I don't know," said Caina again.

"Then it is our task to find out," said Halfdan. "The Emperor himself has commanded it of us."

"The Emperor?" Caina sat up a little straighter. "Why should the Emperor care about some wretched slave merchant?"

"Vanio's death is not an isolated aberration," said Halfdan. "Do you know the city of Rasadda?"

"I've never been there, but I know of it," said Caina. She thought for a moment. "The capital of the Saddai Province. A week's ride east of here, along the coast road. Shorter by ship. It used to be the capital of the old Saddai kingdom, before the Saddai became part of the Empire." She frowned. "During...the War of the Second Empire, I think. In fact, old

Crisius was the Emperor who conquered them. They built this city around his tomb and mortuary temple, didn't they?"

Halfdan nodded. "They did. And over the past year, twenty people have been found dead in Rasadda."

Caina stared at him.

"All of them burned to death," said Halfdan, "in much the same circumstances as you found Vanio. No trace of a fire, no sign that the bodies were moved, and yet still they were burned alive. You can see why the Emperor might take an interest."

"Twenty people?" said Caina. "How is that possible?"

"We don't know," said Halfdan. "The Ghost circle in Rasadda became suspicious, and sent word to the Masters in the capital, asking for assistance. You will be that assistance, girl."

"Me?" said Caina. "Why?"

"Because you are good at finding things out," said Halfdan, "and no one knows how or why these people have been killed. Sorcery of some sort must be involved, but we don't know what kind."

"The Magisterium," said Caina. "It's plain enough. Some rogue magus dabbling in forbidden arts. It's happened before, and it will happen again."

"Unlikely," said Halfdan. "Have you ever heard of an order called the Ashbringers?"

Caina frowned. "Yes. I..."

The door to the Inn's common room swung open.

Halfdan had his crossbow leveled before Caina even had time to blink. "Sign?"

The newcomer stopped, and Caina took a good look at him, her hand slipping beneath her cloak to a knife. The man looked like a killer, his face grim and weathered, his mouth a hard line, his hands marked with faint scars, his balding hair close-cropped. He wore a ragged red tunic, trousers, and worn boots, and a broadsword hung from his belt.

His eyes glittered like ice, or frosted steel, and Caina saw no fear in his face. Then his eyes met hers. For a moment the color drained from his face, and he took a half-step forward. Then he stopped, still staring at her, and something like desolation sank into his grim face.

"Sign?" said Halfdan. "I'd really prefer not to shoot you. The blood would take forever to mop up."

There are Ghosts in the shadows," said the man, speaking High Nighmarian with a heavy Caerish accent, "and let the tyrants tremble in their beds, for the shadows are ever watchful."

"You're late. But good enough," said Halfdan, setting the crossbow aside.

"That gets tiresome," said the man in Caerish, stepping forward. He had excellent balance, and Caina guessed he knew how to use that

12

broadsword. "You know who I am."

"Protocol is protocol," said Halfdan, "and you should have come through the back door. You're lucky I didn't shoot you on sight." He gestured at the casks. "Wine?"

"Do you have any word?" said the man. "And news at all?"

"No," said Halfdan. "I'm sorry."

The man nodded, his expression unchanging, and crossed to the wine casks. He filled a goblet and joined them at the table. His eyes flicked to Caina, cold and sharp, and then moved on, dismissing her.

Caina wondered what that had been about.

"You may call this man Ark," said Halfdan. "He is a member of the Ghost circle in Rasadda, and will assist us." He gestured at Caina. "For reasons that will soon become clear, there is no good reason for you to know this young woman's name. She is a Ghost as well, of nightfighter rank, and you may call her the Countess Marianna Nereide."

Caina outranked him. Ark's left eye twitched, once, but he said nothing. She knew the name Marianna Nereide, as well; she had masqueraded as the Countess in the past, spying for the Ghosts.

"Now, Countess," said Halfdan, "you were telling me about the Ashbringers."

A faint frown flickered across Ark's face, but he remained silent.

"I know very little," said Caina. "Nothing more than what I have read about the history of the Empire, and what you told me about them. They were a band of sorcerer-priests, and they worshipped the Saddai god. The Living Flame, I think. Fire fueled their sorcery, and the Ashbringers were loathed for their brutality. They…tried to enslave all the world, but the Emperor founded the Magisterium to fight their sorcery, and the Ghosts to spy on them, and old Crisius wiped them out below the walls of Rasadda."

"Very good," said Halfdan.

Caina shook her head. "That's ancient history. Centuries gone. What does it matter? Does the Emperor think some Ashbringer has killed these people?"

"We don't know," said Halfdan. "But the Emperor wishes us to find out. Certainly the deaths match the ancient descriptions of the Ashbringers' spells. If some zealous follower of the Living Flame has rediscovered the Ashbringers' arts, the Empire itself could be in danger. The magi of the Magisterium are corrupt and wicked, but at least they do not practice forbidden arts, at least not openly. The Ashbringers did, and if the histories are correct, they were outright madmen, and murderous madmen at that." He shrugged. "Certainly they should remain in the dust of history."

"If only the Magisterium could join them there," said Caina. Ark gave her another appraising glance, but he remained silent. "But I am doubtful. The Magisterium governs the arcane sciences in the Empire, and they do not suffer rival practitioners. If some fool tried to become an Ashbringer, the magi would kill him within a month."

"You do not understand, Countess," said Ark, voice cold and soft. "The Ashbringers are gone, but the Saddai still worship the Living Flame, and they do not love the Empire. If someone appears, claiming to wield the powers of the Ashbringers…"

"Revolt," said Halfdan.

"Then what must we do?" said Caina.

"You will go to Rasadda and find the truth," said Halfdan.

"And if we do find this killer?" said Caina.

Halfdan's smile was cold, almost wolfish. "You know what must be done. And if the killer is indeed a practitioner of sorcery, I think you will enjoy doing it."

"Yes," said Caina, gazing back into her wine. For a moment rage filled her, such rage that she wanted to fling the goblet against the wall, but she closed her eyes and mastered herself. "Yes, I think I will."

"This is what you shall do," said Halfdan. "In three days' time a merchant caravan leaves for Rasadda."

"What are they carrying?" said Caina.

"Salted fish," said Halfdan. "The owners of the local fisheries think they can turn a greater profit by shipping overland. They will, if they avoid bandits, but that is not our concern. You will disguise yourself as the Countess Marianna Nereide and travel with the caravan to Rasadda." He squinted at Ark. "You will act as her captain of guard. The role should suit you well enough, I think."

Ark nodded.

"How many maids will I have?" said Caina.

"Three. And a coachman."

"Three?" said Caina, lifting an eyebrow. "The last time I played this part I had sixteen. And a butler besides."

"Your story is different this time," said Halfdan. "It's common for the sons and daughters of a noble House to go on a tour of the provinces. Except, in your case, your lord father is impoverished, and cannot supply you with a dowry. Therefore he hopes that during the tour, your beauty and wit will capture a suitable young man, preferably one with an ample supply of money." He smiled that cold smile again. "And who will believe that a pretty, charming young Countess has a brain between her ears? You will have access to the wealthy and the powerful, and they might let something slip."

Caina nodded.

"Ark will be your contact for the Ghost circle in Rasadda," continued Halfdan. "They will be able to move among the commoners and the native Saddai, while you deal with the rich and the nobles." He turned to Ark.

"Listen well to our young Countess here. She's quite clever."

Caina saw a flicker of doubt in the grim-faced man's eyes, but he nodded.

"Countess, you'll want to listen to Ark. He knows Rasadda and the Saddai quite well." Halfdan's cold smile flashed again. "And he's quite a useful man to have in a fight."

Ark smiled once, showing his teeth.

"Once we get to Rasadda," said Caina, "where should we start?"

"Go to the Inn of Mirrors, located in the great square outside the Imperial Basilica," said Halfdan. "Ark knows the way, I'm sure. A man named Narmer will arrange rooms for you and await you there. He's a member of the city's Ghost circle. He will give you the latest news, and assist you in whatever way you deem necessary."

"All right," said Caina. She finished her wine and set the goblet aside.

"Get some rest," said Halfdan. "We'll want you to look the part of an Imperial Countess in the morning. After all, your servants have just deserted you, and you're going to have to hire some new maids."

Caina went to her room and fell sleep.

When she slept, the same old dream returned to her.

She was a girl of eleven again, creeping through her father's library, her heart pounding with terror. His chair faced the window, and she saw his limp hand resting on the armrest, the heavy signet ring glittering on his finger.

As she had a thousand times before, she looked at his face.

But this time his body erupted into raging, howling flames, his flesh melting in sizzling rivulets.

CHAPTER 3
COUNTESS MARIANNA NEREIDE

Three days later, Caina swept into to the Inn's common room, her boots clicking against the stone floor. She wore the clothes of an Imperial noblewoman; a dark blue gown to match her eyes, the waist and bodice laced tight, the drooping sleeves marked with intricate embroidery. Jewels glittered on her fingers and at her throat, and her black hair had been done up in an elaborate crown of braids. When she had looked over herself in the mirror, she had been pleased to see that she looked the very image of an Imperial noblewoman of Nightmarian descent; haughty, pale, and proud.

She still carried her father's ring on a silver necklace. And she still kept a pair of daggers hidden in her boots. Caina never liked to go anywhere without at least one weapon. It made her uneasy.

The common room had filled up with teamsters and peddlers, all of them devouring breakfast and drinking cheap wine. Halfdan hurried from table to table, barking orders to the girls he had hired to serve tables. He played the part of the fawning innkeeper to the hilt. Caina swept across the room, her skirts swishing.

"Innkeeper," she said, interrupting his conversation with a trio of rough-looking teamsters, "whatever is the meaning of this?"

Halfdan turned and made a quick bow. "My lady. Is something amiss?"

"Yes there is," said Caina. "What is all this racket? Where did all these people come from? I paid you for peace and quiet, not for the rabble to trouble my ears with their carousing."

"Begging my lady's pardon," said Halfdan, bowing again. He had even managed to work a cringing whine into his voice, "but a caravan is leaving before midday, and the caravan master ordered everyone to eat before he set out."

"A caravan, you say?" said Caina. "Where is it headed?"

"Rasadda, my lady, the capital of this province," said Halfdan.

"I know where the capital of the province is," said Caina. "I have been thinking of taking ship from Rasadda back to the Imperial capital. Where is the master of this caravan? I would speak with him."

"Over there, my lady," said Halfdan, pointing at a balding man by the door, "his name is Rendower, and I'm sure he would be most honored for you to travel with him."

"Of course he would be honored," said Caina. She waved her hand. "You have leave to depart, and to prepare my breakfast."

"Of course, my lady," said Halfdan.

"Wait," said Caina. "Have you seen my captain of guard? If the fool has wandered off to drink, Father will have harsh words for him."

"There, my lady," said Halfdan, "and I fear that he is indeed drinking."

"Oh, bother," said Caina. "That is all."

She left, making her way towards Ark. He stood in the corner, clad in mail and leather, a surcoat with the sigil of House Nereide over his armor. He still wore his broadsword in a scabbard at his belt, and a heavy shield hung over his shoulder.

Among the teamsters and peddlers, he stood out like a wolf among sheep.

"There you are," said Caina. "Why are you here? Father will be cross if I tell him that you've been drinking."

Ark's jaw twitched, just a bit. He had not seen her dressed as Countess Marianna Nereide before. The cold eyes flicked over her once, and then he bowed, stiff and precise.

"Countess," he said. "What do you command?"

"Come with me," she said. "I've decided that we shall journey to Rasadda, and I think it would be best if we travel with this caravan."

Ark said nothing, and followed as she walked towards Rendower.

"You," said Caina in Caerish. "Merchant." She extended her hand towards him. "Your name?"

Rendower took one look and scowled at her. Then he took a better look at her, and he made a hasty bow. "Lady." He kissed her ring. "I am Rendower, a merchant of Rasadda."

"You have the honor of addressing Countess Marianna Nereide," said Caina, doing her very best not to wipe her hand on the side of her gown. "I understand you are leading a caravan to Rasadda?"

"Yes, Lady," said Rendower, straightening up. "A load of salted fish. If I sell the salted cod and haddock in the Rasadda bazaars before summer comes, I shall turn a fine profit."

"I wish to travel to Rasadda myself," said Caina.

"The city is quite a sight, my lady," said Rendower. "Wait until you see the Burning Pyramids, or the Great Pyramid of Corazain. You will never forget the sight, I promise you."

"Yes, I'm sure," said Caina. "I desire to travel with your caravan. The Saddai plains can be dangerous, or so I have been told, and my captain of guard simply insists that we travel with a caravan. He nags like an old woman sometime."

Rendower blinked. "We...ah, should be honored to have you join us, my lady. Though my teamsters and hired guards are a rough lot, and...unfit to spend time in a lady's presence."

"That is quite all right," said Caina with an airy wave of her hand. "Father sent my captain here for just that purpose. Should anyone offer me discourtesy, Ark will teach them the error of their ways. Won't you, Ark?"

Ark said nothing, but his scowl spoke eloquently.

Rendower swallowed. "Very good. We leave in another hour."

"Splendid," said Caina. "My coachman and my maids shall be along with my baggage presently."

She turned on her heel and walked away, Ark trailing after her.

"You seem different this morning, Countess," murmured Ark.

"Why, yes," said Caina, "that is rather the point, wouldn't you say? Now let us find some breakfast before we depart."

Rendower's caravan left in another hour, sixty wagons heavy with barrels of salted fish, dozens of pack mules loaded with supplies, a small army of teamsters, and his mercenary guards.

Caina rode in the coach.

Where Halfdan had found the coach, Caina had no idea. It looked shabby, the sort of thing one might expect an impoverished lesser noble to own, yet the doors had been painted with the Nereide coat of arms. An old coachman named Lasko sat in the driver's seat, muttering to the horses, while Ark sat besides him, broadsword resting between his knees. Caina sat inside with her new maids, listening to them chatter.

She watched the countryside as the caravan rolled eastward. The Saddai plains stretched away to the north, broad and flat and rolling. Most of the land had been under cultivation for long centuries, and Caina saw dozens of small farms. The Alqaarin Sea gleamed to the south, and the Imperial highway wound its way through the plains like a white snake.

The conversation of her maids bored her, but Caina tried to draw them out anyway. She had three of them. Anya and Julia were both younger than Caina, talkative, excitable, and not terribly bright. Cornelia was twice her age, and had outlived two husbands, both of whom had been lazy and shiftless, or so Cornelia claimed.

"I'm just glad to be getting out of Mors Crisius, my lady," said Julia. "I'm honored to have taken service with you, of course, but still…"

"Why?" said Caina. "Why should you wish to leave so earnestly?"

Anya dropped her voice. "The murder, my lady."

"Murder?" said Caina.

Julia's voice fell even lower. "Publius Vanio was found dead in his townhouse. All of his guards had been slaughtered, and Vanio himself was burned to death in his bed."

"How simply dreadful!" said Caina. "Who would do such a terrible thing?"

"It was no less than he deserved," said Cornelia, her sour tone matching her expression. "Old Vanio was up to his arms in the slave trade. Everyone knew it. High time he got what was coming to him."

"Slavery?" said Caina. "But that's illegal."

"Troubled times," said Cornelia. "That's what it is, troubled times. You get all sorts of nastiness in times like these."

"What did you mean?" said Caina.

"It's not my place to trouble my lady with such talk," said Cornelia.

Something in the older woman's voice suddenly reminded Caina of her mother, and she felt a surge of dislike. She pushed it aside. "You may speak freely. When my lord father sent me on this tour of the provinces, he wanted me to learn about the Empire. How else shall I learn?"

"If my lady insists," said Cornelia. "It's those filthy Saddai, if you ask me. I'm not an Imperial citizen, but my folk came here with the Legions, and we've always kept to the ways of the Empire." Her face twisted with disdain. "But those Saddai. They have outlandish ways, and they pray to that fire god of theirs. Little wonder things are so grim. The rich get fat and the poor starve. It's those filthy Saddai, I say."

Julia and Anya nodded their agreement.

"I even hear that the Saddai burn people alive to please their god," said Cornelia. "Maybe that's what got old Vanio in the end, when his wickedness turned upon him."

"Perhaps," said Caina. "It seems that all is not well in Saddai Province."

"The Lord Governor is too lenient with them," said Cornelia. "He ought to give them a good whipping."

Caina considered this in silence.

"May I also speak freely, my lady?" said Julia.

Caina inclined her head.

"Did your lord father send you to tour the provinces," she said, starting to blush, "or to find a husband?"

"Hold your impudent tongue!" said Cornelia.

Caina lifted a hand. "It is all right. My lord father…well, he said he would not be displeased if I should convince some suitable young man to pay me court."

"Some Lord of the Empire?" said Julia. "Maybe even a High Lord?"

"Bother," said Cornelia. "A Lord has more pride than sense, and more honor than money." She shook her finger. "Marry a merchant with money, my lady. Money is all a man is good for. You're quite comely, and you should use your beauty before it fades. If you put your mind to it, you can have the richest merchant in Rasadda wrapped around your finger within a moon's turn. That will please your lord father, I'm sure."

"Yes," repeated Caina, "I'm sure."

The talk turned to husbands and dowries and bride gifts. Caina listened with half an ear. The thought of her father brought up old pain, and Cornelia's resemblance to her mother summoned up the old rage.

But her thoughts turned to Cornelia's sneering contempt for the Saddai, and the dead man lying burned in his bed.

The next morning, Caina rose before anyone else and walked a short distance from the caravan's encampment, the high grasses rustling around her riding skirts.

She had a routine she liked to follow in the morning, whenever the demands of her duty allowed.

She practiced her forms.

The Ghosts' style of open-handed fighting, Halfdan had told her, had evolved from several different forms. The Spinning Blade of the Anshani, the Three Rings of the Disali hillmen, the Storm Dance of the Kyracians. The Ghosts had encountered them all, and learned from them.

She had been practicing for years, ever since Halfdan had taken her into the Ghosts, and she moved through the forms with quick grace. Open-palm strike, closed fist, high kick, sweeping kick, the left dodge, the right throw, followed by the throat strike and the wrist throw. She took the forms slowly at first, stretching her muscles, and then faster, until her arms and legs wove blurring designs around her.

Her arm pulled back for a palm strike, and Caina saw Ark watching her. He wore his mail, leather, and cloak, his hand resting near the hilt of his broadsword. Caina finished the form and waited as Ark crossed the grasses to join her.

"Those unarmed combat forms are interesting tricks," he said. His voice was calm, but his eyes were cold, weighing.

"They have their uses," said Caina.

Ark shook his head. "They are a game. Little good they will do you against an armored man with a blade."

"I am half a foot shorter than you and probably half your weight," said Caina. "So an enemy will expect me to be helpless. If I can catch a foe off-guard, even for a second, that is often enough to win a fight."

Ark titled his head to the side, his cold eyes glinting. "You...sound different. Your accent has completely changed."

"That is the point," said Caina.

"Is it so easy for you to be the Countess one moment, and then a Ghost the next?"

"It wasn't at first," said Caina, "but I've had time to practice."

Ark continued to stare at her. In another man, Caina would have interpreted this as lust. Instead, she suspected that Ark had started to hate her.

"You don't like me very much," she said, after a moment, "do you?"

"Does that displease you?"

"Not particularly," said Caina. "We are both Ghosts, servants of the Emperor, and your opinion of me matters very little so long as we both perform our duties well." Her voice turned cold. "But, do unburden yourself to me. What have I done to offend you?"

"When we reach Rasadda," said Ark, ignoring the question, "what will you do?"

Caina shrugged. "We will try to find whoever is behind these burnings."

"Perhaps I have not been clear," said Ark. "What good are you to us?"

"I have a knack for finding things out," said Caina, "or so Halfdan tells me."

Ark scowled.

Caina waited.

"A knack," repeated Ark. "You seem to have a knack for masquerading as an empty-headed Countess, and nothing more."

"Does that offend you? The Ghosts are the Emperor's spies, not his warriors," said Caina.

"We asked Halfdan for help," said Ark. "For nearly a year now these...burnings have been plaguing Rasadda. If the situation is not taken in hand, the city will revolt. And Halfdan sends us," his mouth twisted with distaste, "he sends us an actress."

Disdain crept into her voice. "And what will you do? Seize people at random and demand the name of the murderers, or you'll cut their throats? That should work very well."

"And how would you find things out?"

Caina shrugged. "I watch. I listen. I observe. That has served me well so far."

"Has it?" Ark's scowl darkened. "Then what do you observe about me, Countess?"

"Very well," said Caina. She looked him in the eye. "You are in your middle thirties, I think, and were born in one of the Caerish provinces."

"Halfdan told you that."

"No," said Caina, "your accent is constant, whatever language you speak, and you seem unable to rid yourself of it. You used to be in the Legions."

Ark blinked, and then tapped his weapon. "The sword, of course."

"Only legionaries and veterans use that style of broadsword. And I can see the scars on your left arm from your shield. You lied about your age to get into the Legions, didn't you?"

Ark flinched.

"You're in your middle thirties," Caina continued, "and you must have served your full twenty year term of service. Desertion in the Emperor's armies is punishable by crucifixion, after all. And if you had deserted and escaped, Halfdan would not have let you join the Ghosts. He hates deserters. Incidentally, Halfdan himself recruited you into the Ghosts, didn't he? He only tells his proper name to those he recruits individually." Caina tapped her lips with a finger. "The age of admission to the Legions is sixteen. So I would suppose you lied about your age and joined at fourteen or fifteen. Probably fourteen."

Ark scowled and turned to go. "You've made your point, Countess."

Caina stepped in front of him. "Don't you want to know more, my captain? Surely you can keep secrets from some silly frivolous noblewoman." Something warned her to stop, but Ark had irritated her, so she kept talking. "You were in the Eighteenth Legion. That Legion tattoo on your right bicep? You should do a better job of concealing it. And I would guess you made at least centurion rank, perhaps even the first centurion of a cohort. You snapped out enough commands at the teamsters during our departure. Which explains why you are so annoyed that you have to take orders from some silly Countess."

Ark kept walking.

"You've been out of the Legions for at least three or four years," said Caina, following him. "That armor is making you uncomfortable, though I doubt you'll ever admit it. Oh, and you're a widower."

Ark stopped. He turned towards her, his eyes wide and wild and full of a terrible pain, and Caina felt a sudden stab of fear. Had she pushed him too far?

"Halfdan told you," he hissed, his voice full of fury, "Halfdan told you, he promised, he swore that he would never tell a soul..."

"He didn't," said Caina, voice quiet. "You talk in your sleep. A woman's name, over and over again. Tanya." She pointed. "And you keep fiddling with that ring on your left hand."

Ark stared at her, breathing hard, and bit by bit he mastered himself.

"Perhaps, Countess," said Ark, his voice toneless and dead, "I may have misjudged you."

Caina nodded.

"But do not speak of Tanya again. Not ever. Not to anyone," said Ark. "Do you understand me?"

Caina heard the threat in his words, and did not like it. But there was no reason to push him any further. She had made her point. So she nodded again.

"We should return to the caravan," said Ark. "They will begin to whisper, if you keep disappearing with your captain of the guard."

"Let them," said Caina. "Silly, frivolous Countesses are rarely known for their chastity, after all."

The eastward journey wore on.

Ark spoke to her very little, and Caina soon grew weary of conversation with the maids, so she took to speaking with the teamsters and the peddlers. A few of them spoke Caerish, but most of them spoke only Saddaic. Caina took the opportunity to practice the tongue, and discovered to her delight that one of the peddlers had some books in his inventory.

Caina bought three. The first was a typical history of the Empire, the second a collection of poetry and songs from the Empire's long-ago wars against the Sea Kings of Old Kyrace. The third, though, described the Battle of Rasadda, when the Emperor Crisius threw down Corazain, the last and mightiest of the Ashbringers. Caina hoped it might have some insights into her current situation.

Cornelia looked shocked that her lady would read in public, but Caina did not care.

Later that day she saw the first abandoned village. It sat athwart the road, the houses crumbling, weeds growing in the streets. The village had once been surrounded by cultivated fields, but the grasses of the Saddai plains were returning. The place could not have been abandoned for more than five or six years, Caina guessed.

"What happened here?" she asked Cornelia. "Plague?"

"No, my lady, no plague," said Cornelia. "This was a village of Saddai farm folk. Lazy and shiftless people. The cattle men have been buying up all their lands and converting them to pasture." She nodded with approval. "They'll finally have to work to fill their bellies."

Caina frowned but said nothing. A mile later she saw the first cattle herd. Hundreds of cows and steers, perhaps even a thousand, wandered across the plains. A few men on horseback tended them, cracking whips and shooting suspicious glares at the caravan.

"What happens to the farmers, once they're forced off their lands?" said Caina.

Cornelia stared at her, then laughed. "Surely my lady doesn't care about some filthy Saddai commoners."

"I am merely curious," said Caina.

Cornelia shrugged. "I'm sure I don't know. They go to the cities, I expect, and try to find work. Probably to Rasadda." She made an exaggerated shudder. "Dirty people, the lot of them."

Caina felt her patience leave her. "My legs are cramped. I think I shall walk for a while."

"Amongst the teamsters?" said Cornelia. "Surely my lady would rather stay in the coach."

"She would not," said Caina, closing the book about Corazain the Ashbringer. "Fear not. My captain will escort me, and if anyone offers impertinence, well…I'm sure he'll know what to do. You may remain here."

Cornelia wilted onto the cushions with relief.

Caina swung out of the coach's door and onto the road. Her skirt and heeled boots made it rather tricky, but she kept her balance. Ark walked alongside the carriage, hand resting on his broadsword, and glanced at her. She beckoned, and he fell into step alongside her, silent and grim.

"Tell me," said Caina. "When did the farmers start getting forced off their lands?"

Ark blinked, but answered the question. "A few years ago. Shortly after Lord Nicephorus became governor in Rasadda. The Imperial nobles began buying the land at cheap rates and giving it over to pasture. Apparently they can make a greater profit with meat, cheese, milk, and leather instead of grain."

"Is that not illegal?"

"Yes, it is," said Ark. He paused. "Why does this concern you?"

"Men do not kill without reason," said Caina. "And desperate, starving men have more reason to kill than most."

"So you think the Saddai peasantry might have something to do with these burnings?"

"Perhaps," said Caina, "but I don't see how." There was a Magisterium chapterhouse in Rasadda, she knew, and if some Saddai peasant had set himself up as an Ashbringer, the magi would have slaughtered him long ago.

"I have had similar thoughts myself," said Ark, "but…"

He stopped, his cold mask hardening further.

"What?" said Caina.

"The donkeys," he said.

Caina looked at the nearest pack donkeys. She knew only a little about animals, but she thought they looked restless. The drivers walked back and forth down the lines of animals, cursing and cracking their whips.

Ark's hand shot out and seized her arm, fingers like iron.

"Don't move," he muttered. "Look, over there. Past the third donkey."

Caina did, and saw the lioness.

She crouched motionless in the grasses, her eyes like twin pools of golden fire. Caina just had time to draw breath, and then the lioness sprang forward. Her leap drove one of the donkeys to the ground, the beast bleating in terror. One of the drivers stumbled back, shrieking in fear, and the lioness whirled to face him, muzzle pulling back from yellowed fangs.

Then Ark moved.

One moment he stood at Caina's side. The next he was springing over the fallen donkey, his broadsword a steely arc. And the instant after that the lioness sprawled prone on the road, her blood gushing into the dirt.

Caina blinked in astonishment.

Ark had just killed a full-grown lioness. With nothing more than a broadsword.

The caravan exploded into pandemonium. The teamsters were all shouting, the drivers running back and forth. It took Rendower the better part of an hour to get everyone back in line.

"Well done, sir, well done," he said, giving Ark a vigorous clap on the shoulder. "The gods alone know how many of my pack animals that beast would have killed."

"None," said the driver, "because it would have been feasting on my flesh. You saved my life."

"It was happy fortune, Countess, that you joined our caravan," said Rendower. "Your man acquitted himself quite well, quite well indeed." Ark sketched a short bow. "I'd never seen a sword move so fast."

"Is it so surprising, master merchant?" said Caina. "Do you think my father would assign my protection to a sluggard or a craven?"

"Indeed not, my lady," said Rendower.

A short time later the caravan renewed its journey, and Caina and Ark walked back to the coach.

"You know, we might work together quite well," said Caina. "If I can find this murderer, clearly you shall have no trouble striking him down."

For the first time, Caina saw Ark grin, and he looked far more dangerous than the lioness.

Black mountains came into sight the next day, looming out of the haze like giants. Rasadda sat at the foot of those mountains, Caina knew, old volcanoes that still sometimes spurted with liquid fire. Rendower squinted at them, and pronounced that they would reach Rasadda by the next day.

That night, before Caina went to bed, she saw a glow to the east. She stepped out of her tent and frowned. The sun had gone down, and there were hours yet before dawn, yet a reddish glow flickered over the eastern horizon. Had the grasses of the plains taken fire? Or had one of the volcanoes burst into flame?

"That?" said Rendower, when she asked. "Oh, that. That's merely Rasadda, my lady. One can see the light of the city from a far way off."

"Surely there must be more lanterns there than in all the rest of the world put together," said Caina dubiously.

"In a way, my lady, in a way," said Rendower. "But I shan't wish to spoil the surprise for you." He grinned. "The first sight of Rasadda is always…something."

"Indeed," said Caina, annoyed, and went to bed.

The next day she rode on the coach's front seat besides Lasko, the book about Corazain the Ashbringer cradled on her lap. The air inside the coach had become close, and she had grown weary of listening to the maids chatter. So instead she watched the scenery roll by, and read about Corazain with interest. The Empire and the Ashbringers had been locked in battle for centuries, and entire cities had been laid waste by the sword and the Ashbringers' sorcery. At last the Emperor Crisius had invaded Saddai itself, intent on bringing the Ashbringers down…

Ark walked past. Caina looked up, saw Ark staring at something off the road. A horseman sat atop one of the nearby hills, gazing down at the caravan. Even as she looked, the rider snapped the reins and galloped off.

"Watch my book," said Caina. Lasko grunted an acknowledgement. She pushed off the seat and walked to join Ark. "Trouble?"

"Perhaps," said Ark, his hard eyes glinting. "That rider."

"A herdsman," said Caina. "We must have ridden past ten thousand cows in the last day."

"But none for the last hour," said Ark. "So either that fellow was looking for a missing steer, or…"

"Or he was scouting for someone," said Caina. "Bandits?"

"Maybe," said Ark, scowling. "There's no place to hide on the Saddai plains, so the bandits hole up in the mountains. They swarm down every so often."

"This is a large caravan," said Caina. "They'd be fools to attack."

Ark gave her a sidelong glance. "What did you tell me yesterday? Desperate men have more reason to kill than most, was that it?"

Caina said nothing.

But they saw no bandits.

###

"My lady," said Ark.

Caina looked up from the book, blinking.

"This is your first visit to Rasadda?" said Ark.

Caina frowned. "You know that it is."

There was something almost like amusement in his face. "Then you'll want to see this."

Caina closed the book and climbed down from the seat. She walked to the head of the caravan, past the drivers and the donkeys and creaking wagons full of fish.

And then she saw it.

"Gods," muttered Caina.

A few miles to the east rose black walls, gleaming in the sunlight. Beyond those walls stood towering black pyramids, their peaks crowned with raging flames.

CHAPTER 4
RASADDA

Caina stared at the black city.

"That's Rasadda?" she said, after a moment.

Ark nodded.

She saw at least thirty of the great pyramids, all of them topped with flames. The smallest rose about two hundred feet tall, while the tallest stood at least four times that. Their sides gleamed black, reflecting the light of their burning crowns. As the caravan drew closer, Caina saw the houses, mansions, and shops of Rasadda clustered around the feet of those pyramids.

"The pyramids," she said. "What are they?"

"Tombs, my lady," said Rendower, who had joined them. "Ancient tombs. Built to house the Ashbringer kings of old."

"Clearly the Saddai hold them in great reverence," said Caina. "The cost of keeping those fires lit must be enormous."

Ark shook his head.

"Ah…no, my lady," said Rendower. "Those are no natural fires. They require no fuel."

"No fuel?" said Caina. "Explain."

"He means," said Ark, "that those tombs house dead Ashbringers, and the Ashbringers' sorcery lit those fires. Some of those fires have been burning for thousands of years."

"And the Magisterium let those fires burn?" said Caina. "I know little of the magi, you understand, but my father said that they hate rival sorcerers."

Ark looked at Rendower.

"Well," said Rendower, "the official story is that the Magisterium let the flames stand as a gesture of respect to the Saddai people."

It took Caina every bit of self-control she had to keep from laughing aloud.

"But I've heard," said Rendower, dropping his voice, "that the Magisterium can't put the fires out. They're not strong enough. Those old-time Ashbringers, they were mighty sorcerers, or so the stories say, and no living magus as the power to undo the spell." He looked around with sudden anxiety. "And don't go repeating that, mind. I don't have any truck with sorcery, and the magi...the magi are not kindly." He reddened. "Forgive me if I have spoken too bluntly."

"Not at all," said Caina with a gracious wave of her hand. "I have heard much the same from others." Rendower bowed and hastened away to take charge of his teamsters. "Ark. Was he telling the truth?"

Ark shrugged. "As far I know. All the tales and rumors I've heard say the same thing."

Caina stared at the pyramids.

Sorcerous fire.

And charred corpses kept appearing in Rasadda.

"Could this murderer...be dragging the corpses to the fire?" said Caina. "Throwing them into the flames, and then abandoning them?"

"We thought of it," said Ark. "But the bodies never show signs of having been moved."

"And that wouldn't explain Publius Vanio, besides," muttered Caina. Everlasting sorcerous fires and a charred corpse lying upon an untouched bed. Too much of a coincidence, and Caina detested coincidences. They were usually signs of a pattern she could not yet see.

"The fires hardly matter," said Ark. "They have burned for a thousand years. Yet it is only in the last year that people have burned to death."

"Yes," said Caina. "Perhaps you're right." But it still it troubled her. She shook her head and walked back to the coach. She needed to act like a noblewoman of the Empire, and no Imperial noblewoman would walk through the gates of a provincial city.

"Open the windows," said Caina, settling into her seat.

"My lady?" said Cornelia, sounding affronted, while Anya and Julia stared at her.

"Do it," said Caina. "I've come all this way to see Rasadda, and I can't see it if the windows are closed and the curtains drawn."

She watched as the Imperial highway rolled up to Rasadda's gates. The walls stood at least sixty feet high, built of basalt and fronted with gleaming black marble. The coach clattered through the gates and an expansive square below the walls, at the foot of one of the smaller pyramids. Looking closer, Caina saw that it was not so much a pyramid as it was a ziggurat, its terraced sides linked by stairs and steep ramps. The flames burned at its crown, bright even in the daylight.

"We part ways here, my lady," said Rendower, looking through the coach's window. "I'm for the East Bazaar, to meet with the brokers. Will you be joining us?"

"No," said Caina, "I sent on a man ahead, to prepare rooms at the Inn of Mirrors. But I wish you good business, master merchant, and I thank you for your hospitality."

"It was our honor, Countess," said Rendower. His face brightened when Caina passed him a few coins for his trouble. After he left, she slid open the front window and looked out at Lasko. "Do you know the way to the Inn of Mirrors?"

Lasko grunted. "Aye, my lady. Across from the Imperial Basilica, below the Great Pyramid of Corazain."

"The Great Pyramid of Corazain?" said Caina. Her fingers brushed the book lying on the seat. "Is that the big one?" She looked at the colossal pyramid looming over the lesser pyramids, rising over the city like a black mountain.

"Aye, my lady," said Lasko. Ark swung up onto the running board, hand on his broadsword. Lasko snapped the reins, and the coach clattered into the streets of Rasadda.

Caina gazed at the alien city around her. It was a dark place, a grim place, and yet had its own solemn beauty. Most of the buildings had been faced with dark basalt, no doubt quarried from the nearby mountains, while the larger houses gleamed with black marble. The Saddai themselves seemed to favor garments of bright red and orange, and went about their business on the basalt-paved streets.

There were a lot of beggars, though, leaning against the walls, ragged and gaunt. Caina had visited many of the Empire's great cities, and all of them had beggars. But she had never seen so many in one city.

"Quite a lot of beggars, aren't there?" said Caina.

"It's very sad, my lady," said Anya. "They've all been driven off their lands, and there's no work to be found, so they come here to live on the Lord Governor's grain dole."

"Very sad," murmured Caina. And desperate, starving men had more reason to kill than most.

"Oh, humbug," said Cornelia. She gave the beggars a disdainful sniff. "Look at them. They're all Saddai. Lazy and shiftless to a man. No doubt they're too lazy to find work, and so come here to grow fat and indolent on the grain dole."

"Perhaps there is no work to be found," said Caina.

Cornelia smiled. "My lady, forgive me for speaking so, but you are young, and quite innocent. A woman my age has seen much of the world, and I can say beyond a doubt that these Saddai are lazy and deceitful."

Cornelia sounded so like her mother that Caina felt again that furious, choking wrath, and she found her hand twitching towards the knives hidden in her sleeves. She hid the gesture by smoothing her skirts. "Yes. An innocent."

The coach jolted to a stop.

"You there!" shouted Lasko, his voice furious. "Get out of the way!"

Ark's colder voice rang out. "Clear the way at once!"

Caina twisted around in her seat and looked out the window.

The coach filled most of a narrow alley between the windowless backs of two sagging, grim houses. This looked like a bad part of town; the houses were not built of basalt but black-painted brick. A dozen men blocked the street. They looked like beggars, but they had weapons. Some of them had clubs, others had swords, and one hefted an enormous steel warhammer.

"Move," said Ark, voice deadly cold, "or get run down. Your choice."

The man with the hammer spat and began speaking in Saddaic. "Aye? Well, this is our street. You want to pass, you'll deal with us. You'll pay our toll."

"How much?" said Ark, drawing his broadsword a foot from its scabbard.

"Bah!" said the man, spitting again. "We don't want your gold. You high-and-mighty Imperial scum, strutting about our streets as if you own them."

"We do," said Ark.

The beggar's lips pulled back from his teeth. "What we want is blood, fool. You give us the highborn bitch in the coach, and we'll let you go. Otherwise we'll kill you all."

Caina's heart beat faster.

"Dear gods," said Cornelia, horrified, "those men are criminals, they're…"

"Shut up," said Caina. Cornelia fell into a shocked silence.

"No," said Ark. "Out of my way, now."

The beggar with the warhammer laughed. "Aye? Or what? You took the wrong street today, you Empire-worshipping fool." The other men raised their weapons.

Ark's sword blurred from its scabbard so fast Caina could scare follow the movement. "Move. Last chance."

The beggar laughed again and lifted his hammer. "I think not. Kill him and take the…"

In the next instant the beggar was on his knees, the hammer ringing against the street, blood pouring from the ghastly wound in his neck. Then Lasko slammed back into his seat, shrieking in pain, a crossbow bolt buried in his chest. Men were bellowing and shouting, and Julia and Anya were screaming in fear. Ark had somehow gotten his shield onto his left arm, and his broadsword sent a spray of bloody drops into the air.

More men burst from the nearby house, bearing clubs, and rushed for the coach.

Caina cursed under her breath and looked up. There was a little trapdoor in the ceiling, opening onto the roof. She pushed open the trapdoor, gripped the edges, and lifted herself up.

The first man stuck his head through the coach's door. "Well, what have we…"

Caina swung down, shoving with her arms, and her heeled boots slammed hard into the man's face. Bones cracked, the man's head snapping back, and he toppled onto the street. Caina fell to one knee, her right hand dipping into her left sleeve.

Another man reached into the coach, seized her arm, and began to yank her out. Caina gave no resistance, so it was the easiest thing in the world to slam her hidden knife into his throat as he pulled her close. The man stumbled backwards with a gurgling scream, wrenching the knife out of Caina's hand. She fell out of the coach, tucked her shoulder, and rolled into the street.

"Marsaidan?" said one of the men, looking down at the man choking on his own blood. "Marsaidan? What the hell…"

Caina disliked her boots, but they added a useful weight to her foot as she whipped her leg around, driving a kick into the nearest thug's knee with all the strength she could manage. Again she heard the snapping crackle of damaged bone. The thug fell with a howl of pain, club rolling from his fingers. Caina scrambled back to her feet, reaching for the knife hidden in her other sleeve.

A hand seized her hair, yanking her back, another arm coming up to reach for her throat. Again Caina offered no resistance, adding the momentum to her own as she spun around. Her palm strike smashed into a man's unshaven face, and he stumbled back with a grunt. But his fist lashed out and plunged into her stomach, knocking the breath from her. Caina struggled to keep her balance, and the man kicked her legs out from beneath her. She hit the street with a painful grunt, a jolt of pain shooting through her limbs. The thug took a step towards her, snarling curses as he reached for a dagger at his belt.

Then his head seemed to collapse on itself as Ark's broadsword swept past in a spray of blood and brains. The thug's face twisted weirdly, and he fell into a twitching heap on the basalt-paved street.

Silence fell. Caina heard nothing but the rasp of her breath and the pounding of her heart.

"Excellent timing," she managed to say at last.

Ark grunted and held out his hand. Caina took it, and Ark pulled her to her feet. She looked around and saw the bodies carpeting the street. Ark had killed four or five men, at least. The man she had kicked in the face lay dead. He must have broken his neck against the street. The man she had stabbed in the throat also lay still, his mouth forever open it a final, futile attempt to draw breath. Caina watched the blood pooling across the basalt flagstones, and again she saw the men lying motionless on the floor of her father's library, her mother's face twisted with insane fury. Nausea stabbed into her aching belly, and it was all she could do to keep her breakfast down.

She looked at Ark, and for a brief moment glimpsed the same sort of thing in his face. It was more desolate, more despairing, yet she saw the same pain in his eyes. They looked at each other for a moment, and then Ark shook his head and turned to the side.

"Look," he said, pointing with his sword. Blood slid from the tip of the blade.

Caina frowned. The man she had kicked in the knee lay against the black house, dead of a sword thrust through the chest. He looked like an average Saddai of unremarkable birth; pale, gaunt, black eyes now glassy and empty.

"My lady!" Anya peered through the coach's windows, wide-eyed with fright. "My lady, are you all right?"

"I'm fine," said Caina. "Stay there and don't move." Anya vanished back into the coach.

"Look," said Ark, again. "What do you see?"

Caina stared at the dead man, but saw nothing remarkable. "What of it?"

"We've seen him before," said Ark. "Remember the horseman outside the city? This is him, I would swear to it."

"Then they were waiting for us," said Caina.

"Robbers, most likely," said Ark. He knelt beside the corpse, ripped open its tunic, and began to clean his sword on the torn cloth. "This fellow was the lookout. When he saw us, he rode back to the city, to let his fellows know that an Imperial noblewoman was traveling with only one guard."

"Wait," said Caina, frowning. "Wait. Tear his tunic open the rest of the way."

Ark looked at her, then shrugged and tore open the red cloth. The dead man had a tattoo on his chest, a stylized image of a flame done in swirling reds and yellows. Blood dripped across the image, but it remained bright and clear against his pallid skin.

"Have you ever seen this before?" said Caina.

"No," said Ark. He shook his head. "I've seen this symbol before, though. It's the Living Flame, the sigil of the Saddai god. But I've never seen it worn as a tattoo."

33

Caina crossed to the man she had stabbed in the throat and wrenched the knife free. There was quite a lot of blood. She cleaned the blade on the dead man's clothes and then cut open his tunic.

The tattoo of a flame marked his chest.

"Check the others," said Caina.

Without exception, the dead men had the tattoo of the Living Flame upon their chests.

"What do you think?" said Caina.

"I don't know," said Ark.

"You wear the tattoo of the Eighteenth Legion upon your arm," said Caina. "Perhaps this tattoo is a similar mark. The sign of membership in a secret society, maybe."

Ark snorted. "A secret society of fools, then, if they all wear identifying marks."

Caina finished cleaning her knife and stood. "To our benefit, then." She stared hard at the dead men. A man found burned to death in his bed. Eternal sorcerous fires crowning the pyramids. And now thugs with flame tattoos upon their chests.

Gods, she detested coincidences.

She walked around the coach. Lasko sat slumped in the driver's seat, eyes wide and empty, blood trickling down his legs. The horses stamped and whinnied at the smell of blood, but they hadn't bolted.

"Damn it," said Caina, looking at the corpse. The deaths of the tattooed thugs troubled her, but they had tried to kill her. Lasko had only been a tired old man looking for work.

Ark stared at her, expression unreadable.

"We should go," said Caina.

Ark nodded, and Caina heard the sound of running footsteps. She saw men in leather jerkins hurrying towards them, spears in hand.

"City militia," said Ark, his lip curling in contempt. "Local Saddai auxiliaries. Not a single veteran of the legions among them. No doubt they hid when they heard the sound of fighting, and only now crawl out of their holes."

Caina nodded. "Let me do that talking."

The militiamen stopped, looking at the carnage with wide eyes. One of them stepped forward, an officer's crest upon his helmet.

"You there," he said, pointing at Caina, "what happened here? Speak quickly, woman." He spoke Saddaic with the same thick Caerish accent as Ark.

"Woman?" said Caina, her voice cracking like a whip. "Do you not know who I am, fool?"

"Ah," said the officer, his eyes skittering over the crest on the coach, and Caina's own disheveled but expensive clothing. "I...fear I do not, my lady."

"I am the Countess Marianna Nereide," said Caina, "recently arrived from the Imperial capital, and no sooner do I set foot upon your streets than I am set upon by robbers and brigands! Did you not hear our cries for help?" She turned a furious glare over him. "Well?"

The officer seemed at a sudden loss for words.

"My captain of guard was forced take up arms in my defense!" said Caina.

The officer blinked. "He...killed them all? By himself?"

Ark gave him a chilly smile.

"I am an Imperial countess, a noblewoman of Nighmarian descent," said Caina in her most affronted tone. "Do you expect me to lift a sword in my own defense? Of course he killed them all! He had no choice." She pointed at Lasko's body. "These murderous villains slew my coachman, a retainer long in loyal service to my family! Your Lord Governor shall hear all about his valiant militia. Oh, yes, he shall hear all about them."

"My lady," said the officer, "it was only ill fortune that we came upon the scene too late. These...insurgents infest the streets of our city, and the militia has only so many men. We cannot be everywhere at once. Please, permit us to escort you."

"What is your name?"

"Ah...Valgorix, my lady, Decurion of the city militia."

"Very well," said Caina, voice cold. "We were making for the Inn of Mirrors. I assume you know the way?

"Of course, my lady," said Valgorix. "We...ah, shall see to the body of your retainer, with your permission." Caina nodded, and two of the militiamen took Lasko's body down. Ark clambered up into the seat, laid his broadsword across his knees, and took the reins. Caina brushed off her skirts as best she could and climbed into the coach.

Anya, Julia, and Cornelia all stared at her with expressions caught halfway between fascination and horror.

"You are all well, I trust?" said Caina. "What is it?"

"You...you killed him," whispered Anya. "That man who grabbed you."

"Of course I did," said Caina. "He was trying to kill me, after all."

"But...you killed him," repeated Anya, half in shock.

This could be a problem. Caina doubted that any of them had realized Countess Marianna Nereide was only a fiction, but best to leave nothing to chance.

"Listen to me," said Caina. They looked at her. "My...mother came to an evil death, when I was a child." That was not a lie, at least. "So my father made certain that I knew how to fight, should I, too, ever face dire peril. It...he said that in Old Nighmar, in the first days of the Empire, it was said that it was better for a man to die on his feet, with his blade in hand, then upon his knees. Why should the same not be true for us women, as well?"

"It is good that you knew how to fight, my lady," said Julia. "They would have killed us all, otherwise." All three of them nodded.

"I would prefer that this remain secret," said Caina. "It…well, if I am to find a worthy husband, it would certainly help if he didn't know."

They nodded again. Caina sighed and sat back as the coach rattled and bounced through the streets of Rasadda, past the grim black buildings and the lines of beggars.

Cornelia did not make a single snide remark, not one.

CHAPTER 5
A PRIESTESS OF THE LIVING FLAME

The coach came to the plaza below the Great Pyramid of Corazain.

The Inn of Mirrors stood on one side of the plaza, a tall building with three wings overlooking a paved courtyard and a bubbling fountain. Inn and courtyard had been covered in gleaming black marble, and it shimmered like a dark mirror in the sunlight. Rich merchants of both Saddai and Nighmarian birth stood in the courtyard, drinking wine, while armed guards kept away the beggars.

The Imperial Basilica stood on the far side of the square. It had been faced with white marble, a stark contrast to the rest of Rasadda. The purple banners of the Emperor hung from the walls, adorned with a golden eagle. It was one of the larger basilicas Caina had seen, a monument to the might of the Empire.

But the Pyramid of Corazain dwarfed both Inn and Basilica.

The great black pile reared against the sky, terraces and ramps and stairs climbing ever higher. Caina looked up, and up, and saw the flames crackling at the Pyramid's distant crest. It was like looking at a mountain. And mere men had raised this thing?

Or, Caina amended, mere men equipped with sorcery.

The coach halted before the Inn, and Caina got out, holding her skirts in one hand. Valgorix approached her and made a polite bow. "Lady. The Inn of Mirrors, as you asked. Have you lodgings here?"

"Yes," said Caina. "A man in my service named Narmer arrived in advance a few days past. He will have made arrangements."

Valgorix hesitated. "I would suggest that you stay off the streets, my lady."

"What do you mean?" said Caina.

"Forgive my bluntness," said Valgorix, "but you are a noblewoman of high Nighmarian blood, and the mob will detest you on sight. If you stray too far into the city you may be attacked again. The Empire is not very popular in Rasadda, because of the..." He frowned. "At least, keep your guardsman with you at all times."

"What were you going to say?" said Caina. "Because of what?"

"The murders, my lady," said Valgorix. "Among other things."

"Those brigands in the street?" said Caina, glancing at Ark.

"Yes. That...and people have been found burned to death," said Valgorix. "Twenty-six total, with the most recent found yesterday." He scratched his jaw. "A horrid way to die. And it's got the city in an uproar." He glanced fearfully at the beggars wandering around the plaza. "There's a rumor going around that sorcery was used in the murders. Ridiculous notion. The Magisterium killed off all the Ashbringers long ago. Some charlatan is playing tricks to make the Saddai rabble think an Ashbringer has returned. Still, the murders are inflaming the populace, and it is not safe to travel the streets alone."

Caina had never considered that. "I see. Well, your counsel seems sound, and I shall leave the city when convenient. I thank you for your service, and you are dismissed."

Valgorix bowed and returned to his men.

"What do you think?" murmured Caina, when Valgorix was out of earshot.

"I don't know," said Ark. "I left Rasadda six weeks ago to seek out Halfdan in Mors Crisius. Things were bad then, but now the city seems on the edge of a revolt. And six more murders?"

Caina nodded. "Then let us find Narmer. Perhaps he shall have more information for us."

She turned to the coach, calling for her maids, and stopped. They still sat hunched inside the coach, staring at everything with wide and fearful eyes. The fight in the streets had terrified them. Caina's training and experiences as a Ghost had inured her to violence. The maids had no such luxury.

That troubled her. Had her heart become so cold, so hard? Could she kill two men and walk away without it affecting her in the least? She remembered the savage emptiness in Ark's eyes as he had butchered the thugs. Was that what she had become?

So be it. Someone had burned nearly thirty people to death. And when Caina found this killer, he would not face a frightened girl but a Ghost of the Empire with cold steel in hand.

Caina walked to the coach and touched Anya's sleeve. "See that the horses get stabled and my things unpacked. Then get something to eat and take some rest. You've had a dreadful shock, all of you. I'll send for you when I need you."

"Thank you, my lady," said Anya. Caina gave the girl a quick smile, and then followed Ark into the Inn.

They walked into a high common room, the wall ringed with a balcony. Volcanic glass covered the walls, smooth and black, and Caina saw her image reflected dozens of times in the dark panels. A pool ran through the center of the room, three statues of nude women standing on pedestals in the rippling waters. Sunlight poured down through an elaborate skylight in the roof, reflecting off the walls and the water. The combined effect was ethereal, both beautiful and disturbing.

A fat Saddai man in flame-colored clothes hurried over. "Welcome, noble Countess, welcome to the Inn of Mirrors. I am Sairzan, master of this house, and I am honored that you have chosen to stay beneath my roof in these troubled times." He bowed, seized her hand, and planted a hasty kiss upon her ring. "All of my rooms are fine, of course, but I shall have my finest rooms prepared for you at once." He clapped his hands, and servants hurried to her side.

"Your hospitality does you credit, master innkeeper," said Caina, "but are not my rooms already prepared?"

Sairzan blinked in sudden consternation. "I fear that my simple mind cannot follow the wisdom of your words."

"My man Narmer was to meet me here, and to have rooms waiting," said Caina. "Is he not here?" She looked over the great common room. Any number of tables stood scattered about, along with cushioned alcoves tucked away in the corners. She saw merchants and nobles discussing their business, but no sign of anyone who matched Ark's description of Narmer.

"Forgive me, my lady," said Sairzan, "but I know of no man by that name. Nor have I received word that a Countess of surpassing beauty was coming to grace my house with her presence."

"Surely you must have seen him," said Ark. "A man of Caerish descent, like myself, about your height, weathered from much exposure to the sun. He would commonly wear leather armor and carry a sword."

Sairzan hesitated. "I have seen such a man. He works as a bodyguard for some of the merchants in the dockside. But I fear I have not seen him here for three or four days."

Ark's cold mask turned into a genuine scowl.

Sairzan swallowed. "My lady, I fear that this rogue Narmer has taken advantage of your generous nature. He took your coin, and then abandoned his duty to you."

"So you have not seen him for three days?" said Caina.

Sairzan shrugged. "Forgive me, my lady, but this Narmer is a small and insignificant man. Had I but known that he was in service to your radiant personage, I would have kept closer watch over his comings and goings.

But, alas, no such news reached my ears."

"This is most distressing," said Caina, wondering what had happened to Narmer. It was not like a Ghost to be late. Some mishap must have befallen him. But what sort of mishap?

"Ah, Countess, it grieves me to see you so distraught," said Sairzan. He bowed again over her hand, planting his lips on her ring. "I beg of you, permit me to prepare my finest rooms for you at once, to make up for this Narmer's faithlessness. Your smile, I am sure, would be more radiant than the sun itself."

Despite herself, Caina laughed. "Your flattery amuses me, shameless though it is. Very well. Have rooms prepared. Also, send some of your servants to unload my baggage. My maids are weary from the journey, and have earned some rest."

"My lady is gracious," said Sairzan. He clapped his hands again, and servants rushed to do his bidding. "Will you take some refreshment while you wait?"

"Yes, of course," said Caina. "Send some food to my maids, as well. Ark, pay him, and then come join me."

Ark handed some coins to the innkeeper. Servants appeared bearing glasses of wine and trays of cheese and fresh fruit. Caina realized that she was ravenous and took the food. A few moments later Ark joined her at the table, his face grim.

"Where's Narmer?" said Caina, voice pitched low.

"I don't know," said Ark. He bit into an apple with too much force. "I spoke with the servants unloading your chests. Several of them know Narmer by name, yet no one has seen him for three days."

"What do you think happed to him?" said Caina. She took a sip of the wine. It was very good. Halfdan would have loved it.

"I don't know. Narmer has always been reliable," said Ark. For the first time since Caina had met him, Ark seemed baffled. "He was in the Legions, as was I. Steady man. Knows how to handle himself." He shook his head. "Something must have gone amiss. Either he's gone to ground somewhere. Or he's dead."

"Doesn't your Ghost circle have protocols for unanticipated disaster?" said Caina. "You should have a meeting point, or a safe house."

Ark's eyes flashed. "Of course we have protocols. We're not fools." He took a deep breath, getting himself under control. "There's more. When I checked on the servants I went outside to have a look. There's another member of the Rasadda circle, a woman named Crastia. She's a ceramics merchant, keeps her booth here in the square, across from Corazain's pyramid. The booth is empty. The servants say that about two weeks ago she didn't show up, and hasn't appeared since."

Caina stared into her wine, thinking hard. "Could the secrecy of the

Rasadda circle have been breached?"

"Possibly," said Ark. "But I cannot see how."

Caina shrugged. "A simple mishap. Treachery, perhaps. And the magi of the Imperial Magisterium have spells that let them pry into another man's mind."

"Absurd," said Ark. "They are forbidden to do so under Imperial law."

"Oh, certainly. And the magi have been ever keen to obey Imperial law," said Caina.

"Is that your answer for everything?" said Ark. "You were quick enough to blame the Magisterium at Halfdan's inn. And on what basis? No magus I have ever met has acted other than honorably."

Caina glared at him. "The magi wield sorcery. And as it happens, sorcery was employed in these burning deaths."

"Sorcery," said Ark, his voice dripping scorn. "Are you a Ghost nightfighter, or some peasant child to blame every misfortune on sorcery? Perhaps those thugs in the alley were conjured up by sorcery. Or some sorcerer summoned that lion out on the plains."

For a moment Caina was so angry that she could not answer. Her fingers tightened hard around the stem of her glass, and she simply stared at Ark.

His dead gray eyes did not waver.

For a moment they did not speak.

"It is clear," said Caina, ice in her voice, "that we shall have to exercise the utmost caution. The secrecy of your circle has been breached, that is plain. Perhaps whoever is behind these burning murders did not appreciate your circle's investigation. We lack information, and until we know more, we shall have regard everyone with suspicion. Even the Magisterium. Despite how eager you seem to lick their fingers."

Ark's eyes got harder. "I put twenty years in the legions, girl. I've killed more men that I can remember, and most of them before you had your first moon's blood. Probably even before you were born. I earned my centurion's plumes, and I led my men through the sort of slaughter that would leave someone like you weeping and broken if you witnessed it. Were you to live through a tenth of the things I've endured, it would break your mind." He leaned closer. "I am no man's dog."

"All that may be true, centurion," said Caina, "but in the Ghosts I still outrank you."

Ark sat back, his hand curling into a fist.

Caina sighed. "So Crastia is gone. Do you have another contact?"

Ark blinked, caught off-guard by the sudden shift in topic. "I do. A man named Aulean. He works as a cook in the Imperial Basilica, for Lord Governor Nicephorus himself."

"Then you shall have to speak to him," said Caina. "It…"

41

Sairzan approached their table, bowing, and Caina fell silent. "My lady. Your rooms are prepared, if you wish to go up."

"Shortly," said Caina. "After we finish eating. Despite this unpleasantness with Narmer, you have done well, master innkeeper. I thank you for your service."

"Ah," said Sairzan, "you accused me falsely of flattery, Countess. Your smile is indeed as radiant as I claimed." He bowed again and walked away.

Ark shook his head. "I shall never get used to how your voice can simply…change. You sound like two different women."

"That displeases you, does it not?" said Caina, her voice icy again.

"Yes. It does," said Ark. "Who are you truly? A Ghost of the Empire, or an Imperial Countess? Or a girl play-acting at being a Ghost?"

"I've already told you," said Caina, "that my name is Countess Marianna Nereide." She stood, tired of the argument. "Now, come. You need to speak with Aulean, and if you go to speak with him directly it will look suspicious. The best way, I think, will be to contrive a dinner invitation with Lord Governor Nicephorus." She smiled at Ark. "And pretty, empty-headed Countesses make for fine dinner companions, do they not?"

Ark said nothing. But he followed her up the stairs as Sairzan led her to her rooms. Caina glanced back at Ark, wondered how best to handle him. He had saved her life in that alley. But, clearly, he was beginning to loathe her, if he had not already. It seemed that the proud centurion rankled at taking orders from a woman sixteen years his junior. But why? Surely Ark was used to taking orders from men he loathed; soldiers were never fond of their commanders.

Or was there something more to it than that?

Caina didn't know, and it annoyed her. They had bigger problems at the moment. But she wished the Rasadda circle at sent someone else to ask for Halfdan's help. Or maybe that was why they had sent him; perhaps he was too unreliable to be trusted with anything other than delivering messages, despite his formidable skill with that broadsword.

"Here we are, my lady," said Sairzan, opening a door. Her rooms were a sprawling suite on the Inn's top floor. It had a sitting room, an expansive bedroom, a set of smaller rooms for the servants, and a large bathtub hewn of black marble, with hot water piped up from below. Caina appreciated that.

She also appreciated the large balcony that opened off the bedroom, looking down on the great square below Corazain's pyramid. For someone with a rope and grapnel, it would make coming and going unseen all the easier. Especially at night. Dark and grim this city might be, but Caina's cloak would blend well with the darkness.

"The rooms are superb, master innkeeper," said Caina. "You have my thanks."

"Simply call if you need anything, my lady, and I shall be at your side in moments." Sairzan bowed and departed.

"What will you do now?" said Ark.

"I shall try to contrive a dinner invitation to Lord Governor Nicephorus's table," said Caina. "You can then find a way to contact Aulean without drawing suspicion."

"And how will you do that?" said Ark.

"I haven't yet decided," said Caina. "I…"

She frowned. Someone was shouting. In fact, a lot of people were shouting. She walked past Ark, into the bedroom, and onto the balcony overlooking the square.

People, thousands of people, were streaming into the square. For a moment Caina thought that the Saddai had risen up in revolt, but no one in the throng was carrying weapons. They walked towards the Basilica, all shouting the same thing in Saddaic over and over again.

Bread and justice. Bread and justice.

"Get off the balcony, now," hissed Ark. "You're too fine a target."

"No," said Caina. "None of them are even armed. And they're all looking at the Basilica."

Ark glared at her for a moment, then strapped his shield to his left arm and joined her on the balcony.

The thunderous chant rolled on and on for some time. A figure in a red robe came to the head of the crowd. A woman, Caina saw, and an old one, to judge from her halting step and the cane in her left hand.

"That robe," said Caina. "Is that…"

"Aye," said Ark. "She's a priestess of the Living Flame. The Saddai commoners will do whatever she says." His voice tightened. "In fact, I think that's…"

"Hear me!" The woman's voice, rich and strong, rolled over the square. The volume of it astounded Caina. "Lord Governor Anatsius Nicephorus, hear me! I am Tadaia, a Sister of the Living Flame, and I have been chosen to speak for the Saddai of Rasadda!"

"You know her?" said Caina.

"Everyone knows her," said Ark. "She is the eldest Sister of the Living Flame, the preeminent priestess in Rasadda, and much loved among the poorer Saddai." He hesitated. "If not for her, the Saddai would have erupted in revolt years ago. But she's never done anything like this before."

Tadaia's great voice rolled on. "We come in peaceful petition as loyal subjects of the great Emperor of Nighmar. The people have been driven from their land so that cattle might graze where once wheat grew, and we are hungry. The grain dole is not enough, Lord Governor. Our men go hungry, our women suffer in silence, and our children go to bed with empty bellies. Give us justice, Lord Governor, and succor to those under your protection."

The crowd murmured approval to her words.

Caina wondered how many of them had flame tattoos upon their chests.

The doors to the Basilica swung open. A troop of militia marched out, Valgorix at their head in his plumed helm. The men gripped crossbows with nervous hands, eyes sweeping over the throng.

"Depart at once!" Valgorix's voice seemed weak compared to Tadaia's, but Caina could still hear it clear enough. "This is an illegal assembly, in violation of Lord Governor Nicephorus's decree. If you depart immediately, no punishment will be leveled upon you, but should you linger, the consequences shall be dire!"

An angry rumble went through the crowd. But Tadaia's voice rang out once more. "The people hunger, and unless the grain dole is increased, we shall soon starve."

"You will have to make do with the grain dole," said Valgorix, his face pained. "Are you starving? Then find work, and purchase your own food."

"There is no work to be had, you know this," said Tadaia. "These people were driven from their lands by the corrupt and wicked, and had no choice but to come to Rasadda. Shall we grow food from paving stones and courtyards?"

"Be off at once!" said Valgorix. "This is your final warning!"

"Look," said Ark, his voice low and urgent. "Horsemen. There, there, and there, at the mouths of those streets."

Caina nodded. "And crossbowmen there, and there, on the parapets of the Basilica."

Ark snarled a vicious curse. "If Tadaia refuses to leave, Nicephorus will slaughter them all. And if Tadaia is killed, the city will explode in revolt." He shook his head, every muscle radiating tension. "And if this city goes up in revolt…it will drown in an ocean of blood before the end."

For a moment neither Tadaia nor Valgorix said anything. Caina saw more horsemen maneuvering in the streets, saw the crossbowmen wind and load their weapons. The tension in the air turned electric.

Then Tadaia took a step backwards.

"We wish for no blood to be spilled today," she called. "And let every man and woman mark it well: we came in peace to our Lord Governor, and he threatened us with death. So be it! But we shall return in a week, and the week after that, until justice is done."

Valgorix said nothing, but his men raised their crossbows. And then Tadaia turned her back to them and faced her people. The sheer courage of it took Caina's breath away.

"Do not be bitter, my brothers and sisters!" said Tadaia. "Let us support each other in our sufferings. Remember what the Living Flame has taught us. Temporal suffering is the fire that refines us. Pain is the crucible that burns away our impurities, so that we might be made pure for our next lives, and may one day join the Living Flame in eternal light. Let us lean on each other, brothers and sisters, in this time of adversity."

She limped from the plaza, head held high, the click of her cane against the ground loud in the silence. The mob followed her, draining back into the streets. The mounted militia moved aside to let them past.

"Gods, that was close," said Ark. "If some fool had squeezed his trigger a little too tightly, we'd have had five years of war."

Caina watched the mob draining away. "It seems that she has legitimate grievances."

"Yet she did not mention the murders at all," said Ark.

"Perhaps she has bigger concerns," said Caina. "Or maybe the victims were unloved by the Saddai."

"Or, perhaps," said Ark, "she wished not to draw attention to them."

Caina frowned. "You think she is behind these murders?"

"Why not?" said Ark. "Her people are starving and desperate. And you yourself said that desperate men have more reason to murder than most. I assume the same would apply to women as well."

"It would," said Caina. Her mother flashed through her thoughts for a moment, and her hand crept towards her father's ring, hidden beneath her clothes. "It would." She shook her head to clear away the memories. "But if this Nicephorus has let matters degenerate to this point, then he is a fool."

A short time later a knock came at the door.

Julia opened it to reveal a liveried messenger from Lord Governor Nicephorus.

"Countess Marianna Nereide?" he said.

"I am," said Caina. "Your business with me?"

"The Lord Governor has heard of your arrival in the city, and wishes to make your acquaintance. To that end, he invites you to a banquet, to be held tonight at the eighth hour in the Imperial Basilica."

"Please convey to the Lord Governor my thanks for his gracious invitation," said Caina. "I am honored, and shall be glad to attend."

The messenger bowed and departed.

"That was quick," said Ark.

"Yes," murmured Caina. "It seems that Valgorix reported to Nicephorus. Perhaps we'll finally have some answers tonight."

CHAPTER 6
LORD NICEPHORUS'S BANQUET

It took a lot of work to get ready for the Lord Governor's banquet.

She started with a long soak in the black tub, the heat sinking into her muscles. She felt better with the sweat and grime of the road washed away. And the festivities in the alley had left blood under her fingernails. The clotted blood came loose and dissolved in the hot water.

Cornelia helped with her hair. For all her sharp tongue, the older woman did a splendid job. She arranged Caina's hair into an elaborate braided crown, and did it faster than Caina herself could have managed.

Two hours later she was bathed, shaved, coiffed, perfumed, and dressed. She chose an elaborate green gown with gold embroidery on the sleeves and bodice. It left, perhaps, a touch too much of her shoulders and chest exposed, but depending on the Lord Governor's character, that could prove an asset. She wore her father's ring on a chain hidden beneath her sleeve. The usual daggers remained hidden in her boots. The gown had large enough sleeves that Caina could strap an extra pair of knives to her forearms. She appreciated that.

At last she emerged from the bedroom and into the sitting room. Ark sat in a chair, working nicks from his sword blade. He looked at her, and his eyes turned colder for a moment.

"You look different," he said.

"As I've told you before," said Caina, "that is the point."

"Our lady looks as lovely as the dawn," Julia told him with a hint of reproach.

It came and went so fast that Caina thought she might have imagined it, but something like pain shivered through Ark's icy eyes for an instant. "Indeed. Master Sairzan has lent us a coachman, and we may leave whenever you are ready."

"Then let us depart," said Caina. She looked at her maids. "Thank you, all. You have liberty for the rest of the evening."

She followed Ark down the stairs, taking care to keep her balance. Damnable skirts! The coach waited in the courtyard, one of Sairzan's servants in the driver's seat. Ark opened the door for her, and Caina climbed inside. It seemed silly to ride the coach across the plaza, but an Imperial Countess would not walk to her destination. Besides, after the attack in the alley, Caina was glad for the extra protection the coach offered.

After a ridiculously short ride, they arrived. Ark opened the door, Caina climbed out, and they walked into the Basilica.

"My lady Countess," said a servant, bowing to her, "this way, please."

Servants pulled open the doors, and Caina walked past a troop of armed militiamen and into the Basilica's judgment hall. The immense groin-vaulted roof arched a hundred feet over her head. The floor had been done in elaborate, massive mosaics, depicting triumphs from the Empire's past. One showed the Emperor Crisius defeating the Ashbringer Corazain.

Dozens of glowing glass spheres sat on intricate bronze pedestals, throwing back the darkness. The Magisterium used their sorcery to enchant the spheres, Caina knew, imbuing them with a spell that would glow for years. The steady light glinted off the polished marble columns and the high ceiling. Dozens of men and women stood in the judgment hall, Lords and Ladies of the Empire, rich Saddai and Nighmarian merchants, all speaking to one another in low voices. There were even some Anshani and Alqaarin merchants from across the Alqaarin Sea, exotic with their dark skins and feathered turbans. Servants hastened to and fro bearing trays of wine and food, and musicians played gentle songs in the dark corners.

The servant led Caina and Ark to a group of men standing near the judgment seat.

My Lord Governor," said the servant, "may I present Countess Marianna, of House Nereide."

Lord Governor Anatsius Nicephorus regarded her in silence for a moment, and Caina took the opportunity to size him up. He was a lean, wolfish man in his mid-forties, with deep-sunk eyes and silver-streaked black hair. He wore elaborate black finery, along with the crimson cloak and the polished ceremonial cuirass of his rank. Sword and dagger hung from his belt, but neither weapon seemed to have seen much use. At last he bowed over her hand and kissed her ring.

"And I," he said, speaking in High Nighmarian, "am Anatsius, of House Nicephorus, Lord of the Empire, and Lord Governor of the Saddai Province." Caina offered him a deep bow in turn. "You do us honor. I have never yet seen a scion of House Nereide in my province."

"Our house is old in honor, my lord, but currently of small renown, alas," said Caina, answering him in the same language. In fact, House Nereide had been exterminated during the War of the Fourth Empire a century and a half past, but Caina doubted that Nicephorus knew that. "Only recently has my father turned his hand to commercial pursuits, and he has sent me upon a tour of our Empire's provinces."

"Ah," said Nicephorus, "your father has my sympathies. It is a crass and undignified age, is it not, when we of high birth must scrabble for coins like any commoner? Still, my affairs have certainly prospered since I came to Rasadda, and I hope your father's do the same."

"You are kind, my lord," said Caina.

Nicephorus gestured to a man standing near him. "This is Septimus Romarion, a merchant of no little renown. We have managed to make each other a great deal of money over the years. Perhaps he can do the same for your father."

Romarion. Caina recognized that name.

She had seen it in Publius Vanio's ledger. The dead merchant had purchased rare artworks, possibly stolen, from Romarion.

Now. How to pry some answers from him?

"An honor, Countess," said Romarion, kissing her ring. He was about thirty or thirty-five, she guessed, with the sun-lined face of a lifelong sailor. He looked vaguely Saddai, but both his name and accent were Nighmarian. "It does me good to look upon your beauty, I confess, and to hear your accent. I grew up in the Imperial capital, but I made my fortune in the provinces. I do grow homesick from time to time, though."

"I am pleased," said Caina, "indeed, doubly so, to meet men of such courtesy so far from the capital." She smiled at him. "I had heard that provincials were crass and undignified, and I shall have the servant who told me so whipped, for clearly he lied to me."

"Well, we are far from the lights and temples of Nighmar," said Nicephorus, "and must dwell among a barbarous and uncouth people, but we carry on the best we can." Two men in black robes moved behind him, speaking to each other in low voices. "Ah. Here is someone else I should like you to meet." He beckoned to the black-robed men.

Caina's smile froze in place.

Two brothers of the Magisterium. No, not brothers, but masters. Both magi wore ceremonial purple hoods trailing down the back of their black robes, and purple sashes around their waists. One was short and lean, his head bald, his eyes bright blue. The other magus was tall and gaunt, his mouth set in a perpetual frown, his dark eyes moving back and forth, his graying hair unkempt.

"We are honored to have two masters of the Magisterium among us," said Nicephorus. "Countess Marianna Nereide, may I present Master Kalastus," he gestured to the bald man, "the head of Rasadda's Magisterium chapter, and his second, Master Ephaeron."

"Learned masters," said Caina. It shocked her, how her voice stayed calm and pleasant. "I am honored to meet you." They both bowed and kissed her ring. Their touch made her skin crawl with revulsion. She could sense the presence their sorcery, like needles pricking against her skin.

The price she had paid to gain the sensitivity was not something she wished to recall.

"My lady," said Kalastus. "Truly, the tales of your beauty have been underestimated." He had a sonorous, strong voice, a voice made for oratory.

"Thank you, learned master," said Caina.

"Kalastus has been with us for some time," said Nicephorus. "Ephaeron only just arrived from the Imperial capital."

"Yes," said Ephaeron. He sounded tired, distracted. "I much would have preferred to remain in the capital, but the study of arcane sciences demanded that I travel here." He took a flute of wine from a passing servant, drank, and fell silent.

Kalastus smiled, whispered under his breath, and crooked a finger. The crawling tension in Caina's skin increased. A flute of wine floated off a startled servant's tray, drifted through the air, and stopped before Caina's hand.

"A glass of wine, my lady?" said Kalastus, smiling. He was looking at her in a way that she did not at all like. For a panicked moment Caina wondered if he had used his spells to pry into her thoughts, to learn her real identity. But, no. There was no suspicion in his gaze, only lust. "You have not had anything to drink."

"Thank you, learned one," said Caina, taking the floating glass. "I fear that wine makes me light-headed. Though how could I refuse a glass brought to my hand by such extraordinary means?"

"I could have just carried it to you," said Romarion. They all laughed, and Caina made herself laugh with them. A bell rang out, and more servants hurried into the hall.

"Ah," said Nicephorus. "Dinner is ready. Please, let us be seated."

Caina sat at the high table, along with Nicephorus, Romarion, the magi, and the wealthier merchants. The servants placed tray after tray upon the table, laden with meats, vegetables, fruits, pastries, and more. It was ten times more food than everyone at the table could eat, and people were starving in Rasadda's streets. It made Caina vaguely sick, but she made herself eat and make polite small talk.

"I understand that you were attacked, my lady," said Nicephorus, spearing a piece of beef with his dagger. "Ambushed on the streets, I understand?"

"A small matter, my lord," said Caina, taking a sip of wine. "My captain of guard dispatched the attackers easily enough. Though, alas, my coachman was slain."

Nicephorus's eyebrows rose. "My Decurion told me that your captain of guard left eight corpses in his wake."

"Oh, yes," said Caina. Ark stood nearby, ostensibly watching over her. He murmured a few words to every servant that passed, and they answered him back. To judge from his annoyed expression, he was not getting good answers. "He has been in my father's service for some years, and is most skilled with a sword."

"It is well that he accompanied you," said Nicephorus. "The vermin in the streets are getting out of hand. Soon, I fear, I shall have to take stern measures."

"There was one strange thing, Lord Governor," said Caina. "All the dead men had a most curious tattoo, a flame upon their chests. Have you ever heard of such a thing?"

Nicephorus looked at Romarion and the magi, and the other men laughed. Except for Ephaeron, who only looked distracted.

"My lord?" said Caina. "Have I said something amusing?"

"Not at all," said Nicephorus. "Forgive me. You ran afoul of the so-called Sons of Corazain."

"Who are they?" said Caina.

"The local troublemakers," said Nicephorus. He took a long drink of wine, and continued speaking. "Are you familiar with the history of the Saddai?" Caina shook her head. "You've heard the name of Corazain, no doubt. He is a hero to these Saddai rabble. He was their last king, before the Empire, and he was also utterly insane. A pyromancer. Or an Ashbringer, as the Saddai called them. The Emperor Crisius crushed him, the Magisterium slaughtered the pyromancers, and the Saddai kingdom became a province of the Empire. These 'Sons' of Corazain have the ridiculous notion that one day the Ashbringers will return, and they shall drive out the Empire."

"A harrowing tale," said Caina.

"A ridiculous one," said Nicephorus. "Were the Saddai to rise, we would crush them utterly."

"I have heard the most fearful tales about Rasadda, I do confess," said Caina. "One of my maids heard a story that people were being burnt alive in the streets."

Nicephorus frowned, and both Kalastus and Ephaeron looked at her.

"Surely it is not true, is it?" said Caina. "My maid told me…well," she lowered her voice, "that sorcery was used in these burnings."

Both Kalastus burst out laughing, while Ephaeron frowned.

"Countess," said Ephaeron, "you should discipline your maid. The art of pyromancy is long extinct."

"Pyromancy?" said Caina. "I've never heard that word before."

"It refers to the discipline of arcane science that deals with fire sorcery," said Kalastus. "It is incredibly dangerous, both to the practitioner and any bystanders, but a man adept in pyromantic arts could achieve dreadful feats of power. The Ashbringers, of course, were the paramount masters of pyromancy in the world. But the Magisterium exterminated them utterly, and destroyed their books of lore. There are no pyromancers left in the world."

"Nor should there be," said Ephaeron. "Pyromancy is an abomination, one of the arcane sciences forbidden by Imperial law. Countess Marianna, you may tell your maid that should some fool dare to practice pyromantic arts, the Magisterium will show him no mercy."

"I shall sleep the easier for it," said Caina.

Nicephorus shrugged. "In truth, we have found a number of burned corpses scattered through the city, but the explanation is simple enough. You've seen those black pyramids, I assume, with the fires upon their tops? They are the tombs of old Ashbringers, and those damnable fires burn eternally through their sorcery. No doubt the murderers slew their victims, threw the bodies into the fire, and then dumped the corpses into the street to incite the rabble." He shook his head. "And it seems to be working, too, from the way the populace seethes."

"It is not hard to see why. The people are desperate and starving," said Ephaeron. "Little wonder they place their faith in phantasms from the past."

Nicephorus scowled. "Their miseries are their own fault, I have told you that before."

"Forgive me," said Caina, "but I have seen more beggars in Rasadda than anywhere else in the Empire. Has there been some sort of famine, or perhaps a drought?"

"They are simply too lazy to find work," said Nicephorus. "When I first received command of this province, my associates and I," he waved his hand at the assorted merchants and lords seated at the high table, "perceived at once that the lands of the Saddai peasantry were underused. So we purchased their lands as cheaply as possible and converted them over to pasture land." His mouth twisted with contempt. "But rather than take the opportunity to better themselves, the fools all drifted into Rasadda to beg, claiming that they could not support themselves."

"Pardon my ignorance, for I know only a little of Imperial law," said Caina, "but is it not illegal for a Lord Governor to purchase lands in his own province?"

She thought he would take offense, or refuse to answer. But instead Nicephorus looked indulgently amused. Caina realized that he did not see her as an equal, and therefore not as an enemy, but only as a pretty, empty-headed Countess. Just as she had intended.

"My dear Countess," laughed Nicephorus, "of course it is illegal! But laws may be purchased, just like anything else. Our new pastures have proved productive beyond our wildest imaginations. We now dominate the markets for beef, cheese, and leather in the eastern Empire, and have even made contacts among the Anshani and Alqaarin." He waved a hand at the foreign merchants. "Someday you will understand that a man must do whatever is necessary to make his own fortune." His indulgent smile widened. "How else could a man hope to win the heart of a lady as fair as you?"

"Of course," said Caina.

"I only wish the Emperor would relax the Imperial ban against slavery," said Nicephorus. "The rabble choking Rasadda's streets are fit for nothing else. I could dominate the Istarish and Alqaarin slave markets, become the wealthiest man in the Empire, and clear the streets of the rabble within three weeks."

"Of course," said Caina again. An icy knot of rage hardened her stomach. She thought of the daggers in her boots, and wondered how it would feel to slam one of those blades into his smirking face. Instead she took another drink of wine. Haeron Icaraeus was dead, and House Icaraeus disgraced, but it seemed that Nicephorus shared the late Lord Haeron's views.

The banquet wore on. Ark finished speaking to the servants and took up position against the wall, watching everything. Caina knew him well enough by now to see the angry glint in his cold eyes. She guessed that he had not been able to find Aulean.

"Your bodyguard is most vigilant, my lady," said Ephaeron suddenly, his eyes flicking back and forth between them. "He seems to have questioned every servant in the hall, and his eyes have left you only rarely. Such vigilance is to be commended."

"It is, learned master," said Caina. "He slew eight of the thugs, after all. I have no concerns for my safety while in his company."

"Come here, man," said Ephaeron. Ark lifted an eyebrow, but crossed the room and bowed before the magus. "What is your name?"

"Ark, of Caer Marist."

"Very good." Ephaeron gestured, and a glass of wine floated from a tray to Ark's hand. "Please drink, and help yourself to any food you desire. Valor is a rare thing, and ought to be rewarded." Nicephorus looked affronted, but he remained silent.

Ark seemed puzzled, but he bowed again. "Thank you, learned master. You do me honor." He helped himself to some meat and cheese, took a drink of wine, and retreated to his corner.

The interminable banquet wore on. Caina's mood darkened, and she said little, but she hardly needed to, as Nicephorus and Romarion continued to flirt with her. At long last the meal ended, and the servants began to take away the uneaten food.

"It is my custom, my lady, to walk the balcony after a meal and take a glass of wine," said Nicephorus. "I would be most honored if you would join me."

Caina suspected that Nicephorus would invite her to his bedroom after the balcony. "Thank you, my lord, but I must decline. The wine has made me light-headed, and I shall need to lie down for a while."

"Of course," said Nicephorus. He looked disappointed, but hid it well. "Do feel free to call upon me at any time, should you feel the need."

"And you may call upon me, as well," said Romarion, "for my door shall always be open to you."

"And you must," said Kalastus, "visit our chapterhouse ere you leave Rasadda. We have many wonders we could show you, Countess."

"Indeed," said Caina. She feigned grabbing at Ark's arm for support, and Ark stepped into the ruse without missing a beat. "Truly, you all have been most kind to me. Thank you, my lord governor. I do hope to see you again soon."

They bowed to each other, and Ark escorted Caina from the hall.

"What a collection of fools," said Caina, once they returned to the coach. She had drunk too much wine, and it had put her into a black mood. "Nicephorus is a thief, and an idiot to boot. A quarter of a million people must live in Rasadda. How is the city to feed itself if he illegally buys the peasants' lands and converts them to pasture? That idiot is pushing the Saddai into the biggest revolt the Empire will see in our lifetimes, and he's too blind and too greedy to see it."

"We may have a problem," said Ark.

"I should hope that is obvious."

"A different problem." Ark settled his broadsword between his knees. "I think Ephaeron might have recognized me."

Caina blinked. "What?"

"I told you I served in the Eighteenth Legion," said Ark. His lip twisted. "Or, rather, you figured it out. But it is common practice for a detachment of magi to travel with a legion, to use their arcane sciences for the defense of the Empire. Ephaeron spent four years with the Eighteenth."

Caina scowled. "Do you think he recognized you?"

"I don't know," said Ark. "We never spoke to each other. The magi dislike associating with common soldiers, even with lower-ranking centurions. But we must have seen each other a hundred times, and even took the field together."

"He had to ask your name," said Caina. "He must not have remembered you."

"And he did not seem upset when I told him my alias," said Ark. "Still, it worries me. If he happens to look into the records of the Eighteenth Legion, he will see that I gave him a false name."

"But only if he had reason to become suspicious," said Caina. "And he has no reason to suspect that you are a Ghost. It's not uncommon for a retired centurion to take service with a noble House."

"You are right," said Ark. "But mark me well. Ephaeron looks like a fussy old scholar, but he is both powerful and dangerous. We in the Legion were glad he was on our side. I once saw him slaughter a score of men with a single spell." For a moment he looked haunted at the memory, and then shook his head. "If he learns that we are Ghost spies, he will kill us both out of hand. If we are lucky."

"Yes," said Caina, "I know." There was more venom in her voice than she would have liked. "I know just what crimes the Magisterium is capable of."

Ark frowned, but said nothing.

"Did you make contact with Aulean?" said Caina.

"No," said Ark, his cold face turning even grimmer. "The servants all knew him, of course. They told me that he vanished without a trace three weeks ago. Just like Crastia and Narmer."

"Almost as if," said Caina, "someone was targeting the Ghost circle in Rasadda."

Ark nodded.

"And if Ephaeron committed these murders," said Caina, "and he knew that Narmer, Crastia, and Aulean were all Ghosts, he might realize that you were a member of the Ghost circle."

"Or he could be investigating the murders himself," said Ark, "and if he realizes that Narmer and the others were Ghosts, he might track me down."

Caina rather doubted that Ephaeron would trouble himself, but she still saw the danger. She thought it over for a moment. "Do you have a list of the victims?"

"My circlemaster did," said Ark, "but I could only contact him through Narmer or Crastia."

"That is where we shall start," said Caina. "It is possible that these killings were random, but I doubt it. Our new friend Septimus Romarion, for instance. His name was in Vanio's ledger." Caina laced her fingers. "I suspect the victims are all linked, and if we follow the chain back far enough, we shall find the killer."

"Where will you get this list?" said Ark. His lip twisted. "Shall you charm it out of Nicephorus?"

"No," said Caina. The coach rattled to a stop, and she felt one of the knives tucked into her sleeve. "Nicephorus is a fool. If I want to find anything, I shall have to find it for myself."

CHAPTER 7
NIGHT HUNTING

"This is folly," said Ark.

"I know what I'm doing," said Caina.

They stood in their sitting room at the Inn of Mirrors. Caina had changed into the loose black clothes of a Ghost nightfighter, her weapons and tools belted about her waist. The shadow-woven cloak hung from her shoulders, darker than the night.

"Do you?" said Ark. "Suppose you are captured. Think of how it will look if Countess Marianna Nereide is caught prowling around the Imperial Basilica at night."

"It would look bad," said Caina, checking the knives in their sheaths. "I suppose I'll have to avoid getting caught, then."

"How clever," said Ark. "Are all your plans so cunning?"

Caina gave him a flat look, and resumed checking her tools.

"It is too much of a risk," said Ark. "Ephaeron may or may not have recognized me. But if you are caught, especially while wearing that cloak, they will realize that we're Ghosts."

"Of course it's a risk," said Caina. "Everything we do here is a risk. But we shall learn nothing if we sit here and hide."

"I ought to contact the other members of the Rasadda circle first," said Ark.

"That is too risky," said Caina. "If the circle has been compromised, they'll have gone into hiding. Trying to find their hiding places could be dangerous, both for us and them."

"This is a foolish risk," said Ark.

"Perhaps," said Caina. She looked up from her tools and met his eye. "But I have the higher rank and you do not. Therefore we are going to do it

56

my way."

Ark's icy eyes seemed to boil for a moment, but he gave a curt nod.

Caina concentrated, and slipped into the voice she used while disguised. "Wait here." Her voice hissed and snarled, and was scarce recognizable as female. "I shall be back by dawn."

Ark stared at her. "How do you do that?"

"Practice," said Caina. She tugged the mask over her face and pulled up the black cowl. "Perhaps I'll give you lessons. If any of the maids wake up, tell them that I do not wish to be disturbed until morning."

"And if you're not back by morning?"

"And if I'm not back by morning," said Caina, thinking, "then tell them that Romarion seduced me. It ought to be worth it, just to see Cornelia's expression."

Ark's eye twitched, perhaps in amusement, and he nodded. Caina closed the bedroom door behind her, barred it, and crossed to the balcony. She pulled a steel grapnel and a coil of slim, silken rope from her belt.

A short time later she crept through the nighttime streets. Thanks to Halfdan's training Caina could move stealthily almost without thought. During her training, she labored from dawn to dusk under his tutelage, sometimes until she was so exhausted she could scarce put one foot in front of the other.

But it had paid off. No one saw her as she left the Inn.

Rasadda had no need of street lamps. The everlasting pyres atop the Ashbringers' black pyramids provided adequate illumination. They also threw all matter of tangled shadows across the streets, shadows that blended with Caina's cloak. The great plaza was too much open space, so she took the long way around, taking the streets behind the Inn and past the mansions of the wealthy.

At last she came to the Imperial Basilica. The great judgment hall was the largest feature, but only part of a larger complex. It linked with the Lord Governor's private mansion and the fortified barracks of the city's militia. Guards strolled along the outer wall, crossbows cradled in their arms. Despite the tumult in the city, the militiamen did not look concerned, and Nicephorus had not bothered to post extra men.

Idiot. But it served Caina's purpose.

She settled into a shadow and watched the guards. They did not bother to alter their patrol, and more than once she saw them pause for conversation. Even better. Caina waited until the guards had gone around the corner, then raced across the street, the grapnel whirling in her right hand. She flung it, and it lodged in the stones of the rampart with a soft click. Caina scrambled up the wall, going hand over hand, and rolled onto the rampart. None of the guards had looked in her direction. She undid the grapnel, looped the rope, crept down the stairs to the courtyard, and pressed herself into a shadowy corner.

Trying to keep her breathing quiet, she forced herself to count to sixty.

No one noticed her. No one even bothered to look into the courtyard. Caina grinned beneath her cowl and mask and started moving, keeping to the shadows beneath the ramparts.

Ark was right, really. This was dangerous. But every barracks in the Empire was built to a common plan. Caina would not have dared it otherwise. And she knew exactly where she was going.

She entered the barracks proper and slipped into the common hall. A long table ran the length of the room, but all the men were either sleeping or on duty. Caina took six steps across the room, and heard voices echoing down the stairwell. She looked left, and right, and seeing no better hiding place, ducked into the cold fireplace, wrapping the cloak around her.

Eight militiamen trooped down the stairs, crossbows in hand. A shift change, then. Caina waited until they had exited the common hall, and sprang out of the fireplace and raced for the stairs. In the upstairs room she found rows of the soldiers' bunks, stacked three high. Caina slid under one of the bunks, tugging her cloak tight around her so it would not show.

A few moments later the militiamen from the wall came in and went to their beds. The bunk above Caina creaked, the thin mattress sinking down to within a few inches of her nose. The men grunted and sighed, settling down to sleep, and bit by bit silence fell. Caina counted to three hundred, and slid out from under the bed. The militiamen lay snoring, oblivious to the world. Caina crept past the beds and into the officers' quarters. The common militiamen each had a bunk, but the officers rated a private room, and of course the Decurion had the largest room of all. Caina listened at the door for a moment, picked the lock, and let herself inside.

Valgorix's room had a comfortable bed, a few chairs, and a desk. The Decurion sat at the desk, scowling at a map of the city. Without his plumed helmet, he looked careworn and worried.

Caina crossed the room with silent steps, sliding a knife from her belt. In one smooth motion she reached down and leveled the blade across Valgorix's throat, her gloved hand clamping over his mouth. For an instant Valgorix struggled in sudden panic, but Caina pressed the knife harder against his skin. He went still, breathing hard through his nose.

"Do not scream," hissed Caina in her disguised voice. "I have not come to harm you. Cooperate with me, and you will live through this night. Am I understood?"

Valgorix nodded, carefully. Caina withdrew the knife and stepped into the corner, cloaking hanging about her. Valgorix stood, looked to where his sword lay across his bed, and then looked back at her.

Caina shook her head.

"Have you come to kill me?" said Valgorix, voice thick.

"I have already told you that," said Caina.

Valgorix took a tentative step towards her. "Gods," he whispered. "What...what are you? A demon come to drag me down into hell, or...or some sort of ghost?"

"A ghost?" repeated Caina. "Yes. You could say that."

Valgorix's face went white, and he dropped back into his chair. "A Ghost. One of the Emperor's spies."

"The Emperor has no spies."

"Oh. Of...of course," said Valgorix. Beads of sweat stood out on his forehead. "And should anyone ask me, the Emperor has no spies, is that it?"

Caina nodded.

"What do you want from me?"

"As I said," said Caina, "merely to talk."

Valgorix stared at her. "This...is about those murders, isn't it?"

"What do you think?" said Caina, hoping to draw him out.

"I told the Lord Governor this was going to be a problem," said Valgorix, raking a hand through his hair, "but he wouldn't listen."

"Perhaps," said Caina, "you ought to start from the beginning."

"This business began a year or so ago," said Valgorix. "Some burned corpses began turning up in the streets. At first we thought nothing of it. Most likely some common criminals threw the bodies into the fires atop the pyramids. It's happened before. But more and more bodies kept turning up." He shook his head. "The damnedest thing. You burn a man alive, it makes a hell of a mess. Ash, soot, smoke damage and the like. And it takes a big pile of wood and a lot of oil. But these bodies are always found without any sign of a fire, nor any sign that the bodies have been moved. Just a burned corpse, appearing out of nowhere."

"How did you identify the bodies?" said Caina.

"With difficulty," said Valgorix. "But the evidence added up. In about half the cases the features were roughly intact, though badly damaged. Often the corpses were found in their beds, yet with no damage to the beds. Sometimes family was able to identify the dead men." He shrugged. "Six, though, we simply could not identify."

"The peasants say that sorcery burned those men to death," said Caina.

"Sorcery?" said Valgorix, scoffing. "Oh, indeed. Sorcery. Never mind that the Ashbringers have been extinct since before my grandfather's grandfather was born." A touch of doubt came into his voice. "But...the way these burned corpses appear without a trace of a fire...I can see why the peasants might think that, yes."

"Who were the victims?" said Caina.

"Merchants, mostly," said Valgorix. "Some of Saddai birth, some of

Caerish. No Nighmarians. And some random people of little importance: a cook, a kettle merchant, and the like."

Like Aulean and Crastia, perhaps, along with the rest of Rasadda's Ghost circle.

"Do you have a list of the names?" said Caina.

"I do," said Valgorix, reaching for a paper on his desk. "Or most of them, anyway. A few were too badly burnt to be identified."

"Later," said Caina. "I have a few more questions for you."

"Oh." Valgorix sank back into his chair.

"Rasadda seems to have more than its fair share of beggars," said Caina. "Why is that?"

Valgorix scowled. "More folly on the part of our honorable Lord Governor."

"Folly of what sort?"

The words started pouring out of him. Valgorix, it seemed, had a lot of pent-up frustration. "This business with the farmers. It's illegal for a governor to buy land in his province, everyone knows that, yet Nicephorus and his cronies have bought up half the farmland in Rasadda. That's bad enough, but he's kicked the peasants off their land and converted it to pasture. There's hardly any food coming into the city. We're just getting by on fish and grain shipped from Alqaarin, but the prices are steep. There's a grain dole for the poor, but a fish will cost a man two days' wages." He shook his head. "It's a wonder famine hasn't struck yet. And when it does, we'll all be murdered in our beds, mark my words."

"Why hasn't there been a revolt yet?" said Caina.

"What? Oh. Sister Tadaia. She's keeping a lid on things," said Valgorix.

"Who is she?"

"Sister of the Living Flame. Ah…priestess of the Saddai god, you could say. She's been helping to feed the poor, all the dislocated peasants who've wound up into the city. They all adore her, and she doesn't want a revolt. She knows what will happen if the Saddai rebel." He scratched at his jaw. "I don't know how much longer she'll be able to keep things together."

"Why not?"

Valgorix looked around, and then lowered his voice. "The Sons of Corazain. It's a brotherhood among the peasants. See, Corazain was this…"

"I know who Corazain was."

Valgorix swallowed. "Well, they're a revolutionary group. They haven't done anything yet, at least not anything drastic. They tried to kill an Imperial Countess this morning, but her bodyguard killed seven or eight of them and the rest ran." Caina smiled behind her mask. "But they're getting worse, and Lord Nicephorus won't bother to crack down on them. Especially since Gaidan joined them."

"Gaidan?" Caina had not heard that name before.

"A priest, Brother of the Living Flame. A lot younger than Tadaia. More hot-headed. He'll give these speeches calling for the Saddai to rise up and throw out the Empire. No one listened to him at first, but more and more of the peasants are coming around to his way of thinking. Tadaia's kept him under control so far, but when the food runs out..." He shrugged. "A lot of people are going to get killed."

"I doubt these burning murders have helped matters."

"No." Valgorix shook his head. "From what I hear, most of the Saddai think Lord Nicephorus is behind it."

"And who do you think is behind it, Decurion?"

"I don't know," said Valgorix. "If I had to guess, I'd say Gaidan. I'd arrest the bastard if I could find any basis for a charge, but he keeps his hands clean. Besides, it'd set the Sons of Corazain off, and then we'd have an insurrection."

"So you think Gaidan is behind these murders," said Caina. "But I thought you said the Saddai blamed Nicephorus."

Valgorix shifted in his seat. "They do. Or, at least most of them do. I've heard that Gaidan's lot think the burning deaths are a sign, an omen that an Ashbringer walks among them. In the old times the Ashbringers killed people with fire spells. In the Battle of Rasadda, Corazain used his sorcery to burn an entire legion to ashes, or so I've heard. And I wouldn't put it past Gaidan to play at being an Ashbringer."

"Of if he is one in truth," said Caina. "Do the priests of the Living Flame wield any sorcery?"

Valgorix shrugged. "Some, like most priests, but nothing significant. None of them could match of a magus of the Magisterium, though. And if they tried any pyromancy, they wouldn't last a week before the Magisterium got them."

"I see," said Caina. She thought about it for a moment. "One final question. Have you ever met or seen a merchant from Mors Crisius named Publius Vanio? A fat man, of Caerish birth."

"Aye, I have," said Valgorix. "He came to the city every few weeks, usually did business with both the Lord Governor and another merchant named Romarion."

"Vanio was found burned to death a week past in his townhouse," said Caina.

Valgorix swallowed.

"You have answered well," said Caina, holding out her gloved hand. "I will take that list now."

Valgorix handed over the roll of paper. "Are you going to kill me?"

"Are you deaf? I already told you that I'm not going to kill you," said Caina. "Assuming you're wise enough not to mention our meeting to anyone."

"I won't," said Valgorix. "What are you going to do now?"

"That is none of your concern," said Caina. "I may, however, contact you in the future for further information or assistance."

"Well, you'll have it," said Valgorix. He glanced at his door. "If you want to kill Lord Nicephorus, I think you'd better do it soon. Too much..."

Caina took the opportunity to walk backwards, seize the windowsill, roll over it, and drop down. There was a thin ledge below the sill, and Caina seized it and pressed hard against the wall, pinning her cloak beneath her legs. She hung there and waited.

And it was not a long wait. A moment later she saw Valgorix lean out the windows, scanning the courtyard, eyes wide with consternation. He stared into the night for a moment, muttered a curse, and disappeared back into his room. Caina waited, counted to a hundred. Her arms began to tremble with the effort, but she saw no sign that Valgorix had raised an alarm.

Caina grinned and let go. There were plenty of hand and footholds in the rough wall, and it did not take her very long to get down to the courtyard. Still she saw no sign that anyone had noticed her, so she unhooked her grapnel and started for the wall.

A short time later Caina walked into her sitting room, wearing a nightgown, the roll of names in one hand.

Ark sat in one of the chairs, dozing. Caina's bare feet made no sound against the carpet, but nonetheless Ark's eyes shot open, his hand flying on the hilt of his sword. He stared at her for a moment, face blank, and then relaxed his grip.

"You're back sooner than I thought," he said.

"I told you I knew what I was doing," said Caina. She sat at the table, smoothing the paper, and beckoned Ark to join her.

"What is that?" said Ark. He crossed to the table and sat down, scowling.

"A list of those burned to death," said Caina, read the names. Twenty-six total, all of whom had died in agony. She felt a twinge of anger, and twisted her father's ring, still on the first finger of her left hand.

"How did you get that list?" said Ark.

"Valgorix."

"You stole it from him?"

"No." Caina shook her head. She recognized several of the names on the list. "I asked."

Ark stared at her.

"He was actually quite helpful," said Caina. "It seems that he hates

Lord Nicephorus, and blames him for Rasadda's recent troubles. So he may be useful in the future." She pushed the list towards him. "You'd better read this."

Ark stared at the list for so long that Caina wondered if she had offended him in some way. Maybe he had never learned to read. Then he pointed at a name, his face grim and hard as a marble mask.

"Narmer, of the dockside ward," said Ark.

Caina nodded. "That explains why he never met us here."

"Crastia, of the north ward," said Ark, still reading, "Aulean, of the Imperial Basilica..." He spat a curse and slammed a fist down on the table, his eyes so full of crazed rage that Caina almost took a step back. "Gods damn it. The entire circle. They killed the entire damned circle."

"Keep your voice down," snapped Caina. "If you wake up the maids, we'll have some awkward explanations." Ark glared at her, but he fell silent. "The entire circle? All of them?"

"Yes," hissed Ark, looking back at the list, "all...wait. There's one missing. Other than myself. Our circlemaster. He must have escaped."

"Or no one's found his body yet," said Caina.

Ark glared at her again, but he nodded.

"So someone targeted the Ghosts of Rasadda," said Caina. "The Magisterium, perhaps."

"Why the Magisterium?" said Ark. "You are always so quick to blame them."

"The Magisterium hates the Emperor's Ghosts, because we have more than once stopped them from taking total control of the Empire," said Caina. "You spoke highly of Ephaeron, I know. But that would not stop him from killing us all if given the chance."

"And any of the Empire's other enemies would target the Ghosts," said Ark. "The Sons of Corazain, perhaps."

Caina nodded. "Have you heard of a Brother of the Living Flame named Gaidan?"

Ark nodded. "Yes. He's a troublemaker. In deep with the Sons of Corazain, I heard."

"Valgorix thought he was behind the murders," said Caina. She thought for a moment. "All right. We have three tasks, then. First, we must find as much information as we can about both Nicephorus and his cronies and Gaidan's Sons of Corazain. Our murderer, in all probability, has contact with one of those groups."

"Very well," said Ark.

"We'll also have to try to find your circlemaster," said Caina. "The Ghosts of Rasadda were murdered for a reason. They may have learned something, or they might have gotten too close to the murderer. If your circlemaster is still alive, he almost certainly knows something that we must know."

Ark nodded again.

"And, lastly," said Caina, voice quiet, "we'll have to wait for someone to kill you."

Ark blinked, hand twitching to his sword.

"If someone's gone to the trouble of killing the entire Ghost circle," said Caina, "then they must have been strongly motivated to do it. And if they realized that you were part of the circle, then they'll come for you, sooner or later. We could catch our enemy in the act."

"If they come for me," said Ark, "they will regret it."

"Oh, they'll regret a lot of things," said Caina, "when we catch them. Which we will. What about these other names? Do you recognize them?"

Ark read over the list. "Some of them. Middling merchants, for the most part. Not quite wealthy, but well-to-do."

"Merchants," muttered Caina. "I can see why someone would want to kill the Emperor's spies, but why random merchants? I shall have to lean upon Romarion. I'd be curious to know what kind of business he was conducting with Vanio," she gestured at the list, "or with these men."

"What now?" said Ark.

"Now? Now I'm going to get some sleep," said Caina, "and you should too. Tomorrow I will see if Romarion's still willing to follow up on that dinner invitation."

Ark nodded and returned to his chair, and Caina went to her bedroom. The bed was huge. Caina suspected it had been built for the sort of nobleman who enjoyed sharing it with several mistresses at the same time. But it was comfortable, at least. Caina lay down, and worn out by the day's exertions, she fell asleep at once.

She awoke to pounding at the door. Caina blinked, morning sunlight streaming into her eyes, and rolled out of bed. She crossed to the door, a knife held tight against her forearm, and pulled open the bar.

Ark stood in the doorway.

"What is it?" said Caina.

"Sairzan just found a burned corpse outside the Inn."

CHAPTER 8
A BURNED MAN

A crowd had already gathered by the time Caina and Ark emerged from the Inn.

Caina had wanted to go out at once, but Cornelia and the other maids protested. They had been scandalized that Caina wanted to go out with so little preparation. After some bickering, they settled on a green riding dress and a light cloak of a similar color, her black hair pulled back with a silver clasp. Caina seethed at the delay, but saw no way around it. Bad enough that the maids had already seen her kill; Caina wanted to give them further hints that she was an Emperor's Ghost.

So by the time they had gotten to the Inn's courtyard, the crowd had already gathered. Mostly wealthier Saddai and Nighmarian merchants, though more poor Saddai peasants than Caina would have expected. Militiamen in leather jerkins held the crowd at bay, spears and crossbows ready in their hands.

The smell struck Caina at once, the same charred, greasy stench she had encountered in Vanio's bedroom. Burned flesh was a hard sort of smell to forget. It was not as strong as she might have expected, but perhaps the odor had dissipated somewhat in the open air.

"Where?" muttered Caina, as they threaded around the edges of the crowd.

"The alleyway behind the Inn," said Ark.

Caina shook her head. "I walked past there twice last night, and saw nothing. It must have happened within the last few hours. How did they find the body?"

"One of Sairzan's serving girls found it," said Ark. "I was eating breakfast and heard her scream. Sairzan and I found her out here, and he sent one of his servants running for the militia."

"You saw the body, then?" said Caina. She saw more militiamen blocking the alley's entrance.

"Aye," said Ark. "No one I recognized."

"The face was intact, then?" said Caina.

Ark frowned. "Yes."

"Odd." Vanio's features had been badly burnt, and Valgorix had said several of the dead remained unidentified. "That's not like the others."

"But I discerned nothing else from the corpse," said Ark. His mouth twisted. "When you look at him, no doubt you'll be able to unravel all his secrets from a single glance."

Caina chose not to respond that. "Let us hope so. We could use whatever we can find."

She spotted an officer's red plume, and saw Valgorix talking to his men. It seemed that the Decurion himself had come to take charge of the investigation. He looked worse than before. Evidently a midnight visit from a Ghost had not improved his nerves.

Caina beckoned Ark to follow her, and began striding towards the militiamen. "Decurion? Decurion!" she called in her most imperious tone.

Valgorix scowled, saw her, and made a quick bow. "Countess. Forgive me, but this is a very poor time."

"I heard another of these dreadful burned corpses was found outside the Inn," said Caina, adding a little quaver to her voice.

Valgorix's expression softened a little. "I'm afraid you are correct. As I told you yesterday, the city's streets are not safe, and you should remain indoors."

"But I must speak with you!" said Caina, letting the words tumble out of her. "I am sorry to interrupt your duties, but one of my maids disappeared last night, along with my new coachman. They haven't returned yet, and I thought…and I thought…"

Valgorix stepped towards her, frowning. "You're sure?"

"I am," said Caina. Her lip trembled just a bit. "It's just…since I've come to the city my coachman was murdered, and now my maid has disappeared."

"Come with me," said Valgorix. "Lady…I warn you, this sight might be upsetting. But if you can identify the corpse, that will be of great help." He glanced at Ark. "If your captain doesn't object?"

"Only if I come with her," said Ark.

"Very well," said Valgorix. "Follow me." He led the way into the alley, and the burnt smell grew stronger. A corpse lay slumped against the Inn's gleaming black wall. "Here it is."

Caina looked at the dead man. Some part of her concentration went to maintaining an appropriate expression of shock and horror, but the rest of her attention focused on the naked corpse before her. It was a man, middle forties, of Caerish birth, most likely. He had been badly burned across the legs, torso, and lower arms, but his head and shoulders remained mostly undamaged. Caina's eyes swept over the corpse, noting the details.

She recognized the man at once.

"Do you know him?" said Valgorix.

"No," she said. "No. I'm sorry. I don't know him." She gave him a tremulous little smile. "I'm just…I'm just relieved it's not my maid."

Valgorix sighed. "Of course. I'm sorry to have wasted your time," he said, in a tone that suggested his time had been wasted.

"It…wait," said Caina. "I don't know him, but I think I might have seen him before. Last night, when I dined with the Lord Governor. I thought I saw him in the Imperial Basilica."

Valgorix turned towards her, eyes intent. "You did? Can you remember his name?"

"I'm…I'm afraid not, Decurion," said Caina. "There were so many people going back and forth, so many servants, and I'm afraid I have little memory for names. But I am sure I saw him in the Imperial Basilica last night. Perhaps he was a servant."

"That is more to go on than we had before," said Valgorix. "Thank you, Countess. And if I were you, I would speak sternly to your maid and new coachman. They have worried you needlessly, and no doubt they simply crept out for a tryst."

"No doubt," said Caina. "May the Imperial gods smile upon your investigations." She turned, and let Ark lead her back to the square.

"You didn't recognize him?" said Ark.

"Keep your voice down. Of course I recognized him," said Caina.

"But you said…"

"A Countess of the Empire cannot be bothered to remember the little people," said Caina. "And before you ask, I gave him that hint on purpose. The poor fool would blunder around for days trying to identify the body otherwise."

Ark took a deep breath. "Who was it, then?"

"I don't know his name. But I did indeed see him in the Imperial Basilica last night. Some merchant. One of Nicephorus's cronies, I think. He spent most of his time talking with Septimus Romarion."

"The same Romarion you saw in Vanio's ledgers?" said Ark. "And this man has been murdered in the same manner as Vanio."

"No," said Caina. "The deaths were nothing alike. This man was not burned to death."

Ark stared at her. "Ridiculous."

Caina stopped, took his arm, and lowered her voice. Ark's arm felt like a bundle of taut steel cables, and his cold eyes locked on her. "He was stabbed to death. You could not see it? Four, maybe five stab wounds to the chest. Either blood loss finished him, or one of the blows found his heart. Then the corpse was thrown into a fire and dragged here. Probably one of the pyramid pyres." She glanced at the Great Pyramid of Corazain's flaming crown. "Not that one. Probably that smaller pyramid on the other side of the square. A shorter climb, and it's about the same distance to walk. No doubt they burned the body to cover their tracks. Twenty-six burned corpses have turned up. What's one more? Then they dumped the corpse here – you could see the soot marks on the street were they dragged it – and they fled."

Ark said nothing.

"Do you disagree?"

He pulled free of her grasp and shook his head. "You have the eyes of a hawk, or perhaps a demon." He thought of a moment. "So, who do you think killed this man?"

"I have no idea," said Caina. "It was not the same person or group behind the other deaths, that is plain. I suspect this man's business rivals killed him, and then made his death look like the others in order to disguise their involvement. Merchants have enemies, after all."

"That makes sense," said Ark. "I wonder...get behind me!"

He shoved her behind him, his broadsword flying into his hand. Caina frowned, caught her balance, and turned, reaching towards the knives hidden in her sleeves.

Saddai peasants were filling the square.

A lot of Saddai peasants. Two hundred, at least. And unlike those who had followed Sister Tadaia, they looked violent, and ready for blood. Some had taken off their tunics, and Caina saw the flame tattoo of the Sons of Corazain. At least a dozen of them were heading towards her and Ark, clubs in hand. This was bad. Caina wondered if they could run for the Inn, or vanish into the streets...

"Imperial-born bitch," snarled one in Saddaic, "you should have never set foot upon our lands."

Ark's broadsword came up, the steel reflecting the sunlight. "Come here and say that, fool."

The Saddai hesitated, and another voice rang out.

"Hold!" Valgorix stalked towards them, a troop of his militiamen behind him. "Our Lord Governor has prohibited public assemblies. Especially of armed men, feeble though your weapons are." He cast a withering glare over the assembled Saddai. "I am feeling clement, however. Depart at once!"

"We will be heard!" A young Saddai man shoved his way to the front of the mob. He looked somewhat plumper than the typical Saddai peasant, and he wore red robes similar to Tadaia's. Despite his soft appearance, his eyes blazed with fervor, or perhaps madness. "We are Saddai, and this is our city. You will hear us!"

"Gaidan," muttered Ark.

"You are under warning, Gaidan!" said Valgorix. "Depart at once!"

"What is your Lord Governor's law to us?" shouted Gaidan, his voice ringing over the plaza. "Does not a lawful ruler protect his people? Does he not shield them from harm? Instead my people are found burned to death in the streets and your Empire does nothing!"

"If you have a grievance with Lord Nicephorus," said Valgorix, "settle it in the courts. Or send a petition to the Imperial Curia or even the Emperor, should you feel so affronted. But unless you something important to say, I have work to do."

"Look!" said Gaidan, pointing at Caina. He did not seem to be speaking to Valgorix, but preaching at his followers. "See the perfumed whores the Empire bring to pollute our city! The Emperor grows fat on our labor and our sweat, and his prostitutes fasten upon us like leeches. Our people lie butchered in the street, and this harlot struts arrogantly amongst us! How long shall we suffer this injustice, oh men of Rasadda?"

"I see no men here," said Caina, filling her voice with icy contempt, "only mewling children, throwing feeble mockery at their betters."

Every eye turned towards her. Gaidan's pale green eyes focused on Caina for a moment. She saw the loathing in them, the utter hatred. Ark's knuckles began to whiten around the hilt of his sword, and a trickle of sweat crawled down Valgorix's face.

"Your miserable Imperial whore!" snarled Gaidan, stepping towards her. "You'll die screaming for mercy, I promise you. When the great day of burning comes at last, you'll scream with the rest of them."

"Stop!" roared Valgorix. He gestured, and the crossbowmen leveled their weapons at Gaidan. "Take another step and you'll be dead before your heart beats again."

Gaidan wheeled to face Valgorix. "Do not threaten me!"

"Do you want to settle this right now?" said Valgorix. "I swear on the names of the Imperial gods that if you take another step I'll gut you, and damn the consequences."

Valgorix, it seemed, had more backbone than Caina had thought.

"Then do it!" said Gaidan, his eyes alight. "Strike me down, if you can. I have four times as many men here. Kill me, and they'll rip you to pieces, and all of Rasadda will rise in revolt."

"And if Rasadda rises in revolt," said Valgorix, "the Emperor will summon his armies. They will tear down the walls and swarm into the streets. The Legions will butcher every last man, woman, and child in Rasadda."

Ark's sword trembled, just a bit. Had Caina not been looking right at him, she would not have seen it.

"So!" said Valgorix, "it is your choice, Brother Gaidan. Either leave, or lead your people to death and horror." He drew his sword and gestured. "Well? Which shall it be?"

For a moment neither man spoke. Tension crackled in the air like a thunderstorm. The Sons of Corazain and the militiamen faced each other down, Caina and Ark caught between them. For a moment Caina was certain that Gaidan would attack, that his followers would surge towards them in a wave of howling bodies. Then Gaidan took a step back, his face slick with sweat.

"The great day of burning will come, and quickly," said Gaidan. "I have some mercy in me. You have a little while yet, foolish dogs of the Emperor. Leave Rasadda while you still can. Before your time is up."

He turned back to his mob and vanished into their midst. Bit by bit, the Sons of Corazain drained from the plaza, departing into the streets and the alleys. A sigh of relief went up from the militiamen.

"What in the hell were you thinking?" said Valgorix. He flung his helm at the ground, and it clattered at Caina's feet. "Provoking him like that? Gods, Countess. One more harsh word and we'd have been butchered like sheep."

"You will speak more respectfully," said Ark.

Caina ignored him. "Am I a daughter of the Empire or am I not? I was sure we were about to die, Decurion. Shall I face death cowering and weeping?" She let her voice tremble and hands shake a bit. It did not take much acting.

"No. No, indeed not." Valgorix sighed. "You comported yourself as well as any man. But, gods, Countess. Try not to provoke Gaidan any further."

"Why was this man not arrested?" said Ark, ramming his broadsword into its scabbard. "He threatened a noblewoman of high Nighmarian lineage, and threatened to revolt against the Emperor. Were I still in the Legions I would have cut him down where he stood."

"Then go!" shouted Valgorix. "Cut him down! And see what comes of it. Had we tried to arrest him, we'd all be dead." He shook his head. "Countess. Please stay off the streets, and leave Rasadda as soon as possible. Gaidan and his rabble will kill you if they get the chance." He scooped up his helmet and shoved it back onto his head. "I have warned you." He turned and walked back to his militiamen.

Caina took a deep breath, let it out. "That was close."

"It was," agreed Ark. "I would have taken Gaidan's head before all was done, though. Still, it is plain who is behind the burning murders, now."

"Oh?" said Caina.

Ark frowned. "Gaidan kept talking about a great day of burning. An admission of guilt, if I ever heard one."

"Perhaps," said Caina. "But this corpse was not killed in the same manner as the others. And if he had committed these murders, why show up to take credit for them? Has he made any effort to do so before now?"

Ark shook his head.

"And he claimed that his people had been found burned to death in the streets," said Caina. "He blamed Nicephorus for failing to protect them." She looked over the plaza, half afraid that the Sons of Corazain would return. "Why do that, if he had killed them?"

Ark shrugged. "To bolster his standing among the Saddai peasants, obviously."

"Maybe," said Caina.

His lip twisted. "Unless the Magisterium reached into his head and made him their puppet. By sorcery, of course."

Caina kept her voice calm with an effort. "Don't speak of things you don't understand." She pursed her lips and took a quick glance over Ark's shoulder. A man in shabby clothing stood in the mouth of a nearby alley, staring at Ark. "Someone's watching you."

"What?" said Ark.

"No, don't turn around, he'll see you," hissed Caina. "I'm going to take a step and then stumble. You'll offer me your arm, and take a look as we turn."

She took a step forward and feigned a stumble. Ark turned and offered her his arm, and Caina took it. She got a good look at the man in the alleyway then. He was thin, almost emaciated, and his hair had turned prematurely white. His clothes had not been washed in quite some time, and the man himself appeared in dire need of a bath. He looked confused, almost bewildered, and seemed quite lost.

Ark's breath hissed through his teeth.

"Do you know him?" said Caina.

"Ostros," said Ark. "Where has he been?"

"Who is Ostros?"

"The Ghost circlemaster of Rasadda," said Ark.

"Finally," breathed Caina. She shook free of Ark's arm. "Finally we can get some answers."

Ostros blinked as they approached, and a spasm went through his muscles. A look of horrified recognition came over his face, and he fell back a few stumbling steps. His mouth opened and closed, but no sounds came forth.

Then he fled, running at a terrific clip.

"Wait!" said Ark.

Caina took a quick glance behind her, but saw nothing that should have so terrified Ostros.

The circlemaster of Rasadda kept running.

"After him!" said Caina. "If he gets away, we might never find out what's happened here!"

CHAPTER 9
PYROMANCY

Ark ran with surprising speed for such a big man. Caina kept pace with him, skirts hiked up with one hand, cloak billowing out. Ostros sprinted through the alley, risking a glance over his shoulder, and then vanished around a corner. Ark raced after him, and Caina tried to follow, but her skirt kept binding up her legs. She almost fell, and took a half-dozen stumbling steps to regain her balance.

Ark glanced back at her.

"Stay after him!" said Caina. He kept running. Caina reached into her sleeve and drew one of her knives.

An Imperial Countess did not run into alleys after shiftless vagrants. Too many people had seen her do it, and too many people had seen her face. If they saw her sprinting through the city's streets, someone might draw conclusions. Besides, she couldn't run properly with the damnable skirt entangling her legs.

Time to improvise.

Her knife ripped through the fabric, tearing the skirt front and back. She cut a strip from the hem, wound it around her face and hair in an impromptu mask, and pulled up the hood of her cloak. It wasn't perfect, and it looked odd, but it would hide her features and let her move without hindrance.

Caina sprinted down the length of the alley, her legs eating the distance, the torn skirts flapping around her. She rounded the corner and burst into another plaza. This one sat below one of the smaller black pyramids, and seemed to serve as a bazaar. Booths and stalls filled the square, roofed with bright fabric, merchandise piled high on wooden counters. Caina saw Ark standing in an aisle between the booths, his head turning back and forth.

Her heart sank. He had lost Ostros. Then she saw Ostros duck behind a nearby wagon. He climbed into the wagon's bed and slid beneath a tarp, all without making a sound. Caina pulled her cloak close, her head bowed to hide her ragged mask, and walked towards the wagon.

She was a dozen paces away when Ostros burst from the wagon, his face filled with unreasoning panic, and took off running. Caina ran after him, dodging and weaving through the shoppers. Ostros collided with a merchant carrying a stack of brass pans. He stumbled and bounced off the side of a booth, the pans clanging and clattering against the basalt flagstones.

"Here, now!" said the man, scowling. "Watch yourself, fool!" Caina pushed past him and reached for Ostros, who sprang back to his feet and threw a palm strike at her face. Caina shoved it aside with her forearm and jabbed for his throat. But Ostros knew the move and countered, slapping aside her hand. He launched a sweeping kick at her ankles, forcing her to jump back.

"Militia!" yelled the pan merchant. "Brigands in the bazaar! Militia! Militia!"

Caina caught her balance just as Ostros snatched a pan and flung it at her. She ducked, and pan struck the bellowing merchant in the face. Men began to shout, and Caina saw militiamen shoving their way through the crowds. Ostros fled at a sprint, and Caina leapt over the clattering pans and chased after him.

Damn it, why was he running? He had never seen Caina before, but surely he must have recognized Ark. The rest of the Ghost circle had been murdered. Why would Ostros flee from the only other surviving member?

Unless the Ghost circle had been betrayed.

Unless Ostros thought Ark a traitor.

No. Speculate later. Caina could pry answers out of Ostros at her leisure, but only if she caught him first. She was faster than him, she saw, and in better physical condition. Bit by bit she closed the distance between them as they dodged shoppers and wagons.

Then Ostros broke to his left, vaulting over a counter and vanishing into a tangled warren of booths and tents. Caina leapt after him, rolling over the counter, dashing down a narrow aisle between booths. She stumbled into a tent. Inside rolled Anshani and Istarish carpets stood in bulging piles, while a wide-eyed fat man struggled to his feet.

"Please!" he said. "Take my money. Just do not kill me!"

Caina looked back and forth. Ostros had vanished. Had he gone out the tent flap? Or had he doubled back and vanished into the bazaar?

There! She saw the tent wall rippling. Caina shoved past the merchant and spun around a pile of carpets just in time to see Ostros finishing cutting a slit into the tent wall. He screamed in frustration and threw himself through the cut, Caina at his heels.

She emerged into one of the bazaar's main aisles. She saw Ostros vanish into a gap between two booths, heard the pan merchant yelling, saw the carpet merchant burst from his tent, crying bloody murder. A half-dozen militiamen ran down the aisle, spears in hand, and Caina saw their eyes focus on her tattered cloak and ragged mask.

Not good.

One of the peddlers had a brazier on his counter, thin strips of meat sizzling over a blackened grill. Caina's leg shot up in a kick, her boot smacking against the brazier. It spun end over end, cinders flying, and the hot coals struck the booth's canvas roof. Flames began to dance over thick cloth.

"Fire!" screamed Caina at the top of her lungs. "Fire! Fire! Bring water! Fire!"

Her shout caused a predictable panic. Some shoppers gaped at the flames, while other merchants erupted from their booths, buckets in hands. The militiamen tangled into the sudden influx of people, cursing and trying to beat a path with the butts of their spears. Caina ran after Ostros.

She came to the edge of the bazaar, saw Ostros sprinting for a three-story mansion fronted in gleaming black marble. He kicked open the front door and vanished inside. Caina sprang up the steps after him and skidded to a stop.

She found herself in a vaulted hall, ringed by balconies, a pair of fountains sparkling and splashing. Soft music drifted from the corners, and perfume hung light in the air. A girl of about sixteen or seventeen lounged on a marble bench, naked but for a twist of silk about her waist, and a pair of women in similar undress sat on either side of a Saddai man in expensive clothes, laughing at something.

A brothel. Ostros had fled into a brothel.

She saw him vanish up a flight of stairs.

"Here, now!" A huge man stalked towards her, scowling. The establishment's resident enforcer, no doubt. "You uppity rabble keep your quarrels outside, you hear?" He reached for Caina's shoulder. "Or I'll…"

Caina seized his wrist, twisted it back, and the man's eyes went wide with sudden pain. She punched him in the throat, and he doubled over, wheezing. The undressed girls and the rich man gaped at her. Caina ignored them, tried to catch her rasping breath, and ran after Ostros.

She almost caught him on the third landing. He looked even more tired than she felt, his face red, his chest heaving with effort.

"Damn you!" he croaked, still running. "Leave me alone! You'll not drag me down to hell with you, not like the others!"

"I'm only…"

Ostros kept running. A flight of stairs opened onto the brothel's roof, and he stumbled up them, Caina at his heels. Exhausted as he looked, he still ran with considerable speed. Caina reached the flat roof just in time to see Ostros leap over the alley, landing on the rooftop of the next building. Caina sprinted to the edge and jumped. She made the leap with a few inches to spare and kept after Ostros.

"Damn you!" rasped Ostros, still running. "Leave me alone, leave me alone…"

The chase went on, and they sprang from rooftop to rooftop, Caina's cloak and torn skirt streaming out behind her like bizarre wings. Caina's breath tore in her throat, her chest heaving with the effort, her arms and legs like lead. Ostros was faltering, but Caina did not know how much longer she could keep up the chase. This had to end soon.

Ostros leapt atop an apartment building lined with wooden balconies. Caina jumped after him, and with a final burst of speed, threw herself at him. Ostros overbalanced with a scream, and they rolled over the edge of the rooftop together. Ostros screamed again…and a balcony broke their fall after only a few feet.

Just as Caina had hoped.

She had not expected, however, that the brittle balcony would tear free from the side of the building. The boards splintered, and the balcony crashed to the alley below. Caina tucked her shoulder and rolled, spinning over a dozen feet of dusty flagstones before she smacked into a brick wall. The breath exploded out of her, every bone vibrating with the impact.

She struggled to her feet to see Ostros lying nearby, panting for breath. His eyes bulged as Caina approached, and he tried to sit up. She slugged him, and Ostros fell back against the broken boards with a strangled cry. Caina put her foot on his neck, and Ostros went still.

"Don't," she spat, "move."

Ostros managed to nod, trembling.

Boots clicked against the flagstones, and Ark ran into the alley.

"Where have you been?" said Caina.

"I lost the two of you in the bazaar," said Ark. "Then I saw you chasing him across the rooftops. So much for secrecy. At least you thought to cover your face."

"No!" Ostros jerked away from Caina's foot and crawled backwards. He huddled against the wall, staring up at Ark with terrified eyes. "No! You're dead. You're dead! Stay away from me! You won't drag me down to hell with the others!"

"What are you talking about?" said Ark. "Do you have any idea how hard we've tried to find you?"

"You won't take me," gasped Ostros, shuddering. "They're all dead. All the others. Crastia and Narmer and Aulean, all of them." He began to rock back and forth, hugging his knees. "And now you've come to take me as well, down to the burning hell with the rest."

"What nonsense is this?" snarled Ark. "What happened to the others? Did you betray them? You did betray them, didn't you? I'll…"

"Ark," said Caina, "stop."

Ark glared at her, lips pulled back in a snarl.

"Look at him," said Caina. "Just shut up and look at him."

Ark did. Ostros kept rocking back and forth, weeping and clutching at his knees.

"Look at him," said Caina. "He's gone mad."

"How?" said Ark.

For a moment Caina thought a magus had broken into Ostros's mind and shattered his sanity. But no. Ostros had shown a great deal of cunning in the bazaar, even though his panic. Had a brother of the Magisterium invaded his mind, Ostros would not be able to feed himself, let alone think. Caina had seen it before.

"Fear," said Caina at last. "Something's so terrified him that his reason has been overthrown."

"He snapped," said Ark. He sounded incredulous. "I've seen it before, in the Legions. But Ostros was always a cool hand." He shook his head. "Gods, what happened to him?"

Caina took a quick glance around. No one seemed to have noticed the racket. Perhaps the surrounding apartments were abandoned. Or, more likely, the residents had hidden from the noise. Caina knelt besides Ostros, who pulled away from her, shivering.

"Ostros, listen to me." She sighed and undid the improvised mask, revealing her face. "Listen to me."

Ostros blinked. "You're…you're a woman. You're that noblewoman I saw with Ark's shade."

"How terribly observant," said Caina. "But Ark's not dead. You sent him for help, remember? Well, help has come. I am a Ghost nightfighter, and I've been sent to stop these burning murders."

"Ark?" said Ostros, blinking at the younger man. "Is…that truly you? You're not dead?"

"It is," said Ark.

"How do I know you're not a demon, come to trick me?" said Ostros, his voice beginning to tremble again.

"I swear it to you," said Ark. "And not on the name of any gods." He lifted his left hand, touched the cheap ring on the third finger. "I will swear it to you on Tanya's name, Ostros. You know what that means to me. I swear on her name that I am telling you the truth."

Ostros gave a slow nod. "Yes. It…yes. I know what that name means to you. Not even your shade would lie upon such an oath. I thought…I thought you were dead, though. Like the others. Gods, like all the others." He rubbed the heels of his hands across his forehead. "I saw them burn, I saw them burn. Oh, Crastia. I heard her scream…"

"What happened?" Caina grabbed his hands, pulled them away from his face. "Tell us what happened."

"It's so jumbled," said Ostros. "A nightmare, over and over again."

"Then start from the beginning."

Ostros nodded, closed his eyes. "It…was a year ago. Yes, I remember. Things weren't nearly so bad in Rasadda then. We had orders from the Emperor. We were to spy on Lord Nicephorus, to find irrefutable proof of his wrongdoing. Once we had it, the Emperor would remove him from office and bring charges before the Imperial Curia." He rubbed his chin, the stubble making a rasping noise. "And if we couldn't find anything, we were to kill him."

"What?" said Ark. "You never told me that."

"I was the circlemaster," said Ostros. "Our orders were secret. And it's easier for one man to keep a secret than seven."

"So you were spying on Nicephorus," said Caina. "When did the murders start?"

"There were only a few, at first," said Ostros. "I didn't think anything of them. Sometimes a murderer will throw his victim's body into the pyramid pyres to disguise his crimes. But there were more. And Nicephorus's policies grew harsher. And still more burning murders. The city started to seethe. Something had to be done." He shuddered. "I heard rumors. The victims…simply caught on fire. Burned with flames that no water could quench." He giggled. "I thought it foolishness at the time." He burst into peals of despairing, shaking laughter. "I know better now! Oh, gods, I know better!"

Caina gave him a violent shake. "Stop that! What did you do then?"

Ostros's wild laughter trailed into despondent whimpers. "I…I knew we needed help. Nicephorus's crimes had pushed the city towards revolt. Those murders were only making things worse. So I…so I sent Ark to request help. A nightfighter, we needed a nightfighter. And I. The Magisterium…"

"The Magisterium?" said Caina. "What about the Magisterium? Are they behind this?"

"No," said Ostros. "In fact, they offered to help. The masters. Ephaeron and Kalastus. They both feared that some Saddai priest had rediscovered the Ashbringers' lost art…pyromancy, they called it. Fire sorcery."

"But the Ghosts and the Magisterium have been enemies for centuries," said Caina.

Ostros shook his head. "They said pyromancy was incredibly

dangerous. So dangerous that they would set aside our differences to stamp it out. Ephaeron especially." He shook his head. "They thought…they thought that this pyromancer, this new Ashbringer, was someone in Gaidan's rebel band. A Son of Corazain. We began to investigate. And then…and then…"

Ostros curled into a ball and began to weep.

"What happened?" said Caina. "Tell us."

"My circle," said Ostros. "They killed my circle. All of them. Everyone except Ark, I suppose."

"How were they killed?" said Caina.

"They burned," whispered Ostros.

"We know that," said Caina. "But how?"

"Sorcery," said Ostros. "Too strong. The Magisterium couldn't stop it. We are just men of flesh and blood. How can we battle sorcery?" He turned panicked eyes towards Caina. "You must flee the city! You must! Otherwise they'll kill you too, they'll kill you too…"

"Listen to me!" said Caina, grabbing his shoulders, suddenly angry. "Sorcery can be fought. I have done it. A magus once tried to kill me, but I killed her first. I swear to you, on the name of my father, that I will find this murderer, and he will answer for what he has done! Do you hear me?"

Ostros nodded, still trembling.

"Now, how were they killed?" said Caina. A breeze blew through the narrow alley, set her tattered skirt and cloak to dancing. "How were they burned to death?"

"I…I don't rightly know," said Ostros. "They…burned. Gods, how they burned. One moment they were alive. The next they were burning. I watched Crastia burn to death, Ark. Oh, gods, the screams." He pawed at his dirty sleeve suddenly, revealing a shallow cut. "They took their blood, I see it now. For the spell. Don't you see? They took my blood, too." His voice rose to a shriek. "They took my blood, too!"

Caina opened her mouth to ask a question, and all at once she felt it.

Her skin crawled, the hair on her neck standing up on end, and she felt the electric snarl of unseen power crackling in the air, like lighting about to strike. She jumped to her feet, drawing knives in either hand. The breeze picked up to a steady wind, and the air seemed to buzz around her.

Sorcery.

"No!" shrieked Ostros, clawing to his feet. "No, no, gods, please, no, not like this, not like this…"

He took a step towards her, then another.

The howling power in the air surged.

And Ostros exploded into raging flames.

Sheets of fire erupted from his arms, his chest, his face, and yet even over their roar Caina heard Ostros's scream of agony. He flung himself against the wall, trying to beat out of the flames, but still they chewed into his flesh. Caina saw his clothes dissolve into cinders, his hair wither into ashes, his eyes shrivel. And still Ostros screamed and screamed.

"Move, damn you!" Ark shoved her aside, a barrel of rainwater in his arms, and flung it over Ostros. It did nothing. The flames did not even flicker as the water splashed over him, did not even steam. Ostros lurched towards Ark, arms outstretched in supplication, and stumbled. Caina tried to get out of the way, but the burning man fell against her.

She expected the agony of heat, expected her clothes to catch fire, but nothing happened. She felt no heat, not pain. To her horror, she felt Ostros's arm shriveling and twisting beneath her hand, felt the blackened skin crumbling beneath her fingers, but still she felt no heat. The black smoke poured off him in waves, but she could not smell it.

Ostros stumbled away from her, the unnatural flames still eating into his flesh. He crumpled to the ground, mercifully, and did not move. Smoke poured from the blackened ruins of his face. The crackling power drained from the air, and all at once the smell, the awful, reeking smell, struck Caina like a fist.

A charred, ruined husk lay at her feet, just like Vanio.

CHAPTER 10
THE SONS OF CORAZAIN

"Countess," said Ark.

Caina stared at Ostros's smoking corpse, unable to look away.

"Countess."

She had seen death before, more than she cared to remember. She had killed men, watched them die on the end of her knife. She had even seen her father and mother die in the space of a few hours.

But she had never seen anyone die so horribly.

"Countess!" Ark seized her arm. His eyes were wild and fierce. "We have to get out of here. Now."

Caina looked at the corpse, at Ark, back at the corpse.

"Someone will have seen the smoke, heard the screams," said Ark. "If we are still here when the militia arrives that will be bad. We have to go. Now!"

"Yes," said Caina. "Yes, you're right. But...oh, gods, to die like that..."

"I know," said Ark. "But we have to go."

Caina nodded. She tore her eyes from Ostros's smoldering husk, suddenly grateful that she had not eaten breakfast. "Which...which way?"

"Anywhere but here," said Ark. He broke into a run, and Caina urged her aching legs to follow him. They rounded a corner, crossed a street, and raced down a narrow alley between sagging, black-painted apartment buildings. Caina heard a sudden scream behind her, followed by a frantic voice calling for the militia. Ark kept running, and at last they came to a courtyard behind between a pair of crumbling warehouses. Abandoned crates and barrels lay strewn across the ground, weathered and splintered, and weeds poked between cracked flagstones. Two of the smaller black pyramids rose in the background, their tops crowned with fire.

"This ought to be far enough," said Ark. "Give me a moment. I need to catch my breath."

Caina nodded and leaned against a wall, raking a hand through her sweaty hair. The stench of Ostros's burned flesh saturated her clothing. She could still hear his hideous scream, the ghastly sizzle as the flames consumed his flesh.

"So," said Ark, "you're not made of ice after all."

Caina blinked. "I've seen men die before. But...but I've never seen anyone burn to death before, Ark."

"I have." His voice was quiet. "Boiling oil, poured from a wall. It's not the sort of thing you forget. The scream. The smell." His voice got even quieter. "Gods, the smell."

"No." Caina took a ragged breath. "I hope no one saw us chasing him."

"We'll say he knocked you down and stole some jewelry from you," said Ark. "If anyone noticed."

"Yes, of course." Caina should have thought of that herself.

"You covered your face, at least. Which was clever. Your clothes are so torn up that you look like a thief."

"At least we know one thing," said Caina. "Sorcery was used to kill these men."

Ark stared at her.

"You saw it, didn't you?" said Caina. "You dumped a barrel of water on him. Nothing. No steam, not even a sizzle. And he fell onto me, Ark. I should have been burned. But I didn't feel any heat." Her hands rolled into fists. "The Magisterium will pay for this."

"The Magisterium?" said Ark, incredulous.

"Do you know any others who use sorcery?" said Caina.

"You heard Ostros. He thought Gaidan, or one of Gaidan's disciples, was behind it. So do Kalastus and Ephaeron. I've seen Ephaeron in action, and he's no fool. If he thinks the Sons of Corazain are behind these murders, I'm inclined to believe him."

"Of course the Magisterium would say that," said Caina, more scorn in her voice than she would have liked. "How better to conceal their crimes?"

"Indeed," said Ark. "What basis do you have for accusing the Magisterium? The victims all burned to death. The Saddai worship a god called the Living Flame. The Ashbringers used to practice fire sorcery. Both the magi and Ostros thought the Sons of Corazain were behind the murders. And we just saw a man killed with pyromancy in front of our eyes. So tell me, clever Countess. How does this evidence damn the Magisterium?"

"If you won't see their villainy, then you are blind," said Caina.

"And you are blind to anything else," said Ark.

Caina took a deep breath, tried to still the rage and pain. "Enough. Enough! We cannot quarrel among ourselves. If we do, we are lost."

Ark's scowl did not waver, but he nodded. "Very well."

"Let's get back to the Inn," said Caina. "The sooner we're off the streets, the better..."

She heard footsteps, and turned.

Ark's broadsword rasped from its scabbard.

A half-dozen Saddai peasants walked into the courtyard, clad in ragged clothes. They stared at Caina with hard, glittering eyes, clubs in their hands. The lead man's shirt hung open, and Caina saw the flame tattoo upon his chest.

"You'll want to idle elsewhere," said Ark.

"I know you," said the lead man in Saddaic. "I saw you in the plaza, below great Corazain's tomb. Gaidan renounced you, whore of the Empire."

Caina said nothing.

He looked her over and laughed. "What's this, then? Out for a tumble with your guardsman? Perhaps a feather bed wasn't good enough for you?" His followers laughed. "Or maybe you wanted to do it on a hard surface, since he wasn't hard enough to please you."

"What wrong I have ever done you?" said Caina. "I have never even spoken to you before this day. If my presence so offends you, I'll go."

The Saddai laughed. "Oh, no. We'll burn the infection of the Empire from our ancestral lands. Starting with you."

"Try it," said Ark, lifting his broadsword, "and you'll be face to face with your precious Living Flame before this day is done."

The Saddai laughed again. "The Living Flame? A false and corrupt god, a lie told to weaklings. We follow the Burning Flame, the true Saddai god."

The Burning Flame? Caina had not heard that one before.

"We'll kill her in front of you," said the Saddai man, the other Sons of Corazain fanning out behind him, "make her squeal and beg for her life..."

Any other time, Caina might have tried to talk her way out of it, or just run. But Ostros's death had filled her with a vicious fury, and that fury had found an outlet.

"Throw down your weapons and run," said Caina, her voice ice. "Once chance is all I'll give you. Otherwise I'll kill you where you stand."

The leader blinked, then began to laugh with his followers.

Caina slipped a knife from a sheath and stepped forward, her back arched, her arm swinging back. Her entire body snapped like a bowstring, sending the knife hurtling at the leader. He had titled back his head to laugh, which meant Caina had a lovely path to his neck. Her blade ripped his throat open and slashed the major vein. Blood gushed over his tattered cloak, and the leader fell to his knees, drowning in his own blood.

Ark gave her a surprised glance. The Sons of Corazain gaped at their dying leader.

"Well?" snapped Caina. She snatched the dagger from her right boot and raised her weapons, dagger in right hand, and knife in her left. "Who's next?"

"She has murdered Baizair!" shouted one. "Kill them!"

The Sons of Corazain came in a rush. Ark roared a war cry in Caerish and ran to meet them, his broadsword blurring in a steely arc. One of the Saddai tried to parry with his club, and Ark's blow shattered the crude weapon and tore a gash down the man's side. Ark twisted, and his spinning backhand opened another man's belly. The man fell with a strangled shriek, clutching his dislocated innards, while the other three backed off in a wary circle. They did not look at Caina at all, which gave her a marvelous opportunity to throw another knife, which she did. Another man toppled, his lifeblood soaking into the cracks between the flagstones.

"Last chance," growled Ark. "Run away, now, or you'll get to join your precious Living or Burning Flame or whatever the hell you call it."

The last two men backed away. The man on the left glanced at Caina, and then looked at a stack of crates leaning against the warehouse wall. Caina followed his gaze, saw the flash of metal atop the crate.

"Ark!" she shouted, diving for the ground, "down!"

Ark threw himself sideways just as two crossbow quarrels stabbed down from the crates. The first one shattered against the ground. The second ripped past Ark's flank, and he grunted in sudden pain, landing on one knee. The surviving Sons of Corazain rushed him.

Caina leapt back to her feet, saw two Saddai men in militia garb standing atop the stack of crates, reloading their crossbows. She ran at the stack, and the nearest militiaman cursed and swung his bow around to face her. Caina jumped and threw out her legs, her feet smacking into the crate. The entire stack shuddered, and the crossbowman lost his balance, his bolt flying wild. Caina kicked out again, and the stack of crates began to lean sideways. One of the men jumped off the stack, while the other fell backwards with a scream.

She sprang to her feet as the militiaman swung his bow to face her. She slashed with her dagger, and the man dropped the crossbow with a snarl of pain, blood welling from his hand. He pawed for the dagger at his belt, but Caina stepped forward and drove her blade into his throat. She heard noise behind her, and ducked as the second militiaman came at her, using the stock of his crossbow as a club. Caina spun and kicked him in the knee as he went past. Something snapped, and the militiaman spilled to the ground, screaming. Caina stomped on his wrist as he reached for his dagger, and he flopped onto his back, moaning.

"You can fight," gasped the astonished Saddai. "But...you're just a woman, and you can fight!"

Caina looked down at him and drew the dagger from her left boot.

"I swear I won't tell," he babbled, "I swear, I swear..."

"You won't," said Caina, and she bought his silence with steel.

His gurgling scream ended, and Caina looked for Ark. She found him kneeling besides one of the dead Saddai peasants, and for a moment she thought he had been killed. But he was only cleaning his sword on the dead man's shirt.

"Are you hurt?" said Caina.

Ark looked up at her without blinking, and Caina glanced down at herself. Her clothes were splashed with blood, and shredded almost to the point of indecency. Suddenly self-conscious, she tugged her dirty cloak closer.

"No," said Ark, standing. He fingered a gash in his leather jerkin, his mail shirt visible through the tear. "That bolt almost skewered me, but the mail turned it." He frowned at her. "I've never seen anyone throw a knife like that."

"Thank you." Caina began collecting her knives from the corpses.

"Where did you learn how to throw like that?"

Caina glanced at him. "Remember when you saw me practicing open-handed forms in the morning? I told you that they weren't useless." She crossed to the dead militiamen. "Militiamen? Why would militiamen try to kill us?"

"Maybe they were aiming for the Sons of Corazain," said Ark.

"No," said Caina. "I don't think so." She wrenched the dagger free from the dead man's throat and used it to cut open the front of his leather jerkin and shirt.

A tattoo of swirling flames covered his chest.

"So they stole the uniforms and weapons," said Ark.

"Or," said Caina, "the Sons of Corazain have infiltrated the Rasadda militia. You've seen Valgorix's men. They're mostly Caerishor Disali, but quite a few are Saddai." She cleaned the dagger on the torn cloth and stood up with a wince. Now that the fight was over, her entire left side hurt from the balcony collapse. She would have some ferocious bruises.

"They were spies?" said Ark.

"No doubt," said Caina. "And if Gaidan does decide to revolt, he'll have men in place in the militia." She looked at the tattoos on the dead men's chests. "The Burning Flame, they said. I thought the Saddai god was called the Living Flame."

"It is," said Ark. "As far as I know, anyway."

"Burning Flame," repeated Caina, this time in Saddaic. She thought of

Ostros's horrible death and shuddered. "I wonder what that means."

"I know what it means," said Ark. "We just saw Ostros burned to death. And now the Sons of Corazain are talking about the Burning Flame? For someone so clever, I cannot understand why you remain so blind. Someone in the Sons of Corazain is behind these murders, I'm sure. Maybe even Gaidan himself cast the spell that killed Ostros. And if he did, he will pay for it."

"Blood," said Caina.

"What?"

"Ostros said that they had taken his blood," said Caina. "I wonder…I wonder if the blood of the victim is an integral part of this fire sorcery."

"That cut on his arm, you mean? How could someone take some of his blood without him realizing it? Or, for that matter, why didn't he see who took it?"

"For someone with sufficient skill in sorcery, that wouldn't pose a problem," said Caina. "A magus could numb his mind, or even destroy the memory entirely."

"Then why bother with burning people to death?" said Ark. "Why not just put a blade into his chest while his mind was numbed?"

Caina opened her mouth, closed it again. "That," she said at last, "is a very good question."

"It's a statement, a dramatic gesture," said Ark. "The Sons of Corazain pray to a Burning Flame, and their enemies die in flames."

"There must be more to it than that."

Ark looked scornful. "How?"

"If they wanted to make a statement, why not knock out their victims, tie them up, and burn a house down on top of them?" said Caina. "Why bother with all the effort of pyromancy. You heard Kalastus and Ephaeron. Pyromancy is incredibly dangerous. And I don't know how…sensitive you are to the presence of sorcery."

"What do you mean?"

Caina shrugged. "I can feel it when a magus casts a spell. My skin crawls, my hair starts to stand on end, and it feels like a bolt of lightning is about to fall from the sky."

Ark stared at her. "I've never felt anything like that."

"Well, I have." Not many people had that sensitivity. And Caina would not tell Ark how she had acquired that sensitivity, how she had suffered for weeks in Maglarion's hidden lair. "That spell, the pyromancy used to kill Ostros took a lot of power. It must have been excruciatingly difficult to work. If the only wanted to make an example out of their enemies, why go to all the trouble and risk of using pyromancy when they could do the same thing with a coil of rope, a jar of lamp oil, and a lit candle?"

Ark said nothing, but his eyebrows creased.

Caina rubbed sweat from her forehead. "And how does Romarion tie into all of this?"

"Are you sure he's involved?"

"I'm certain he's involved," said Caina. "His name was in Vanio's ledger, and you know what happened to Vanio. We need more information. Or we have too much information, and nothing to bind it together." She shook her head, and took a quick look around. "We'd better get out of here. I'm exhausted. We were lucky only a small group came along."

"It was my fault," said Ark. "I should not have led us here."

"I should have kept my wits about me," said Caina. "I'm supposed to be the clever one."

"You had just seen a man burn to death," said Ark. "That was a horror. It would scramble anyone's wits."

"Horror. I ought to be used to horror by now," said Caina. All at once her knees felt weak, and her hands started to shake. The memories stormed through her mind, finding her father in his study, her mother's mocking laughter, and what had come afterwards. For a moment the memories flooded so vividly through her mind that she could not move. Except in her mind's eye she saw her father burst into flames, screaming horribly, while her mother laughed.

"Countess?" said Ark. "Countess!" He shook her shoulder, and Caina looked at him. She could only imagine what her expression must have looked like. Her eyes stung. Was she crying? No, she would not cry. She would not cry! It must have been the smoke from Ostros's corpse, which was even worse.

"We all have our horrors to remember," he said. His face was haunted, bleak. He had been in the Legions for twenty years, and cried out the name of a woman in his sleep. Caina knew her horrors. She wondered what horrors Ark carried with him.

"Yes," whispered Caina. She closed her eyes, collected herself.

"Damnable luck, though," said Ark, steering her towards the street. "These men finding us here."

"Oh, it wasn't luck, I'm sure," said Caina. "You saw how Gaidan was staring at me. He might have seen us run off. He probably sent a few of his followers to trail us, and they must have found us when we were running from Ostros's body."

"But why kill you?" said Ark. "You only just arrived here."

"Because they hate the Empire," said Caina, "and Lord Nicephorus is too well guarded. I'm just a helpless woman with one guard. How does that Anshani proverb go? Kill the chicken while the monkey watches? But we've lingered too long. Let's go."

Ark held up a hand. "Wait. Someone's coming." He pressed against the wall. "Militia."

"Valgorix must have seen us running after Ostros, sent someone after us," said Caina, tugging her sleeve to hide the knife sheaths strapped to her forearms. "We'll tell him what you thought up, that Ostros tried to rob me and we chased him."

"I hope he believes it," said Ark. "We've run a long way."

He was right. It was a long way to run down a thief over a piece of stolen jewelry. And an Imperial Countess would not chase a thief.

"Carry me," said Caina.

Ark looked shocked. "Excuse me?"

"We'll tell them that we ran into the Sons of Corazain. They knocked me down and tried to kill me, but you drove them off. I am too frightened and shocked by the experience to move, so you gallantly decided to carry me. That will win their sympathy, and they'll believe our story."

"Ridiculous," grumbled Ark. But he put one arm around her shoulders and the other below her knees, and lifted her as if she weighed nothing at all. "But after a few streets you're going to feel better and insist that you can walk. You'll say it's beneath the dignity of an Imperial Countess to be carried through the streets like a bag of potatoes or some such excuse. Because I am not carrying you all the way back to the damned Inn, understand?"

"Agreed," said Caina. She did feel ridiculous. But the ruse worked. When Valgorix himself hurried into the courtyard, at the head of twenty militiamen, he looked at the corpses, and then at her, and he yanked off his helm and walked over, swearing all the while.

"What the hell are you two doing here?" he said. "I told you to stay off the streets, Countess. And now I find you surrounded by corpses in the middle of the slums!"

"Watch your tone," said Ark.

Valgorix's tired face reddened, and he looked as if he was about to order Ark arrested then and there.

"I'm sorry, Decurion," said Caina, letting her voice tremble. "It's just that after we looked at that dead body, a man knocked me down and took my brooch, and that brooch belonged to my mother. Ark chased him, and I followed, but...but I don't know my way around the city, and I got lost. Then those...those men found me," she glanced at the corpses and shuddered, "and they said I was Imperial swine and had no business in their city. Then they hit me and knocked me down and started kicking me. I was sure I was going to die. But Ark came and saved me."

Valgorix looked at the corpses. "You killed...all these men?"

"My duty is to protect the Countess," said Ark. "So I did what was necessary."

"They all have the tattoo, sir," said one of the militiamen, kneeling by the bodies.

"Gods," said Valgorix. "Remind me not to get between you and your duty. We'd best get you back to the Inn. There's been another burning murder, and word's gotten out already. We'll have a riot on our hands if we're not careful."

"You mean the body by the Inn?" said Caina.

"No," said Valgorix, shaking his head. "Another one. Found it just a few minutes ago, on the edge of the slums. It was still smoking. The poor fool had been cooked alive." He gestured to his men. "Enough talking. We have work to do. We'll escort your back to the Inn, Countess, but quickly. We'll be needed to keep order on the streets soon enough."

###

It was almost dark by the time they returned to the Inn. Valgorix bid them a hasty farewell and left at once. Even during the walk back to the Inn of Mirrors Caina had seen Saddai men gathering on street corners, muttering to one another. She wondered how many of them had flame tattoos on their chests.

When they came to the plaza below the Great Pyramid of Corazain, Caina saw that a crowd of several hundred people gathered before the Imperial Basilica. For a moment she thought that a riot had broken out, and Valgorix and his men readied their weapons. But Sister Tadaia stood on the steps of the Basilica, preaching.

"Suffering is the very lot of all who live," she called, her strong voice ringing over the plaza, "and we all suffer, aye, I deny it not. But suffering is the refining force of the Living Flame, to purify our souls for our next lives, and the next, until at last we can be one with the Living Flame for all time. But if you would ease your suffering, do not do so by creating more suffering. Stand with one another. Aid one another in your trials. Ease one another in your burdens, for by these acts you can refine your soul for the Living Flame."

Many Saddai in the crowd nodded at her words. But more looked sullen, and quite a few looked downright angry.

"She's not going to be able to restrain them for much longer, is she?" Ark muttered.

Caina shook her head.

When they returned to her rooms, she told her maids what had happened, and they began to fuss over her. Caina made Ark go get something to eat and drink for himself, and let the maids draw a bath. She had a nasty purple-green bruise down her left hip and thigh, her legs were covered with scratches from rolling in the dirt, and every muscle in her body ached. She hoped she had broken no bones.

A long soak in the hot water drained some of the ache away, and the dried blood dissolved from her fingers and nails. Afterwards Caina refused food and drink, wrapped herself in a heavy robe, and barred the door to her bedroom.

She sat with her head in her hands for a long time, trying not to weep, before she at last went to bed.

CHAPTER 11
ASHBRINGERS

Caina had nightmares.

She had nightmares quite often, usually the same six or seven. Halfdan had once told her that while flesh carried scars, the mind carried nightmares, and some scars lingered longer than others. Caina had believed him.

Her mind had a lot of scars.

In one nightmare she stepped over the men lying on the floor of her father's villa, their glassy eyes staring at nothing, and she tried to race to her father's study, but it kept getting farther and farther away. In another she stood in her father's library, reaching for his chair. She knew the horror that would greet her when she turned his chair around, but she could never stop herself. In another she heard her mother's final, shrill laughter over and over again. Sometimes she dreamt that she was alone and naked in the dark, while Maglarion and his necromancer students reached for her bare flesh with cold hands.

But, tonight, a new nightmare.

In this dream she walked through her father's library, but the men on the floor were charred husks. Yet their eyes remained intact, and stared up at her. And when she entered her father's study, her mother was waiting for her.

"You meddlesome little brat!" she screamed, and burst into flame. She lunged at Caina, opening wide her burning arms. Caina shrieked, but she could not move, and the flames reached out to consume her.

###

Caina sat up with a scream caught in her throat, the blankets falling away. She looked around in a wild panic, half-expecting to see the room on fire. But she only saw the morning sunlight coming through the balcony doorway. The Inn. Of course. Caina's mouth compressed into a hard line, and for a moment she felt such fury that she could not think straight.

Whoever had killed Ostros and the rest of the Rasadda circle would pay dearly. One did not do such things and live. Not while Caina yet drew breath. Caina stood, stretched, and her arms flowed into the opening stance of the Ghosts' open-handed fighting style. She moved through the forms Halfdan and his various associates had taught her, the movements fluid and graceful with long practice. At first her arms and legs remained stiff and sore, but as she moved from the high blocks to the palm strikes to the stabbing elbows, the ache worked itself out. A second time she started, moving faster, her arms and feet a blur.

When she finished, breathing hard, a thin sheen of sweat on her forehead, she felt better. Her mind was clear, and she knew what she must do. She washed her face and hair, put on a robe, and sat down to write two letters, sealing them with the signet ring of House Nereide. After they were written, she unbarred the door and went into the sitting room.

Ark sat in a corner, facing the door, his broadsword on his lap and a whetstone in his hand. The stone made a grim, rasping noise as it slid down the blade. Anya hurried over, face expectant.

"My lady," said Anya. "Do you wish some breakfast?"

"Yes," said Caina, "but have Julia or Cornelia do it. I need you for something else, and Ark as well."

Ark rose, sheathed his sword, and crossed the room to join them.

"Put on your finest clothes," said Caina, handing Anya the letters, "and deliver these. Ark will accompany you, since I don't want you wandering the city alone."

Ark frowned, but Anya asked, "Where should the letters go, my lady?"

"Take the first to the house of Septimus Romarion, a merchant of the city," said Caina. "You will take the second to the chapterhouse of the Magisterium. Both are nearby, and Sairzan can give you directions."

"Of course, my lady," said Anya.

Ark lifted an eyebrow.

"Both Romarion and the masters of the Magisterium graciously invited me to dine with them," said Caina, "and it would be churlish to decline, would it not?" Ark looked puzzled, even a bit annoyed, but Caina was not going to explain herself in front of the maids. They had seen her do too much already.

Anya left with Ark, and Cornelia brought a plate of bread, bacon, and fruit, with a pitcher of mixed wine. Caina retrieved the book she had purchased from the peddler about Corazain and the Battle of Rasadda, and sat down to read while she ate. Cornelia seemed shocked that Caina would read at the table, but at least she kept her mouth shut.

Caina had only given the book an idle glance on the road, but the experiences of the last few days had added meaning to the words, and she read with interest. The Emperor and the Magisterium, the book claimed, had waged war against the sorcerer-kings of the Saddai for centuries, driving the Ashbringers back step by step even as their pyromancy turned the plains to ash and the forests to charcoal. Entire cities were put to the sword, or devoured in storms of raging, spell-driven flame, their citizens transformed into living, shrieking candles.

She remembered Ostros's death, and shuddered.

At last the Emperor Crisius besieged Corazain, King of the Saddai and last of the Ashbringers, within Rasadda. Corazain, it seemed, had already raised his great tomb, anticipating defeat at the hands of the Empire. Even as Crisius broke down the gates, Corazain withdrew to the pyramid's apex, his followers gathered around him.

"Hear me well, my children," the book recorded him as saying. "For the Empire is upon us, and all is lost. But by the wrath of the Burning Flame, we shall have our revenge. You shall see the unveiled fury of an Ashbringer, and tremble! Defeated we may be, but we shall have revenge. For I shall return from death one day, and bring ruin upon the Empire, and lead the Saddai people to glory."

And Corazain cast his final spell, devouring himself in the flames of his pyramid's funeral pyre. But death unleashed the full fury of his arcane power, and his wrath exploded in a firestorm unequaled by any before. Flames erupted from the earth, and fire poured from the very sky itself. Two-thirds of Rasadda burned, Caina read, and most of the city's population perished in the holocaust. Her mouth twisted in contempt. The great hero of the Saddai had roasted most of his people alive. Over a hundred thousand Imperial legionaries died in the flames, along with most of the Magisterium's masters, and Crisius died of his burns soon thereafter. The Empire fell into a century and a half of civil war as the noble Houses squabbled for the Imperial throne, but the Ashbringers and their pyromancy had been destroyed, never to rise again.

Caina closed the book, unsettled. Corazain had possessed the power to kill a quarter of a million people? Men had been dying one by one in Rasadda, but suppose the murderer grew stronger? She crossed to the window and looked at the great black bulk of Corazain's pyramid. In her mind's eye she saw it wreathed in flame, tens of thousands of men screaming as Ostros had screamed. The image disturbed her, and she looked away.

She doubted Corazain had the power to return, after so long. Caina knew that a necromancer could use his black and forbidden science to cheat death –she had seen Maglarion do it with her own eyes- but she doubted an Ashbringer could do the same. Yet suppose some Saddai priest had rediscovered the secrets of pyromancy, and now presented himself to the Saddai peasants as Corazain reborn? Brutalized by Nicephorus's tyranny, they would be easy prey for his lies.

But where would a Saddai priest have learned fire sorcery? Pyromancy, Ephaeron and Kalastus had said, was a magical science forbidden to the Magisterium. But so was necromancy, and all the necromancers Caina had ever encountered or heard about had been former brothers of the Magisterium.

"You seem distressed, my lady," said Cornelia. The older woman sat in a corner, embroidering. She was quite good at it, actually.

"I am," said Caina. "There is much wrong with this city, and it troubles me."

"A husband would do much to ease your mind."

Caina chose to ignore that. "Tell me. How long have you lived in Saddai Province?"

Cornelia's needle hesitated for a bit, then resumed. "Most of my life. My husband was a discharged veteran from the legions, and I followed him to Mors Crisius. Unfortunately, the fever took him ten years ago, poor man."

"In your time here," said Caina, "have you ever heard the Saddai refer to their god as the Burning Flame?"

"My lady shouldn't concern herself with the customs of these uncivilized folk."

"I am curious," said Caina. "Indulge me."

Cornelia frowned, her needle slowing. "You know…I'm not certain. They've always called their god the Living Flame, at least in my hearing. But from time to time I've heard about religious squabbles among the Saddai. It may have had something to do with the title of their god, I suppose."

"Thank you," said Caina. She sat back down to finish her breakfast and resumed paging through the book. A short time later Anya entered the room and did a curtsey.

"It's done, my lady," said Anya. She handed over two formal letters. "Both Master Romarion and the magi sent back word. Master Romarion hopes to dine with you tomorrow evening, and the masters of the magi the night after that."

"Very good," said Caina, looking around for Ark.

"I'd never seen a place so strange as the inside of the Magisterium chapterhouse, my lady," said Anya. "All those lights…are they truly magical?"

"They are enspelled, yes," said Caina. "The magi use their arcane science to make the lights glow."

"Unnatural folk," muttered Cornelia. For once, Caina found herself in complete agreement with the older woman.

"I thought they were pretty," said Anya.

"Thank you, Anya," said Caina. "Where did Ark get to?"

"Oh," said Anya, "he left."

Caina blinked. "He made you walk back here alone?"

"Oh, no, my lady," said Anya. "He brought me back to the Inn, and then went about his business."

"Business?" said Caina.

"He said you had given him tasks, and that he would return once they were accomplished," said Anya. She wilted a bit. "Did…did I do something wrong, my lady?"

"No," said Caina, "you did well. Thank you again."

She stared at the book for a moment, puzzled. What was Ark doing? Had he decided to strike out on his own? He disliked her, she knew, but so far he had always listened to reason. Or had Ostros's death upset him more than she had thought?

He had been adamant in his belief that Gaidan and the Sons of Corazain were behind the murders. Had he gone to take justice into his own hands? Maybe Ark was right, and Gaidan was really guilty. Yet Caina doubted it. It just did not feel right. Perhaps Gaidan was involved, but Caina suspected the truth was deeper, darker, than just a disgruntled rebel with some skill at sorcery. And if he was innocent, and Ark killed him, his murder might very well touch off a revolt.

Or had Ark been killed? Might his burned corpse now lie smoldering in an alley?

Damn him. Not for the first time, Caina wished that Halfdan had sent her alone, or given her a different contact in Rasadda. But all the other Ghosts in Rasadda had been murdered. And Ark had saved her life, twice. She sighed again, and wished that she knew what to do.

"Is my lady upset?" said Anya.

"No," said Caina, "merely tired."

She resumed reading, paging through the book, turning the facts over and over in her head. A few hours later a knock came at the door. Julia opened it, and Sairzan the innkeeper entered, bowing in Caina's direction. After him came a Saddai peasant clutching a roll of paper in one hand.

"Begging your pardon, my lady," said Sairzan, "but this man here claims to have a message for you."

"Do you?" said Caina. "Come here."

The Saddai peasant came closer, looking nervous. His loose shirt and vest hung open in the front, and Caina saw no sign of a flame tattoo on his chest. He made a quick bow and set the roll of grimy paper on the table. "Your guardsman gave me a coin to bring you this, my lady."

"So he did," said Caina, unrolling the paper. The message was in High Nighmarian, written in hard, blocky script.

"Countess," read the message. "For haughtily the stag runs, yet the wolves watch unseen from the shadows. The Pyramid of Arzaidanir. The Lane of Ashes. The Ninth House. Midnight. Your servant, Ark."

"Thank you," said Caina. "Give the man a coin, Cornelia, and see him on his way."

"Was the message from Ark, my lady?" said Anya after Sairzan and the peasant left.

"It was," said Caina. "He did what I sent him to do." Or, at least, she hoped that he hadn't done anything rash.

She spent the rest of the day in the sitting room, reading, while her maids attended to minor tasks and amused themselves with gossip. Shortly after dinner, Caina stood and said, "Tomorrow will be a long day, I think, and I am still weary from yesterday. I will go to bed early." Caina bid them good night, refused their offers of help, and barred the bedroom door behind her.

She lay down and went to sleep for a few hours. Whatever Ark had in mind, Caina suspected, was bound to be exhausting.

When she awoke it was dark outside, save for the endless funeral pyres atop the black pyramids. Caina rose and dressed in her loose black nightfighter garb, slipping the mask around her face and pulling the cowl of her shadowy cloak low. She felt better with the knives strapped to her forearms, and the belt of weapons and other useful tools around her waist. The weight of steel felt reassuring.

Once she was ready, Caina strode onto the balcony, hooked one of her grapnels to the stone railing, slid down the slender rope, and vanished into Rasadda's shadow-choked night.

Ark's message had been in code. "For haughtily the stag runs, yet the wolves watch unseen from the shadows." That was a line of Nighmarian poetry from the earliest days of the Empire. The Ghosts used it when they planned to spy upon a target. The Pyramid was the tomb of Arzaidanir, one of Corazain's predecessors, and stood in the heart of Rasadda's slums. The Lane of Ashes, Caina presumed, was a street that ran below Arzaidanir's pyramid, and she assumed that Ark wanted to meet there.

Unless the message had been faked, of course. Or if Ark had indeed become a traitor to the Ghosts, though Caina doubted it after seeing Ostros's murder. Her gloved hand dipped into her cloak, brushing the throwing knives sheathed at her belt.

Well, if someone wanted to offer her trouble, she could repay them in kind.

As ever, the burning pyramids bathed the city in their fiery glow, casting all kinds of lovely shadows over the streets and alleyways. Caina moved from the stately mansions (and, she supposed, the high-class brothels) surrounding the Imperial Basilica and Corazain's pyramid, and into the slums. The buildings changed from marble to brick and sagging wood, and Caina saw more and more people slinking on the streets and the alleyways. Women selling their bodies, and hungry men looking for prey. Lord Nicephorus's seizure of the peasants' lands had put a lot of desperate, starving people on Rasadda's streets. Just thinking about it made Caina angry, so she put the thought aside. She needed to focus on remaining unseen.

They never saw her.

She came to Arzaidanir's pyramid. It was only about a third of the size of Corazain's, and weathered with age, but its crowning fire burned as brightly as ever. The neighborhood around the pyramid seemed the worst that she had seen in Rasadda so far, block after block of sagging, crumbling apartment houses alongside a row of charcoal works. Caina stared at the charcoal works for a moment, and then nodded. The Lane of Ashes. Of course.

Caina moved through the shadows until she came to the ninth house overlooking the street. Like all the others here, it looked abandoned, the windows empty, the boards sagging and splintered. Someone had even stolen the door. Caina went up the front steps and looked around, listening. She saw nothing but dust, heard nothing but her own breathing.

She saw recent footprints in the dust, though, going up the stairs. She followed them, her boots making no sound against the boards, and came to the fourth floor. A door opened into an empty room, and Caina saw Ark standing by the windows, staring down at the street. He was waiting for her.

"Ark," said Caina in her disguised voice.

She had the immense satisfaction of seeing him flinch in surprise. He whirled, broadsword flying into his hand, the blade coming up. His eyes fell on her, and he took a step back in sudden alarm.

"Don't you recognize me?" said Caina, in her normal voice. She walked into the room, the cloak blending and blurring with the darkness.

"No," said Ark. He shook his head. "In the dark, when you are dressed like that...you look and sound like the very shadow of death itself." He scowled. "How did you sneak up on me? No one has ever been able to do that."

"I've told you before," said Caina, her voice snarling and hissing, "practice."

His lip twitched.

"Now, what is going on?" said Caina. "Why did you want me to meet you here?"

"There's something you need to see," said Ark.

Caina waited.

"A meeting of the Sons of Corazain," he said.

"How did you learn of this?"

"When we delivered your response to Romarion. Some of Romarion's servants are Saddai. I spoke only in Caerish to Romarion, so I suppose they assumed I couldn't understand Saddaic. I heard them speak of it, and I went to find a convenient place to observe."

"You should have told me," said Caina.

"I did. You're here, aren't you? You must have gotten the note."

"You should have told me before you did this," said Caina. "For all I knew you had been killed."

"The opportunity was there and I took it," said Ark. "It needed to be done. Something had to be done. The Ghosts of Rasadda have been slaughtered, the city is on the edge of revolt, and all you are doing is accepting dinner invitations."

"That is because Romarion and the Magisterium are plainly involved in this," said Caina, "and if I am to find..."

"Plainly?" said Ark. "For someone so clever, you have a remarkable gift for deluding yourself. Gaidan has all but confessed to the murders in front of us, and yet you insist upon chasing this merchant and the magi..."

Suddenly furious, Caina stepped closer to him. "Gaidan is probably involved in this, yes. But there's more to it than that. Romarion's name was in Vanio's ledger. And I have ample precedent for believing the Magisterium guilty of forbidden practices."

Ark's scowl deepened. "Do you really..."

"Enough," hissed Caina. She held up her hand for silence, and listened, but heard only the old house groaning. "What's done is done. This is not the time and the place to argue about it. So the Sons of Corazain are meeting. Where can we watch?"

Ark nodded. "This way." He led to the opposite wall. "These houses are abandoned, and they're all built up against each other. The house next door overlooks where the Sons will meet. The place is a complete wreck. The bottom three floors have collapsed, and the doors have been blocked." He gripped something on the wall, and wrenched. A wooden panel came away with a groan, revealing a jagged gap in the wall. "I found another way in, though." He beckoned. "Careful. The floor is...uneven."

That was an understatement. Caina saw that the house's bottom three floors, and most of the fourth, had collapsed into a pile of shattered timber and broken bricks. What was left of the fourth floor jutted from the wall in a precarious tangle of sagging beams and shattered floorboards. It was a long fall to the rubble heaped below.

Ark climbed onto one of the more solid-looking beams, and Caina followed him. It felt sturdy enough, but she still took careful, hesitant footsteps. She did not want to trust her weight to what remained of the floorboards. Bit by bit they made their way to the wall. A good chunk of the wall had collapsed, and they had an excellent view of the square below Arzaidanir's pyramid.

A square that was full of people.

Caina leaned over, put her arm over Ark's shoulders, and put her mouth against his ear. He flinched, and then she began to whisper. "Cover your head."

"Why?" Ark breathed back.

"Your forehead is reflecting the light. And keep your cloak closed. You shouldn't have worn a mail coat."

Ark scowled, but pulled up the hood of his cloak. Caina settled into a comfortable position and waited. More and more people filed into the square, facing the first terrace of the worn pyramid. Most of them had torches.

"They dare to meet so openly?" whispered Caina.

"There's no risk," said Ark. "The militia never comes into this part of the city after dark."

There was movement on the pyramid. Caina saw Gaidan in his red robes, climbing the lowest stairs, flanked by a number of tough-looking Saddai and other red-robed Brothers of the Living Flame. Gaidan lifted his hands, and the crowd in the square fell silent. There were at least two thousand people there, Caina saw, with more packed into the alleyways.

"Hear me, my fellow Sons of Corazain!" said Gaidan, his voice booming. "I have heard your grumblings, and your complaints. Your lack of faith shames me. Have I not promised you, again and again, that the great day of freedom is near at hand? The great day of burning, when the Empire shall fall!"

A rumble went through the crowd. Someone shouted a question, which Caina could not quite hear.

"I will tell you why," said Gaidan, gesturing. "I did not know, at first. When the first burned corpses appeared, I blamed the Empire and its running dog Nicephorus. Why were the victims only Saddai, and foreigners of no importance? Why did Nicephorus not burn, or any of his pack of fat, thieving merchants? This troubled me, and I spent long hours in prayer to the Burning Flame. And, at last, the answer came to me."

He paused, leaning towards the assembled Sons of Corazain. An expectant hush came over the gathered Saddai. Gaidan, Caina had to admit, knew how to play a crowd.

"Great Corazain has been reborn!" thundered Gaidan. A stunned silence fell over the crowd, and a dozen men shouted questions at once. "Yes! Corazain himself has been reborn." Gaidan pointed at the great dark mass of Corazain's pyramid, its pyre bright in the darkness. "Did not our lord Corazain stand there and predict his return, even as he unleashed the mighty spell that struck down the murderer Crisius and his legions? He spoke truly!" Gaidan's voice rose to a scream. "Corazain himself appeared to me, and promised me that he would soon return openly. The burning deaths, my brothers, are the signs, the harbinger of his return. Those Saddai who burned were weak in their faith, and the others were only foreigners. Mighty Corazain will return, my brothers, and when he does, the Empire will burn!"

A roar of approval met his words.

"I think," Caina murmured, "that we've heard enough. And we'd better go before somebody sees us and they decide to celebrate with a bonfire."

CHAPTER 12
A SIMPLE MERCHANT

An hour later they returned to their rooms the Inn of Mirrors.

"How can you possibly think that?" said Ark.

"Keep your voice down," said Caina. "You'll wake the maids."

Ark began to pace. "You heard the same thing I did. Gaidan all but took credit for the murders. He and the Sons of Corazain are behind this."

"I don't doubt that Gaidan is a scoundrel and the Sons are dangerous," said Caina, "though it is Nicephorus's fault for creating them. And it is possible that Gaidan is involved. But I didn't think he was directly responsible, and I am more certain of that now."

"Why?" said Ark.

"Weren't you listening?" said Caina. "His followers were grumbling. They asked him why some Saddai were among the victims. And Gaidan didn't know."

Ark opened his mouth, closed it. He was not happy, Caina saw, but he was listening.

"So then he prayed and suddenly realized that Corazain had returned," said Caina. "I'll wager he made the entire story up so that he had something to tell his followers. Else he would look powerless, otherwise." She looked at him. "Unless you actually think that Corazain has been reborn."

Ark said nothing.

"No doubt in a few months Gaidan will claim to be Corazain reborn, and take credit for any more murders."

"Perhaps he is," said Ark. "Not literally Corazain, of course. But perhaps he has enough skill at sorcery to have managed these deaths."

"I doubt it," said Caina. "Gaidan doesn't strike me as all that clever. If he had any talent at pyromancy, I suspect he would have gone after

Nicephorus, or tried to burn the Imperial Basilica to the ground. Then the Magisterium would have killed him. There are more arguments against it as well. Gaidan's sent the Sons to have me killed twice now. Why not just burn me to death if he knows pyromancy?"

"I don't know," said Ark.

"Which is part of the reason I'm suspicious of the local Magisterium," said Caina. "These burning murders have been going on for at least a year, correct? Why haven't they found our pyromancer yet?"

Ark shook his head. "We haven't, either."

"We haven't. I, however, have only been looking for a few days," said Caina. "If I am still looking in a year, we have problems."

Ark snorted.

"The truth is, we do not have enough information," said Caina. "Gaidan knows something. Romarion knows something. The Magisterium knows something. Together, they might know everything."

"And just how are you going to learn that?" said Ark.

"I told you," said Caina, "I'm going to start accepting dinner invitations."

She went to bed. Tomorrow was going to be busy.

The damned grooming and beauty regimen, as usual, took forever.

The maids clucked over the collection of bruises and scratches Caina had acquired. They washed her hair, complaining at how sweaty and tangled it had gotten. After the bath was done, she wound up in a dark blue gown in the old Imperial style, which Julia claimed matched her eyes. It left her arms bare, which Caina disliked, since it had no sleeves for concealing weapons, but it looked charming, which she supposed was the point. She could still keep the daggers in her boots. She also chose silver bracelets and earrings, and a silver coronet set with pale sapphires. Anya shaped her hair into an elaborate pile, and Caina was ready.

"My lady looks lovely," said Cornelia.

"Let us hope so," said Caina, examining her reflection. "I'd hate to have done all this work for nothing."

"You will surely capture this rich merchant's heart," said Anya, "and live in comfort for the rest of your days."

"Indeed," lied Caina. She had no use for his heart. She needed his head, and the secrets it held.

Ark escorted her to the coach, and they rode to Romarion's house. The streets were quiet, guarded by numerous patrols of militia. Caina suspected that Valgorix wanted to make a show of force. She doubted they dared to venture into the slums. Romarion's house stood on the far side of

Corazain's pyramid, and it was only a short ride.

"Well," said Caina, climbing out of the coach, "it seems that Romarion has done well for himself."

Larger than the Inn of Mirrors, Septimus Romarion's mansion had been built in the classic Imperial style. That meant lots of marble columns, a red-tiled roof, and numerous statues of Emperors and the Imperial gods standing in alcoves. Four armed guards stood by the doorway, keeping a cool eye on the street. Servants hurried from the front doors, and led her and Ark into the house.

Romarion met her in a cavernous atrium, sunlight pouring through the skylight and into a sparkling fountain. His coat and boots and shirt looked only slightly less expensive than the house itself, and he wore a bejeweled rapier at his belt. He bent over her hand and kissed her ring, and Caina gave him a polite bow in response.

"Welcome, Countess," he said, speaking in High Nighmarian. His weathered face creased in a smile, but Caina thought she saw a bit of tired strain around the eyes. "It was good of you to come. My humble house is honored by your presence."

"And it was good of you to have me," said Caina in the same language. "Indeed, your house is most beautiful. Certainly a refreshing change, seeing as how the Saddai so enjoy unrelieved black."

Romarion burst out laughing. "You're quite right. For a people who worship fire, you'd think the Saddai would enjoy using different colors in their architecture. But, no. Permit me to give you a tour of my home."

Caina followed Romarion deeper into the house, with Ark trailing a discreet distance behind, along with several of Romarion's bodyguards. Romarion took great pride in his residence. He pointed out how the marble for the columns had come from the Tauseni Mountains, how glassmakers from Jear had constructed his windows, how the wood for his doors had come from the cedars of the Disali hills, how he had brought in the finest artisans from Nighmar itself to fashion the mosaics on the floor. Caina paid very close attention. She did not care about his building materials, but the layout of the house interested her a great deal. It would come in handy later.

"I grew up in Nighmar," said Romarion, "but I came to Rasadda and the Saddai provinces to make my fortune." He smiled. "Now that I have made my fortune, I have tried to bring some of the Imperial capital here."

"It must have cost a great deal," said Caina.

Still, Romarion had a lot of money. Caina wondered how he'd earned it.

He also had a mania for artwork. There were paintings on the walls and mosaics on the floors. Practically every doorway had a bust of some long-dead Emperor gazing down from the frame. Statues stood on pedestals and on alcoves. Most of the artworks were Nighmarian pieces in marble and bronze, but others looked to have been carved out of obsidian and basalt.

"What is this one?" said Caina. The statue seemed to show a naked woman stepping forth from an amorphous blob of black glass. Or she was melting into nothingness. Either way, she found the statue oddly disturbing.

"This?" said Romarion, pacing around the piece. "This is Saddai artwork, Countess. Created during the reign of Arzaidanir, or possibly Morazair. Striking, is it not?"

"It is," said Caina, looking closer. "Is that…obsidian? I didn't think it was possible to sculpt obsidian so smoothly."

"It isn't," said Romarion. "At least not by conventional means. A Saddai Ashbringer used pyromancy to sculpt this statue."

Caina remembered Ostros screaming in agony, and resisted the urge to cringe away from the statue. "Indeed? How does one use sorcery to create a statue? Did they merely wiggle their fingers and say the magic words?"

Romarion laughed. "Not quite. The records from that time are only fragmentary, but from what I understand, an Ashbringer would gather a quantity of volcanic sands. He would then use his pyromancy to heat it to melting, and then would mold it into whatever shape he desired. I believe the funeral pyramids in the city were reared in a similar method, though on a much larger scale."

"It's…almost disturbing to look at," said Caina. "The poor woman looks as if she's melting."

"Oh, yes," said Romarion. "The sculptures of the Ashbringers are always powerful, and frequently disturbing." He shrugged. "It was apparently quite common for an Ashbringer to go insane. All that power must scramble a man's brains." He hesitated. "Though don't repeat that in the hearing of a magus, please."

Caina laughed. "I quite understand. You have my word." She thought for a moment. "But there haven't been any Ashbringers for centuries, which means there are no new statues. So I suppose the statue is quite valuable?"

"It is," said Romarion. "This particular statue could easily fetch a quarter of a million denarii. Perhaps three hundred, four hundred thousand."

"Four hundred thousand?" said Caina. In some parts of the Empire a man counted himself lucky to earn a hundred denarii a year.

"The buying and selling of antique artworks is quite remunerative," said Romarion.

"I should say so," said Caina. "If I may ask, where does one obtain antique Saddai artworks? I rather doubt the Saddai themselves are eager to part with them."

Romarion shrugged. "A number of sources. Some of the wealthier

Saddai still have some pieces, and will sometimes sell them. A huge amount was looted during Crisius's conquest, and remains in circulation throughout the civilized world. But all that can be costly. The best way to obtain Ashbringer sculptures is to find them in the ruins."

"Ruins?" said Caina. "There are Saddai ruins?"

"Quite a few, actually. You see, the Saddai Ashbringers used to rule over a great empire themselves. Nearly the entire eastern third of the modern Empire, along with most of the islands in the Alqaarin Sea, and large portions of the Alqaarin mainland. And an empire means fortresses and palaces and cities, many of which were destroyed in the war and now lost. No one knows where they all are, and if you find an untouched ruin, you can lay claim to any relics or artifacts found within."

"That would be quite a windfall," said Caina.

"It is," said Romarion. He smiled, some of the strain vanishing from his face. "That was how I got my start, Countess. I started out as a merchant captain, trying to turn a profit trading cargoes between Rasadda and the Alqaarin cities. I was thrown adrift in a storm, and came across an uncharted island. Apparently the old Saddai empire had once maintained a fortress there, because we found a rich cache of statues that we sold for a tremendous profit." He shrugged. "My business partners gambled and drank away their shares. I invested mine, and came to prosper."

"A fine story," said Caina.

"I rather enjoyed it," said Romarion. "May I tell you more of it over dinner?"

"Certainly," said Caina.

Romarion set a fine table. There was meat in sauce, spiced vegetables, chilled fruits, breaded mushrooms, and host of other delicacies. Caina even liked the wine, and she hated wine. All this food must have cost a fortune, especially with prices so high, but Romarion could afford it.

Which no doubt explained why six guards stood watch over the meal.

"My father threw me out of the house when I was twelve," Romarion said. "So, of course, I went to sea. I thought it would be romantic." He laughed. "I was whipped on my first day, and almost drowned the second, so I soon lost that notion. But I made my way up, and I soon had enough money to buy a share on a merchant ship. When the captain retired, I bought the ship outright. Then I got lucky and found that cache of old Saddai art. I started buying cargoes in bulk, and as you can see," he waved a hand over the opulence of his mansion, "I have done quite well."

"I can see that," said Caina. "The wine is very good, after all."

Romarion laughed. "What about you?"

"What about me?"

"What brings you to Rasadda?"

Caina shrugged. "My father sent me on a tour of the provinces, as is the custom for the children of noble Houses. I stopped at Mors Crisius, and hope to take ship from Rasadda back to the Imperial capital."

"By yourself?"

"Well," said Caina, glancing to where Ark stood silent and unmoving. "Not quite. My captain of guard is most direct with anyone who tries to take inappropriate liberties."

"So I have heard," said Romarion. "I shall strive to be the perfect gentleman, then."

They both laughed.

"My life has not been nearly as adventurous as yours, in truth," lied Caina. "House Nereide is an old House, founded shortly after the Saddai war. Yet we do not have much wealth, and consequently have stayed out of politics. No son of House Nereide has held a provincial governorship, a legion command, or an Imperial magistracy for generations."

"Distressing," said Romarion.

"It troubles my father more than it troubles me," said Caina. "There is something to be said for living quietly."

"But the greatest rewards come from risk," said Romarion. "Had I not taken risks, I would still be counting jars of wine at my father's tavern. Risks have taken me very far in life." He shrugged. "All I truly lack at this point is a noble title."

Caina hesitated just a bit, and then sipped her wine. "Do you?"

"I am ready to leave Rasadda," said Romarion. "I have made all the money I can make here, I think. And Rasadda is turning sour." He lowered his voice. "It is Lord Governor Nicephorus's fault, I'm afraid. The Saddai province used to be peaceful and well-ordered. Even prosperous. Not the slightest hint of insurrection. Then the Imperial Curia appointed Nicephorus governor, and everything has gone downhill since. His greed has driven the province into the ground."

"I thought you might approve," said Caina, "or have profited from our Lord Governor's dealings."

"No," said Romarion, shaking his head. "No. Nicephorus is a fool. He might make some money, but he'll ruin the Saddai. There is a difference between shearing the sheep and slaughtering them." He hesitated. "I will admit that Lord Nicephorus's mismanagement is one of the reasons I wish to leave Rasadda. The province is going to explode into revolt sooner or later, probably sooner, if he is not removed from office."

"Rasadda does seem mismanaged," said Caina. "I am only a woman, of course, and know little of governance, but I have never seen so many beggars and vagrants."

Romarion seemed to reach a decision. "My lady, may we be candid with each other?"

"Of course," said Caina. "I certainly don't wish for you to lie to me, after all."

"The real reason your father sent you on this tour was to find a wealthy husband, was it not?" said Romarion. "I am not so innocent of the world."

"It was," admitted Caina. "I confess that my prospects were less than desirable in Malarae itself. I do not have enough money to attract of a husband of high birth, and our title is not venerable enough to interest a wealthy nobleman of less ancestry."

"I see," said Romarion. "My lady, I would make you a worthy husband."

"Would you?" said Caina. "So direct, master merchant. You shan't try to flatter my vanity, first? Perhaps praise my beauty, or write a poem about my eyes?"

"You do not seem, Countess, to be a woman who would appreciate flattery," said Romarion.

"No," admitted Caina, annoyed at his observation. Caina cared nothing for flattery. Countess Marianna Nereide was supposed to enjoy it. Romarion should not have seen that.

"Then I will be honest, though you are very lovely," said Romarion. "And clearly a woman of uncommon resolve, too. You have been attacked, what, twice since you came to Rasadda? And yet you have not fled the city."

"That is more my captain of guard's doing than mine," said Caina, glancing at Ark.

"But, still," said Romarion. "I know I am not of high birth, but I have money, and know how to make more. I can bring great wealth to your house, and with a noble title, I could stand for Imperial office." He hesitated. "I…am not a bad man, Countess. I am not cruel. I know some husbands enjoy lording over their wives, but I am not such a man." He spread his hands. "We could go on to great things, you and I, as husband and wife. Permit me to travel with you when you return to the Imperial capital, so that I might meet your lord father."

Caina could not decide to be amused or annoyed at his presumption. "Master merchant, if you wish to pay court to me, you may do so. Though any final decision, of course, will come from my lord father."

"Of course," said Romarion, smiling. "But I think you'll find that I can be very persuasive."

And he spent the rest of the evening trying to persuade her.

###

Later Romarion walked Caina to the coach and made her promise to return soon. She settled into the seat, Ark opposite her, as the coach rattled into motion. Caina fiddled with one of her bracelets, lost in thought.

She felt an odd pang. Romarion had indeed been very charming. That counted for little, of course; Caina had met men who smiled and whistled as they cut out an enemy's heart. And she doubted that Septimus Romarion had amassed his fortune entirely by fair means. Yet Caina wondered what it would be like to take a husband, to have children.

But that was something she would never know, and that awareness put her into a black mood.

"Countess?"

Caina blinked, looked up. "Yes?"

"I was surprised," said Ark.

"Surprised by what?"

Ark hesitated.

"Oh, just come out and say it," said Caina.

"I am surprised you didn't go to bed with him," said Ark. "You probably could have gotten him to tell you everything."

"No doubt," said Caina. "But I didn't. Why does that surprise you?"

Ark shrugged. "I thought you would do it." His tone hardened. "You…seem like the sort of woman who would use sex as a weapon."

Caina glared at him, but could summon no real anger. Ever since she had met him, she had been pretending to be someone else. She could see how he might have drawn that conclusion.

"I did do it that way, once," said Caina, her voice quiet as she remembered Alastair Corus, her first and only lover, a man who had died because of her decisions. "My first assignment for Halfdan. It…didn't go well." She shook her head. "It was wrong, and I shouldn't have done it. I won't do it again."

"I see," said Ark. "So this entire evening was a waste of time?"

"Oh, no, not at all," said Caina. "I learned two things, both of them valuable."

She waited.

Ark sighed. "And what two things are those?"

"For one thing, why is Romarion so eager to get out of Rasadda?"

Ark frowned. "He said business had turned sour…"

"Did you see that mansion?" said Caina. "That big pile of marble and glass? And all those statues? It must have cost a fortune, maybe several fortunes. It's not the kind of thing you can pack up and take with you. And if he moves to Nighmar he'll incur huge losses in his business. The established merchants in Malarae won't exactly step aside for him."

"So?" said Ark.

"So," said Caina, "something has him so badly frightened that he's willing to flee the city at once. The fact that he's so charmed by my beauty that he wants to follow me is simply a convenient excuse."

Ark frowned. "He said he thought the Saddai would revolt against Nicephorus."

"In which case he is unusually far-sighted," said Caina. "The coming revolt is plain, yet neither Nicephorus nor his cronies are able to see it. No, something else has terrified Romarion. I'd rather like to know what that is."

"And what second thing did you learn?" said Ark.

"The interior layout of his mansion," said Caina. "It was most helpful of him to take me on that tour." She smiled. "The knowledge will come in handy very soon."

That seemed to puzzle Ark, but Caina said no more.

A short time later they returned to the Inn, and went to the sitting room. Ark yawned, rubbed his face, and reached for the carafe of wine sitting upon the table. Caina glanced into the maids' room, made sure they were asleep.

"Don't get comfortable," said Caina.

Ark took a quick drink of the wine. "Why not?"

"We're going back to Romarion's mansion."

"What?"

Caina shrugged. "He did invite me back, didn't he?"

CHAPTER 13
BOX OF BLADES

"This is a bad idea," muttered Ark.

They waited in the shadows of an alley across the street from Romarion's splendid mansion. Caina stood wrapped in her shadow cloak, steel at her belt and strapped to her arms. Ark had hidden the gleam of his mail coat beneath a jerkin, his face likewise hidden beneath a hood and mask.

"It will work," said Caina.

"You didn't need me to stand lookout before," said Ark.

"This much more dangerous," said Caina. "The militia is lax. Valgorix's heart is in the right place, but he's not terribly competent. Romarion's not stupid, whatever else he might be, and I think his guards might actually know their business. So I need backup."

"What are you looking for?"

"I'll know it when I find it." Caina wanted a good look at Romarion's ledgers. She suspected she might find all sorts of interesting things there.

"How will I know if you need help?" said Ark.

"Trust me, you'll know," said Caina, checking her weapons and tools one last time. "Use your judgment. You did yesterday, after all."

Ark stepped back in sudden alarm, and Caina did the same. A troop of mounted militia rode past, torches in hand, and Caina waited until they had passed. She counted to twenty, took a deep breath, and stepped into the street.

She saw no one.

"If I'm not back by midnight," said Caina, "return to the Inn."

Ark nodded and vanished into the alley. Caina hurried across the street and plunged into the shadow of Romarion's mansion, her cloak blending with the darkness. A low ornamental wall surrounded the mansion and its grounds, and Caina hopped onto the corner, wrapped her cloak around her, and waited.

She did not wait long. A guard strolled through the mansion's well-kept grounds. He wore a studded leather jerkin, sword and dagger at his belt, and carried a crossbow ready in his arms. All his weapons were in good condition, and he looked as if he knew how to use them. Caina remained motionless, watching the guard.

When he vanished around the corner, Caina moved. She raced across the grounds, grapnel and thin rope spinning in her right hand. She flung the grapnel, felt it catch on the red tiles of the mansion's roof. After a few cautionary tugs, Caina scrambled up the line, her boots scrabbling against the smooth marble walls. The guard came around the corner again, and Caina swung into a darkened window frame, huddling into her cloak.

The guard did not see her. People never looked up. Caina waited until he had passed, and resumed her climb. She stopped at a high window just below the roof. Caina swung into the frame, pulled down the rope, and returned it to her belt. She scrutinized the shutters for a moment, then slipped a knife into the gap and popped the latch. They swung open, and Caina jumped inside, pulling them closed behind her.

She found herself in a bedroom, perhaps a guest room. Her boots sank into a thick carpet, and polished furniture gleamed in the faint light leaking through the shutters. The bed was empty. Caina listened for a moment, but heard nothing. She crossed the room and opened the doorway.

A high-ceilinged hallway stretched the length of the upper floor. Nighmarian and Saddai statues stood in alcoves, while unlit iron chandeliers hung from chains. If Caina remembered right, Romarion kept his offices on the east side. Still listening, she started down the corridor.

She had gone no more than six steps when she heard the voices approaching. Caina looked back and forth. The door was too far away, but a massive statue of an Emperor in antique armor stood to her left, and one of the iron chandeliers hung right over her head. Caina scrambled up the statue, perched on the dead Emperor's shoulders, and jumped to the chandelier. It rocked a little, but the massive chains held it in place, and with the candles extinguished she cast no shadow. She settled into place, like a spider in an iron web, and waited.

Romarion and another man walked down the hallway, speaking to one another in low voices, four guards trailing after them. Caina tensed, but they didn't notice her. People simply never looked up. She settled down to listen.

"It could just be a coincidence," said one of the men. To judge from his dress, Caina supposed he was Romarion's steward.

"No," said Romarion. "It's not a coincidence." He clutched a letter in one hand.

Caina blinked in surprise. Romarion had always had spoken High Nighmarian with a cultured, elegant accent. Now he spoke Caerish, his accent rough and harsh. He sounded like a lifelong sailor.

"They got all the others," said Romarion. He sounded angry, or frightened, or perhaps both. "They've been turning up dead one by one in their beds. I never thought to die in bed, you know. I always thought I would drown, or hang, but to die like that…no, gods, no."

"I still think…" said the steward.

"No!" said Romarion. "All the others are dead, and then we receive word that Vanio is dead in Mors Crisius?"

Caina blinked in surprise.

"It could have been an accident," said the steward. "The letter didn't say."

"No," said Romarion, shaking his head. "It's not an accident. I'll wager the poor bastard was found burned to death in his bed, just like the others. First he came for the others. Then he got Vanio. And he's going to come after me next, I know it."

They stood in silence for a moment.

"What are you going to do?" said the steward.

"Get out of Rasadda as soon as it's feasible," said Romarion. "Hell, I ought to get out of the Saddai province entirely. Vanio was in Mors Crisius, and he got to him anyway. As soon as I can convert enough of my solid assets to ready money, I will leave. If I can convince that charming young countess to marry me, all the better. It'll make it easier to land on my feet." He shrugged. "But if not…I am leaving before the month is out. I can always rebuild my fortune. I can't bring myself back from the dead."

"Very true," said the steward. "But you may not have a month."

"Perhaps," said Romarion. "But I don't think he suspects that I know anything. If I sail steady and calm, I can get away before the storm comes. And if not…well, I've got a few hiding places around the city." He clapped the steward on the shoulder. "You can always loot the mansion after I flee."

"That was always the plan, sir."

Romarion laughed. "Enterprising man, I like that." They kept walking, and Caina soon heard the sound of them going downstairs. She counted to a hundred, but no one else appeared, and she dropped from the chandelier, cloak pooling around her legs.

Interesting. Caina wished that Romarion had mentioned more names. But clearly he feared falling victim to this unknown pyromancer, just like all the others. Caina wondered who the "others" might have been.

Time to find out.

She crept down the hallway and reached the door to Romarion's study. He had left it locked, and Caina knelt before the door, pulled the appropriate tools from her belt, and set to work. She soon realized that Romarion had not scrimped on security. The lock was damnably good, so good that Caina almost decided to go out the window and crawl along the ledge. But at last the lock released with a click, and the door swung open.

Unlike the rest of the mansion, Romarion's study was simple, almost austere. A pair of cutlasses, the blades notched with use, hung on the wall, alongside a shark's jawbone. Bits of coral and exotic shells sat on the writing desk. Relics from Romarion's days at sea, Caina supposed.

She walked around the desk, intending to read the papers covering its surface, and stopped. A huge iron box sat below the window, massive enough that it would take five or six strong men to move. Dark, solemn designs covered its sides, along with dozens of ominous black slits. Three different keyholes adorned the massive lock.

Caina whispered a curse.

A Strigosti trapbox.

This was very bad. The Strigosti were a reclusive, unfriendly people, but none could match their skill with machinery and intricate mechanical devices. They specialized in siege engines, locks, and cunning traps of ghastly lethality. Romarion must have paid dear for the iron chest, but thieves who tried to break into a Strigosti trapbox without the proper keys almost always wound up dead.

Caina had disarmed Strigosti trapboxes twice before, but it had almost killed her both times. She ought to just find the keys, but Romarion no doubt kept them on his person. If she stole them, Romarion might panic and flee the city before Caina could learn anything useful from him. She was sure Romarion kept things in this chest that he wanted kept secret, which meant that Caina wanted to know them.

She had to try. Caina closed and locked the study door and took a moment to clear her head. Then she unpacked her tools, knelt before the iron box, and set to work.

Of the three keyholes, Caina guessed that the first two disarmed the traps, while the third would undo the lock. Turning the keys in the wrong order would undoubtedly trigger all the traps at once. Caina had no way of knowing the correct sequence, so she had to try other methods.

She examined the front of the chest until she found a slender seam in the carvings. After several minutes of prying with a dagger, a metal plate popped away, revealing an intricate maze of gears, springs, cogs, and wound springs. The logical course would have been to smash the intricate machinery. Logical, and suicidal; smashing the machinery would release all the traps at once. Instead she stared at the gears for a moment, thinking. It looked as if one trap would fling darts from the dark slits on the box's sides. To judge from the small steel bottles Caina saw, the blades would have a coating of poison. The second trap would send dagger blades stabbing from hidden compartments, taking the fingers and eyes of any clumsy thieves.

She selected a small prybar from her tools and set to work. Bit by bit she worked her way through the machinery. A spring loosened, a gear wound back here, and Caina began to feel more confident.

Then something clicked. The gears began to spin, faster and faster, the cogs working up and down. Caina cursed and threw herself backwards, rolling over Romarion's desk to land on its far side. A heartbeat later she heard another, louder click, followed by a silvery hiss. Her heart thudding, Caina peered around the desk.

Foot-long steel blades had erupted from the Strigosti trapbox, making it look like a freakish metallic porcupine. Yellow grease coated the blades. A poison, no doubt. After a moment the clockwork innards began to spin again, pulling the blades back into the chest. Another click, and the trap reset itself.

Caina took a moment to steady herself. When her heart had slowed and her hands stopped trembling, she took a deep breath and resumed work. This time she knew what gears and cogs to avoid. One by one, she disarmed the box's traps. Then she stared on the chest's lock. It was a masterpiece of the locksmith's craft, and sweat began to drip down Caina's face as she worked. She had been working for at least an hour, and very soon she would run out of time. Ark might take direct, and dangerous, action.

The lock shuddered, releasing. Caina flung open the massive iron lid, and rolled backwards, half expecting a rain of razor blades to erupt from the iron chest. But nothing happened. Caina sighed, straightened up the desk, and started rifling through the box, taking care to memorize the arrangement.

She found several leather pouches of precious gems and platinum coins, along with a few small jade statuettes. No doubt Romarion planned to take them when he fled. Caina left them alone, and turned her attention to the stacked ledgers. She lifted them free, opened them on the floor, and began flipping through the pages.

The records only went back four years, but Romarion's business interests included gold, silver, gems, ivory, ebony, marble, rare woods, fine wine, and other valuable luxuries. But it seemed that the foundation of his great wealth came from dealing artworks. He had sold dozens of rare Saddai statues for vast sums of money. A lot of Romarion's statues had gone through Vanio in Mors Crisius. Caina's mouth curled into a crooked smile. No wonder Romarion kept his records under lock and lethal trap. He smuggled his statues into Mors Crisius, avoiding the Imperial customs agents in Rasadda's harbors. From there he shipped the statues overland to Rasadda, and then sold them through his partners.

Caina blinked. She read over the list of partners again.

Her breath hissed through her teeth.

The names of Romarion's business partners, every last one of them, had been on Valgorix's list of the burned dead. Caina's eyes scanned the ledger's pages, doing the math in her head. In fact, if she added it up, there had been only two groups of identified victims on Valgorix's list of the slain. The Ghost circle of Rasadda, and Romarion's business partners. And Caina would wager that the unidentified bodies on the list were connected to either the Ghosts or Romarion's partners; spouses, perhaps, or servants who had been in the wrong place at the wrong time.

Caina could almost see the sequence of events. Four years ago Romarion and his partners began dealing in ancient Saddai artwork. Then someone started to murder his partners using pyromantic sorcery. The Ghost circle under Ostros noticed and investigated, until this pyromancer killed them all lest they interfere.

She stared at the ledger for a moment, thinking hard.

Romarion looted ruins for his artworks. He must have found something valuable, something priceless. But someone else must have learned of his discovery, and was willing to kill to claim it. What could possibly be worth such carnage? Some old statue? Caina didn't know.

For a moment Caina considered breaking into Romarion's bedroom and demanding the truth, or kidnapping him and taking him to a safe place for interrogation. No, too risky. Caina and Ark could not pull it off between them. And Romarion surrounded himself with armed guards. Too much could go wrong.

Caina still needed more information, so she resumed flipping through the ledger. Two things caught her eye.

First, Romarion had been frantically converting his assets to coin, even selling numerous artworks below cost.

Second, Romarion had sold a huge amount of Saddai artwork to the Magisterium, even several pieces to both Kalastus and Ephaeron personally. One piece, in particular, had commanded a truly enormous price.

Very interesting.

But she could think about that later. It was past time to go. Caina returned the ledgers to the trapbox and closed the lid. She heard a series of clicks as the lock and the traps reset themselves. With any luck, Romarion would not notice anything amiss. She jumped atop the Strigosti trapbox, opened the shutters, and gazed into the grounds below until she found the patrolling guard. Once she saw his pattern, she climbed into the windowsill, closed the shutters behind her, and rappelled down the side of the mansion. From there she raced across the grounds, jumped the ornamental wall, crouched into the shadows, and waited.

No cries of alarm. No sign of pursuit. Caina crossed the street, her cloak flowing into the darkness of the night. Ark waited in the mouth of the alley, staring at the mansion. He did not see her until she was four or five paces away. He flinched, reached for his sword, and lowered his hand.

"I was ready to go," said Ark. "What took so long?"

"There were complications," said Caina. The mask covering her face felt hot and sweaty, and she wished she could take it off. "Romarion invested heavily in his security. All his records were in a Strigosti trapbox."

Ark frowned. "You opened it?"

"Yes."

"And you're still alive?"

"Either that, or my shade has come to haunt you," said Caina.

Ark's eye twitched. "And did you find anything?"

"Oh, yes," said Caina. "It seems that Romarion's business partners, every last one of them, have been found burned to death over the last year." She wrapped her cloak tighter, sinking into the shadows of the alley. "Between them and the Ghost circle, they account for every last identified name on Valgorix's list. Which means that these killings are not random. Someone started killing Romarion's business partners, and slaughtered the Ghost circle once Ostros started investigating."

"Why hasn't Romarion been killed yet?" said Ark.

"I'm not sure," said Caina. "But he guards himself night and day. If some of the victim's blood is required to work the fire sorcery, then our pyromancer might not have been able to get close enough to get some of Romarion's blood. Still, he knows someone is after him, which is why he's preparing to flee the city."

Ark growled. "We should take him and make him talk."

"A fine idea," said Caina. "And if you can figure out a way to do that without getting killed, let me know."

"Why?" said Ark. "Why kill Romarion's business partners?"

Caina shrugged. "I don't yet know. Romarion made most of his fortune selling Saddai artworks plundered from old ruins. It probably has something to do with that."

"Then Gaidan did it," said Ark. "He must view Romarion and his partners as tomb robbers. So he started killing them with pyromancy, and killed the Ghost circle when they realized what was happening."

"Perhaps," said Caina, "but where did Gaidan learn pyromancy?"

Ark said nothing.

"And Romarion sold a lot of art to the local Magisterium, and received a great deal of money for one piece in particular," said Caina. "I'd like to know what that was."

"I still think you refuse to see the obvious," Ark said.

"We can discuss this later," said Caina. "We'd better get off the streets. Someone might find us here if we loiter."

They started back towards the Inn.

"All this butchery over some damned statues, then," said Ark, shaking his head.

"Maybe," said Caina. "I wonder…"

"You wonder what?"

"I wonder," said Caina, "if Romarion found something…worse." She shrugged, wrestling with the idea. "There are dozens of nations in the Empire, and all of them had their own arcane traditions until the Magisterium suppressed them. Halfdan has told me of incidents where tomb robbers dug up something that should have remained buried."

"Like what?"

"Some fearsome thing of old sorcery, some enspelled artifact," said Caina. "Maybe Romarion found something darker than an old statue. A weapon, perhaps. Some sorcerous relic of the old Saddai empire."

"Do you have any proof of this?"

"No," said Caina. "Just a suspicion."

Ark shook his head. "Then…"

He stopped, reaching for his sword.

A score of men blocked the street, staring at Ark and Caina. All of the men wore gleaming chain mail beneath jerkins of black leather, polished steel helmets, and armored boots. Broadswords rested ready in their hands, round shields on their left arms. They had the look of seasoned, hardened veterans. Mercenaries, most likely, and competent ones.

"State your business," said Ark, pointing with his sword.

"Right where the old man said he'd be," said the leader, shaking his head. "Uncanny, I tell you."

"Matches the description," grunted another.

"What about the other one, the little fellow in the black cloak?" said a third mercenary, looking at Caina with cold eyes.

"What of him?" said the leader. "Kill them both. Now."

Caina just had time to wonder why these men wanted to kill Ark. And then they rushed forward, swords raised.

CHAPTER 14
RIOTS

Caina's arm snapped up, a knife in hand. She took a step backwards, her back arched, her arm flung back, and hurled the knife with all her strength. It flew true, making for the mercenary leader's face. Or, at least, it would have, had his shield not snapped up, sending the blade spinning into the darkness.

"Run!" roared Ark.

Caina spun, snatched the heavy daggers from her boots, and took off after Ark, her cloak snapping out behind her. She heard the heavy pounding of the mercenaries' boots, and risked a quick look back. Despite their heavy armor, they kept pace.

"Have to slow them down," said Ark. "The alley on the right. In there, then turn."

Caina nodded. The alley would force the mercenaries to come at them one and two at a time. Within any luck, they could force them off balance, and make their escape. Ark veered to the right, dashing into the alley between two fine houses, and Caina followed, the mercenaries hot on their heels.

"Now!" said Ark.

Caina whirled, dropping to one knee as Ark's broadsword stabbed over her head. The blade plunged into a mercenary's mouth in a spray of blood and broken teeth, and the man sagged with an agonizing gurgle. Ark struggled to wrench his sword free, and another mercenary sprang at him, sword raised over his head for an overhand blow. Caina sprang to her feet, driving her left dagger into the armpit of the mercenary's upraised arm. He stiffened, and she slashed her right blade across his throat and stepped back besides Ark. The dying man collapsed across his slain companion, and for a moment the mercenaries hesitated.

"Kill them both!" roared the leader.

Another man stabbed at Caina. She jerked to the right, slamming into the wall, and the sword whistled past her. She spun, stepping within his weapon's reach, and stabbed for his face. But he stepped backwards, his shield coming up, and Caina's blow clanged away. Caina heard a scream and a gurgle, and another mercenary fell dead atop the others, blocking the narrow alleyway.

"Run!" shouted Ark. He turned and sprinted, blood falling from his sword, and Caina raced after him, daggers in hand. The far end of the alley opened into another square, below one of the lesser funeral pyramids. A half-dozen streets branched out from that square, and they could escape.

Or so Caina thought, until more armored mercenaries appeared, fanning out to block their escape.

They were almost trapped. But Ark roared at the top of his lungs and leapt forward, his broadsword a bloody arc over his head. One mercenary fell dead, the top half of his head reduced to bloody mush, and Ark crashed into the into the rest. They swarmed around him, and one presented his back to Caina, so she took the opportunity to plunge a dagger into his neck. He fell, and Ark wrenched free of the tangle, blood flowing down his jaw. Caina saw more mercenaries racing to meet them, at least a score more, and some of them had crossbows.

"Go!" Caina shouted. She and Ark ran across the square, Ark moving with a faint hitch to his stride. He must have been wounded in the leg. "Here!" She turned towards a small temple to one of the gods of the Empire – Markoin, the god of soldiers - its white marble stark against the dark Saddai buildings around it. By ancient custom, no blood could be shed within the sanctuary of an Imperial temple. Caina raced up the stairs, Ark following, and darted between the marble columns and into the temple proper. A marble altar stood before a statue of an armored man with a greatsword, the braziers filling the chamber with a dim glow.

"You there!" A fat young man in formal robes hurried over, his face filled with annoyed chagrin. "Arms are forbidden with a temple. Leave at once." He turned just as the leader of the mercenaries stormed through the doorway. "What is this? A riot? Take your brawling..."

The leader ran the priest through, kicked him off the blade, and left him to die on the floor.

The mercenaries, it seemed, cared little for the ancient custom of sanctuary.

A crossbow went off, and Ark grunted, his free hand going to his side. Caina rolled as more bolts came whistling through the doorway and bounced off the marble floor. She dropped one dagger, snatched a knife from her belt, came to one knee, and let the blade fly. This time she caught the nearest crossbowman right in the neck. He dropped his weapon, clawing at his throat as the blood welled up. Ark snarled and whipped his broadsword back and forth, but the mercenaries pressed them back.

"Altar!" shouted Caina. She raced across the temple, jumped up onto the altar, and seized one of the metal braziers, pulling it up after her. The thing was heavy, and almost too hot to hold, even through her gloves. Ark saw her, his eyes going wide, and he sprinted for the altar, a dozen mercenaries trailing after him.

It gave Caina a lovely target.

She hurled the brazier at them, a glowing arc of hot coals spilling out. The mercenaries fell back with cries of alarm, throwing up their shields to cover their faces. Fires caught in some of their clothes, and the men beat at the flames with curses. Caina jumped from the altar, swung around the statue of the god, and ran for it, Ark following after her. She went through a doorway and found herself in a comfortable bedroom; the unfortunate priest's, no doubt. A window opened onto the street. Caina kicked open the shutters, threw herself over the sill, and dropped the six feet to the street. Ark came after, grunting with pain, his face lined with tension.

"Are you hurt?" said Caina.

"I'll manage," growled Ark. "We have to find a place to hide, now. If they catch up to us again it's over."

"I know, I know," said Caina, scanning the street. She heard the pounding of boots and the mercenary leader's angry shouts. "Follow me. Quickly!"

A bathhouse stood further down the street, an odd amalgam of Saddai and Imperial architecture. Caina dashed towards it, Ark following. He was slowing, Caina saw, and she wondered how badly he had been hurt. If she did not think of something clever, the mercenaries would kill them both.

Well. She would just have to be clever, then.

Caina ran at the door, dropped her shoulder, and slammed into it. She was not heavy, but she had a good deal of momentum, and the door splintered its frame. Caina bounced back several steps and recovered her balance. She saw the mercenaries racing around the temple, swords in hand. Caina kicked in the door and staggered into the bathhouse, Ark behind her.

The air inside was hot and steamy, the brick walls wet with condensation. Perhaps two dozen men lounged in the steaming waters, several of them dallying with prostitutes. An unkempt Saddai attendant near the door staggered to his feet, eyes wide.

"You have ruined my door!" he bellowed. "What cause have you for…"

"Shut up!" said Caina, gesturing with a bloodstained dagger. The attendant went quiet and shrank back into his corner. Caina looked around, saw stairs leading to the second story. She hurried up the slick stairs, trying to keep her balance, and Ark followed.

She threw open another door and found herself in a large room. Close to forty men crowded the room, all gathered around a speaker on a central podium. None of the men wore their shirts. All of them had the flame tattoo of Corazain upon their bare chests.

"Damn it," muttered Ark.

For a moment the Sons of Corazain stared at her in shocked silence.

"Who are you?" said the speaker. "Why do you dare to intrude upon this gathering of the servants of the Burning Flame?"

A wild notion seized Caina.

"Behold, for I am the wrath of the Emperor!" she roared in her loudest voice. "You have dared to rebel against your lawful sovereign. His patience is great, but you have exhausted it at last, and I have come to bring just retribution upon your heads!"

They gaped at her. So did Ark.

"What foolishness is this?" said the man nearest Caina, stepping closer. "There are only two of you!"

Caina slugged him, the hilt of her dagger cracking into his jaw. The man stumbled back with a cry, spitting blood.

"Fools!" Caina bellowed. "Perish all!"

"Kill them!" screamed the speaker. As one of the Sons of Corazain seized weapons and surged towards them.

"What..." said Ark.

"Shut up and run!" said Caina, grabbing his arm.

They stumbled back down the stairs, the Sons of Corazain in hot pursuit, just as the mercenaries stormed into the bathhouse. The attendant fled screaming past the pools, while the patrons and the prostitutes blinked in surprise. Caina leapt down the rest of the stairs and landed with daggers in hand, cloak billowing out behind her.

"Get them, get them, get them!" yelled the mercenary leader, pointing with his broadsword.

"Slay these infidels, my brothers," screamed Caina in Saddaic, "in the name of the Burning Flame and great Corazain!"

The Sons of Corazain came howling down the stairs and crashed into the shocked mercenaries. Swords rang and men screamed. Caina ducked and dodged and tore her way free of the wild melee, almost losing her balance on the damp floor. She grabbed Ark's arm and dragged him towards the pools. The bathers stared up at her in alarm.

"What are you looking at, you fools?" she said. "The Saddai have come to purify their city of prostitutes and their customers! Run, if you value your lives!"

Naked men and women surged from the water, yelling in fear, and began a panicked run for the exits. The bathhouse erupted into sheer chaos, with the Sons of Corazain howling, the mercenaries screaming orders to each other, and naked bathers fleeing in all directions. Caina tightened her grip on Ark's arm and threaded her way through the madness. She saw a naked man vanished though a door in the back, followed him, and found herself on the streets. Men were shouting, and Caina saw a troop of militia racing for the bathhouse.

"Now's our chance," said Caina. "Run!"

She and Ark fled through Rasadda's streets, taking turns at random, putting distance between themselves and the mercenaries. At last they stopped in the bazaar where Caina had chased Ostros, now closed and empty for the night. Caina slumped against an empty booth, her breath ragged and quick, while Ark slumped to the ground, face wet with sweat.

Caina opened her mouth to speak, and a strange sound met her ears.

Ark was laughing.

She gaped at him. Ever since Caina had met him, she had never seen him so much as chuckle. He barely smiled. Yet now he was shaking with laughter, his cold eyes alight with wild mirth.

"What the devil are you laughing about?" said Caina.

"Did you see their faces?" said Ark. "When…when you told the Sons of Corazain to kill the mercenaries? Gods! I have never seen men so surprised. And when…and when you told the prostitutes that the Saddai had come to kill them." He almost doubled over, still shaking. "We ought to be dead! A dozen times over. Yet you talked them into fighting each other! Gods!" Another burst of laughter erupted from his mouth.

"I fail to see how this is possibly funny," snapped Caina.

Ark stared at her, still chuckling.

Caina stared back at him. All at once she remembered the expression of stupefied shock on the Saddai man's face when she had punched him, and she found herself chuckling with Ark. Then the sheer absurdity of their escape struck her full force, and she began to laugh. Ark saw her laughing, which made him laugh, which made her laugh harder.

It took a while to calm down.

"How…how did you know the Sons of Corazain would be meeting upstairs?" said Ark.

"I didn't!" said Caina.

They looked at each other, and both burst into laughter again.

"You're a madwoman," said Ark, wiping sweat from his brow. He laughed once more, and shook his head. "An utter madwoman."

"Perhaps," said Caina. She tugged down the mask concealing her face for a moment, and grinned at him. "But a madwoman who's still alive. As are you."

Ark snorted and shook his head. "I cannot argue with that."

"Come," said Caina, standing and returning her mask to its place, "let's get back to the Inn. We need to get off the streets."

He nodded, and they vanished into the night.

"Stop whining," said Caina, giving the needle another tug.

Ark grunted, but did not move.

Caina sat cross-legged on the massive bed, Ark lying facedown besides her, his trousers off. He had taken a nasty gash to the hip, and another to the back of his thigh, and could not reach the wounds himself. So Caina had cleaned them with boiling wine, and was now stitching them closed.

"You're not very good at this," said Ark.

"No," said Caina, "but good enough. Finding a surgeon would attract attention. And you can't do it yourself. So lie still and stop complaining. If you wake up the maids, we'll have to explain why I'm dressed all in black and armed to the teeth. And we'll also have to explain why you're lying half-naked on my bed."

Ark's lips twitched. "I'm not sure which would be harder."

"Let's not find out," said Caina.

She worked in silence for a moment. Ark had numerous old scars on the thick muscles of his legs, including a long reddish-white one that looked as if it should have taken his left leg entirely. She finished stitching the cut on the back of his thigh, wrapped bandages around the leg, and began on the gash in his hip.

"I know those mercenaries," said Ark.

"Oh?" said Caina, hesitating.

"Years ago," said Ark. "I thought they looked familiar, but I couldn't place them. I saw them when I was still with the Eighteenth Legion. The Black Wolves, they're called. They were hard men. Brutal. They would kill anyone for the right price. They used to do a lot of work for the Magisterium, hunting down rogue sorcerers."

"The Magisterium, you say?" said Caina, holding the needle over a candle flame.

"Or anyone else who would pay," said Ark. He closed his eyes. "About...ten years ago, maybe twelve, they killed a High Lord. The Emperor declared them outlaw, and they fled to Alqaarin, or perhaps Istarinmul."

"Apparently, they're back," said Caina. Ark winced as she jabbed the needle into his skin. "Any idea why they would want to kill you?"

"Me?" said Ark. "They came to kill you."

"No," said Caina, stitching the wound. "Weren't you listening? They had come for you. You, Ark. They said that you matched the description. They were surprised to see me. The 'little fellow in the black cloak', remember?"

"You're right," said Ark, voice quiet.

"Why would they want to kill you?" said Caina.

"I...don't know," said Ark. "It can't be a personal grudge. I only saw them once, at the start of my term of service with the Eighteenth. That was twenty years ago, and I never spoke with any of them."

"Did someone hire them to kill you?"

"Why?" said Ark. "I am a discharged veteran of the legions. I used to be a blacksmith. Ostros had me masquerade as a caravan guard. I'm not important enough to kill." His voice hardened. "Unless someone learned I am a Ghost."

"The only one killing Ghosts in Rasadda is our pyromancer," said Caina, "and if he had come after you, you would have burned to death. He wouldn't have sent mercenaries."

"No," said Ark. "Then who sent the Black Wolves after us?"

"I haven't the slightest idea," said Caina, concentrating on the gash. "Our pyromancer wouldn't have done it. Gaidan couldn't afford them. I just don't know. But what's one more mystery? It's not as if we have any shortage of them." She finished stitching up the gash, and began making a poultice for the wound. "One thing troubles me."

"What's that?"

"You were disguised. No one saw us leave the Inn, and no one followed us, I'm sure of it. Yet they still knew where to find you. How?"

She folded the poultice, her fingers working over the cloth.

"Countess?"

Ark sounded odd, almost melancholy.

Caina looked at him, surprised at his tone. "Yes?"

"Those men we killed tonight," said Ark, his head on the pillow, his eyes staring at nothing. "Do you regret it? Does it weigh upon your conscience?"

"Do I feel guilty about it, you mean?" said Caina, laying the poultice over the stitched gash. "No. Not at all. We were only defending ourselves. If we had not fought back, they would have killed us both. But do I regret that we had to kill them?" Caina sighed. "Yes, I regret it. Keenly. I have too many nightmares already. This shall be one more."

"I understand about nightmares," muttered Ark, his voice growing thick. "I have many myself."

"I know," said Caina. "I have heard you shout in your sleep. Halfdan told me once that as our flesh bears scars, our mind bears nightmares."

Ark made no answer, and Caina bound the poultice in place with bandages. When she had finished, she saw that Ark had fallen asleep. She looked down at him, and felt a peculiar gratitude towards him. He had saved her life tonight, again. Ark might have been able to claw free of the

Black Wolves on his own, but Caina could not have done so, not in a stand-up fight. Nor could she have escaped the Sons of Corazain twice now. He might hold her in disdain, but she had come to admire his unyielding courage and his terrible skill with the sword.

Caina tugged a blanket from the bed and laid it over him. Let them maids think what they want, but Ark deserved a night's rest. She changed into a nightgown, settled into a chair, and went to sleep.

The next morning she submitted again to the grooming and beauty regimen as she prepared for her dinner with the masters of the Magisterium.

"I heard the most dreadful rumor," said Anya. "It seems that there was a riot in the city last night."

"Oh?" said Caina.

"Yes, at a public bathhouse."

"Not surprising," sniffed Cornelia. "Only wicked men frequent bathhouses. One of them was behind it, undoubtedly."

"Oh, undoubtedly," said Caina, doing her very best not to laugh.

CHAPTER 15
A MASTER OF THE MAGISTERIUM

As dusk fell, Caina and Ark rode to the chapterhouse of the Magisterium.

Caina had thought herself ready for this. She suspected at least one of Rasadda's magi was involved in the murders, and when Ark had mentioned that the Black Wolves had worked for the Magisterium, her interest had only sharpened. Yet as the coach drew closer to the chapterhouse, black dread settled on her heart. Old memories, dark and rotten, fluttered in her mind, and her hands tightened beneath her soft gloves.

She hated the magi, hated them more than she could ever say.

The coach stopped before the chapterhouse, and Caina climbed out. She had chosen a formal green gown with a high collar, and a jacket with embroidered sleeves. It was not nearly as alluring as the dress she had worn to Romarion's house, but that was by design. Romarion might have been a rogue, but at least he had been polite and charming. Caina doubted that Ephaeron and Kalastus would share his courtesy.

The chapterhouse itself looked like a smaller version of the Imperial Basilica, though built of black Saddai marble. The sigil of the Magisterium, a pair of eyes looking from an open book, had been carved into the lintel. A wave of nausea went though Caina as she looked at the sigil, and she desperately wanted to leave.

No. She had her duty, and she would do it. Her face remained a calm mask as she walked to the doors, Ark at her side. He had insisted upon wearing his armor, and walked with only the faintest trace of a limp, his face grimmer than usual.

Two soldiers stood besides the chapterhouse doors, dressed all in black. Even their breastplates and helmets had been enameled black. The Magisterial Guard, the bodyguards of the magi. They were just as brutally murderous as their masters. But they bowed to her and pulled open the doors, and Caina entered into the chapterhouse.

She found herself in a great hall, similar to the Imperial Basilica but smaller in scale. Long tables stretched the length of the hall, covered in strange mazes of glass tubing, odd mechanical devices, and piled books and scrolls. The enchanted glass spheres so favored by the magi lit the hall with unnatural light. Caina's skin began to crawl. Somewhere very close, she knew, someone was performing sorcery.

A brother of the Magisterium, in a black robe with a red sash, hurried over and bowed.

"Countess Marianna Nereide, I presume?" the magus said.

"I am," said Caina.

"The masters awake you eagerly." He lifted his hand and whispered something under his breath. The crawling on Caina's skin intensified, and she felt the faint surge of sorcerous power. An apple-sized sphere of blue light appeared between them. She resisted the urge to recoil. "Simply follow this simulacrum to the masters' chambers. It will guide you there."

"Thank you," said Caina.

The magus bowed, and the blue sphere began to drift forward. It led them across the hall and up a flight of stairs. The globe spun all the while, pulsating like a living heart. Petty showmanship, to be sure, the same way Ephaeron had floated a glass of wine to Ark's hand at the Imperial Basilica. The Magisterium adored their little tricks.

They passed along the balcony and into a sitting room, adorned with overstuffed chairs and low wooden tables. The sphere of light pulsed once more and vanished. Another door stood open on the far side of the room, and Caina heard angry voices.

One of them was Septimus Romarion's.

"Wait here," she murmured to Ark, and crept forward, trying to keep her heeled boots from making any noise against the marble floor.

"I must insist, learned master, upon prompt payment," said Romarion. "After all, I have fulfilled my end of the bargain, and I have a right to my money."

"The payments will continue as we have agreed," said another voice, deep and rich. Caina could not place it for a moment, and then the memory came. Kalastus, the bald master she had met at Nicephorus's dinner. His sonorous voice hardened with contempt. "The artifacts you supplied were satisfactory, and you ought to be honored to conduct business with the Magisterium. Instead you come here and grovel for more money ahead of our agreed schedule."

"I have need of the money now," said Romarion.

"Don't be ridiculous," said Kalastus. "You shall receive your money when we agreed and not a moment before. Why are you so impatient? The

Magisterium keeps its word, merchant. It…ah!" Kalastus laughed, long and mocking. "These 'burning murders' among the Saddai rabble have you frightened like a child, do they not?"

Romarion said nothing.

"I had thought better of you, Septimus," said Kalastus. "Pyromancy is extinct. The notions of the Saddai rabble are nothing more than feebleminded delusions. They cling yet to the foolish belief that their precious god will save them – the Living Fire or the Smoking Ember or whatever they call it."

"The city is on the verge of rebellion," said Romarion, his voice so quiet Caina could scarce hear him. "Surely you must see it, even if the Lord Governor does not."

Kalastus laughed again. "Let the Saddai revolt! Yes, you heard me. Let them rebel! If they dare, we shall slaughter them like the dogs that they are. If they dare, we of the Magisterium will show them such sorcery that the Ashbringers of old will look like mewling children. Sorcery that you shall see, merchant, if you continue your impudent demands for early payment."

Caina's mouth tightened.

"I see," said Romarion, almost snarling.

If he left now, he would see Caina listening at the door. She knocked on the doorframe and stepped into the next room. It was a study, she saw, dominated by Kalastus's massive desk of dark wood. Papers and various knickknacks covered the desk, along with a massive book bound in black leather and polished steel. A few ancient Saddai statues stood around the room, no doubt the pieces Kalastus had bought. Romarion stood before the desk, his stance stiff with anger, while Kalastus lounged in his chair. Both of them looked at her with surprise.

"I do hope I am not interrupting your business," said Caina, "but I know how men are. If I leave you alone, you'll discuss business all night, and we shall never have dinner."

Kalastus smiled at her. He must have been over sixty, yet he remained lean and fit, his black robe hanging loosely off his frame. "Not at all, Countess. I am honored that you could join us."

"And you are quite right," said Romarion, bowing over her hand and placing a kiss upon her gloved fingers. "Though so lovely a noblewoman as yourself is a welcome distraction from the cares of business. I do hope you will again join me for dinner."

"I would be glad," said Caina, "if you are willing to entertain the poor daughter of a lesser House."

Romarion laughed. "Humility? It does not suit you. But still I should be very glad."

"Countess," said Kalastus, "the merchant and I were just concluding our discussion." His smile was not at all friendly. "I will join you presently.

Please, make yourself comfortable." He made a gesture at the door.

It was a slight, but Caina smiled anyway. "Of course." She smiled at Romarion, walked back into the sitting room, and paused. Another doorway opened off to her right, and she glanced into it. Sudden wonder stole her breath, and Caina walked into the room.

It was a library. Massive bookshelves lined all four walls, ladders climbing up towards the ceiling, every shelf stuffed with books. Two tables sat in the center of the room, piled with still more books. Caina approached the nearest shelf, running her fingers over the spines. She had always loved to read, even as a child. Some of her happiest memories were in her father's library, poring over his books…

Her father's library.

Sudden tears came to her eyes, and she blinked them away. She had found her father's servants lying on the floor of that library, their eyes empty. She had found her father in his chair…

And now she stood here in this den of serpents.

Distressed, struggling to keep her calm mask in place, Caina turned. One of the books caught her eye, and she reached for it. "The Catechism of Minaerys", a book of prayers and rituals to the goddess of wisdom and learning. Caina flipped through it, trying to distract herself.

Someone yanked the book from her grasp. Caina flinched and saw Kalastus standing near her, too near. He closed the book, looked at the cover, and gave her an incredulous look.

"This book?" he said, chuckling. "What a collection of tripe. Why anyone would worship a myth is beyond me." He tossed the book onto the table. "Ridiculous, really."

Caina said nothing, not trusting herself to speak.

Kalastus looked at her, still standing too close, and his eyes widened. "Do not tell me you were praying? Surely you do not believe such nonsense?"

Caina shrugged. "It seems foolish to anger the gods."

"Folly," said Kalastus. "That a noblewoman of the Empire would follow such a…such a contemptible superstition is quite beyond me. Perhaps that is the problem with the Empire."

"You skirt dangerously close to treason, learned one," said Caina.

"Not at all," said Kalastus. "Indeed, no one cares more for the greater good of the Empire than the Magisterium. But reason must rule our Empire, and not the shopworn creeds of past ages, or the petty moralities that constrain small-minded men. It is criminal, I think, that the Magisterium does not have a greater voice in the rule of the Empire, as we did in more enlightened ages. Reason must rule the Empire! And who better to wield reason than the magi, we who have mastered arcane sciences? Think of the good a council of ruling magi could do." "Surely that is a comforting thought," lied Caina.

"Comfort?" Kalastus burst out laughing. "Comfort, my dear Countess, is for the weak. Those too feeble to see that man must rule himself without mewling before nonexistent gods. Those who lack the strength to reshape the world to their liking."

"You sound," said Caina, her voice colder than Countess Marianna Nereide had any right to speak, "exactly like my mother."

"Then your mother was a wise woman," said Kalastus. "Ah. I see that I have offended you. If my blunt speech has caused you to take offense, then I suppose courtesy demands that I apologize."

Caina felt a surge of hot fury, but rebuked herself. Her purpose here was to gather information, not to relive the horrors of her past. And Kalastus reminded her all too well of those horrors. But arrogant and haughty as he was, he might hold some of the answers locked within that bald head of his. She would endure his speech if she must.

And perhaps the pyromancer, this new Ashbringer, slept beneath this very roof.

Ark stepped into the library. "Countess," he rumbled. "Is anything amiss?" Kalastus glared at him, lip curling back from his teeth, and Ark returned a flat stare.

"Oh, all is quite well," said Caina. "Master Kalastus had just offered an apology. Which I do accept. By the way, will Master Ephaeron be joining us for dinner, learned one?"

"No," said Kalastus. "He had urgent business, I'm afraid. It will just be the two of us."

"Ah," said Caina. "Splendid."

Dinner with Kalastus did not go well.

Kalastus had insisted that Ark remain in the sitting room, so they ate alone. Romarion, and even Nicephorus, had known how to carry on a conversation, but Kalastus's talk was a never-ending series of rambling lectures, jumping from topic to topic almost at random. The learned master, it seemed, was quite bitter. He held most of the Lords of the Empire in scorn. He loathed the unwashed and unlettered commoners. Soldiers, with their unlearned ignorance, annoyed him to no end. He detested the Saddai, and hated the smell of their cooking. And he did not like Ephaeron very much, either.

"I have been a master of the Magisterium for twenty-three years," said Kalastus, "and the high magi see fit to send this…this boy to advise me."

"Oh?" said Caina, making herself take another bite. As if Kalastus's unending ranting wasn't trial enough, the food wasn't terribly good either.

Caina reminded herself that people were starving in Rasadda and made herself swallow. "Forgive me, learned master, but it I thought Ephaeron was in his forties at the least. Certainly not a child."

Kalastus barked a laugh. "I forget how young you are, Countess. Ephaeron is a child, at least compared to my experience. Oh, he always likes to mention his time with the Legions as a battle magus, but what is mere experience of war compared to a deep understanding of the arcane sciences?"

Caina realized that he expected an answer. "I...am not sure, learned one, as I do not even have a shallow knowledge of the arcane sciences."

"Exactly right," said Kalastus, as if she had just agreed with him. "Exactly right! And now I have Ephaeron looking over my shoulder at every turn, questioning the way I do things. It never stops! I am the preceptor of the Rasadda chapter, not him!" He shook his head with disgust, the unnatural light glinting off his bald head. "And he has turned his attention to these murders. Such petty affairs are beneath the concern of a master of the Magisterium."

"The murders, learned one?" said Caina, hoping to get his rambling turned to that topic.

"Yes, these murders," said Kalastus with disgust. "All these burned corpses found in the street. Ephaeron has taken it upon himself to investigate their deaths. As if the murder of some Saddai peasants and Caerish merchants were a concern for the Magisterium!" He snorted. "He has this ridiculous notion that one of the Saddai priests has become an Ashbringer and has gone on a rampage."

Caina thought of Gaidan, and Ark's suspicions. "Why is that ridiculous, learned one?"

"Because both the Ashbringers and the practice of pyromancy have been extinct for generations."

"Can you be certain of that?" said Caina. "I...saw one of the bodies near the Inn, when the Decurion of the city militia found the corpse. The poor man had been burned horribly across his body."

"I can be utterly certain of that," said Kalastus.

"But no one could say how he had been killed," lied Caina. "Might not sorcery have been used in his death?"

"Absolutely not. The Ashbringers are extinct, Countess. The Magisterium saw to that after the Saddai war, after Corazain himself was killed. And a good thing, too." His eyes turned distant. "If our records are correct, the Ashbringers were...insane. Raving madmen. Men who killed at whim. But powerful, though. Corazain killed every last living thing in Rasadda to empower his final spell. The Ashbringers worshiped the Burning Flame, a god even more implausible than the gods of the Empire, and sought to set the world aflame at his command."

"The Burning Flame?" said Caina. "I have never heard that name before. I thought the Saddai referred to their god as the Living Flame."

"They do now," said Kalastus, making a dismissive gesture. "From what I understand, it was a theological dispute among the Saddai. A schism of sorts. Some interpreted their god as the Living Flame, and others as the Burning Flame. Those who espoused the way of the Living Flame eventually won out." He laughed. "Especially since the Magisterium slaughtered the Ashbringers and all others who favored the path of the Burning Flame."

"I see," said Caina. "Master Kalastus, you set my mind at ease." She let a little quiver into her voice. "So…there's no way pyromancy could have been used in these terrible murders? I needn't fear being burned to death in my sleep."

"Absolutely not," said Kalastus. "I have told you before, Countess. There are no more pyromancers."

Caina, who had seen Ostros burn to death, knew better.

"It vexes me to no end that people can even think that," said Kalastus. "It merely proves that the Magisterium should rule the Empire."

Caina blinked. "The Magisterium did rule the Empire, once, and were overthrown, if I remember my history aright."

"You do," said Kalastus. "And the rule of the magi was a golden age." Caina had read rather differently, but said nothing. "A time of unprecedented order and prosperity. And it can be so again. The Lords of the Empire are corrupt, blind fools. The Emperor is weak. The Empire of Nighmar needs better rulers. And who better than men whose minds have been trained to the pinnacle of reason, men who are steeped in the arcane sciences?" His eyes glittered. "We can reshape the Empire. We can even reshape the world."

Caina thought that a drunken pickpocket would make a better ruler than the masters of the Magisterium, but she said nothing. She wanted to find an excuse to leave.

"You ought to marry a magus," said Kalastus. He took a long drink of wine.

Caina desperately hoped that Kalastus did not have himself in mind. "Oh? Why is that, learned master?"

"The Magisterium ruled the Empire once before," said Kalastus, "and it shall be so again. Sooner or later. As the wife to a magus, you would command great respect and power. Perhaps you even have skill for sorcery that you have not realized, hmm? Both men and women may join the Magisterium, though few women do so."

"My father," said Caina, "will have to make the final decision, of course."

They ate in silence for a moment.

"You are so lovely," said Kalastus.

"Thank you," said Caina, disquieted.

"I mean that truly," said Kalastus. "You will see." His fingers moved, and he began muttering under his breath.

Caina felt her skin begin to crawl, and felt a surge of alarm. He was casting a spell at her, and she reached for one of the knives strapped to her forearm. Then Kalastus moved his hand in a sweeping gesture, and a strange, placid calm fell over Caina. She settled back into her chair with a relaxed sigh, all the tension leaving her body.

Something was terribly wrong, she knew, yet somehow it did not seem to trouble her.

"So lovely," murmured Kalastus. He gestured again. "Stand."

That seemed like a splendid idea. Caina stood.

"Come here," said Kalastus, beckoning. Caina walked to join him, and Kalastus stood. He seized her shoulders and pulled her close, running hands up and down her.

Something was very wrong, but Caina still could not place it.

"Yes," muttered Kalastus, making another gesture. He stepped back. "Open your clothes for me."

That seemed like another good idea. Caina's fingers worked at her bodice, undoing the laces, until she pulled the front of her gown open. Kalastus stared at her for a moment, smiling, then stepped forward and put his hands on her breasts. His pupils shrank, his breathing coming hard and sharp, and sweat stood out on his forehead.

His concentration wavered, and some of the placid calm smothering her splintered.

In a horrified rush she realized what was happening. He had pushed his sorcery into her mind, dulling her thoughts, numbing her emotions, and making her susceptible to his commands. Kalastus pushed his face against hers and put a rough, wet kiss on her mouth. Caina wanted to pull away, tried to pull away, but she could not. Kalastus's will held her mind fast, kept her from breaking away.

But he had reached into her mind. That meant there was an excellent chance he could feel whatever she felt. It took every ounce of effort she could muster, but she dragged her hand to the right, till it hung over the table.

Directly over one of the candle flames.

"I can feel you struggling," murmured Kalastus, still fondling her breast. "You shouldn't. It will go easier on you." A stab of pain shot up Caina's hand. "Or it can be rough for you. It...ahh!" He wrenched his hand back and looked at it, stunned.

And the strange calm filling Caina's mind vanished as Kalastus's concentration broke.

He was standing right in front of her, so Caina slammed her forehead into his face. Kalastus's head snapped back, and she heard his nose break. His hands flew to his face, so Caina punched him in the gut. Master of arcane science Kalastus might have been, but he knew nothing of hand-to-hand fighting. He doubled over, and Caina kicked his legs out from under him. Kalastus fell with a strangled groan, and Caina kicked him in the face. Again. And again. And again.

Then Kalastus screamed a word and thrust out his palm. Caina just had time to feel her skin tingle before an invisible force slammed into her, throwing her back. It flung her the length of the room, smashing her into the opposite wall. She felt the invisible weight of Kalastus's sorcery pressing down upon her, crushing her, her ribs creaking with the strain. Kalastus staggered to his feet, his face bloody, his eyes wild with rage.

"You dare to strike me?" he screamed.

"I dared only to strike a craven fool!" Caina spat back at him, too furious to care. "A murderer and scoundrel and a liar, just like every other magus!"

"You dare!" roared Kalastus. There was no hint of rationality in his face, only molten rage. He stalked towards her, He was not going to try and force himself on her, Caina saw. He was going to kill her. She could not pull away from the wall, but she jerked her leg up, her hand curling around the hilt of the dagger in her boot. If he came within reach she would ram the blade right through his eye.

Kalastus began to snarl an incantation, pointing at her, and Caina's skin began to tingle so violently it felt as if someone had jabbed needles into her arm. Kalastus moved closer, almost within reach, and Caina's hand tightened around the dagger...

The door banged open. Ark stepped into the room, broadsword in hand, and looked back and forth between them. Kalastus froze, his hand still hooked into a claw, and the tingling against Caina's skin began to subside.

"What's going on here?" Ark said.

Some hint of reason returned to Kalastus's eyes, and he stepped back. The invisible pressure pinning Caina to the wall vanished, and she struggled to keep her balance, breathing hard.

"What is this?" said Ark. He looked at Caina, saw the front of her bodice hanging open, and seemed shocked.

"We're leaving," said Caina, still glaring at Kalastus, "now." She tugged at the front of her gown, holding it closed. "Right now."

Kalastus said nothing, his bruised face filled with enraged, poisonous hate. Caina thought he would raise his hand and began another spell, but he said nothing, did nothing.

She turned and left, Ark following her.

CHAPTER 16
CONFESSIONS

"What happened?" said Ark.

Caina said nothing as she hurried into the night, still holding her gown closed. The coach was nowhere in sight. She pointed at one of the black-armored Magisterial Guards with her free hand. "You. Where is my coach?"

The Guard blinked. "It...ah, we it sent around to our stables, my lady..."

"Get it! Now!" said Caina, fumbling her bodice closed. "No, have it sent to the Inn of Mirrors. I'm not spending another minute in this wretched place." The Guard gaped at her. "Are you deaf? Are you too stupid to understand me? Go!"

The Guard bowed and hurried away. Caina stalked down the stairs, intending to walk the rest of the way back to the Inn. Ark hurried after her, hand still on his sword hilt.

"What happened?" said Ark, again.

Caina did not answer. She did not trust herself to speak. Not since the night of her father's death had any enemy gotten so far within her defenses. Kalastus had frightened her badly, and that filled her with choking fury. She kept walking, almost running, and had gotten nearly a hundred yards by the time Ark caught up to her.

"Stop!" snapped Ark, his hand closing around her left arm. He dragged her into the shadow of a deserted alleyway.

Caina wrenched away from him. "Don't touch me."

"Then tell me what happened."

She turned away.

"You tried to seduce him, didn't you?"

Caina glared back at him. "What?"

Ark shook his head, voice full of disgust. "Do you think me a fool? You were standing there half-naked."

"He tried to force me, you idiot," said Caina. "He put a spell on my mind."

"I'm sure," said Ark. He looked angry, angrier than Caina had ever seen him. "We asked Halfdan for help, and he sent us you. You're a liar and a charlatan, Countess." He spat the last word like a curse. "Anyone with half a brain can see that Gaidan and the Sons of Corazain are behind these murders, and you're wasting time chasing the Magisterium. The Ghost circle is slaughtered, and you're trying to climb into bed with Kalastus."

"I told you," snarled Caina, "he tried to force me. And I told you that the Magisterium is a collection of arrogant and murderous fools, but you won't listen to that, either."

"So you say," said Ark, "but I've never seen any basis for it. Why do you hate them so badly, Countess? Hmm? Maybe they didn't bow deep enough? Or they slighted you at a ball once? Perhaps they didn't kiss your ring?" He sneered at her. "Maybe they…"

His tone made something in her snap.

"I told you!" screamed Caina, and shoved him. He stumbled a half-step, stunned. "What more proof do you want? They're murderers!" She shoved him again. "They'd be tyrants if they could, and they kill people for enjoyment. You saw Ephaeron slaughter people, Ark." She gave him another shove. "Or maybe you enjoyed that. You were in the Legions, maybe you enjoyed killing people, maybe…"

He caught her wrists in a grip like iron and pushed her away. "You're mad. What did they do to you to make you hate them so badly?"

"They killed my father!"

Ark let go her of her wrists.

"Is that what you wanted to know?" said Caina. "That I watched my mother kill my father? Is that a good enough reason for you, centurion?"

"What?" said Ark. He seemed caught between confusion and horror.

Caina was not going to tell him anything. But the words flooded out of her, kept coming in a rush of rage and pain. "My parents were both of noble birth. My mother trained early as sister of the Magisterium, and had no wish to marry. But my grandfather forced her to marry my father. My mother hated me." Her voice had turned flat, hard, hollow. "I didn't understand it at the time. Now I know that she saw my father and me as hindrances, chains that kept her from reaching the pinnacle of arcane power. When she became frustrated, she would scream at me, hit me. So I spent more time with my father. He was more of a scholar than a nobleman. He taught me to read, to speak a dozen different languages. I loved the learning. I loved his library. I loved my father."

Caina blinked. She was not crying. Her eyes just stung, that was all.

"Well, my mother was eager for more sorcery, more power. She fell in with a group of magi who practiced forbidden arts. Necromancy, to be precise. Blood magic. Sorcery that drew its power from blood and death and torment. My father found out. Tried to stop her, threatened to report her. So she put a spell on his mind, him and all his servants. Tried to make them into puppets. But she wasn't as nearly as skillful as she thought herself. Instead of making them into puppets, she wiped their minds. Made them into vegetables. They would lie there and drool until they died."

Still Ark said nothing, his face frozen into something more brittle than its usual mask.

"I went to meet my father, and found him in his chair, his mind gone," said Caina. She no longer recognized the sound of her own voice. "My mother found me as I tried to rouse him. She laughed at me, told me what had happened, told me that she would be free of her chains soon. I...went mad then, I think. There was a fireplace in my father's study. A hot poker. I seized it and hit her. She lost her balance, fell, and broke her neck."

Her mother's eyes still filled her memory, still full of hatred.

"So you see, Ark. A liar and a charlatan I may be, but I'm also a murderer. A matricide. The very first person I killed was my own mother."

"What," Ark closed his eyes, swallowed, "what did you do then?"

"Nothing. But my mother's teacher found me. You see, the magi, the necromancers, do not share their teachings without a price. And my mother had already made a payment." Caina stared into the night. "She sold me to the necromancers in exchange for their teaching."

Ark still stared at her.

"Maybe my father found out about it, why he finally confronted her," said Caina. "Not five minutes after my mother died, they came, and took me away to their lair. Do you want to know what they did to me?"

"I..."

"Surely you want to know," said Caina, "what your magi, so learned and so noble, would do to a girl of eleven?"

"They forced themselves on you?" said Ark.

"I thought they would, at first," said Caina. "They took my clothes. But they chained me to this metal table. It was so cold. They would...they would cut me. Across my belly and hips. Draw out the blood." She remembered lying in the darkness, screaming into her gag as Maglarion approached, knife glittering in his hand.

"Why?"

"They were necromancers. And I was a virgin. The blood and heart of a virgin can be used to fuel potent sorcery. That is what they had in mind for me eventually, I think...to kill me and use my heart and blood to empower some spell. They...kept cutting, and healing the wounds, and cutting again." She did feel the tears on her face now, but did not care.

"They cut too deep, and made me barren. I shall never bear a child. Nor will I ever have a husband, or a home, for who would wed a woman who cannot bear a child?" Her voice dropped to a grating whisper. "Sometimes I see women with their children, and it is all I can do to keep from screaming."

There was a long pause.

"How did you get away?" said Ark.

"Halfdan," said Caina, and she smiled for the first time since leaving the Magisterium's chapterhouse. "He killed the necromancers. All nine of them."

"Nine?" said Ark. "He killed nine magi? By himself?"

"They were monsters," said Caina, "but still mortal men. They ate and drank. And Halfdan was posing as a wine merchant, and he sold them poisoned wine. They all died choking and clawing at their throats. Halfdan hadn't expected to find me, and he didn't know what to do with me, so he brought me into the Emperor's Ghosts. He trained me, and found others to train me."

She stepped closer to Ark. "You wanted to know how I learned to throw knives? I learned from the best knife-thrower in the Empire. He made his living wandering from village to village, betting the local farmers that he couldn't split an apple at fifty paces. How I learned to fight? I studied under a Kyracian master of the storm dance, and it was six months until I could block one of his punches. How I learned to disguise my voice, to speak in different accents? My father began it, but I spent a season with the Grand Imperial Opera. I was even on stage once. Though I didn't sing. I never learned to carry a tune. I spent a year with an Imperial noblewoman, who taught me to dress and speak as a lady, since my mother had never bothered to show me. And Halfdan himself taught me how to move quietly, how to pick locks, and how to learn those secrets than men wish hidden. I learned it all quickly. I had a lot of rage, and it gave me the will to learn. And what I wanted to learn was how to stop people like my mother and her teachers."

Ark let out a breath. Caina scrubbed the tears from her face and glared at him.

"So that is why, Ark, that I hate the Magisterium so much. I hope the answer satisfies you." She turned to go.

"Wait."

Caina paused.

"I am sorry," said Ark. "I should not have pushed you like that. And I can see that you have good cause to hate the Magisterium. And I should not…I should not have implied that you tried to seduce Kalastus."

"Why did it disturb you so much?" said Caina.

"It's just that…" Ark shook his head. "It is not important."

"I think it might be," said Caina. "I think you hated me from the moment you laid eyes on me. Is that it? Or are you jealous? Did you want me for yourself, was that it?"

"No," said Ark, "and no. It...I do not wish to speak of it."

"Too bad," said Caina. "You know why I hate the Magisterium. Well, it's time for payment, and I want to know once and for all why you hate me."

"I do not hate you," said Ark.

"Convince me otherwise," said Caina.

Ark sighed, closed his eyes. "Very well."

Caina waited.

Ark opened his eyes, cold and empty and dead. "You have to understand," he said, "that I am a monster. In the Legions, I...I did things that I am not proud of. I committed every crime it is possible for a solider to commit. I slew men in fair battle, yes. But I also butchered unarmed prisoners. I slaughtered those who begged for mercy. I put old men and women to the sword." He could not meet her eye.

Caina kept waiting.

"Some of the men in the Legions grow hard and cold," said Ark. "I wished I could, but I did not. The guilt weighed on me. By the end of my term of service I was a centurion. Had I reenlisted, I would have made first centurion, almost certainly. But I could not. The guilt was too much. When my term ended I took my service bonus and left. I had no family, no purpose, and no reason to live. I decided to see the ocean one more time, and then fall upon my sword. I went through Marsis, and into Varia Province." He blinked a few times. "Then I came upon a young widow. She was traveling to the market in Marsis, when she was attacked by bandits who wanted her cattle and her virtue. I found her, and that was the end of the bandits. Since I had nowhere else to go, I traveled with her to Marsis.

"Her name was Tanya."

Caina nodded, understanding.

"I traveled back with them to her father's village. Her husband had been killed by Anshani slavers, and her father crippled in the same attack. That was why she had to go to market herself. They needed a strong man...and I needed something. Anything. A reason to live." He smiled at the memory, one of the few true smiles she had ever seen on that grim face. "We were married four months later. I had never been a happy man, Countess. But for the first time, I was happy. All the men in the legions are trained in a craft, and I was trained as a blacksmith. I became the village smith, and Tanya didn't have to grub in the fields any more. We had a child, a son. It was a good life."

His story sounded like a dark mirror of her own. "And what happened?"

Something ugly kindled in Ark's dead eyes. "I went into the woods to hunt. When I returned, I found the village burned to the ground, all the women and children gone, the men lying dead. Her father lived long enough to tell me what had happened. The Anshani slavers had returned. I followed them, but they had horses. They made it to their ship and got away with their captives. I tried to find a ship to follow them, and then I met Halfdan."

"Halfdan?" said Caina, frowning. She worked out the dates in her head. "This was…what, three, four years ago?"

Ark nodded. "He had come to bring down the slavers. Since I needed the help, I joined him. We found their base, raised a unit of local veterans, and destroyed it. Killed them all. But the slavers' ship was not to be found. I was ready to chase it to hell and back. But Halfdan told me that it could have gone to twelve different ports, that I'd never find it without his help. So I joined the Ghosts, and he sent out word." Ark closed his eyes and let out a shuddering breath.

"What happened to the ship?" said Caina.

"I don't know," said Ark. "Nineteen different ports have slave markets in the western sea, and the Ghosts have agents in them. Halfdan checked with them. All of them. The ship never put in. It simply vanished. Most likely it sank in a storm. My wife, my son, and my stepson are all dead. They drowned." His hands curled into fists. "They drowned, after enduring gods know what torments, because I failed to save them. I had a second chance, and I lost it, because of my folly, because I wasn't there to protect them."

His breathing came hard and sharp, but no tears. Ark was not the kind of man to cry, Caina suspected. Instead he would drown his grief in blood. Not even the gods themselves could save those slavers if Ark ever found them.

"I'm sorry," said Caina. She hesitated, and touched his shoulder. "At least…at least I know what happened to my father. Awful as it was. But not to know…" She shook her head. "I'm sorry. I should not have forced you to tell me."

Ark barked a harsh laugh. "Why not? I forced you to tell me your secrets, didn't I?" He laughed without mirth again. "But aren't we a pair, though? The orphan and the widower. Does Halfdan only recruit the bereaved?"

"We have more reason to fight tyrants than most," said Caina. "But you didn't answer my question."

Ark frowned. "Question?"

"Why you hate me."

"I don't hate you," said Ark quietly, miserably. "I did at first, though. I thought you were a seductress, the sort of woman who would unlock a man's secrets by seducing him and stabbing him in the back. But then I saw that you are brave, and clever, far cleverer than I could ever be. Then I simply did not know what to make of you."

"But why did that make you hate me?"

Ark looked her in the eye. "Because you look like Tanya."

Caina had no answer for that.

"You have black hair. Blue eyes. So did Tanya. You even resemble her in the face somewhat. She was a little taller, and not so lean, but still..." Ark sighed. "When I came to Halfdan's inn and saw you sitting there...for a moment I thought that Halfdan had found Tanya. That she had not died after all, that she had come back to me. For just a moment...and then I came closer, and saw that you were not her."

He fell silent.

"So you were angry with me that I was not your dead wife?" said Caina.

Ark snorted. "It sounds foolish when you say it that way." He shook his head. "It was foolish."

"No," said Caina. "Not foolish. Sad. But not foolish."

They stood in silence for a moment.

"My real name," said Caina, "my true name, is Caina. Of House Amalas, my father's House."

"Caina?" said Ark. "It suits you, I think. My true name is Arcion. Once of Caer Marist, then of the Eighteenth Legion, and then the village of Hruzac, and now of the Ghosts."

"Arcion," said Caina.

"Caina," said Ark.

"If it will make you feel better," said Caina, "I suppose I am technically an Imperial Countess. Or at least I would be, had my father lived."

Ark laughed. "I cannot tell you what a comfort that is to me."

"Then perhaps this will comfort you," said Caina. "You were right."

Ark blinked. "About what?"

"Neither Ephaeron nor Kalastus had anything to do with these murders," said Caina.

"But Kalastus just tried..."

"Yes," said Caina. "He just tried to rape me. Which was stupid. Marianna Nereide is an Imperial Countess. You were right there, and there had to have been at least a dozen witnesses within earshot. It was a stupid risk, and men that stupid do not commit nearly thirty murders undetected. I doubt he's clever enough to have pulled it off, or even clever enough to have actually learned pyromancy. And he said that Ephaeron is actively investigating the murders. So neither of the masters of the Magisterium are behind this."

Ark nodded.

"They're still villains, though."

"I shan't argue," said Ark. "Could one of the lesser magi be behind it?"

"Possibly," said Caina, "but I don't know for sure. If we're going to find this Ashbringer, the place to start looking is the Sons of Corazain."

"And just how are we going to do that?" said Ark.

"Sister Tadaia is a fine speaker," said Caina. "I think that it's past time that we heard her preach, don't you?"

Ark nodded. "I do."

"And when we find this pyromancer," said Caina, her voice soft, "this murderer who is cut from the same cloth as my mother and your slavers, we'll know what to do."

"Indeed." Ark's gray eyes glinted. "We will."

They walked back to the Inn together, side by side.

CHAPTER 17
CHARITY

The next morning, Caina began the day with a hot bath.

"How was your dinner with the magi, my lady?" asked Anya.

"Unpleasant," said Caina, closing her eyes and leaning back, her hair fanning out on the water.

"Are they truly as wicked as everyone says?" said Anya, voice low.

"No," said Caina, glancing at Anya. "They're actually much worse. I would have gladly skipped the dinner, if not for the obligations of my rank. Stay far away from them, for your own sake."

Anya's eyes got wide, and she nodded.

Caina brooded. She still felt Kalastus's clammy palms closing around her breasts, and she wanted to scrub the skin raw. There had been female servants in the Magisterium's chapterhouse, she remembered. Did Kalastus make a practice of enspelling and abusing them? Caina badly wished that she had killed him last night. It would have destroyed her secrecy, but the man surely deserved it.

After the bath, she wrapped herself in a heavy robe and went to the sitting room. Julia brought her breakfast. She was eating when Ark returned, still walking with a faint limp.

"Any luck?" said Caina. She pushed the plate towards him. "Here, eat."

"Yes, my lady," said Ark, taking some cheese and a slice of bread. "It took some asking, and I had to bribe a few people, but I found it. Sister Tadaia preaches to the people every day at noon, in the plaza before the Temple of Living Flame."

"The Temple of Living Flame?" said Caina. "I haven't heard of it."

Ark shrugged, took a bite, swallowed. "It's across the plaza below

143

Narzaiden's pyramid, in bad part of the city. And it's not a large building, not compared to the funeral pyramids. A little smaller than the Imperial Basilica. Apparently there used to be a huge Temple, but it was destroyed after Corazain was killed. The governors never let the Saddai build a large one."

"Think they'll attack us?" said Caina.

"Possibly," said Ark. "From what I heard, Gaidan always attends the sermons, along with many of his followers. But Tadaia disapproves of them, and she is still higher in the people's hearts than Gaidan and the Sons of Corazain. I don't think they'll try anything with her there."

"My lady?" said Cornelia, who had been listening. "Surely you are not going to listen to this Saddai priestess? It is too dangerous to visit the streets."

"Perhaps," said Caina, deciding upon a suitable lie. "You remember when she preached in the square here, below Corazain's pyramid? She alone in this city cares for the poor and destitute, and her words have touched my heart. I wish to hear more from her."

Cornelia looked aghast. "You are not converting to the Saddai faith, my lady? Are you?"

Caina laughed. "Of course not. But I still wish to hear Tadaia speak."

For more reason than one.

The coach rattled through Rasadda's streets, making for the plaza below Narzaiden's pyramid. Instead of Sairzan's servant, Ark drove. There was an excellent chance that the Sons of Corazain might attack them, and Caina remembered poor Lasko's demise. She sat besides Ark on the driver's seat, clad in a green traveling gown. The long sleeves and skirt concealed the knives strapped to her forearms, and the daggers hidden in her boots. Ark drove with one hand on the reins, the other on the hilt of his broadsword, which was tucked between his knees.

"Where did you learn to drive a coach?" said Caina.

"The Legion," said Ark. "Everyone learns a trade in the Legion."

"I thought you were a blacksmith."

"Eventually," said Ark. "I started as a wagon driver and an animal handler. That lasted until the day I accidentally ran over my centurion's foot."

Caina laughed in surprise. "You didn't!"

"I did," said Ark. "He had me beaten, of course, but the men of our century could not stop laughing, so he swore that I would never again handle one of the Legion's wagons. Instead he sent me to the smithy, and that was that."

"I'll make certain to stand well clear of the coach while you're driving, then," said Caina.

Ark grunted. "That's not funny." Caina laughed anyway.

A short time later they came to the plaza between the Narzaiden's pyramid and the Temple of Living Flame.

"So many of them," murmured Caina.

Thousands packed the square. Caina saw ragged Saddai peasants, tired and lean, mothers holding infants, and fathers carrying their children on their shoulders. Old men and women leaned on canes, staring at the black, domed temple across the plaza from the burning pyramid. It was an impressive building, the dome perhaps seventy-five yards across.

"Why don't they go into the temple?" said Caina.

"There's not room," said Ark. "From what I understand, Sister Tadaia stands upon the stairs and preaches to the crowd."

"Ark," said Caina, "look."

Here and there Saddai men stood scattered through the throng. The front of their shirts and vests hung open, revealing the flame tattoo upon their chests. Most of the Saddai paid no attention to the coach, and shuffled out of its way. But the Sons of Corazain glared at them, eyes icy, and many of them wore daggers and short swords on their belts.

"I see them," said Ark. "If they want to live, they won't try anything."

"Stop the coach," said Caina. She grabbed his arm. "Stop the coach! It's too crowded. If we try to force our way through we'll touch off a riot."

Ark nodded and reined in the horses.

"We can listen on the roof," said Caina, "and see better, besides."

"And have a better defensive position against anyone who comes at us," said Ark.

"That too." Ark swung up onto the coach's roof. Caina followed him, her movements hampered by her long skirt. Ark stood, surveying the crowd, while Caina settled cross-legged besides him, throwing knives readily at hand.

"Look," said Caina, "there's Gaidan." The red-robed priest stood near the steps to the temple, ringed by a dozen thugs. They nodded at his every word. "No doubt he hopes to borrow some of Tadaia's prestige."

One of the nearby Sons of Corazain took a hard look at the coach, turned, and started shoving his way through the crowd. He was heading towards Gaidan, Caina saw. No doubt he went to warn his master that an Imperial noble had come to listen to Tadaia.

"That fellow, there," murmured Caina.

"I saw him," said Ark.

"Keep an eye on him," said Caina. "And Gaidan. If they start coming we may need to leave in a hurry..."

A hush went over the crowd. Caina looked towards the black-domed temple, saw an old woman hobbling from the doorway, leaning upon a cane, her red robes flapping around her.

Sister Tadaia.

"Hear me, my brothers and sisters!" said Tadaia. From a distance, she looked weak and withered, yet her rich voice rolled over the plaza like a thunderclap. "Hear me, I beg, and heed well my words, for the words I speak to you are the words of the Living Flame."

She called her god the Living Flame. The Sons of Corazain spoke of the Burning Flame. Caina wondered what the difference was. Though she remembered the terrible story of Corazain's final spell, and suspected that she knew.

"I am grateful, so grateful, that you have come on this day," said Tadaia. "For indeed this world and this life is harsh and full of pain and sorrow. And I know that you suffer, I know it sorely. There is not enough food to be had, despite the grain dole. Our children go hungry. There is no work to be had. We cannot earn enough to buy food for our children."

A murmur went through the crowd. Caina saw the Son of Corazain reach Gaidan, saw them speaking together in low voices. Gaidan looked her way, and even across the distance she felt the burning hatred in his gaze.

"I know that some of you whisper against the Empire," said Tadaia, her voice pleading. "I know that some of you yearn to take up arms, to rise up against the Lord Governor and throw out the Empire." The Sons of Corazain raised their arms and cheered. Some of them brandished their swords.

Tadaia lifted her hands for silence, and the scattered cheers faded. "My brothers and sisters, such a path is folly." Some of the Sons jeered, and received glares from the other Saddai. "No, hear me! Hear me! If we raise our sword against the Emperor it shall be a time of torment and tribulation such as we have never known. You may not be able to feed your children, but they shall perish if we rebel. Your wife may weep for their suffering, but she shall die in the fire if we revolt. If we rebel, Rasadda will perish, and the destruction shall be even worse than the time of Corazain's fall."

An angry mutter went through the assembled Saddai, but not very loud. Most of them seemed to agree with Tadaia.

"And we forget who we are," said Tadaia. "We are the Saddai, the children of the Living Flame. And we forget the purpose of our lives, the purpose of our sufferings. We bathe in the heat of the Living Flame. Our souls are flawed, riddled through with weakness and darkness. Through suffering, our souls are refined, made pure, like steel at the forge. And we shall be reborn, to finally break free of the endless cycle of birth and rebirth, and to at last become one with the Living Flame."

"You don't seem to agree," said Ark, glancing at Caina.

"No," said Caina. "There is only one mortal life, and then the life beyond death, this I believe. I've already endured enough pain in this life. I would not want to repeat it all over again. Would you?"

"Not really."

"Let us aid each other in our sufferings," said Tadaia. "I am an old woman, and must lean upon my cane to walk." She thumped it against the black marble stair for emphasis. "So too must we lean upon each other. We must bear our sufferings with joy, and aid each other. For such acts will help the Living Flame to reforge our blackened souls, to burn away the dross until the bright steel shines like the very sun itself."

"You disagree?" said Ark.

Caina nodded. "Too passive. Too…fatalistic. Nihilistic, even. We must all die in the end." She thought of her of mother, and then of Kalastus. "But I would rather die fighting, rather than to wait feebly for the end to take me." Her voice hardened. "But at least she cares for the poor of this city. Nicephorus would let them starve, and never lift a finger to help them."

"I…" Ark frowned.

A dozen men pushed and shoved their way through the crowd. Caina saw the flame tattoo upon their chest. They stopped before the coach, glaring up at them, daggers and short swords in hand. Caina stood, looking down at them with a haughty expression as Tadaia continued to expound of upon the virtues of generosity.

"What do you wish of me?" said Caina. Ark slid his sword from its scabbard with an ominous rasp.

"You aren't welcome here," said one of the Sons of Corazain.

"We have merely come to hear the Sister of the Living Flame speak," said Caina. "Surely all are welcome."

"All true sons of the Saddai are welcome," said the leader, "but not the painted whores of the corrupt Empire."

"You are mistaken," said Caina.

The leader blinked. "What?"

"I'm not wearing any makeup," said Caina. "A whore I may be, but painted? I most certainly am not. Use your eyes, man."

Ark gaped at her, and she saw Gaidan staring at them from the temple steps. Caina reflected that coming here might not have been the best idea. She looked over the crowd, seeking an exit. They were not all that far from the nearest street. If Ark whipped the horses to a run, they might be able to break free before the mob closed around them…

"Do not play word games with the Sons of holy Corazain!" thundered the leader, pointing his short sword at her. "Wise men do not trifle with the Burning Flame."

"Oh, certainly not," said Caina, "but you, sir, are more of a sputtering ember than a Burning Flame."

"Blasphemer!" shrieked the leader. "Take her, take her, take her now!"

The Sons of Corazain surged towards the coach. Ark whipped his broadsword around, a thrown dagger bouncing from the blade and falling against the basalt flagstones. Caina dipped her hand into her sleeve, reaching for a knife.

"And someone continues to abuse the holy flames, to use them to murder," said Tadaia. "Such an act is a blasphemy against the Living Flame, and...hold! Hold! What is this violence? I said to hold!"

Her voice cracked with displeasure. The Sons of Corazain froze, looking at Sister Tadaia, and back to Gaidan.

"There are foreigners among us!" shouted Gaidan, stepping towards Tadaia. "A noblewoman of the Empire and her pet brute. They defile us with their presence, and have come to mock your words. Let them be removed from us!"

"No!" called Caina in her loudest stage voice. "Hear me!"

The Saddai looked towards her in sudden shock. Evidently they had not expected her to speak.

"I have heard the people speak well of Sister Tadaia, of her kindly words and learned wisdom," said Caina, "and I wished to hear them for myself. For I have traveled to many cities in the Empire, from Marsis in the west to Rasadda in the east, and rarely have I seen anyone who cared so deeply for the widow and the orphan. If I am not welcome, then I shall go, but I thought that to care for the poor was a concern of all men of good heart. Perhaps I was mistaken."

"Let us eject them!" said Gaidan.

"No!" said Tadaia, "for they have come in peace. What is your name, young woman?"

"Marianna, of House Nereide," said Caina.

"Please, come hither," said Tadaia, "for I would speak with you more, and learn the truthfulness or falsity of your words."

Caina looked at Ark, and he rammed his sword into its scabbard and clambered down. She started after him, and he reached up and lifted her down. Together they walked through the throng of Saddai to the temple steps. The Saddai parted, staring at them, and Caina walked through them, keeping her face calm. Ark kept pace behind her, his eyes darting back and forth, his hand resting on the hilt of his broadsword.

Sister Tadaia awaited them. She was in her fifties, perhaps in early sixties, her face lined with care and fatigue. She leaned hard upon her cane, her gray hair floating in the morning breeze. Despite her worn appearance, her green eyes were sharp, almost bright. Caina met them and felt a sudden crawling tingle along her skin. Tadaia had some ability at sorcery. Valgorix had claimed that the priests of the Living Flame could work minor spells. Still, her presence did not have the harsh, snarling power of either

Kalastus's or Ephaeron's spells.

And it did not feel the same as the furious spell that had killed Ostros.

Gaidan stood a short distance away, watching. Again Caina saw the seething hatred in his gaze. She knew that had Tadaia not been present, he would have ordered both her and Ark killed on the spot.

"Countess," murmured Tadaia. "You speak with an eloquence that belies your youth."

"You are too kind, honored Sister," said Caina.

Tadaia's eyes flicked over her, up and down. They were penetrating, and Caina had that odd feeling that the old woman's gaze could pierce flesh and bone to view the heart beneath. "Why have you come here? Truly?"

"Because your concern for the poor has touched me," said Caina, "and I wished to prove it." It was not entirely a lie. She reached into her cloak and withdrew the purse from her belt. "Please to take it to buy bread for the hungry."

Tadaia took the purse, hefted it, and glanced inside. She seemed surprised at the amount of money within, and turned to face the crowd of Saddai once more. "Let it not be said that all the people of Nighmar are cruel and grasping! For the Countess has seen our plight, and donated a sum of money to help buy bread for the poor. Now go, my brothers and sisters, go and support one another in our sufferings."

Most of the Saddai seemed pleased, but the Sons of Corazain looked furious. No doubt taking charity from an Imperial noblewoman insulted their pride. Gaidan continued to glare at her, and Caina was certain that the Sons of Corazain would try to kill her again, soon.

"This was a noble gift, Countess," said Tadaia. "Thank you."

Caina shrugged. "It is not nearly enough, that is plain."

"No," said Tadaia, "but it is still needed." She smiled. "Tell me. Have you chosen to convert to our faith? Such is a thing is rare, but it has been known to happen."

"No," said Caina.

"Ah," said Tadaia. "Do you have a god, then? Do you pray to the stern gods of the Empire? The storm gods of the Kyracians, perhaps, or the hard and cruel gods of the northerners? Or are you haughty like the magi, certain that the gods are only a crutch for the weak and feeble?"

"No," said Caina. "I do not know what gods reign in heaven, or what follows this life. I only try to live as best I can."

Tadaia inclined her head. "We are doomed not to just one life but many, to be reborn again and again until our souls may join with the Living Flame."

"I disagreed, honored Sister," said Caina. "There is but this one life, and then eternity. And I am glad of it. One life has enough pain to it; who would want to relive it over and over again."

"Pain?" said Tadaia. "Forgive me, but what does an Imperial noblewoman know of pain?"

"More than you might think," said Caina.

Tadaia nodded slowly. "It has been given to me to see the hearts of men. A gift from the Living Flame, though it is often more curse than blessing." Caina suspected that Tadaia's gift was a sorcerous ability, but she said nothing. The old woman's gaze fastened upon Caina, and the gentle prickling against her skin intensified. Her eyes actually seemed to brighten, like pools of liquid jade.

Tadaia shivered and took a step back, her cane rasping against the marble step.

Caina wondered, with some unease, just what the old priestess had seen.

"Yes," whispered Tadaia, "you know more of pain that I had thought. Much more. And more of many other things." She shook her head. "Your mind is like ice, cold and hard and sharp, but your heart is filled with pain. And rage, rage like a furnace."

Ark grunted. He did not sound impressed.

Tadaia's eyes flicked to him. "And you are much the same way. But your pain paralyzes you, leaves you bereft of purpose and will." Her gaze returned to Caina. "But not you, Countess. Not you. You wield your wrath like a weapon, a brand of fire in your hand. A heart of fire and a mind of ice...you would make a terrible enemy, Countess. A terrible enemy. Who are you, truly?"

"I told you," said Caina, putting as much uncertainty into her voice as she could. The priestess's level of insight had unsettled her. "I am Countess Marianna Nereide. Who else would I be?"

Tadaia shook her head, and some of the sharpness faded from her eyes. "No one, I suppose. Forgive an old woman's foolish fancies, I pray. Thank you for the generous gift, Countess. You are right that it will not buy enough bread to feed all those who hunger." She smiled, some of the lines easing from her face. "But it will still buy quite a lot of bread. And that is by far better than nothing." She lifted her hand in benediction. "May your pain reforge you in the image of the Living Flame."

"the same for you," said Caina.

Tadaia smiled, they bowed to each other, and the old woman began limping back towards the temple. Gaidan gave Caina one more venomous glance, then hastened to Tadaia's side and began whispering in her ear. Caina looked around, saw the crowd dispersing.

"A crock," said Ark.

"Hmm?" said Caina, watching Gaidan whisper at Tadaia. The priestess shook her head, making a dismissive gesture.

"This business about reading your heart," said Ark. "Any charlatan at a fair can do as much. A cold-read."

"I know what a cold-read is," said Caina.

"Surely you don't believe her?" said Ark.

Caina shrugged. "She has some ability at sorcery, though nothing like what a magus could do. Couldn't you feel it?"

Ark shook his head, glanced around, and kept his voice low. "Do you think she is our Ashbringer?" The prospect seemed to displease him. "I would hope not. Despite all her religious mummery, her actions are those of a virtuous woman."

"No," said Caina. "It doesn't seem to suit her. And I can...feel a spell, for lack of a better word. It makes my skin crawl, my hair stand up. Like a lightning stroke. And the spell that killed Ostros felt nothing like what Tadaia did just now."

Tadaia stopped in the entrance to the temple, looked Gaidan full in her face, her expression angry. Their voices rose, and Caina could almost hear them.

"Wait here," murmured Caina, and she began walking closer, taking care to keep her footfalls silent. Neither Gaidan nor Tadaia noticed her.

"It would have been a criminal act," said Tadaia. "To murder an unarmed woman in our midst. Shall we dishonor ourselves so before the Living Flame? The purpose of our path is to purge our souls of impurities, Gaidan, not to tarnish them further."

"And our souls were tarnished by her presence, Sister," spat Gaidan, his sweating face red with his fury. "Bad enough that Nicephorus rules over us with a crushing hand. Now his whores are to strut among us unchallenged."

"She gave us money to buy food for the hungry," said Tadaia. "That is hardly the act of a whore."

Gaidan sneered. "You speak foolishness, Sister. We are to reforge our souls and purge them of dross, yes. But the fire must also cleanse other things. We must rid Rasadda of the Empire and of its vile works."

"Now you speak blasphemy!" said Tadaia, rapping the tip of her cane against the steps. "You would follow in the errors of the Ashbringers, who brought our people to ruin and the brink of destruction. You would follow in the path of whatever murderous thug litters the streets with burned corpses."

"I told you," hissed Gaidan, "that these deaths are a sign. A sign that the Saddai shall be ascendant once more. Corazain himself will be reborn, and he will restore our people to their past glory."

"Corazain laid Rasadda waste with his pride and his folly, and nearly brought our people to annihilation!" snapped Tadaia. "I will not let you follow his path, and drag our people to ruin."

"You should not speak of 'letting', Sister," said Gaidan. "Very soon you will no longer be in a position to dictate to me. I…"

He blinked, and saw Caina watching them. He sneered at her and stalked into the temple, his red robes swirling around him. Tadaia sighed and continued her tired limp, the cane rapping against the marble steps. Caina watched her go, and then returned to Ark.

He looked almost amused. "I suppose you learned all sorts of dark secrets."

"Eavesdropping is a profitable activity, I'll have you know," said Caina. "Tadaia is not behind the murders, I'm almost certain. She rebuked Gaidan for trying to use them to stir up a revolt against the Empire." She thought for a moment. "Which would imply that he isn't behind them, either. He's only trying to exploit them. He may know who's behind it, though. Remember? He claimed to have spoken with a reborn Corazain, though that might have been a lie. And I'm certain Tadaia knows much more than she happened to mention."

"We ought to put Gaidan to the question," said Ark.

"Certainly," said Caina. "Just like Romarion. And if you can figure out a way to get at either of them without getting killed, I'd like to hear it."

Ark shook his head.

"Sister Tadaia, though," said Caina. She smiled. "I wonder if she'll be more forthcoming if she receives a visit from a Ghost of the Empire."

CHAPTER 18
WRATH OF THE MAGI

They rode back to the Inn of Mirrors, Ark at the reins, Caina sitting besides him. She stared at nothing, rubbing at her father's ring. Gaidan. Tadaia. Romarion. Nicephorus. Ostros and the Ghosts of Rasadda. Corazain reborn and Saddai statues looted from ancient ruins. So many pieces, and yet she lacked the single piece to bind them together.

Or perhaps she had all the pieces already, and could not see how to assemble them. The timeline flashed through her head. Romarion had made his fortune selling ancient Saddai artworks to rich Lords and the Magisterium. Then someone started using pyromancy to burn Romarion's partners alive, and did the same to the Ghosts of Rasadda when they investigated. The Sons of Corazain appeared, agitating for a revolt, and Gaidan claimed to have spoken with Corazain reborn. What tied it all together?

What was she missing?

Caina had the vexing feeling that it ought to be obvious, yet she could not...

Ark hissed and tugged the reins, bringing the coach to a halt.

"What?" said Caina, snapped out of her thoughts. She half-expected to see a dozen Sons of Corazain running at them. "What is it?"

"Something's wrong," said Ark. "Look."

They had reached the plaza before the Inn, and a crowd stood before the doors of the Imperial Basilica. There were the usual ragged Saddai commoners that seemed to turn up for every public disturbance, but Nighmarians in fine clothes stood among the crowd, along with the richer Saddai merchants. A troop of militiamen blocked the doors, and Caina saw the plumed helm of Valgorix himself among them.

And before them all, Caina saw the black robes of a magus.

Ark frowned. "What do you think is happening?"

"Look at them," said Caina. "Saddai commoners, Saddai merchants, Nighmarians, and militiamen together, and they're not killing each other. They're more interested in something else, and that can be only one thing."

"What?"

"Another murder," said Caina. "Romarion. They must have gotten Romarion." She slapped the wooden seat in frustration. "If only I had gotten him to talk first! Stop the coach. I want to take a closer look."

Ark nodded, and they climbed down and walked towards the crowd. As they drew closer, Caina heard a voice ranting and cursing, and she recognized it with a sudden shock.

Kalastus.

"Damn you, Nicephorus!" snarled Kalastus. His deep voice thundered in fury. Caina drew closer, and saw with some satisfaction that Kalastus looked terrible. A livid blue-black bruise covered most of his face, and he paced back and forth before the stairs. Caina wished that she had punched him harder. Or used a dagger. Four black-armored soldiers of the Magisterial Guard flanked him, their expressions cold and hard.

"I told you to come out!" said Kalastus. "Do you think I will stand for this, Nicephorus? I will not! Come out at once!"

"What's happening?" said Caina to one of the onlookers, a Nighmarian-born merchant she remembered from Nicephorus's banquet.

He shrugged. "Another of these burning murders, I understand."

Caina frowned. "Do you know who…"

"A brother of the Magisterium lies dead!" thundered Kalastus. "Found burned to death in his own room. You have failed to keep public order, Nicephorus! Come out and answer to me!"

"A magus?" said Caina, astonished. "A magus was murdered?"

"So I've heard," said the Nighmarian merchant.

Caina shared a look with Ark. A magus had been found burned to death? But why? Had Ephaeron's investigation gotten too close to the truth? Would the pyromancer start slaughtering the magi one by one? But surely the magi were powerful enough to protect themselves from hostile sorcery. For that matter, how had the pyromancer collected the dead magus's blood for the spell? If neither Kalastus nor Ephaeron were the Ashbringer, could one of the lesser brothers have turned to forbidden arts?

"I said to come out!" shrieked Kalastus, and Caina's skin crawled as the magus began to draw in power.

"Learned master," said Valgorix, stepping closer to the enraged magus, "the Lord Governor comes and goes as he pleases. He will see you, but at his convenience…"

"Silence!" said Kalastus. He made a gesture. There was a thunderclap, and Valgorix and his militiamen stumbled back a few steps, their cloaks billowing in a brief wind. "Do not think to give me orders, do not presume! I will speak to Nicephorus, or by the gods I'll spill your blood upon the ground!"

The doors to the Basilica swung open, and Nicephorus marched out, flanked by bodyguards. The Lord Governor wore his black finery and crimson cloak, and glared down at Kalastus with all the hauteur of his rank. Yet Caina saw the faint trembling in Nicephorus's hands, the tightness around his eyes.

The Lord Governor was afraid.

"Well, learned master," he spat, "you have summoned me and I have come. What is your business with me?"

"Last night one of the brothers of the Magisterium was found burned to death in his bed," said Kalastus, stepping closer to Nicephorus. "What have you to say about this travesty?"

Nicephorus shrugged. "Perhaps you ought to be more attentive to your security."

"This is your failure!" screamed Kalastus, shoving a finger into Nicephorus's chest. The bodyguards reached for their weapons, but Kalastus did not notice or did not care. "You have failed to keep public order in this hive of rabble, and now one of my brothers lies dead for your errors!"

"My errors?" said Nicephorus. "Perhaps the magus simply miscast a spell and burned himself alive. Such things have been known to happen, have they not?"

"The Magisterium does not make mistakes," said Kalastus. "And this failure is yours, fool."

"I do not have time to listen to the incoherent ramblings of an old man," said Nicephorus. "I have a province to govern. If you have a point to make, state it quickly. Otherwise return to your books and cease wasting my time."

"I demand restitution!" said Kalastus. "I demand vengeance. A magus has been murdered. A price must be paid."

"A price?" said Nicephorus. "You demand blood money now?"

"Only blood may pay for blood," said Kalastus. "Find this murderer and bring me his head."

Nicephorus laughed. "And if you can find the head, you are welcome to it! Frankly, this magus is the first person of importance to have been murdered." Out of the corner of her eye, Caina saw Ark's hand close into a fist. "The Saddai have been burning each other alive for over a year now, no doubt squabbling over money and liquor. Perhaps your magus was robbed, hmm?"

"I will have justice!" said Kalastus. "The life of a magus is worth a hundred strutting Lords of the Empire like you. And it is worth ten thousand of these stinking, slovenly Saddai!"

An angry murmur went through the crowd. The militiamen gripped their weapons. Nicephorus edged towards the doors, his eyes darting back and forth.

"If you are too stupid to find this murderer, then I shall still have a blood payment!" said Kalastus. "Ten thousand of these Saddai animals for one brother of the Magisterium! Yes, that sounds fair. We will teach these Saddai vermin to know fear. Send out your soldiers, have them go house to house, and butcher every last man, woman, and child of the Saddai they find. That will teach these dogs a lesson."

"The mad idiot," hissed Caina, risking a look around. There were hundreds of Saddai in the plaza, and none of them looked happy. "He'll touch of a revolt here and now. I can only imagine what Gaidan will say when he hears of this."

Nicephorus, it seemed, had taken a better gauge of the crowd's mood than Kalastus. The Lord Governor turned and almost ran back up the steps, vanishing into the Imperial Basilica, the doors booming shut behind him. Kalastus spat a curse, and took a step after him, when the abuse of the crowd reached his ears.

"Murderer!" shouted one man. "Murderer! Sorcerous dog!" The cry came from a dozen more men.

Kalastus spat derisive laughter. "And what do you intend to do about? Please. I am as far above you rabble as a hawk is above a worm. Disperse, and I'll choose to ignore your insult..."

Caina never saw who threw the stone.

It clipped Kalastus across the jaw. The magus stumbled back with a cry of surprised pain, hands clamped to his bruised face, blood welling between his fingers. The Saddai yelled and jeered, and they rushed at him. Valgorix bellow a command to his men, and for a moment Caina thought the plaza would explode into a riot around them...

Then Kalastus reared up, face twisted with fury, lips pulled back from his bloody teeth in a snarl, and made a chopping motion.

The surge of power came so fast and so hard that it hit Caina like a slap. There was a roar, and suddenly seven or eight Saddai were tumbling through the air, their limbs flopping. Kalastus chopped again, and the power of his will sent another dozen Saddai flying. One landed with a sickening crunch a dozen feet from Caina, neck twisted at a sharp angle. The Saddai crowd broke and ran, the militiamen staring in stunned horror, but still Kalastus unleashed his powers. He gestured again, and a Saddai woman froze in place. He made a fist, and the woman's terrified screams stopped as every bone in her body shattered at once. Blood burst from her mouth, and she toppled to the basalt flagstones in a crimson puddle.

"Countess," said Ark. "We've got to get out of here."

Caina shook herself, horrified at the carnage Kalastus had unleashed. "Yes, yes, you're right, he's lost his..."

"You!"

Kalastus stood not twenty paces away, and Caina felt a sudden surge of fear. Then anger smothered her fear. Kalastus's face was flushed, his eyes wide and wild, sweat glistening on his bald head. He looked almost exhilarated, as if murdering a dozen had been like a wine to him.

"Master Kalastus," said Caina, trying to keep her voice cold, "I see you are..."

"Shut up!" said Kalastus, stalking towards her. "Shut up! I've come to detest honeyed words. Especially yours. I hope you choke on them. I hope they rot in your throat."

Ark drew his sword, the steel rasping. Kalastus did not seem to care. More likely he did not consider Ark a threat.

"Come to laugh at me?" Kalastus said, stopping ten feet away. "Did you whip the crowd against me? Have you heard that one of the magi was murdered in the chapterhouse? Did you laugh at that as well, Countess? Well? The Saddai will pay for it." He looked at the broken corpses strewn across the plaza and laughed. "They've already started."

"You murderous animal!" said Caina, no longer bothering to mask her contempt, her rage. "One man threw a stone at you. One man! And for that you slaughter a score of men, and women too! I doubt you even killed the one who threw the rock, you stupid, blind..."

"The strong can do what they wish, and weak have no choice but to suffer it," said Kalastus. "And they dared to attack me. Me! A master of the Magisterium, and they dared to raise their hands against me! They've paid for it."

"And the dead magus at your chapterhouse?" said Caina. She knew that she ought to not provoke him further, but she was too furious to care. "Was he strong?"

The rage in Kalastus's eyes sharpened. "The Saddai will suffer for it. For every drop of a magus's blood that they spilled, I shall take a thousand gallons. All who defy the will of the Magisterium will pay." His voice dropped to a purring snarl. "And you defied my will, dear Countess."

Caina said nothing. Would Kalastus dare to attack her here, in public view? But, then, he had already slaughtered a score of Saddai, hadn't he?

"You'll scream before I'm done with you," said Kalastus. "I'll show you such pain that a strong man would weep to hear of it. I'll reach into your mind and fill your eyes with nightmares. And when I'm done, you'll get on your knees and beg me to take you to my bed." He smiled. "You'll beg for it."

Ark stepped before Caina, sword in hand.

157

Kalastus gaped at the weapon for a moment, and then burst out laughing. "Do you think your pet thug frightens me, Countess? Please. If he is foolish enough to stand against me, then I will sweep him from my path like an insect. Run away, fool, or I'll break every bone in your arms and legs and make you watch as I tame the Countess."

"Go to hell," said Ark.

"Hell?" laughed Kalastus. He gestured at the corpses lying in their own blood. "I can show you hell, if you like…"

His voice trailed off, and he looked to the side with irritation. Caina saw Ephaeron hurrying into the square, black robes whipping around his thin frame, followed by a half-dozen other magi. Kalastus's face twisted with contempt.

"Run away, little Countess," said Kalastus. His voice had gone quiet, almost calm, and that was almost more frightening than his towering fury. "Run away, and hide in your rooms, and cry into your pillows. But I promise you, you'll be kneeling at my feet. Begging for it. Soon."

He laughed once more, and strolled off to meet Ephaeron.

"Gods," muttered Ark, returning his blade to his scabbard. "We should have killed him. We really should have killed him." He looked at the dead Saddai. "All these people…"

"And nothing will happen to him for it," said Caina. "Nicephorus is too much of a coward. Kalastus will claim he acted in defense of his life, and our valiant Lord Governor will agree with him. And Gaidan will hear of this, and if he does not whip the Sons of Corazain into a frenzy over this massacre I will be amazed." She shook her head. "Do you see why I hate the magi so much?"

Ark scowled. "The only magus I've ever really known was Ephaeron. Are they all like that?"

"Probably," said Caina, "though most have more self-restraint than Kalastus."

She shivered, his threats still ringing in her ears. He had the power to make every last one of them come true. Her mother had tried to do it, and reduced her father to a drooling imbecile. But her mother had never been able to throw men like broken toys with a gesture, either. Kalastus could reach into her mind, break her will and reshape it as he pleased, until she knelt at his feet and begged him to take her to his bed. To do so would violate the laws of the Empire, of course, but Caina doubted that would trouble Kalastus in the least. Or his fellow magi, if he was smart enough not to get caught.

She realized that she had erred, badly, in going to the Magisterium chapterhouse. Kalastus had become her mortal enemy. He might very well kill her before she had a chance to find the pyromancer.

Or do worse than kill her. He could do much, much worse.

"Get the coach," said Caina. Her throat was dry. "We'd better go back to the Inn."

CHAPTER 19
BRIBES

Ark returned the coach to the Inn's stables, and Caina walked to her suite. To her surprise, the maids were nowhere to be seen. She found them in her bedroom, gazing in horror out the balcony doors.

"My lady!" said Julia. "You're safe!"

"What happened here?" said Caina.

"There was a crowd outside the Basilica," said Anya, "and we saw your coach coming, and you and Ark get out. And then something started throwing men into the air. They screamed so horribly. Are...are you well, my lady? Were you hurt?"

"I'm fine," said Caina. She took a deep breath. "A magus was found murdered, burned to death, at the Magisterium chapterhouse. One of the masters came to demand justice of Lord Nicephorus, someone in the crowd threw a stone, and...the master went berserk. He loosed his sorcery and killed at least twenty people."

"Good gods," said Cornelia. "Those magi were not to be trusted, I've always said so. No good can come from meddling with dark powers."

"You have no idea how much I agree with you," said Caina.

"My lady...forgive me for asking, but that master," said Anya, "was he the same one who dined with you?"

Caina nodded. "Listen to me very closely. If you see a magus, do not talk to him, and try to find a hiding place. The master...bears me a grudge, and he might try to do me harm."

"A grudge?" said Cornelia. "Why?"

Caina sighed. "He made...indecent advances, and I refused him." That was an understatement, to say the least. But the maids were sympathetic, which made Caina feel absurdly better. She wound up sitting in a chair by the window, a glass of wine in her hand. She hated wine, but hoped it would steady her frayed nerves somewhat.

Ark returned, and closed and locked the door behind him. "The coach is in the stables."

"Good," said Caina. "You know my plans for tonight." She did not want to speak openly in front of her maids. "I shall…"

The lock undid itself, and the door swung open.

A man in a black robe with a purple sash filled the doorway.

Caina scrambled to her feet in sudden alarm, reaching for the knives in her sleeve, while Ark whirled, his broadsword flying free from its scabbard.

The man held up his hands. "Hold! Hold, I say."

It was Ephaeron, not Kalastus. Ark slid his sword back into the scabbard, still keeping his eyes on the magus, while Caina sat back down. The maids stood frozen with sudden fear. Ephaeron walked into the sitting room, glancing around. He looked tired, more tired than Caina remembered, his eyes bloodshot and sunken, jaw rough with stubble.

"I have not issued you an invitation," said Caina in her iciest tone.

Ephaeron ignored her. "You three." He pointed at the maids. "Go downstairs and have something to eat. Your mistress and I must have words, but she shall summon you when our business is finished."

Cornelia glanced at Caina.

"Go," said Caina. She looked at Ephaeron. "This won't take long."

Cornelia, Julia, and Anya filed out, trying to stay as far from the magus as possible. Ephaeron stared at Ark, his bloodshot eyes intent.

"Send your guard away as well, Countess," said Ephaeron. "We must speak privately."

"No," said Caina, her tone still cold. "You magi have given me little reason to trust your honor. Ark shall stay."

She expected Ephaeron to argue. But he only nodded. "Very well."

"What do you want of me?" said Caina.

He sighed and crossed to the center of the room, rubbing his jaw. "It has come to my attention that Master Kalastus may have made inappropriate advances towards you. Is this true?"

"It is," said Caina.

Ephaeron sighed again and closed his eyes. "What happened?"

"We were eating dinner," said Caina. "He must have put drugs into the wine, because I started to feel fuzzy." Countess Marianna Nereide would know nothing of mind-spells. "Then…he opened my gown and started to fondle me. I was frightened, and tried to pull away. He did…something, some magic thing, and I was thrown into the wall. He looked so angry, and I was sure he was going to kill me. But then Ark found us, and we left."

"Damn it," muttered Ephaeron. He glanced at Ark. "What else happened? Master Kalastus looks somewhat battered."

"I was very upset," said Caina. "And my captain of guard becomes...direct when I am upset."

"Evidently," said Ephaeron. He picked up the carafe, poured himself some wine, and took a drink. "Countess, I must apologize to you for Master Kalastus's actions, which were...inappropriate."

Caina blinked in astonishment.

Apologies? From a magus? This was unprecedented.

"Kalastus has been in Rasadda for nearly twenty years," said Ephaeron, "while I only just recently arrived. In truth, Countess, I have been sent to replace him. The high magi feel that Kalastus has spent entirely too long in the Saddai province. We fear that he has become acclimated to Saddai customs and mores. In short, we fear that he has gone native."

"Kalastus hates the Saddai," said Caina. "He told me so himself. At some length."

Ephaeron shrugged. "Perhaps he is simply getting old. Regardless of the cause, his behavior has become increasingly...erratic, and he is no longer fit to head the local chapter."

"Erratic?" said Caina, incredulous.

Ephaeron blinked. "Certainly that may be the wrong word to describe his advances towards..."

"Erratic?" repeated Caina. "He just murdered almost twenty people in a fit of pique, and you call that erratic? What would you say if he took up the murder of children for a hobby? That he has become somewhat unreliable?"

Ephaeron's face hardened. "Master Kalastus was merely defending himself. The crowd assaulted him."

Caina stood, too angry to sit. "Someone in the crowd threw one stone at him. One! And that was only after Kalastus had threatened to kill ten thousand Saddai in repayment for the magus murdered last night. I doubt he even killed the man who actually threw the stone."

"His response may have been somewhat excessive..."

"Somewhat excessive?" said Caina, almost shouting. She took a breath to bring her tone back under control. "The man is a murderous criminal and ought to stand trial for this. Assuming you magi follow any laws but your own whims."

"I do not agree," said Ephaeron. "His actions were excessive, yes. But he had the right to defend himself. Many of the Empire's commoners, and more than a few of the nobles, hold the Magisterium in fear and contempt." He titled his head to one side. "Yourself included, I would guess."

"If the magi did not use their arts to butcher Saddai peasants in the street," said Caina, "perhaps you would be a little more loved."

"Science, Countess. Science, not art." The use of the wrong term seemed to annoy him more than a flat-out accusation of murder. "We in the

Magisterium study and practice the arcane sciences. Only mummers and fools describe the arcane sciences as an art."

"Science or art, it was still murder," said Caina.

Ephaeron shook his head. He seemed not to have heard her. "Kalastus had a right to defend himself, and no magistrate in the Empire will think otherwise. But, yes. He overreacted, and badly. A man who kept his wits about him could have defused the situation without resorting to bloodshed. Instead, I have another mess upon my hands. Between this, the burning murders, and Lord Nicephorus's gross incompetence, it shall be a miracle if we do not have a revolt before the month is out."

Ephaeron thought Nicephorus incompetent? Interesting.

"But that is none of your concern," said Ephaeron, his bloodshot gaze returning to Caina. "Simply put, this latest incident only proves that Kalastus has spent too long in Rasadda, and is no longer fit to head the local chapter. That, along with your...unpleasantness."

"Unpleasantness?" Caina sat back down. "Such a delicate word for it, learned master."

Ephaeron sighed. "I will be blunt. Did he succeed in forcing himself upon you?"

"No," said Caina.

"Very well, then," said Ephaeron. "Do you plan to bring charges against him?"

Caina blinked. She hadn't planned on it. After all, Countess Marianna Nereide did not actually exist. And neither she nor Halfdan wanted the kind of attention a trial before the magistrate would bring. But, then, Ephaeron didn't know that, did he?"

"My father will be furious when I tell him what happened," said Caina. "He has always hated the Magisterium, for he considers you to be cruel, reckless, and full of hubris, and this will only confirm his opinion. He will insist upon bringing charges before an Imperial magistrate, perhaps even the Emperor himself. We are not a wealthy or a powerful House, learned master, but our name is old in prestige. We will be heard."

"I see," said Ephaeron. "The Magisterium can ill-afford embarrassment at this time. I propose a bargain."

"I'm listening," said Caina.

"You will not tell your father of the wrong done to you, and you will never speak of it to anyone," said Ephaeron. "In exchange, we shall give you this."

He reached into his robes, produced a bulging leather purse, and set it on the arm of her chair. Caina tugged it open, and her eyes got wide. The purse was filled with platinum coins! A noble could live in comfort for thirty years off this kind of money. A common man could retire, and his descendents could live in ease for five or six generations.

"This is a fortune," said Caina.

"The Magisterium is concerned with loftier matters than mere material goods," said Ephaeron. "Let us continue to be candid. You went on a tour of the provinces to ensnare a wealthy husband with your beauty, did you not? It seems you have met with little success. These funds, however, can supply you with an ample dowry. You can then easily find a husband of suitable rank and social standing in Nighmar, or even in Malarae itself."

"This is...unexpected," said Caina. "Why do you simply not use your magic to erase my memory?"

Ephaeron seemed affronted. "To violate another's mind without writ is a violation of Imperial law. Despite your opinion of the Magisterium, I would not do such a thing. And," he shrugged, "in truth, you suffered injury at the hands of Kalastus. Perhaps this will serve as some recompense."

A magus with a conscience? Caina was astonished.

"And suppose I do not take this bribe," said Caina, "and tell my father anyway, and he brings charges against Kalastus. What will you do then?"

"If you should choose such a foolish and unprofitable course," said Ephaeron, "I shall do nothing. However, certain rumors will arise that you seduced Kalastus, became pregnant, purged your womb of his child, and now level false accusations against him to defend your honor. And since Imperial noblewomen in general are not known for their chastity or temperance, such a story will be easily believed, and your father's charges against Kalastus will collapse."

Well. So much for conscience.

"I see," said Caina. "Very well. I will take your money, and not speak of what happened to anyone. I suppose I will at least have some profit from the whole miserable affair." Caina had little use for the money herself. But the gods knew Halfdan and the Ghosts needed it. It would please her to use the Magisterium's money to fund the Magisterium's enemies. And perhaps she could give some more to Sister Tadaia.

"Good," said Ephaeron, "very good. You have chosen well, Countess." He turned and started for the door. Then he stopped, as if a thought had occurred to him. "May I offer you some counsel?"

"If I said no, would that daunt you?"

"Leave Rasadda," said Ephaeron. "Immediately. This very day, if possible."

"Why?" said Caina.

"You are not stupid, Countess," said Ephaeron. "I have heard that you were attacked twice. Surely that is reason enough to leave this city."

"Both the roads and the seas are equally dangerous," said Caina, "infested with bandits and corsairs."

Ephaeron made an annoyed noise. "Very well. I shall tell you the truth,

Countess. Rasadda is going to revolt. Perhaps before the month is out."

"Why do you say that?" said Caina.

"Nicephorus's incompetence and malfeasance is a great part of it," said Ephaeron. "But of late, a faction within the Saddai priesthood has been aggravating the situation. They call themselves the Sons of Corazain, after the last king of the old Saddai empire. They believe that Corazain has returned to drive out the Empire and reestablish the Ashbringers, and interpret these burning murders as a sign of his return. Discontented rebels are one thing. Revolutionaries who believe that a god-figure from their past has returned are quite another."

"But these burning murders are the works of charlatans," said Caina, "you told me so yourself, when I asked if sorcery could have been used in these deaths."

"It appears I was mistaken," said Ephaeron. "Pyromancy has almost certainly been used in most of the murders. Someone within the Sons of Corazain has managed to rediscover pyromancy. I suspect Gaidan, the leader of the Sons of Corazain. Last night this pyromancer killed a brother of the Magisterium. This is a sure sign that a revolt is imminent. I shall have to deal with Gaidan soon."

"I see," said Caina. Ephaeron's words made a compelling amount of sense. But why would Gaidan have gone after Romarion's business partners? Surely he would have attacked Nicephorus and the other high officials first. And Caina remembered Gaidan's speech below the ruined apartment building. Gaidan himself didn't seem to know why the murders had been committed. Caina was still missing some vital piece of the mystery.

"Countess, listen to me," said Ephaeron. "Your life is in terrible danger so long as you remain in Rasadda. The men who attacked you on the street were not just robbers. They were Sons of Corazain, Gaidan's men, and they hoped to make a statement with your death. The pyromancer himself may try to kill you. I suspect his spells require a sample of the victim's blood, and if he can lay hands upon even a drop of your blood, he will use his powers to burn you alive. And when the city revolts, if you fall into their hands, you will almost certainly be beaten, raped, and possibly tortured to death."

"I see," said Caina again. His warning chilled her. Yet her duty demanded that she remain. "You are right, learned master. I will make arrangements to take ship to the Imperial capital as soon as possible."

"Good. Very good," said Ephaeron. He paused, and stared at Ark for a moment. "I think I recognize you."

Ark bowed. "Yes, learned master. I am Ark, of Caer Marist. We met when Countess Marianna attended the Lord Governor's banquet."

"Yes, yes" said Ephaeron, "but I recognized you then as well."

Caina blinked, glanced at Ark in sudden alarm. If Ephaeron happened to recall Ark's real name...

"I spent some years with the Eighteenth Legion, serving as their battle magus," said Ephaeron. "You served in the Eighteenth Legion, did you not?"

"I did," said Ark.

Ephaeron frowned. "You...were a centurion, as I recall."

"I was," said Ark.

"When your term of service was up, why did you not reenlist?" said Ephaeron. "Centurions almost always reenlist, as I understand. You could have achieved high rank by now, perhaps command of your own cohort."

Ark shrugged. "I had grown weary of the military life, learned master. In truth, I was happier as a common soldier. Once you gain a centurion's rank...there was too much politics for my taste, and I am a simple man."

Ephaeron's mouth twitched, perhaps in amusement. "I can understand that. How did you come to the service of House Nereide?"

"I took my discharge bonus and traveled to Malarae," said Ark. "I had intended to open an inn. Instead I came across Lord Nereide on the road while he was under attack from brigands. I helped drive them off, and Lord Nereide offered me a position with his House. The work seemed amenable, so I took it."

"Ah," said Ephaeron. "You were fortunate. Every year, dozens of veterans open new inns and taverns in the Imperial capital, and most of them go out of business within the year. There is something about the soldier's life that must make innkeeping an attractive profession."

"The beer, I'm sure," said Ark.

Ephaeron barked with laughter. "No doubt." He turned to Caina. "Countess, I am pleased that you chose to embrace reason and accept my offer. I urge you to follow reason once more. Leave Rasadda quickly." He sketched a bow, turned, and left.

Ark and Caina looked at each other.

"Well," said Caina, "that was close."

Ark nodded. "I was certain that he would recall my real name."

"It's good he didn't. You lied quite admirably, by the way."

Ark smiled. "I have been watching you."

Caina laughed, hefting Ephaeron's purse. "Very good."

"Are you going to leave Rasadda?"

"Of course not," said Caina. She thought it over. "Countess Marianna Nereide might. I can disguise myself as someone else, if necessary. I'll send the maids back to Mors Crisius, tell them that I'll take ship with you. I could easily masquerade as a woman of common Caerish birth, a peddler maybe, or as your wife, perhaps."

Something flickered in Ark's eyes.

"I'm sorry," said Caina. "That was thoughtless of me."

"I know that you meant no ill," said Ark. "And it would be an effective disguise, in truth."

"But too soon," said Caina. "Countess Marianna Nereide can speak with the Lord Governor and with Romarion. A lowborn Caerish peddler, or the wife of a discharged veteran, could not. No, I'll not change my alias, at least not yet."

"What will you do now?" said Ark.

Caina glanced out the window. The day was wearing on. "Now? I'm going to go take a nap. Then it's past time I had that private chat with Sister Tadaia."

CHAPTER 20
THE BURNING FLAME

When night fell, Caina prepared. She barred the bedroom door, and donned her black clothes, her weapons, her tools, the gray mask, her father's signet ring, and the shadow-woven cloak. Then she crossed onto the balcony, hooked a grapnel to the stone railing, and vanished into the night.

She did not need Ark's help for this one. Caina doubted that the Temple of Living Flame possessed the same sort of rigorous security as Romarion's mansion. And the Black Wolves had been looking for Ark, not for her. That still troubled her. Why had the mercenaries been looking for Ark? For that matter, how had they even managed to find him in a dark alley at the middle of the night? It was a tremendous coincidence, and Caina detested coincidences.

No. Think later. Right now she had to focus.

Rasadda's streets were crowded. The better neighborhoods crawled with militiamen, both foot and horse patrols. No doubt Valgorix hoped to stave off a potential insurrection. Saddai commoners thronged the streets of the poorer districts. Caina heard angry muttering about Kalastus's massacre, heard men with flame tattoos upon their chests chanting the name of Corazain.

Caina kept to the shadows, her cloak blending with the darkness.

At last she stood before the Temple of Living Flame. She saw a fiery glow coming from within the Temple's opened doors, the same glow rising from the oculus at the apex of the dome. Between the light from the Temple and the light from the pyramids, tangled shadows filled the plaza before the doors. Caina crept from shadow to shadow, until she could peer into the Temple's opened doors. She saw no one, and heard nothing, and so hurried through the doorway on silent feet.

Black marble gleamed beneath her boots, and a great fire crackled in the center of the domed chamber, the smoke rising through the oculus. Bas-reliefs covered the walls. Caina expected them to show glorious scenes from the old Saddai empire. Instead they showed men and women submitting humbly to their sufferings as the Living Flame purified their souls. There were odd scratches here and there on the carvings, and Caina looked closer.

They had been gilded, she realized. Tadaia must have ordered the gold pulled off to buy bread for the poor.

Caina circled around the wall, trying to keep to the shadows, and made her way around the chamber. Living quarters rested along the Temple's outer wall, and Caina suspected that she would find Sister Tadaia there. The door was locked, but the lock was old and rusting, and it took only a moment's work to release it.

She found herself in a narrow hallway, wooden doors lining either wall. The nearest door was open, candlelight spilling into the darkness, and Caina heard rasping, groaning sobs coming from inside. Curious, she glided forward and peered through the door.

Gaidan knelt over a bed, weeping. His shoulders shook with sobs, and he mumbled a prayer over and over again in Saddaic, asking the Living Flame to scour the corruption from his soul. He did not look like the proud, contemptuous priest Caina had seen. Instead he looked horrified, as if he had seen some nightmare that had shaken the foundations of his soul.

A knife appeared in Caina's hand. For a long moment she considered stepping into the room and driving the blade into his neck. It would be quick, easy, silent. If she made sure to close the door and extinguish the candle, no one would discover the corpse until morning. And the man deserved it. He was raising an insurrection against the Empire, and he was almost certainly the pyromancer, the new Ashbringer, behind the murders.

Almost…

Caina did not know for sure. She would kill to defend her life, and if her duty demanded it. But she would not murder a man bent weeping over his bed. She moved carefully down the hallway. At the third door, she saw light glimmering through the cracks. Caina took a deep breath to steady her hands, and pushed the door open.

The room beyond had a bed, a chair, and a desk. Sister Tadaia sat sleeping in the chair, a book open upon her lap. Caina closed the door behind her, crossed the room, and placed a gloved palm over Sister Tadaia's mouth.

The old woman awoke with a sudden shock, her hands flailing.

"Do not scream, do not call out," said Caina in Saddaic, her voice rasping and disguised. She began to feel a tingling sensation. "And do not attempt a spell. I will know if you do. I wish only to talk. Do you

169

understand me?"

The tingling subsided, and Tadaia nodded. Caina stepped away from the chair, and circled around it so Tadaia could see her.

"The Living Flame preserve me," she whispered. "Someone has been sent at last to murder me."

"I said I wanted to talk," snapped Caina. "I do not speak with the dead." There was a window overlooking the street. If Tadaia decided to call for help, Caina could go out the window and escape easily enough.

Tadaia closed the book on her lap. "You…I know you."

"Do you, now?" said Caina, keeping the alarm out of her voice. If Tadaia recognized her from this morning…

"You are one of the Ghosts," said Tadaia. "The spies and servants of the Emperor. I had heard that your brotherhood prowls the night, wrapped in shadow…but I never thought to meet one of you."

"The Emperor has no spies," said Caina. "Only Ghosts that lurk in shadows."

"So I see," said Tadaia. She frowned. "I…cannot see your heart."

"Since it is still inside my chest, I should hope not."

"No," said Tadaia. "It is a gift of the Living Flame, that I can see the auras of men as their spirits burn within them. And I cannot see yours. Are you…ah, your cloak. It blocks my sight. How am I to know your motives? How I am to know if you mean good or ill towards my people?"

"You shall have to use your wits and your judgment," said Caina, "like those of us who are denied such gifts. But I will say this to you. I do not mean you or your people harm, and nor does the Emperor. Word of these…burning murders has reached his ears, and I was sent to find the truth behind them."

Tadaia sucked in a breath.

"You know of them?" said Caina.

Tadaia said nothing, her lips working, hands trembling in her lap.

Caina went to one knee before the old woman's chair. "Listen to me. I have watched you long from afar. I know how you have labored to feed the poor, how you stripped the gold from the very walls of this temple to buy bread."

Tadaia blinked. "How could you know that?"

"We are the Ghosts," said Caina. "We know much. I know you are a woman of character. I saw one of the burning murders, Sister. I saw it with my own eyes. I watched as a man screamed and gibbered as his flesh crisped and his skin turned to ash. Help me find this murderer, and I swear to you that he will answer for the horrors he has wrought."

Tadaia closed her eyes. "Very well. If you so swear. I will tell you what I know, if you will use it to stop these horrors. And the horrors that are yet to come."

Caina stood, backed away.

"I am not surprised," said Tadaia, "that these murders are happening. Rasadda is falling apart. Nicephorus's hand is cruel and heavy. He has stolen our lands and impoverished our people. The poor cry out for bread, for justice, but there are none to hear. And desperate men fight, sooner or later." She looked at Caina. "Do you know the difference between the Living Flame and the Burning Flame?"

"No," said Caina. "I thought you Saddai worshipped the Living Flame. But I have heard the Sons of Corazain speak of this Burning Flame."

"Corazain." Tadaia closed her eyes again. "Yes. Corazain." Her eyes flicked open. "The difference is this. The Living Flame is the true god of the Saddai people. If you have been watching me from afar you will have heard me speak of him. The goal of our lives is to be reunited with the Living Flame in eternal harmony. But our souls are corrupted, and must be purified. And suffering is the instrument of the Living Flame, the hammer of his forge. By patient endurance, our souls are reforged, are tempered and made new."

Caina nodded, titling her shadowed cowl.

"But the Burning Flame," said Tadaia, "is…different. It is a different interpretation, a different way of looking at our god. A darker way. Those who follow the way of the Burning Flame argue that the world is corrupt, wicked, ruined. The world must burn, they say, all nations and all peoples must burn. Only when this rotten world has burned to ashes can it be rebuilt anew."

"The Ashbringers," said Caina. "They followed the Burning Flame, did they not?" She remembered Ostros screaming in his veil of flames and tried not to shudder.

"Yes," said Tadaia. "When the Ashbringers ruled our people, and went to war against other peoples, the way of the Burning Flame ruled, and those who followed the Living Flame were persecuted. But your Empire threw down the Ashbringers, and the Saddai turned to the way of the Living Flame."

"So the Sons of Corazain," said Caina, "they follow the Burning Flame."

"Yes," said Tadaia. "I pity them, but they do. Nicephorus created them. He drove them from their lands, denied their families food, and their desperation turned to despair and rage. So they have embraced the nihilism of the Burning Flame. They would see Rasadda burn, see all the Empire burn, just to take their revenge upon Nicephorus."

"And among the Sons of Corazain," said Caina, "is this new Ashbringer." Tadaia flinched at the word. "I know that sorcery is behind these deaths, Sister. I told you. I saw a man burn to death in unnatural fire before my eyes."

"Yes," whispered Tadaia, her voice choked with grief. "Yes. I am certain of it. Someone among the Sons of Corazain has chosen to walk the ruinous path of the Ashbringer."

"Who?" said Caina, leaning forward. "Do you know who? Is it Gaidan?"

"Gaidan? No. Gaidan is a fool," said Tadaia. "Yesterday, an Imperial noblewoman came to hear me preach. At first I thought her a silly child, but she had been touched by the misery of the hungry, and donated a large sum of money to buy bread for the poor. Gaidan wanted to kill her for it! He said it was an insult to the dignity of the Saddai people." Tadaia shook his head. "Besides, he lacks the talent for it. Some of the Brothers and Sisters of the Living Flame have some ability at the arcane, as do I, but Gaidan does not."

"I have heard him speak to his followers," said Caina. "He thinks that Corazain has returned, that the burning murders are an omen of his coming."

"Then let us hope and pray that he was wrong," said Tadaia. "If Corazain has truly returned, it would be a disaster for the Saddai, and for the entire world."

"Indeed?" said Caina. "I thought Corazain was a hero to you Saddai."

"There are some who think that," said Tadaia, "and they are fools to do so."

"Why?"

Tadaia paused for a long while. "There are things you must understand, about the Ashbringers and the pyromancy they practiced. Pyromancy is dangerous, incredibly dangerous, to both body and soul alike."

"I know this," said Caina. "I watched a man burn to death. And every magus I have spoken with has told me that same."

Tadaia's eyes narrowed. "You are a friend of the magi?"

"Of course not," said Caina. "The Magisterium is cruel and corrupt. But when even they say that pyromancy is dangerous…"

"Indeed," said Tadaia. She took a deep breath. "Listen to me. You think there are understandable purposes behind these murders. That the victims were killed for political reasons. Or for mere money. It may have started out that way, but no longer. The practice of pyromancy bestows tremendous power. But essence of pyromancy is fire, and the essence of fire is to burn. To burn! An Ashbringer can bring fiery death down upon his enemies. But at the same time, the power is devouring him. Burning him. Burning away his body, his soul, and his mind. An Ashbringer always goes insane. Inevitably. Sooner or later, the power burns away his reason."

"Then the old Saddai kings…"

"Oh, yes," said Tadaia. "Every last one of them went mad, and

Corazain was the maddest of them all. They tortured children for their own amusement. They took what women they pleased, and none dared defy them. They would kill on whim, or for no reason at all. And they discovered the deeper truth within the flames."

"What truth is that?"

"That death can unlock powers even more terrible," said Tadaia. "A man will burn a coal for heat and light. For fuel. The Ashbringers discovered how to burn a man to feed their strength. If they used pyromancy to kill a man…they could drain his strength, his very life force, into their own bodies. They used that stolen strength to heal their wounds, to augment their sorcery, to extend their own lives. The mightiest Ashbringers could live for centuries, cruel, mighty, and insane, nightmares made flesh, until at last their powers devoured them from within."

"Gods," whispered Caina. She remembered how powerful Maglarion had grown on stolen life force. Little wonder that the Empire had fought to bring the Ashbringers down so long ago.

"And Corazain was the maddest of them all," repeated Tadaia. "Do you know the story of his final spell?"

"Yes," said Caina. "When Crisius besieged the city, Corazain withdrew to the pinnacle of his funeral pyramid. He unleashed his powers in a final spell that destroyed most of the city and Crisius's army."

"You are almost right," said Tadaia. "Corazain did indeed withdraw to the pyramid. But he unleashed his powers against the Saddai, not against Crisius's army."

"His own people?" said Caina, horrified. With an effort she remembered to keep her voice disguised. "Why?"

"He burned them all to fuel his own strength, his own sorcery," said Tadaia. "A hundred thousand people, and he burned them all to feed his power. He thought it would transform him into a living god, and then he would strike down Crisius's host with a thought. But the power was too much for him. Mortal flesh could not contain it. It destroyed him, and the ruin of his destruction burned Rasadda to the ground. Crisius's army was destroyed only by accident."

"He tried to slaughter his own people to become a god?" said Caina, appalled. Yes, it did indeed remind her of Maglarion.

"Yes," said Tadaia. "For that was the Ashbringer way, the inevitable end of the path they walked. And now you know why I dread that a true Ashbringer might stalk Rasadda."

"A magus was burned to death last night," said Caina. "Does that mean the killer could…devour the dead man's arcane strength, add it to his own?"

"It does," said Tadaia. "And this Ashbringer has murdered nearly thirty people. Probably more. By now he has grown mighty, so mighty that only the strongest magi of the Magisterium could dare oppose him. And the stolen power has undoubtedly driven him mad."

"So that means he'd be stronger than a normal man," said Caina, "tougher, too."

"If you can find him," said Tadaia, "you will have to kill him quickly. Perhaps before he even sees you. For if he has a chance to employ his powers against you, you will almost certainly perish. And even killing him may prove difficult. All the men and women he has burned to death will have given him a…a reserve of stolen life force. A reservoir, you might call it. It will heal all but the most grievous wounds quickly. This Ashbringer could take enough punishment to kill ten men before he even began to slow down."

"Splendid," said Caina. "Do you have any idea where I can find him? Or even where I can start looking?"

"It is someone in the Sons of Corazain," said Tadaia. "I am sure of that. Beyond that, I cannot say. I have tried to use the sight granted to me by the Living Flame, but I have met with no success. The Ashbringer is strong enough, I think, to cloak himself from my sight. But I have a suspicion where he might be hiding."

"Where?" said Caina.

"The Sign of the Anchor," said Tadaia. "It is a tavern and an inn, located near the docks. The poor fill the city's streets, and they tell me things. Lately I have heard that men have been seen carrying burned bodies from the Inn's back door, and the place stinks of burnt flesh."

"I see," said Caina, disappointed. She remembered the half-burned corpse Valgorix had found behind the Inn of Mirrors. The man had undoubtedly been burned to cover up a common killing, not as part of some mad arcane ritual. But, still. What if the pyromancer was hiding there? Caina could not risk overlooking anything. "Thank you, Sister. You have been most helpful."

"Ghost," said Tadaia, rising. "Listen to me. If you are going to find the pyromancer, you must do so quickly. Things are going to become much worse very soon. I can feel it in my bones. If you do not find him soon…I fear it will be too late."

"I understand," said Caina. "We may speak again."

She stooped, snatched the blanket from the bed, and flung it over the old woman in one smooth motion. Tadaia sputtered in surprise, pawing at the blanket. Caina swung past her, opened the shutters, rolled out the window, pushed the shutters closed behind her, and broke into a run. A few blocks later she paused, ducking into a doorway to catch her breath and to think things over.

Doubt tugged at her. Was it too late? Even if she found the pyromancer, even if she stopped him, would Rasadda explode into revolt anyway? Nicephorus had pushed the Saddai too hard for too long. Perhaps nothing could stop the revolt. And had the pyromancer grown too strong, too powerful, to be stopped?

Caina looked at the everlasting pyres raging atop the pyramids, envisioned them devouring all of Rasadda, and shivered.

CHAPTER 21
ASSASSINS

It was well past midnight when Caina climbed the wall and returned to her bedroom at the Inn of Mirrors. The maids were asleep, and so was Ark. He needed his rest, and no further work could be done tonight, so Caina returned to her bedroom, stripped off the her nightfighter's garb, and went to bed.

Her usual nightmares were jumbled. In one she reached her father's chair, only to see him erupt into flames, screaming as Ostros had screamed. Her mother tried to cast a spell on her, shrieking curses, only she turned into Kalastus, and his clammy hands pulled her close. The magi chained her to a table, only they became the Sons of Corazain, knives glittering as they slid the blade into her belly, digging, digging, digging, Maglarion's laughter filling her ears…

Caina awoke that morning with her head pounding and her mouth dry. She rose, washed out her mouth, wrapped herself in a robe, and went to the sitting room. Ark sat alone at the table, running a whetstone down the length of his broadsword. The steady rasp of stone against steel made her feel better, oddly enough.

Ark glanced at her. "You slept poorly, didn't you?"

"Yes," said Caina, sitting across from him. "Too many scars on the mind."

Ark nodded his understanding, testing the edge of the blade with his thumb.

"Where are the maids?" said Caina.

"The common room," said Ark. "I told them to go eat something. They wanted to wait until you awoke, but I told them you would call for them. I figured you would want to speak privately."

Caina nodded.

"What did you learn from Sister Tadaia?"

"Nothing good," said Caina. "She thinks the pyromancer is hiding at the Sign of the Anchor."

Ark looked dubious. "There? I know the place. It's a tavern. Sailors favor it. Along with independent merchant captains."

"And by independent merchant captains," said Caina, "I assume that you mean smugglers."

"And pirates of all stripes," said Ark. "They'll sell their cargoes in Mors Crisius, where the customs agents are not so vigilant, and then return to Rasadda to keep up appearances. Most of the sailors are who frequent the Sign are foreign-born, Caerish and Istarish and Anshani, and they detest the Saddai. If the pyromancer is one of the Sons of Corazain…the Sign seems like a strange place for a Saddai Ashbringer to hide."

"I agree," said Caina. "Yet Sister Tadaia says that the beggars have seen men carrying burned bodies in and out of the Sign."

Ark frowned. "Like the one Valgorix found outside the Inn. I thought you said that was only an imitation killing."

"I did," said Caina. "And I doubt the Sign of the Anchor has anything to do with the pyromancer. But it's the only lead we have at the moment. I want you to go there and look around. I'd do it myself, but there's no way an Imperial Countess would ever go to a sailors' tavern, and I can hardly walk in there hooded and masked."

Ark nodded. "I'll say I'm looking for work. The pirates are so rife that merchant ships are always looking for guards. And pirate ships always want swords." A brief smile flashed over his face. "And if anyone realizes that I work for you, I will say that you are a cruel and capricious mistress, and I wish to leave the serve of House Nereide as soon as possible."

Caina laughed. "Oh, very good."

"What will you do?" said Ark.

"I'll have to wait here," said Caina. "If you see anything interesting at the Sign, we'll go back together, after dark."

Ark nodded. "I'll leave at once."

"Don't do anything rash. And if you do find the pyromancer, don't try to fight him. Tadaia thinks the pyromancer can absorb the strength of those he's murdered, which might have made him too strong to kill without doing something clever."

Ark snorted. "See? A cruel and capricious mistress, indeed. It's past time I fled from you and went to sea."

"I'm pleased that you see reason," said Caina. "Be careful."

Ark nodded, returned his sword to its scabbard, and left. A short time later Cornelia, Julia, and Anya hurried into the room. Ark had sent them back up. They insisted on drawing a bath, and Caina gave in without too much arguing. It eased some of the ache from her overexerted muscles. Afterwards Caina locked herself in her bedroom and went through the open-handed forms. It made her feel better, cleared her mind.

After, Caina donned her robe again, returned to the sitting room, and ate breakfast, paging idly through her book on the siege of Rasadda. Perhaps an answer would leap out at her. None did, though. Caina sighed and gazed at the book itself. For some reason it seemed to stick into her mind.

A book. Why did that seem so important? Caina frowned, but the answer hovered just out of reach, the like the words to a song she could not quite recall...

Someone screamed.

Caina looked up in sudden alarm.

"My lady?" said Anya. "What was that noise?"

"It came from the common room," said Caina, getting to her feet.

The door smashed open, and men hurried into the sitting room. Four Saddai men, to be precise. They carried shortswords in their hands, and beneath their opened shirts and vests Caina saw the swirling flames of Corazain upon their chests.

Four of them. Oh, this was bad.

Caina suspected that she was about to die.

"How dare you enter here?" raged Cornelia. "How dare you..."

The nearest man backhanded her, sent her sprawling to the carpet. Anya and Julia shrieked and retreated towards the far wall. Caina watched them, cursing herself for a fool. She bore no weapons. Why hadn't she at least tucked a dagger into her robe's sash?

"What is your business here?" said Caina, putting ice into her voice.

The Sons of Corazain looked at each other and laughed.

"Countess Marianna Nereide?" said the man who had backhanded Cornelia. He gave Cornelia a vicious kick as she tried to crawl away.

"I am," said Caina. "State your business with me, immediately."

They laughed again.

"Foolish bitch," said the lead man. "We're here to kill you, to make you pay for your crimes."

Gaidan's work. Still smarting from Tadaia's public rebuke, no doubt. Caina wished that she had killed him when she had the chance.

"Crimes?" said Caina, hoping to stall. "What crimes?" Surely Sairzan, or one of his servants, would call for the militia soon. Unless the Sons of Corazain had killed everyone in the Inn.

"The crimes of the Empire," spat the man. "You have stolen our lands and left us to starve."

"Have I?" said Caina. "That was quite a feat, one woman stealing lands from so many strong men."

"You will pay for your crimes."

"I have committed no crimes, you fool," said Caina. "Yesterday at this time I gave a small fortune to buy food for your starving people. Tell me again how this is a crime. Speak slowly. I am, after all, only a foolish bitch, and might not understand."

"Enough talk," said the man.

"Yes," said Caina. "I'll give you one chance. Walk away. Now. And nobody will die. Else I swear that at least one of you will die before another hour has past." Maybe two, if she was lucky.

They looked at each other, and roared with laughter.

"Kill her," said the man. "Leave the maids alive. We can have some fun with them before we kill them."

Caina snatched up some silverware from the table and held a butter knife out at an awkward angle. She let fear flood into her expression, her hand trembling as she waved the knife back and forth.

"Stay back," she said, "I'm warning...I'm warning you, stay back!"

The Sons of Corazain laughed at again, and leader stepped forward. He seized her wrist with his left hand and twisted, and the knife fell from her fingers.

"Careful," he said, raising his short sword, "you might hurt yourself."

"You're right," said Caina, stabbing with fork she had hidden in her left hand. It plunged into his eye, and the leader reeled back with an awful scream, hands flying to his face. Caina caught the shortsword as it fell, reversed it, and stabbed into his gut. She wrenched the glistening blade free, blood splashing across her robe, and the leader toppled to the carpet, screaming.

The three survivors stared at her in stupefied shock. Caina could have put a knife into any one of their throats, and again she cursed herself for leaving her weapons in the bedroom. She circled around the table, keeping the heavy slab of wood between her and them.

"Well?" said Caina, raising the bloodstained sword.

The Sons of Corazain roared and came at her. Caina wheeled and ran at the man coming on her left. She felt a tug and a wash of pain across her back she did. The man on her left yelled and slashed, and Caina ducked under his blow, the blade whizzing past her hair. Strong and fast these Sons of Corazain might have been, but none of them knew how to fight. Caina stabbed, her blade biting into his neck, and the man's hands came up to his throat. She felt another blow coming behind her, and ducked, but too slow.

The crosspiece of the sword caught her on the jaw, and Caina spun around. Her bare foot slipped on the bloodstained carpet, and she fell with a grunt of pain. She saw a sword descending and rolled away. The blade pinned the skirt of her robe, and Caina tore the cloth free with a desperate yank. She sprang back to her feet, the tattered robe swirling around her legs, while the two remaining Sons of Corazain stalked after her.

She was right next to the bedroom door. Caina turned and raced through it. The Sons of Corazain bellowed and followed her. She always hid her nightfighter clothes in hidden compartments at the bottom of a chest, but her weapons were a different story. Her belt rested on a chair, knives waiting in their leather sheaths. Caina snatched up the belt, yanked out a knife, wheeled, and flung the blade in one smooth motion. The Sons of Corazain were almost on her, and the whirling knife sheared away most of the nearest man's right cheek. He screamed, blood spraying from his teeth, and the last man reached Caina.

She tried to twist away as he stabbed, but a line of hot pain erupted along her left hip. Her assailant grunted and tried to recover his balance, and Caina hit him in the face. He stumbled back, sputtering, which gave Caina just enough time to slide another knife free of the belt and bury it in his neck. He fell, blood pouring from his wound, and tumbled back into the sitting room.

Caina picked up a fallen short sword and walked towards the last man.

"You can fight?" he mumbled, his words muffled by the necessity of holding his ruined cheek together. "But...but you're a woman, and you can..."

"Yes," said Caina, cutting his throat, "surprising, isn't it?"

She stepped into the sitting room, looked at the dead bodies, doubled over, and threw up her breakfast. Caina gripped a chair for support, shuddering, the wounds on her shoulder and hip aching. Her robe, wet with both her blood and the blood of the dead men, hung limp and sodden around her. That had been close. If those men hadn't been so stupid and incompetent. So close. Another inch, and she would lie dead on the carpet.

The carpet. It was ruined. Caina wondered if Sairzan would charge extra, and laughed. Lightheaded. She really ought to sit down. No. Work to do first. She retrieved her knives from the dead men, cleaning the blades on their clothes.

"My lady?"

Julia and Anya approached, supporting Cornelia between them. Caina had forgotten all about them.

"Cornelia," said Caina, "you're hurt."

"I'll live," said the older woman, hand pressed to her side. "You're...you're hurt worse, my lady. Gods, all that blood..."

"It's not mine," said Caina. She winced as the cut in her hip throbbed, and she wadded the skirt of the ruined robe against it. "Mostly."

They stared at her in horrified amazement, and again Caina felt the absurd urge to laugh.

"What...what should we do now?" said Anya.

"Now?" said Caina. "Now we hide in the bedroom and wait for

someone to rescue us."

It did not take long.

Sairzan had sent his servants running for help, and Valgorix himself arrived in short order with a troop of militia. He looked angry, and frustrated, and very tired.

"What happened?" he demanded as his men dragged the bodies out.

"I don't...I don't really know," said Caina, wrapped in a blanket, makeshift bandages pressed against her cuts. "I was eating breakfast, and...and those men burst into my room, and screamed that they were going to kill me in the name of Corazain, and, oh, gods, they cut me...and I ran and locked myself in the bedroom, and there was all this screaming..." Caina made her voice quaver, her lip trembling. She didn't have to try very hard.

Valgorix raked a hand through his sweaty hair. "Do you know who killed these men? Did you see anything?"

Caina gave a timid shake of her head. "I didn't...I didn't see anything. All I heard was fighting, and screaming. I was so sure that they would break down the door and kill us all."

"Damn it," said Valgorix. He paced around the room for a while. "Countess, it is inappropriate for someone of my rank to speak bluntly to a woman of your rank. But speak bluntly I must. I told you to leave Rasadda. I told you that the Sons of Corazain were going to target you. Was I not right?"

Caina gave him a tremulous nod.

Valgorix sighed. "Countess. You must leave Rasadda, immediately. Matters are bad, and I fear that they are going to get much worse." He dropped his voice. "I expect a revolt any day now. And the Lord Governor is no help at all. Every night when I go to bed I expect to be slaughtered in my sleep. This city is going to drown in blood. You can escape it, Countess, but only if you leave at once."

"You were right, Decurion," said Caina. "I should have listened to you. I'm sorry." She took a deep breath. "I will leave for the Imperial capital on the morrow. I have had enough of this miserable city."

"Good," said Valgorix. "What happened to your captain of guard, anyway? Where is he?"

"I sent him to buy some food," said Caina.

"That was extremely foolish," said Valgorix. "Keep him with you at all times now, understand?" Caina nodded again. "I'll keep a few of my men on guard at the Inn's door, until tomorrow morning."

"Thank you," said Caina. Valgorix bowed and stalked out of the ruined sitting room. Caina stared after him, worried. In the excitement she had forgotten all about Ark. Suppose the Sons of Corazain had ambushed him on the streets? Ark could handle himself in a fight, better than Caina could. But suppose some mishap had happened?

Or suppose the pyromancer had found him?

Sairzan hurried into the room, bowing with every step. Before Caina could interrupt him a profuse stream of apologizes erupted from his lips. He had failed in his duties as an innkeeper and a host, and begged her forgiveness for his many misdeeds.

"It's not your fault. No one was killed," she remembered the blood on her fingers and shuddered, "at least no one of mine, and if you'd tried to fight them they'd have killed you."

"Please," said Sairzan, "I beg of you, though, to accept my second-finest suite of rooms while these chambers are cleaned. Only in this way may I expunge my grievous shame."

And keep his good name, no doubt. "Very well," said Caina.

She looked up, and saw Ark in the doorway. His sword was in hand, and he looked over the bloodstained room with cold eyes.

"What the hell happened?" said Ark.

"We need to talk," said Caina.

"Get on with it, already," said Caina.

She sat naked on the bed in her new rooms, a blanket wrapped around her legs and clutched to her chest. Ark sat beside her, cleaning the wound on her shoulder with boiling wine.

"Shallow," muttered Ark. "Didn't reach the bone. It ought to heal well. Should be stitched up, though."

Caina nodded.

"This will be a lot easier for both of us if you lie down," said Ark.

Caina grimaced, but nodded and lay face-down on the bed, shifting the blanket to keep her modesty preserved. She felt deeply uncomfortable, exposing so much of herself, but she supposed that dying from an infected cut would be even more uncomfortable. Besides, she'd stitched up Ark's wounds, so fair was fair.

A moment later she felt the stab as the heated needle entered her skin. Caina gritted her teeth against the pain, and Ark began stitching. It hurt, but she'd felt worse. Much worse.

"Are you truly planning to leave Rasadda?" said Ark.

"Yes," said Caina, her voice tight, grateful for the distraction. "Or, at least, Countess Marianna Nereide is. This false identity has become a liability. The Sons of Corazain want to kill the Countess, and they won't stop until they do." She took a deep breath. "We'll leave tomorrow. I'll hire some trustworthy servant from Sairzan to serve as coachman. Once we're out of the city, we'll send them to Halfdan at Mors Crisius and double back to the city. I'll have to think of a suitable disguise, but it should work."

"And what then?" said Ark.

"First," said Caina, "tell me what you saw at the Sign of the Anchor."

Ark was silent for a moment. Caina endured the needle jabbing in and out of her flesh. Then he said, "Something's happening there."

"Such as?"

"There are three dozen ships in port right now," said Ark. "Usually the crews mingle and get drunk and brawl together. From what I gathered, there's only one crew at the Sign of the Anchor right now. They drive off anyone else who tries to drink there."

"Is that odd?" said Caina. "Maybe they don't like company."

"It's very odd," said Ark. "Sailors usually hate landsmen, not each other."

"So there's something at the Sign that they don't want anyone else to see," said Caina.

"I asked around," said Ark. "Apparently they come from a ship called the Lynx, which has been in port for the last three months."

"Three months?" said Caina. She thought for a moment. "They must be trying to sell something, and haven't had any luck. Which means they're smugglers."

"Or pirates."

"Or pirates," agreed Caina. "I don't see why Sister Tadaia thinks the pyromancer might be hiding there."

"I looked around," said Ark. "The building stinks of burned pork."

"Or flesh," said Caina. This time her grimace had nothing to do with the damned needle stabbing into her shoulder.

"In the alley behind the Sign, there are char marks on the flagstones," said Ark. "And grease stains, as well. As if a burned corpse was dragged into the alley."

"Just like the man Valgorix found outside the Inn," said Caina. "I'll bet we'll find his killers inside the Sign of the Anchor." She sighed. "But probably not our pyromancer."

"Done," said Ark, straightening up. "We ought to do the one on your hip."

Caina nodded, adjusted the blanket, and rolled to a sitting position. She hiked up the blanket far enough to expose her left leg and wounded hip, and managed to keep the rest of herself covered.

Ark stared at her leg, his face expressionless. He stared for so long that Caina felt the blood begin to burn in her cheeks. What was he seeing? His dead wife, perhaps? For a stunned instant Caina thought he was going to lean over and kiss her. This had been a mistake, she should have found a woman capable of treating her wounds…

Or had it been a mistake? If he kissed her now, should she stop him? Did she even want to?

And then Caina realized what he was staring at.

A rope of twisted, pinkish-white scars wound its way around her hip and across her belly. It almost looked like a belt. They thickened as they sloped downward across her stomach. It had been almost eight years, and sometimes Caina could still feel the scalpel blades digging through skin and muscle.

"Those are cruel scars," said Ark quietly.

"They started on the hips," said Caina, "drawing blood, bit by bit." Her voice seemed to come from very far away. "But from what I understand, blood drawn from the womb of a virgin girl has the greatest utility for necromancy. So they moved there. I thought I was going to die. I hoped I would die." She blinked a few times. "Have you…have you ever screamed for so long that you couldn't remember ever doing anything else?"

"No," said Ark. "Gods."

Caina looked away. "Let's talk about something else."

Ark nodded and stood up. He knelt beside the bed and started cleaning the gash on her hip. Caina gritted her teeth as the hot wine splashed into the wound. "It's longer than the other, but shallower. It should heal even quicker than the other."

"Good," said Caina. "I want to go to the Sign of the Anchor tonight."

"It won't heal that quickly," said Ark.

"That doesn't matter," said Caina. Despite herself, she winced as Ark began stitching the wound. "We've got to act now. If the pyromancer starts killing the magi one by one, and consuming their strength…he'll be too strong for us to stop. He might be too strong for us to kill now. And something has to be done. Tadaia and Valgorix are right. Rasadda's going to revolt, and the Legions will come and slaughter the Saddai, unless something is done."

Ark said nothing for a while, concentrating on the work. Then he said, "Do you really think the revolt can be stopped?"

"I don't know," said Caina, "but we have to try."

"If the Sign of the Anchor turns out to be a dead end," said Ark, "what are we going to do then?"

"Then we're going after Gaidan," said Caina.

Ark froze for a moment. "I thought you said it would be too risky."

"It is too risky," said Caina. "But we're running out of time. I saw him last night, when Tadaia and I had our little chat. He was weeping. Begging the Living Flame for forgiveness."

Ark snorted.

"He knows the truth," said Caina, "and if we have to, we'll tear it out of him. And if not him, we'll find Romarion. He knows more than he said, too. One way or another, we're finding the man who killed the Rasadda Ghost circle."

Ark finished and stood up. Caina glanced at her hip, brushing the stitches with a fingertip. "That looks good."

"I've had a lot of practice," said Ark. "You should get some rest."

"And so should you," said Caina. "We're going to need it."

CHAPTER 22
DEAD MEN AND ALLEYS

Fortunately, Sairzan's second best suite of rooms had a balcony as well, one that looked towards Corazain's pyramid. After night fell, Caina and Ark went over the balcony and down the rope, into Rasadda's pyre-lit nights. Caina's shoulder ached, forcing her to take extra care, but Ark's stitches held. She dropped into the street, cloak blurring around her.

"Which way?" murmured Caina.

"We'll go around the west side of Arzaidanir's pyramid," said Ark. "The longer way around, but we'll avoid most of the slums that way."

"And hopefully the Sons of Corazain," said Caina.

"Yes," said Ark. He beckoned, and they went into the night. Ark had a solid knowledge of Rasadda's layout, and he led Caina through a maze of alleys and back streets. More than once they saw groups of men prowling the streets, swords and torches in hand, and Caina and Ark lurked in the shadows until they had passed.

The air began to smell of salt and tar, and they came to Rasadda's docks. They lacked the unrelieved black of the rest of Rasadda, and Caina supposed that foreigners had built most of the structures here. She saw dozens of ships floating in the harbor, dimly illuminated in the pyramids' fiery glows. They passed warehouses, and taverns filled with the sound of laughter and carousing.

"Here," said Ark.

The Sign of the Anchor was a three story building of timber and mortared stone, a board painted with a gray anchor swinging over the door. No lights shone in the windows. Very faintly, just over the smell of salt and tar, Caina caught the stench of burnt meat. She stared at the tavern, thinking.

"What is it?"

"Hear that?"

Ark frowned. "I don't hear anything."

"Exactly. Are sailors' taverns usually quiet places?"

Ark shook his head.

"We'll go through the back," said Caina. They crossed to the alley behind the tavern. Empty crates and barrels leaned up against the walls, worn and splintered. The burnt smell was stronger back here, the air almost greasy with it. Caina saw a dark door in the wall, and reached into her belt for her lockpicks.

Then the door swung open. Caina froze, and light flooded into the alley. Two men backed out, carrying one end of a wrapped bundle about the size of a corpse. Both had the rough, tanned looks of sailors. Or pirates, more probably. Two more men came out, holding the front end of the bundle, followed by a fifth man.

"Damn it, lift," said one of the men. "My back is killing me. Lift, damn your hide."

"I am lifting," said another man, "maybe you ought to…"

"Gentlemen, gentlemen," said the fifth man, leaning against the door. His voice was smooth and cultured, and his clothes looked finer. "If you keep opening your mouths to whine, I am going to have to hit you, and that will be unpleasant for us all."

"Why don't you carry these bastards?"

"Because I am the captain, and I don't carry things," said the fifth man. He took a quick sip from a flask, which vanished into a pocket of his coat. "The cart's just around the…"

He saw Caina and Ark right about then. He snarled a curse, yanking a cutlass from the scabbard at his belt, while his men yelled and drew their weapons. Ark's broadsword flew from its scabbard, but Caina was faster. She yanked a knife from her belt, threw back her arm, and flung.

The blade buried itself in the wood of the door, quivering a half-inch from the captain's ear.

"If I had wanted to kill you," said Caina, disguising her voice, "that would have been in your throat."

No one said anything for a few moments.

"Indeed it would have," said the captain, stepping away from the door. "And since I remain among the world of the living, I can only assume that you and your hulking friend desire something else. I do hope that you're not selling anything. I detest merchants. Only scoundrels become merchants. Honest men become thieves."

The captain both looked and sounded Nighmarian. He reminded her, oddly, of Septimus Romarion.

"A Ghost," said one of the pirates, voice strangled. "That short fellow.

He's one of the Emperor's Ghosts."

"He?" said the captain, frowning. He squinted. "No. That's a woman."

Caina blinked. "I…"

"A gentleman can always discern a lady, and I am nothing if not a gentleman," said the captain. He yanked the knife from the door, swaggered to Caina, and presented it to her handle-first with a sweeping bow. "Maltaer, captain of the Lynx, at your service."

Caina took the knife and slid it back into her belt. To her surprise, Maltaer took her hand and planted a kiss upon the gloved fingers.

"I suppose you'll be unable to reveal your name?" said Maltaer. "Alas." He straightened and took step back. "And since you have not come to kill me, nor are you trying to sell me shoddy merchandise of questionable provenance, I can only conclude that you have come to talk."

"I have questions for you," said Caina, trying not to let his unusual talent for observation rattle her.

"Splendid!" said Maltaer. "As you might have guessed, I myself am very fond of talk. Let us therefore retire to my chambers for civilized conversation. I have a very fine wine on hand, and you may rid yourself of those cumbersome clothes. I am entirely certain that you have a lovely face under that cloak, which I would like to see, perhaps along with the rest of you, which is no doubt just as lovely."

"For a gentlemen," said Caina, "you are unusually forward."

"I prefer to think of myself as bold. And the ladies prefer to think of me as dashing. Which I am, of course."

The pirates developed amused expressions during their captain's soliloquy. No doubt they were used to his rambling grandiloquence. Still, they looked like hard men, and hard men rarely followed a leader unworthy of respect. He was playing a game with her, Caina realized. Well, if Maltaer wanted to play, then Caina could play.

"Very well," said Caina, "but if you are trying to charm me, you are doing a poor job of it."

"Would you care for flowers, perhaps?" said Maltaer. "Or shall I write you poetry? Or bring you jewels, or rare wines?"

"I have no use for flowers," said Caina, "and poetry bores me. Jewels are of no use for a Ghost, and wine gives me a headache. If you wish to charm me, no, there is only one thing that I truly desire."

"The embrace of a strong man, perhaps?" said Maltaer. "Vigorous children to look after you in your old age? It is in my power to give you both."

"No," said Caina. She did want children, though, and his words had stung her, but long practice kept it hidden beneath the snarling hiss of her voice. "No, I am a simple woman, of simple tastes and needs. I merely desire the answers to a few questions."

Maltaer sighed. "Alas, that is frightfully dull. Though at least cheap."

"Some kinds of knowledge are not cheaply bought."

"No," said Maltaer with a sudden grin. "Very well, my dark lady. Ask your questions, and your humble servant shall answer to the best of his limited powers."

"First, what's in that bundle?" said Caina.

Maltaer gestured, and one of his men bent over the bundle and pulled open the canvas.

The faces of two dead men stared into the night. Caina walked closer, examined their features. After a moment she recognized both men. They had been with Lord Nicephorus at the banquet.

"Since I doubt that you are grave robbers," said Caina, "I assume you killed these men?"

"And cheerfully, I might add," said Maltaer.

"Who were they?"

"The fat fellow on the left is Sontanus, the one of the right Malaphon. Both were Nighmarian-born merchants of considerable wealth, and close confidants of our beloved Lord Governor."

"And why did you kill them?" said Caina.

"Because they were the honorless scum of the earth," said Maltaer. "In short, because they were slavers."

Ark stepped to her side, his face an empty mask, his eyes on fire.

"Slavers. These men were slave traders?" said Caina.

"Oh, yes," said Maltaer. "Rasadda is so overcrowded these days, and so many people are going hungry. Sontanus and Malaphon could find men and women willing to sell their children for a few coins. But less than you might think. So they snatched people off the streets, locked them in fetters, and shipped them away. They especially liked to go after girls and young women. It seems there is a taste for Saddai girls among the Alqaarin and the Anshani."

"Does Nicephorus know about this?" said Caina.

"Nicephorus?" laughed Maltaer. "Nicephorus is in on it. He's taking ten percent off the top."

"What?" said Caina. She remembered Nicephorus complaining that he could not legalize slavery. Apparently he had decided to dispense with the law.

Maltaer licked his lips. "When our enterprising Lord Governor came to Rasadda, he decided to wring every last coin he could from his devoted subjects. So he expelled the Saddai peasants from their humble homes and converted their lands to pasture. He did not expect the peasants to flood the city. But, alas, Nicephorus saw a chance to make even more money. So he invited certain slave traders to the city and promised them protection from Imperial law, in exchange for ten percent of their profits." He gave the corpses a casual kick. "Since then, fellows like this have been harvesting their merchandise from the hungry and the desperate."

"Do you have proof of this?" said Caina.

"Of course," said Maltaer. "I always thought someone like you might turn up one day." He pointed to one of his men. "You. Go get the papers."

The pirate nodded and vanished into the Sign, returning a moment later with a small bundle of papers. Caina took them, stepped closer to the light, and leafed through them. Letters. Pages torn from ledgers. Bills of sale and lading. Nicephorus had made a fortune from selling beef and cheese and leather, but he had made another fortune from selling children kidnapped from Rasadda's streets.

Caina decided, then and there, that she was going to kill Nicephorus. The Emperor had sent Ghosts to kill governors who supported slave traders before. She would need to work out a proper way to do it.

But once she had, Nicephorus would not live out the day.

"I do so enjoy reading," said Caina, "and a bundle of letters would indeed be a charming gift."

"I thought so," said Maltaer. "Do keep them." He grinned. "May I assume that Lord Nicephorus's residence in the realms of the living shall be...ah, brief?"

"Of course not," said Caina. "The Emperor keeps neither spies nor assassins. When Nicephorus has a tragic yet fatal accident, the Emperor will have had nothing to do with it. Nor will anyone suggest otherwise. Am I clear?"

"As a lagoon on a bright day," said Maltaer, "and no doubt just as lovely, beneath that cloak."

Caina resisted the temptation to roll her eyes. "Fine words, my dashing captain. But I would prefer different words. Specifically, the answers to more questions."

Maltaer sighed. "Like all women, you are insatiable. But ask your questions, dark lady, for if anyone can satisfy you, it is I."

Caina doubted that he meant the questions. "Why are you killing slavers?"

Maltaer smiled, but his eyes glittered, the same sort of menacing glower she saw in Ark's eyes. "I am an honest pirate, dark lady. And I detest slavers. Pity the crew of the slave ship that crosses my bow. For the sharks feast well on that day. And then I deliver a load of free men to my next port."

"During your raids," said Ark, cutting in to Caina's response, "have you ever freed a woman named Tanya? She would be of Szaldic descent, with blue eyes and black hair."

"Tanya?" said Maltaer, face thoughtful. "No, I am afraid not, my hulking friend. Szaldic slaves are rare in this part of the world. Most go to

New Kyre, or to Anshan, but not to Istarinmul or to Alqaarin. Especially now that Nicephorus has flooded the market with Saddai slaves."

"I see," said Ark, lapsing back into silence.

"Ah, a loved one?" said Maltaer. "I am sorry, my hulking friend. You see, my dark lady? Slave traders are the scum of the world, and any honest man who finds one should put him to the sword. So that is why I killed these men."

Caina nodded. "You burn the corpses. Why?"

"About a year ago people started turning up dead, burned to death," said Maltaer. "The work of some mad sorcerer, I presume. A horrible way to die. Naturally I thought of doing the same to the slave traders. But fuel is expensive, and dragging them up the pyramids while they are alive is far too much work. So instead we kill them, drag their bodies up the stairs, and roast them for a bit in the sorcerous pyre. Then we deposit the corpse in a convenient location and make our escape. That way the mad sorcerer takes the blame for our heroic deeds, and we escape to fight another day. He already has much blood on his hands, so why not a little more? Lord Nicephorus would not appreciate our valiant acts."

"No, he would not," said Caina. "I commend your cunning."

Maltaer bowed again. "You warm my heart, my dark lady."

"How many have you killed in this way?" said Caina.

"Seven scoundrels have met their just fate at our hands. Not counting the fine gentlemen at our feet, of course."

Caina did the calculations in her head. With seven dead...that meant the only people the pyromancer had killed were Rasadda's Ghost circle, Vanio and Romarion's business partners, and the one magus. That meant the pyromancer had had contact with the magi, the Ghosts, Romarion's circle of merchants, and most probably the Sons of Corazain. But who fit that description?

"Who do you think is behind the other burning deaths?" said Caina.

Maltaer shrugged. "Some mad sorcerer, no doubt."

"Yes," said Caina, "but which mad sorcerer?"

"I do not know," said Maltaer, "but were I to guess, I would blame someone within the Magisterium. They are almost worse than slavers, cruel and wicked."

"I know it well," said Caina. Better than he knew it, probably.

"In the Empire we have the Magisterium," said Maltaer, "and in Istarinmul they have alchemists, in Anshan occultists, in New Kyre storm dancers and storm singers, and in Rasadda they used to have Ashbringers. But they are all sorcerers, if different kinds, and sorcerers are always wicked men. And since the Ashbringers are all dead, that leaves only the Magisterium."

He made a compelling sort of sense, if not for the fact that neither

Kalastus nor Ephaeron could have been behind the deaths. Caina doubted that Maltaer knew anything useful about the Sons of Corazain or the Ghosts of Rasadda. But Romarion had been a merchant captain, hadn't he? Perhaps Maltaer knew something of him.

"Another question," said Caina. "Do you know of a merchant named Septimus Romarion?"

Maltaer blinked.

He looked at his men.

His men looked back at him.

And they all burst into roaring laughter.

"A merchant?" said Maltaer. "Is he calling himself a merchant?"

"From what my sources have told me, yes," said Caina.

"Septimus Romarion the merchant," said Maltaer, still shaking his head. "My dark lady, Romarion is a pirate. He likes to masquerade as a respectable merchant now, but he's still turns quite a profit on stolen cargoes smuggled through Mors Crisius. He even has a full time agent there, a man named Vanio. Romarion used to ply the Alqaarin Sea, and has a price on his head in every port from here to Istarinmul. We worked together from time to time, and helped each other out when the Alqaarin got it into their heads to hunt us down." He sighed. "Romarion was a fine pirate, generous with the loot, and wouldn't do business with slavers. I liked him until he turned to a dishonest line of work."

"Why did he retire from piracy?" said Caina. She wondered if Romarion had known about Vanio's slave-dealing on the side.

"About five years ago, a storm drove him to an island about two hundred miles south of here," said Maltaer. "Unmapped island. Off the charts. Probably no one had set foot on it for centuries. Romarion and his crew found a ruin there. Some old-time Saddai fortress, still intact. Apparently it was old Corazain's secret retreat, and when Corazain burned down Rasadda, everyone who knew of its location perished with the city. Full of those ugly Saddai statues, and old books, too…"

His words hit Caina like a thunderbolt.

"Wait," said Caina. "Wait, wait just a minute. Did you say books?"

Maltaer bowed. "That I did. The library of Corazain the Ashbringer himself. Even a couple of books written by old Corazain himself, from what I gather. Well, rich fools will pay a pretty penny for both old Saddai statues and old Saddai books, so Romarion and his crew made a killing. They all retired and went into business together. Poor fools."

"Those books," said Caina. "Corazain's books. Who did Romarion sell them to do?"

"Alas, I know not," said Maltaer. "Some rich scholar, no doubt." He laughed. "He got enough money for them, and those old statues, that's for certain. I'm jealous."

"Don't be," said Caina, her mind racing. "I can tell you right now that those books brought Romarion nothing but woe."

"Ah," said Maltaer. "My answers have failed to charm you, I see."

"Not at all," said Caina. "You've been a tremendous help."

Maltaer brightened. "Have I?" He bowed over her hand again, kissing the gloved fingers. "Then perhaps we might withdraw to…"

Caina opened her mouth to answer, and a breeze whispered through the alley.

Her skin began tingling.

Caina stepped back in alarm, looking back and forth. She half-expected to see Maltaer, or perhaps Ark, erupt into raging flames. But the tingling was faint, distant, rather like the breeze itself. Maltaer looked up at the sky, his face troubled.

"You can feel that?" said Caina.

"Aye," said Maltaer. "That's sorcery."

"I can feel it too," said one of the pirates. "Like a prickling in my bones."

Caina frowned. This did not feel nearly as violent as Ostros's death, nor even the spell Kalastus had flung at her, yet it felt somehow…larger. Like the first hint of a mighty ocean swell.

Or the first few gentle drops of rain that heralded a storm.

"Someone is working mighty sorcery," muttered Maltaer. "Alas, my dark lady, I fear our courtship will have to wait until another time. Best to be indoors tonight, I think."

"And I thank you for your answers," said Caina. "But my business has become urgent."

"One warning, my charming dark lady," said Maltaer. "Your hulking friend. Someone is looking for him."

"Who?" said Caina.

"Mercenaries," said Maltaer. "The Black Wolves. A bad sort. They wandered past the Sign earlier today, and asked for someone who matched your friend's description. And they were led by a strange fellow, wrapped up in a cloak with a hollow voice. I was sure they meant your friend harm, which means that they undoubtedly mean you harm. I would beware them, for they are dangerous men."

"I know," said Caina. "I thank you for the warning."

Maltaer bowed, and he and his sailors retreated back into the Sign, dragging the dead slavers after them. Caina whirled and ran to the street, Ark hurrying after her.

"What is it?" said Ark.

"I'm a fool, I'm a blind fool," said Caina. "How could I have not seen it earlier?"

"Nicephorus is a slaver," said Ark.

"I know, but that's not important now," said Caina.

"What?" said Ark. "The man is a monster, and..."

"Listen to me!" said Caina, looking around. "I couldn't figure out how someone had learned pyromancy. The Magisterium slaughtered all the Ashbringers and no doubt destroyed their books and scrolls. But Romarion got lucky, found an untouched ruin. I thought he had only plundered statues from the ruins. I never thought he might have found a book. How could I have been so blind?"

"What's so important about these books?" said Ark.

"Because our pyromancer learned his spells from those books."

Ark blinked, and then his breath hissed through his teeth.

"That explains how the pyromancer learned his art," said Caina. "And that's how we're going to find him, Ark. When Romarion tells us who bought those books, we'll have our pyromancer. Think about it. The murderer knows that pyromancy is a forbidden art, so he starts by killing Romarion's partners, everyone who knows he bought the book. And when the Ghosts start investigating, he kills them too. And if Tadaia is right and a pyromancer can devour stolen life force, he's started killing the magi to steal their arcane strength. But we've got to find Romarion, now."

The breeze increased in strength for a moment, and the tingling against Caina's skin pulsed.

"The breeze," said Ark, his voice troubled. "It's blowing in the wrong direction for this time of night."

"Remember Ostros?" said Caina. "There was a breeze right before the spell killed him. Whatever's causing this can't be good. We've got to get to Romarion at once."

"How will we get into his mansion?" said Ark.

"Oh, we'll find a way," said Caina. "We'll find a way even if I have to tear down his doors with my bare hands."

CHAPTER 23
BURNING SWORDS

Maltaer had promised her charming gifts, so Caina stole his wagon.

It was a battered light wagon, harnessed to a pair of sturdy horses. No doubt Maltaer had planned to use it for convenient corpse transportation. Caina needed a fast way to reach Romarion's mansion, and the empty wagon fit the bill. Ark swung into the driver's seat, taking the reins, and Caina climbed up beside him.

"This isn't stealthy," said Ark. The wagon creaked and groaned with every step of the horses. He drew his broadsword, gripping it in one hand while he held the reins with the other.

"The time for stealth has passed," said Caina. "Cover your face, though. If Romarion sees you, he might realize who I am."

Ark nodded and tore a strip from his cloak, winding it about his face in a crude mask. Then he snapped the reins, urging the horses to a run. They surged forward, the wagon rattling. Every bounce and jolt made Caina's hip and shoulder ache, but she didn't care. The strange breeze still whistled through the streets, and her skin tingled and crawled with the presence of sorcery.

She thought the pyromancer might have decided to rid himself of Romarion.

They passed a few knots of people. Some were Sons of Corazain, looking for trouble, torches and weapons in hand. Others were common Saddai peasants, drawn out by the strange breeze. Yet all looked fearfully at the sky as the flames of the torches danced and flickered.

They came to Romarion's home. The mansion lay silent and dark, the windows empty, the grounds draped in shadows. Ark reined in the horses, and the wagon creaked to a stop.

"Ark," whispered Caina, "look."

The gate to the grounds stood open and unattended.

Ark nodded and climbed off the seat, sword raised. Caina gripped a knife in either hand, and followed him. The mansion's front doors lay in shattered ruin. Someone had taken an axe to them.

The faint smell of burnt flesh drifted in the air.

Caina hissed and stepped through the shattered doors.

A crimson glow from the pyramid fires shone through the skylight, illuminating the cavernous atrium. Dark, huddled shapes lay motionless on the floor. Dead bodies, Caina saw. The burned smell was stronger in here, though not so overpowering as it had been in Vanio's townhouse.

"Guards," muttered Ark, turning one of the corpses over. "Romarion's guards."

"That one was his cook," said Caina. "They died fighting. All of them have weapons. But…there's no blood." Caina frowned, knelt, and tore open a dead guard's tunic. "Look at this."

A sword thrust between the ribs had killed the guard. Yet there was no blood. Instead the wound looked seared, the flesh around the cut charred and blackened.

"It's like he was stabbed with a red-hot iron," said Caina.

"Who fights with a hot iron?" said Ark.

"I don't know," said Caina. She took a quick look over the rest of the bodies. All of them had the strange wounds. "This is still sorcery, I'm sure…but different. Something new."

"Romarion is probably dead, then," said Ark.

Caina felt a dead neck. "Still warm. They can't have been dead for more than an hour." She rose. "Romarion might be alive. We'll check his…"

A boot clicked on the mosaic floor.

Caina whirled, her blades coming up, while Ark lifted his sword. A man walked into the atrium, a sword dangling from one hand. His face was slack, expressionless, his eyes glassy. Caina had last seen that expression on the face of her father. He wore black armor, the sigil of an opened book with two eyes upon the pages enameled on the breastplate.

A Magisterial Guard, one of the guards of the magi.

"Name yourself," said Ark.

The Magisterial Guard took another step forward, lifting his sword. Caina felt a sudden crawling tingle against her skin, a wind whipping through the atrium.

And the sword's blade erupted into snarling flame, filling the atrium with stark light.

Ark raised his sword, and the Magisterial Guard ran at him. Caina flung her knife, aiming for his throat, but her blade dug a furrow along the

Guard's jaw. The Guard staggered for a half-step, but his blank expression did not change. The burning sword hammered at Ark, and he ducked and blocked, flinching away from the flames, squinting into the weapon's glare.

Caina yanked the dagger from her boot, darted forward, and drove the blade into a gap in the black armor. The Guard staggered again, but still showed no sign of pain. Ark took advantage of the opening and brought his sword down in a massive blow. The Guard's sword hand fell to the floor, still clutching the burning blade. The Guard did not blink, did not even scream. Instead he merely ducked to reach for the burning weapon with his left hand.

Ark's sword came down on the back of his neck.

The burning sword sputtered and went out. Caina stepped around the pooling blood and snatched up her throwing knife. Ark wrenched his sword free from the dead man's neck with a crackling noise, the blade red and wet.

"Gods," said Ark, "what was wrong with him?"

"He was mind-controlled," said Caina. "Sorcery. He had no will left of his own, was nothing but a puppet. The Magisterium does it sometimes."

"And that sword?"

"Pyromancy," said Caina. "That much is plain." Ark reached for the weapon. "No! Don't touch it." She waved her palm over it, and felt a sudden, stabbing tingle in her fingers. "It's been enspelled. I don't know what it will do if you touch it. Maybe that's how the Guard's mind was enslaved."

"The magi want Romarion dead?" said Ark.

"Or the pyromancer enslaved the Magisterial Guards and sent them to kill Romarion," said Caina. She gritted her teeth in frustration. "Damn it. If he's still alive, we've got to find him. Let's…"

Harsh firelight flooded the atrium.

Four more Magisterial Guards stood in the doorway, their faces slack and empty, swords burning like the fires of hell. More Magisterial Guards stepped out of the doors leading to the dining room. They lifted their swords, the weapons ablaze with sorcerous fire.

"The stairs!" said Caina. "Go!"

They raced for the stairs, and the Magisterial Guards followed in silent pursuit. Halfway up the stairs Caina whirled and flung a knife. It caught the foremost Guard in the throat. The man took another step, and another, and then fell to his knees, face expressionless as his life drained away. Ark sprang past her, sword meeting their burning blades once, twice, a third time. Then a Magisterial Guard tumbled down the stairs, crashing into the others. Another Guard's clothes caught fire, but the man showed no pain as his tunic sizzled and smoldered beneath his breastplate.

"Go!" said Caina.

"We'll be trapped!" said Ark, his sweat pouring down his brow.

"We've got to cut our way out."

"No," said Caina. "No, there's too many of them."

"Out the windows?" said Ark. He crossed blades with a Magisterial Guard, tripped the man, and stepped back. The Guards hesitated for a moment as the fallen man clambered back to his feet, and then resumed their climb. "They'll cut us down, or burn through the rope."

"I have a better idea," said Caina. At least, she hoped it was a better idea. "Get ready to run."

She backed to the second floor landing. A tapestry hung from the wall there, thick and heavy, and Caina cut it free with her daggers. She took the heavy folds in both hands, ran past Ark, and flung the tapestry as hard as she could. The Guards raised their burning swords to block, and the heavy cloth settled over their blades.

And promptly caught fire.

The Magisterial Guards thrashed, trying to tear free of the burning tapestry. Yet their faces remained eerily calm, and not one of them screamed, or even so much as grunted.

"Go!" said Caina. "The third floor."

She raced up the stairs, daggers still in hand, Ark following after her. She saw more bodies lying on the stairs, some in servants' livery, others in the garb of Romarion's hired guards. A dead Magisterial Guard lay over the corpses. Apparently Romarion's men had gone down fighting.

As Caina reached the third-floor landing, the Magisterial Guards cut their way free of the tapestry. She ran, boots hammering against the marble floor, and came to a locked door beneath an iron chandelier. Romarion's study.

"This one," said Caina, shoving the daggers back into her boots and fumbling for her tools. "The lock…"

Ark bellowed a curse, shoved her aside, and hammered the pommel of his broadsword into the door. The wood shuddered, and he brought his pommel down twice more. The door splintered away from the handle and lock, and swung open with a groan.

"I should have brought you along the first time," said Caina.

Firelight flooded into the hallway as the Magisterial Guards reached the top of the stairs. Caina kicked past the ruined door and into Romarion's study. The shutters stood open, the strange breeze blowing into the room. Otherwise, it looked much the same as she remembered, with the simple furniture, the cutlasses and the mementoes of the sea dangling from the walls.

And the massive Strigosti trapbox sitting against the far wall.

"Move that desk," said Caina, hurrying to the trapbox. She yanked out a dagger and began prying at the carved plate covering the machinery. "Get it against the wall but leave enough room for us to fit behind it."

Ark scowled at her, but he obeyed, dragging the desk towards the wall. Caina pulled on the dagger. The plate began to peel away from the chest. The sound of running footsteps in the hallway grew louder, and firelight began to leak through the open door.

"This is a dead end," said Ark. "What are you doing?"

"Get behind the desk," said Caina. "Right now."

"That's a Strigosti trapbox!" said Ark. "If you're not careful it'll go off in your face! What…"

Caina wrenched away the plate.

"Oh, gods," said Ark. He dove behind the desk.

Caina stood and smashed her boot into the box's mechanical innards just as the Magisterial Guards stormed through the door. The trapbox gave a horrid mechanical screech, and the exposed workings began to move, spinning faster and faster. Caina rolled over the top of Romarion's desk and landed squarely on atop of Ark.

A heartbeat later there was another screech, followed by a long series of clicks and hisses. The desk shuddered as something slammed into it. Caina waited until the noises stopped, and then levered herself up on an elbow to look.

Empty black slits, dozens of them, now covered the Strigosti box. Gleaming razor blades, coated with green grease, quivered in the furniture and walls. The Magisterial Guards stood motionless, burning swords hanging loose in their hands. Their armor had stopped the storm of blades, but the razors had driven into their uncovered faces, their skin slowly turning black from poison. One by one they toppled, falling to the carpet, which caught fire.

"What's happened?" said Ark, trying to sit up. Caina stood, taking care to keep from touching any of the grease-smeared blades.

"They're all dead," said Caina. "Don't touch any of the razors."

Ark stood, his eyes a little wild. "It killed all of them?"

"I think so," said Caina, hurrying to the Strigosti trapbox. The foot-long blades had sprouted from its sides again. Taking care to avoid them, she opened the massive lid and reached inside. The money and gems were gone. No doubt Romarion had taken them when he fled, but the papers and ledgers remained. Caina scooped them up and hurried to the door, leaping over the flames.

Ark waited in the hallway. "I have said it before, Countess, and I shall say it again. You are an absolute madwoman."

"Oh, yes," agreed Caina, "but we're still alive, aren't we?" For now, anyway. She tied the papers into a bundle and tucked them under her arm. "We can look over these later. Let's try to find Romarion, or his corpse, before the place burns down around us."

"Those Magisterial Guards," said Ark, "who did this to them?"

"I don't know," said Caina. They passed another dead servant lying on the floor. "You saw those swords. The pyromancer, probably. It wouldn't surprise me if there were a lot of dead magi lying around the Magisterium chapterhouse."

"Unless the pyromancer is a magus," said Ark.

"Either way, we've got to stop him," said Caina. She still felt the distant tingle, and knew that somewhere the pyromancer was summoning a tremendous amount of arcane force. "This isn't like the other murders. I wonder if his reason has finally been burned away, and so…"

She heard a soft thump, not very loud. Caina turned, dagger in hand. She crossed the hallway and threw open a door. It opened into a bedroom, the same bedroom she had used to break in a few days ago. Caina caught a glimpse of motion, saw someone ducking under the bed.

"Hold!" Caina shouted, disguising her voice.

The dark shape froze, and Caina heard a terrified sob.

Moving closer, she saw a young woman huddled in the corner, dressed in a soot-smudged nightgown. The face looked familiar, and Caina realized the young woman was one of Romarion's cooks.

"Don't kill me," sobbed the young woman, raising her hands to shield her face, "please, please don't kill me, not like the others, not like the others…"

"Who are you?" said Caina. "Speak."

"My…my name is Lucia," she said, "I'm a cook, I'm a cook in Master Romarion's service. I don't know anything, I swear I don't, please, please don't hurt me…."

"We're not going to hurt you," said Caina. "We have come to rescue your master." It was close enough to the truth.

Lucia looked up. "You have?"

"Tell us what happened here," said Caina.

Lucia nodded, began to speak, and sobbed again. She took a deep breath. "It…it…Master Romarion was scared, was planning to leave Rasadda before the week ended."

"Why?"

"I don't know properly, but I heard him speaking," said Lucia. "All his business partners were being murdered, found burned to death, and Master Romarion was afraid they would come for him next. So he was going to sail for the Imperial capital."

"What happened here tonight?" said Caina.

"I was in bed," said Lucia, "and then I heard screaming, so I got up and went to look. All those men in black armor had hacked down the door and were killing the guards and the other servants. Their swords…their swords were burning! I've never seen anything like it. They'll kill you if they find you."

"They tried," said Caina. "We killed them all."

Lucia shuddered and shrunk against the wall.

"Romarion," said Caina. "What happened to Romarion? It is urgent that we find him. Is he dead?"

"I don't know," said Lucia. "I...don't think so." She swallowed. "Did you find his...his body?"

"No," said Caina.

"Then he probably fled," said Lucia. "Master Romarion was always afraid that his enemies would come for him. He kept money in an iron box in his study, along with a rope, so he could go out the window if they ever came to kill him."

Caina glanced at Ark. "The window was open in his study." She looked back at Lucia. "Where do you think Romarion might have gone? Does he have a hiding place prepared in the city?"

"I don't know," said Lucia. "I suppose that Master Romarion would go to his friends, if they were not all dead already."

"I see," said Caina, straightening up.

"Don't kill me," said Lucia, "I've told you everything, I swear."

"I already said I'm not going to kill you," said Caina, annoyed. She reached for the purse tucked into her belt. She had not wanted to leave Ephaeron's money sitting around the Inn, and one never knew when bribe money might come in handy. She produced a single platinum coin, and Lucia's eyes got wide. "Take this, and get out of the city immediately. The Saddai are going to revolt soon, and if Romarion's enemy knows that you are still alive, he might kill you. Do you understand me?"

"Yes, sir," said Lucia.

"Take only what you need, and go now."

Lucia gathered up her nightgown and fled.

"She's probably going to loot a few things on her way out, you know," said Ark.

"Let her rob the entire place, for all I care," said Caina. "We've got to go."

"Where?" said Ark.

"I know where Romarion is."

Ark frowned.

"A man in trouble flees to his friends," said Caina, walking back into the hall. "But the pyromancer killed Romarion's friends and partners. So that leaves only his old business associates."

Fortunately, no one had stolen their stolen wagon. Caina secured Romarion's papers alongside Maltaer's documents, and Ark started the horses into motion, pushing them as fast as he dared.

The breeze still whistled through Rasadda's streets, the tingles pressing against Caina's skin.

CHAPTER 24
BOOK OF THE ASHBRINGERS

The wagon stopped before the Sign of the Anchor. The windows were shuttered and barred, though Caina saw faint glimmers of light leaking through the cracks. Ark tied the horses and drew his broadsword.

"How are we going to do this?" said Ark.

"Easily," said Caina. "You're going to kick down the door, I'm going to tell Maltaer to take us to Romarion, and if he's here, he's going to tell us who the pyromancer is."

Ark's mouth twisted. "And if they disagree?"

"That's what this is for," said Caina, pointing at Ark's broadsword. "Oh, keep your face covered, and don't speak unless you must. If Romarion is here, I don't want him to recognize you."

Ark nodded and tugged his improvised mask back into the place. They walked to the Sign's front door, and Ark began hammering with the pommel of his sword. "Open, in the name of the Emperor!"

The door remained closed.

Ark shrugged, and started kicking. After four or five blows, the door splintered in its frame, and Ark put his shoulder to it. The door shuddered open, and Ark went through, Caina right behind them.

The Sign's common room was spacious, well-lit from a pair of fireplaces, and held a dozen pirates, all of whom were holding weapons. Caina stepped past Ark, a knife ready in her hand.

"Let's remain civil," she hissed in her masked voice. "There's no sense in bloodshed."

"There's a score of us and two of you," said one pirate.

"This is so," said Caina. "But come at us and at least one of you is going to die. Maybe more. Well, who wants to volunteer? Anyone?"

No one volunteered.

"Or someone could go get Maltaer," said Caina.

"My dark lady, I am here," said Maltaer, appearing at the top of the stairs. He descended, smiling. "You stole my wagon, you know."

"I happened to need it," said Caina. "And you did promise me many charming gifts."

Maltaer laughed, and pressed his hand to his heart. "Alas! That is just like a woman. Give, and give, and yet she demands ever more." His men laughed. "So, my dark lady, shall we resume our courtship? What would you have of me now?"

"I want to talk to Septimus Romarion."

Maltaer's face went still. "Why would he be here?"

"Because all his business partners have been murdered," said Caina, "and he has nowhere else to go. Remember the mad sorcerer we discussed? He tried to kill Romarion this very night. But you know that already, don't you?"

Maltaer sighed. "I am sure, my dark lady, that you are very beautiful beneath that cowl and mask. But while Septimus and I have our differences, he is still a friend, and it is a grievous thing for one man to betray another."

"I mean Romarion no harm," said Caina. "But I must speak with him. You can still feel the spell coming, can't you? The mad sorcerer is doing something, and I need Romarion's knowledge to stop it."

Maltaer thought it over. "While I am certain that your word is good, my dark lady, I require more. Will you swear to me on whatever you hold dear that you truly mean Romarion no harm?"

Caina nodded. "I swear by the name of the Emperor I server that I have not come to do Romarion harm."

"Very well," said Maltaer. "If you betray your word, may swift ruin befall your Emperor." He beckoned. "This way."

Caina followed Maltaer, Ark trailing after them. The pirate captain led them up the stairs and down a hallway, stopping before a door. Maltaer pushed it open, and they entered a spacious bedroom. Septimus Romarion sat on the bed, head in his hands, his clothes scorched and rumpled.

"Septimus," said Maltaer.

Romarion looked up, blinking. His eyes flicked over Ark and Caina, and grew wide with fright. "Maltaer, you bastard! You brought them here to kill me! No!" His face was almost deranged with terror, just as Ostros's had been. "I won't go without a fight." He surged to his feet, drawing his rapier. "I won't!"

Romarion came at her with the blade, and Caina dodged. As he stepped back to recover his balance, Caina hit him across the jaw with her knife's handle. Romarion stumbled back, spitting blood, and Caina reached inside his guard, seized his wrist, and twisted. The rapier fell from his stunned hand, and Caina turned, sweeping his legs out from under him. Romarion fell with a heavy thump. Caina snatched up the rapier and leveled the blade at his throat. The weapon was a good fit for her hand.

"Ah," breathed Maltaer in admiration. "You must dance exquisitely. Among other things."

"Don't do anything foolish," said Caina. "My friend and I have gone to a great deal of trouble to find you, and it would vex me to no end if you got yourself killed."

"Finish it, then," spat Romarion.

"Do none of you people ever hear a word I say?" said Caina. "I'll repeat myself. I don't want to kill you. I want you to talk. Which would be rather difficult if you were dead."

Confusion replaced fear in Romarion's expression. "Then who are you?"

"That is not important," said Caina. "Suffice it to say that we are Ghosts."

"Ghosts?" said Romarion. "You mean the Emperor's Ghosts? I though that the Ghosts were a story, a fable."

Caina gave his throat a gentle tap with the rapier. "Can a fable hold a blade to your throat? Now get up. You're going to tell us everything you know."

Romarion stood, his face tight. "Why?"

"Because," said Caina, "otherwise the pyromancer is going to cook you like a pig on a spit. Just like he did to your former crew."

Romarion swallowed, his eyes darting back and forth, but nodded. "Can you help me?"

"I won't lie to you. You're in a lot of trouble. We're all in a lot of trouble. But if it is in our power to kill the pyromancer we will do so."

Romarion sighed. "Good enough."

Caina lowered the rapier. "I suggest that you start from the beginning."

Romarion's mouth twisted. "If the rumors about the Ghosts are true, you probably know everything already." He sighed again. "But I used to be a pirate, working the Alqaarin Sea. A few years ago a storm came up, blew my ship off course, and drove us to an uncharted island."

"Where you found an untouched Saddai ruin," said Caina.

Romarion nodded. "And not just a ruin. A palace. A fortress, the stronghold of old Corazain himself. It must have been forgotten after Corazain was killed. The place was stuffed full of statues and treasures. We found the royal insignia of the old Saddai kings, at least a hundred valuable statues, and an entire room full of books…" He shuddered. "I should have thrown the books into the sea when I had the chance."

"I agree," said Caina.

Romarion's eyes were haunted. "And we found Corazain's private chapel. The Ashbringers...everyone says they were insane, but I saw it firsthand. There were statues in that chapel...I think Corazain used his spells to melt blocks of stone around living women, so the stone would harden over their bones. The chapel was full of those stone skeletons."

"He probably stole their lives to fuel his own strength," said Caina. "If a pyromancer uses his art to burn a man alive, he can use the victim's life force to empower himself. Which is what he probably did to your crew. And wanted to do to you."

Romarion shuddered, and nodded.

"So you started to sell the statues," said Caina, gesturing for him to continue.

Romarion rubbed his face. "My crew and I made a pact. We would sell the statues, the jewelry, and the books, and split the profits between us. Since I was the captain, I would take a double share, of course, but otherwise we would split everything. Publius Vanio, my first mate, set himself up in Mors Crisius as a merchant. We smuggled the loot into Mors Crisius's harbor, and Vanio and I found buyers. The jewelry, of course, had no trouble finding a buyer. Nor the statues. It seems that wealthy men in a dozen different nations appreciate Saddai art."

"How much money did you make?" said Caina.

Romarion gave her a little smile. "We made an absolutely enormous amount of money. Even divided among us, it was still a substantial sum. Most of my crew drank and whored their money away, but some of us invested it, went into business. I did well, and so did Vanio. I had thoughts of obtaining a noble title, perhaps founding a minor House. I even tried to seduce a minor noblewoman visiting the city, but it did not go well, alas."

"You never did know how to speak to the ladies," said Maltaer.

"When did the killings start?" said Caina.

Romarion looked away. "A year ago. My crew began turning up dead, one by one. All of them were burned to death. I figured out what was happening. I knew that the pyromancer needed to steal some of my blood for the spell to work, so I kept myself guarded night and day. I tried to warn the others, but they laughed at me, and they all died. I am the last one left. I was about to flee the city when some men attacked my house..."

"Yes, the Magisterial Guards," said Caina. "Sorcery had been used to wipe their minds."

"How did you know?" said Romarion.

"We came from your mansion," said Caina.

Romarion flinched. "And the Guards?"

"All dead."

The blood drained from Romarion's face.

"But they're not important," said Caina. "The books, Romarion. What happened to Corazain's books?"

"Most of them were...just books," said Romarion. "They were written in Old Saddaic, true, but they were just books. There was one that was...different, though. All the books were centuries old, but this one looked as if it had been written yesterday. And it...when I touched it my hands tingled, my skin crawled."

Sorcery. The book had been protected by a warding spell, guarding it from the ravages of time.

"I was curious, so I touched a candle to the cover," said Romarion. "Nothing happened. I tried to light the pages on fire, but the flames could not touch it. Finally I threw it into a fire for an hour. It came out untouched. The statues were valuable. But this...this was priceless."

"So you tried to find a wealthy sorcerer who would buy it," said Caina.

"I had to be careful," said Romarion. "Sorcerers are dangerous, and usually mad, all men know that. But foreign sorcerers are worse. The Magisterium at least pretends to follow the laws of the Empire."

"They do not," said Caina. She felt the pieces beginning to fall together in her head, like a lock opening at last. "So you approached the Magisterium."

Fool, fool, fool.

Romarion seemed to pick up on her sudden anger, and he backed away. "I...started by approaching the local Magisterium, the masters. I did not tell them outright, of course, but asked about the Ashbringers. Ephaeron was adamantly opposed. He spent the better part of an hour lecturing me on the evils of the Ashbringers, how any trace of pyromancy had to be scoured from the face of the earth."

"How fortunate that he was wrong," said Caina.

Romarion flinched. "But the other master...Kalastus. He had bought a dozen of my statues. He seemed at least open to the idea. Finally one night about two years past I mentioned the book...and he insisted upon buying it at once. I sold it to him, then and there, in his study."

In his study.

And at last, all the pieces came together in Caina's mind.

She remembered standing in Kalastus's study, watching the master magus and the merchant argue.

A massive book bound in black leather and polished steel had rested on his desk.

He had tried to rape her, despite the dozen witnesses within ready earshot.

He had slaughtered a score of Saddai before the Imperial Basilica, screaming curses all the while.

Ephaeron claimed that Kalastus had become erratic, unreliable, acting like a man gone provincial.

Acting like a man who had lost his reason.

Or one whose reason gradually had been burned away.

Fool, fool. How could she not have seen it earlier? But she had, hadn't she? She'd known all along it had to be one of the magi, even if she had only now found the proof.

"Kalastus," said Caina, her harsh voice cold and hard. "You sold that damned book to Kalastus." She felt Ark's gaze on her. "You damned fool."

Romarion looked desperate. "You have to understand. I didn't know what would happen. He told me that he intended to destroy it."

"Oh, certainly," said Caina. "Maybe he even intended to. But he looked inside and had to try one of Corazain's spells. Then another, and another, and he became addicted to the power that would burn away his sanity. He knew the other magi would kill him for it. That's why he slaughtered your old crew, to keep the magi from ever finding out about his new powers. All because you didn't throw that book into sea when you had the chance."

"I didn't know," whispered Romarion. "I couldn't have known."

"Oh, no, no one ever does," said Caina. "Not until it's too late." She closed her eyes and mastered herself. Romarion had been a fool, but the blood was on Kalastus's hands.

"Are you going to kill me?" said Romarion.

"For the last time," said Caina, "I already told you that I'm not going to kill you, even though I should. Publius Vanio was trading in slaves, and if Kalastus doesn't kill you, the Ghosts will. Get out of the Empire, Romarion. Go to Istarinmul, or Alqaarin, or even into the barbarian north for all I care. But if Kalastus ever finds you, he will kill you."

Romarion started to answer. "I…"

The tingling against Caina's skin grew stronger, almost to the point of physical pain. The breeze rattling against the windows exploded into a howling gale. A flash of brilliant orange-yellow light came through the window.

Followed an instant later by the roar.

The deafening concussion shook the Sign, dust falling from the rafters, the floor trembling. The roar, louder than any thunderclap, seemed to go on and on. Caina grabbed at the wall to keep her balance, Romarion's blade dangling from one hand.

"What the hell?" said Romarion.

"My dark lady," said Maltaer, "the balcony, this way."

Romarion stared at her in shock. "You're a woman?"

Caina ignored him and followed Maltaer. She heard sounds of shock and surprise coming from the streets below. Maltaer walked to the end of the hallway and threw open the door, and Caina followed him onto the balcony.

She looked into the night sky and blinked in astonishment.

A billowing plume of smoke rose over the city, lit from below by roiling flames. She saw people standing in the streets, gaping in terrified awe at the sky. Caina squinted at the flames, calculating the distances in her head.

It was coming from the Temple of Living Flame.

Caina turned to Ark. "I know where to find Kalastus."

CHAPTER 25
WRATH OF THE BURNING FLAME

Chaos reigned in Rasadda.

Families fled through the streets, clutching their children and their possessions, determined to get away. Others simply stood and stared at the glowing pillar of smoke. Here and there militiamen screamed orders, but no one heeded them. Caina saw Sons of Corazain among the crowds, terror on their faces as they raced for the city's gates. Perhaps the revealed fury of an Ashbringer did not quite meet their expectations.

Ark drove like a madman, reins clenched in one hand, sword in the other. He bellowed threats at anyone who got in their way, waving the broadsword, and they made good time.

"What are we going to do when we find Kalastus?" said Ark.

"That's easy," said Caina. "We're going to kill the murdering bastard."

Ark snorted. "Yes. Very easy. How?"

Good question.

"It will have to be quick," said Caina. "We have to surprise him, kill him before he even knows where there. If he gets a chance to use his powers against us, he could kill us both in the space of three heartbeats. You saw what he did to that crowd, and he didn't even use pyromancy." Caina glanced at Romarion's rapier, lying where she had thrown it into the back of the wagon. "And it will have to be a fatal wound. Tadaia said that he's murdered so many people that he likely has a reservoir of stole life force. He can probably recover from anything less than a killing blow in a few moments."

"And how do we land that killing blow?" said Ark.

"We stab him in the back," said Caina.

"Yes," said Ark. "Easy."

Caina looked up at the fiery plume.

But why had Kalastus attacked the Temple of Living Flame? Caina doubted that his hatred of the Saddai had been a ruse to cover his study of pyromancy. Had he finally decided to kill them all? Or had the last threads of his sanity burned away, driving him to lash out at random?

The wagon rattled into the plaza before the Temple of Living Flame.

"Gods," muttered Ark.

The Temple stood in ruin. Half the dome had been blasted away, jagged fingers of broken stone clawing at the sky. The Temple's living quarters lay in a heap of shattered stone and burning timbers. The explosions had shattered many of the buildings surrounding the plaza, flames dancing in their ruined shells

"Stop here," said Caina. Ark brought the horses to a stop, and they climbed out. Caina had not taken three steps before she heard the sounds of fighting over the crackle of the flames. There were bodies lying motionless on the Temple's cracked steps. Caina drew knives in either hand and hurried towards the Temple, Ark besides her with sword and shield ready.

Most of the corpses were Saddai, unarmored and equipped with crude weapons, the flame tattoo blazoned across their chests. But a few of the corpses wore steel helms and gauntlets, mail shirts hidden beneath black leather jerkins.

The Black Wolves.

"What are they doing here?" said Caina.

"Killing the Sons of Corazain, it seems," said Ark, tapping one of the corpses with his boot. He listened a moment. "It sounds like they're still fighting. The back of the Temple, maybe inside."

Caina wondered if Sister Tadaia lay dead beneath the rubble.

"Let's look around," said Caina.

The Temple's doors had been blasted to twisted shards. Heaps of rubble lay on the Temple's circular floor, fallen from the ruined dome. The fire at the center of the Temple still blazed, though it had been half-buried beneath broken stone. More Sons of Corazain lay dead atop the rubble and cracked floor, along with the occasional Black Wolf.

Steel rang on steel.

Caina darted around a pile of rubble, keeping low, Ark besides her. She saw four Black Wolves fighting near the circular wall. Five Sons of Corazain struggled against them, their clubs and shortswords little use against steel mail and broadswords. Gaidan was with them, blood trickling down his neck, his face slack with terror. One by one the Black Wolves butchered the Sons of Corazain, and advanced on the Brother of the Living Flame. Gone was the furious orator who had rallied the Sons of Corazain. In his place trembled a man driven out of his mind by fear.

"Hold! Hold, I say!"

Caina knew that voice. And then she knew who had hired the Black Wolves to kill Ark.

Ephaeron picked his way through the rubble, the Black Wolves walking to his side. He stopped and pointed at Gaidan. "Priest. Where is the Ashbringer?"

"I don't...I don't know," sobbed Gaidan.

Ephaeron hissed in irritation. "Don't lie to me, fool. The hour for games is long past. The Ashbringer was here, and used his powers to level the Temple. Where is he?"

Gaidan drew himself up, some courage returning to his face. "He...he will kill you all, he is Corazain reborn, he will set the Empire to burn!" He thrust out his hand, and Caina felt a faint, feeble prickling as Gaidan tried to work a spell.

Ephaeron's lip curled in contempt, and he gestured. Caina felt the sudden rush, and Gaidan fell against the walls, screaming, his hands clenched to his temples. Ephaeron made a hooking motion, and Gaidan floated into the air, still screaming.

"Your charlatan's mummery is no match for a master of arcane science. Now. Where is the Ashbringer?" said Ephaeron.

"I don't know!" said Gaidan.

Ephaeron sighed, and gestured. Caina heard Gaidan's arm break, and the priest's scream redoubled. "I say again. Where is the Ashbringer?"

"I don't know!" sobbed Gaidan. "I don't know, I don't know, I don't know..."

Ephaeron repeated the gesture. Gaidan's other arm snapped with such force that the bones tore through the flesh.

"He came here," babbled Gaidan, "he did come here, he did come here, but...but he demanded that Sister Tadaia come with him. She refused. And then he started casting a spell...and the whole Temple exploded around us."

"Where did he go?" said Ephaeron.

"The pyramid...Corazain's pyramid, the very top...I don't...I don't..."

"Good enough," said Ephaeron, voice dripping with contempt. "I thank you for your honesty."

He made a pushing motion. Gaidan hurtled through the air, screaming, and smashed into the wall with terrific force. He collapsed in a boneless heap to the floor, blood pooling around him.

Ephaeron sighed, and sagged a little. Perhaps the effort of sorcery had tired him. "Captain Dio," he said to the nearest Black Wolf. Caina recognized the man. He was the leader of the Black Wolves who had tried to kill her and Ark. "Gather your men. We leave for Corazain's pyramid at once."

"We didn't sign up to fight sorcerers," said Dio.

Ephaeron's eyes flashed, and Dio took a cautious step back. "If you fail to do as I have bid, you will find yourself fighting a magus soon enough! But fear not. I am the only one capable of dealing with this rogue Ashbringer. You shall merely have to keep any of his followers from interrupting me."

Dio nodded, and then Ephaeron frowned, and looked around.

"Wait." Ephaeron closed his eyes for a moment, concentrating. Again Caina felt the tingle of sorcery. A sudden smile crossed his face, and he looked right at where Caina and Ark were hiding. "There you are. I was wondering when you would turn up."

"Damn," muttered Caina.

"I know you're there. You may as well show yourselves," said Ephaeron, "before my men drag you out."

Caina hesitated, and then stood, Ark besides her. Dio looked at them, and laughed in surprise.

"That was clever," said Dio, "that business at the bathhouse."

"Silence," said Ephaeron. "So Dio's eyes did not play him false. There are two of you. I should have known. The Ghosts never operate singly."

"How did you find us?" said Caina, making sure to keep her voice disguised.

"I offered your companion a glass of wine at Lord Nicephorus's banquet, and he drank. The wine was quite harmless, along with the tincture I added to it. Of my own design, I might add. Once it entered his blood, my spells could locate him anywhere in the city."

That, at least, explained how the Black Wolves had found them.

"Why are you trying to kill us?" said Caina.

Ephaeron's face hardened. "Don't play the fool with me, Ghost. I know that you are behind everything that has happened here."

Caina blinked. "What?"

"This entire affair, from the start, has been a Ghost plot to discredit the Magisterium," said Ephaeron. "When you realized that Nicephorus was a corrupt fool, you saw your chance. You encouraged the Saddai to rebel against his depredations, forming the Sons of Corazain. And then, no doubt, you gave safe haven to some Brother of the Living Flame to train as an Ashbringer, little dreaming of the horror your folly would unleash."

Caina stared at him in astonishment. "You thundering idiot," she said. "Kalastus is the pyromancer. He found one of Corazain's books and..."

"Kalastus?" said Ephaeron with a bitter laugh. "Kalastus is too stupid to clean himself, let alone to study forbidden arcane sciences. He spends half his time ranting about the Saddai, and the other half molesting the servant women. No, I knew that the Ghosts were behind this plot. And proof came when I saw him," he pointed at Ark, "at Lord Nicephorus's banquet. He was a decorated centurion in the Eighteenth Legion, and I served as battle magus for the Eighteenth. Such a coincidence captured my attention. When I observed him spying upon the Sons of Corazain, I knew that he was a Ghost, sent to incite the Saddai to rebellion."

"Idiot," said Caina, "Kalastus slaughtered every Ghost in Rasadda. His sanity has gone and I don't know what he'll do next. If you have any wit at all you'll help us to stop…"

"Enough," said Ephaeron. "I will not listen to your lies. It is clear that the Ghosts instigated this revolt to discredit the Magisterium before the Imperial Curia and the Emperor." His mouth tightened. "You fools could not even see the danger in unleashing an Ashbringer upon the city, could you? All these deaths are upon your heads. But you will answer for them, I promise." He gestured to the Black Wolves. "Captain, take them. Cripple them if you must, but I want them alive. I can interrogate them at leisure in the chapterhouse after I've dealt with the Ashbringer."

The four mercenaries started forward, swords ready, shields held out before them. Caina flung the knife in her right hand, not at the mercenaries but at Ephaeron. Her aim was true, and the blade struck home at the soft skin of his throat.

Only to bounce away in a shower of sparks.

"Please," said Ephaeron. "I was a battle magus. Did you think I would take no precautions against weapons of steel?"

Dio and two of the Black Wolves converged on Ark, who backed away, shield raised and face grim. The fourth came at Caina, shield ready to block any thrown knives, sword drawn back for a stabbing thrust. Caina snatched a dagger from her boot, watching the sword. The mercenary was too well-armored, too well-trained. No way could she take him in a straight fight.

Fine. So she would have to do something clever.

Caina tossed the dagger to her right hand and held it out before her. With her left hand she reached up and undid the black brooch holding her cloak shut. The shadow-woven cloth came close without a sound, draping over her left arm. The mercenary's eyes creased in a faint frown, but still he stepped closer. A dead Son of Corazain lay behind Caina, a short sword still in his grasp. She stepped over the corpse's left arm, and let herself stumble.

Instantly the mercenary came at her, his sword a blur of steel. Caina twisted as she fell, the blade shooting past her face, and flung the cloak at him. It billowed over his outstretched sword arm and fell over his head. Cursing, the mercenary stepped back, clawing at the cloak. Caina rolled, came to one knee, and stabbed. The mercenary yanked off her cloak just in time for her dagger to angle beneath the skirt of his mail shirt and plunge into his belly. He doubled over with a groan of pain, and Caina leapt to her feet, bringing the pommel of the dagger onto the back of his helmet. The metal dented, and the mercenary fell.

She whirled, saw Ark pressed hard by the Black Wolves, his shield gashed and torn, blood running down his face. More Black Wolves ran through the Temple doors, weapons in hand, and ran at Ark. If they saw her they would cut her down in a heartbeat.

Ephaeron. She had to deal with Ephaeron. If she could kill him, she might be able to talk the Black Wolves out of killing them. No sense fighting if Ephaeron couldn't pay them, after all. She spotted the master magus watching the fight with an impatient expression, drumming his fingers on his leg. Moving silently, Caina crept up behind him, bloody dagger ready in her hand. She drove the dagger between his shoulders, aiming for his heart.

She felt the blade rip through his cloak and robes, but when it touched his skin, there was a burst of sparks, and the dagger clanged away as if Caina had stabbed a stone wall. Ephaeron spun, pointed two fingers at her, and barked a word. Invisible force slammed into Caina's torso and flung her back a dozen steps. She rolled, trying to slow her momentum, and slammed into a pile of rubble.

"I commend your persistence," said Ephaeron, making a hooking motion with his right hand. Again Caina felt unseen force seize her, and she floated into the air, as Gaidan had floated. "But I told you that I am warded against steel."

Steel, yes. But would his spells stop a rock? Caina seized a chunk of stone as Ephaeron's sorcery lifted her into the air.

"I confess that I have failed in one respect," said Ephaeron. "I have absolutely no idea who you are. Someone else in that flirtatious minx of a Countess's household, I expect. Let's see what is under that mask, shall we?"

She heard Ark growl in sudden pain.

Ephaeron beckoned again, drawing Caina closer, and she flung the broken stone at him as hard as he could.

It hit him right in the mouth, and his head snapped back with a spray of blood. The force holding Caina vanished, and she hit the floor again. Ephaeron stumbled back, clutching at his face, and Caina scrambled to her feet. A rock, she needed a bigger rock. She looked up at the jagged fingers of the shattered dome, and wild idea took her. She yanked the grapnel and the slender knotted rope from her belt and flung it. The grapnel caught on the very edge of one of the jagged fingers, and Caina began to scramble up.

The ruined shard of dome made an ominous groaning noise.

"Get back here!" She looked down and saw Ephaeron standing below her, his mouth a bloody ruin. He raised his hand, fingers hooked into claws. Invisible power wrapped tight around Caina, and she gripped the rope tighter.

Then the shard collapsed.

Caina just had time to see the surprise on Ephaeron's face. Then she hit the ground and rolled, rocks raining around her. Fist sized stones bounced off her wounded hip, her shoulder, her arm, and Caina came to a stop with a groan. She managed to get to her knees, looking for Ephaeron.

He lay a short distance away. His head and neck had disappeared beneath a chunk of stone the size of a wagon wheel. Blood oozed out from beneath the stone, along with a gray soup that Caina realized had been Ephaeron's brain.

She climbed to her feet and saw the mercenaries staring at her. Ark lay motionless between them. She took a step towards him, and the mercenaries raised their swords.

"You killed him," said Dio, shocked. "You actually killed him."

"I'd planned it all along," lied Caina. "Shall we fight? A dead man can't pay you for it."

"He killed Pitor," said one of the mercenaries. "Stabbed him right in the belly, he did."

Caina walked to the man she had stabbed – Pitor, presumably – and retrieved her cloak. She desperately wondered if Ark was hurt, or even alive. Feigning unconcern, she settled her cloak back in place and turned to face the Black Wolves.

"I never liked Pitor," said Dio.

An inspiration struck Caina. "We could fight." She reached into her belt and produced two of the platinum coins Ephaeron had given her. "Or, you could work for the Ghosts."

She tossed the coins. They rolled across the floor and came to a halt at Dio's feet. The mercenary captain scooped them up.

"Of course," said Dio, "there's no reason to be unreasonable."

Caina walked past him and knelt besides Ark.

His armor and the left side of his face were wet with blood. His eyes were glassy, unfocused, and darted back and forth. He trembled and shuddered with every breath.

"Tanya?" he rasped, a shaking hand closing on Caina's forearm. "Is that you?"

"Your name's Tanya?" said Dio.

"Tanya, I'm sorry," said Ark. "I'm so sorry."

"No," said Caina. "Tanya's the name of his dead wife. How badly is he hurt?"

Dio hesitated. "Bad. Not so much from the wounds, but because he took so many of them. He wouldn't go down. He's a tough bastard, I'll give him that."

Caina stood. "You'll get a lot more money from me if he's still alive when I come back."

"Where are you going?" said Dio.

Two things happened then.

The tingling struck Caina again, her skin crawling, but stronger than ever before. Kalastus was working pyromancy again, but on a far larger scale.

And she heard someone make wet, thick groans of pain.

She turned, and saw Gaidan crumpled against the wall. His arms and legs rested at grotesque angles, and odd bulges deformed his belly and chest. Yet he was still alive. Caina walked to his side and knelt over him.

Gaidan's feverish eyes widened. "Are you Death, come for me?"

"I might be," said Caina, "if you don't tell me what I want to know. Why did Kalastus take Sister Tadaia to Corazain's pyramid?"

Gaidan laughed, and wept at the pain it caused him. "Or what? You'll kill me? I'm going to die anyway. You can do nothing to threaten me, nothing to stop what's coming. Nothing!"

"Yes," agreed Caina. She remembered the fear on Gaidan's face as he had prayed weeping over his bed. "You're about to die. And Kalastus is about to kill a lot of people, I'll wager. Probably a lot of Saddai. Unless I stop him. And I can't stop him unless you tell me. Which means that unless you tell me, the blood of all those people will be on your soul. When you stand before your god in another hour or so, how are you going to explain that to him?"

Gaidan's gray face crumpled in sudden horror.

"Tell me," said Caina.

"He didn't say why he wanted Tadaia," said Gaidan, sobbing. "But...but I figured out what he's going to do. Corazain's final spell."

"What?" said Caina, horrified. Corazain's final spell had leveled Rasadda, devouring the city in a colossal firestorm. Hundreds of thousands had perished as the flames devoured their flesh, no doubt screaming as Ostros had screamed. "He's going to cast Corazain's final spell?"

"Yes," said Gaidan. "It requires blood of great power. Tadaia has power, and he will use her blood to fuel the spell. Kalastus will burn every last man, woman, and child in Rasadda, and draw their life forces into himself. And then he will become Corazain reborn...and the Empire will burn!" He began to giggle, tears streaming down his face. "He will become the Burning Flame made flesh, and the Saddai will be freed from Empire."

"You fool," said Caina, "he'll burn the Saddai along with everyone else."

But Gaidan only laughed at her, sobbing at the same time, blood and tears dripping down his face.

The tingling against Caina's skin got worse. How long until Kalastus finished his spell and everyone in Rasadda died as Ostros had died?"

She had to act now.

She stood, leaving Gaidan to die, and rejoined Dio. Two of his men labored over Ark, stripping away the ruined armor and cleaning his wounds. "Stay here at the Temple and keep him under guard. As I told you, if he's still alive when I return, I'll pay you double what I've already paid. Also, there's a wagon outside, with some papers inside. Bring the papers here and don't let anything happen to them. Am I understood?"

"Perfectly," said Dio. "But where are you going?"

"I've already killed one mad sorcerer today," said Caina, running for the doors. "What's one more?"

CHAPTER 26
A FINAL CHARGE

Storm clouds raced overhead.

Caina's mount, one of the wagon horses she had stolen from Maltaer, galloped through the streets. If chaos had reigned before, now outright pandemonium gripped the city. Men and women fled for the gates, clutching their children, and few stopped to stare at the horrors taking shape in the sky.

It was not hard to see why.

The clouds were black, and flickered with ruby lighting. They moved faster than clouds had any right to move, the wind howling through Rasadda's streets. The writhing clouds spun like water pouring down a drain, whirling around a central point.

The apex of Corazain's pyramid.

The funeral pyre blazed brighter than it had before, the flames leaping higher, as if reaching for the clouds. Caina heard men shout that the end of the world had come.

They weren't far wrong.

At last she thundered into the plaza below the Great Pyramid of Corazain, the Inn of Mirrors on right, the Imperial Basilica on her left. The pyramid's raging inferno filled the plaza with bloody light. Caina urged her mount towards the pyramid, towards the steps climbing the first terrace. The climb would probably kill the poor horse, but Caina had no time.

Twin points of flame erupted atop the stairs.

Caina saw two black-armored Magisterial Guards standing atop the terrace, burning swords held out before them. The wind made the fires of their blades dance in billowing trails. Apparently Kalastus had not sent all his mind-slaved Guards to die at Romarion's mansion. Caina's mount shied at the sight of the flames, dancing sideways across the steps.

She soothed the horse, stroking its trembling flank, and the Magisterial Guards walked towards her. Caina put her boots to the horse's sides, and the terrified animal leapt forward. She leaned to the right, steering towards the nearest Guard. The blank-faced man came at her, raising his sword for an overhand blow.

Caina snatched Romarion's rapier from the saddle, braced herself, and whipped the blade around. The sword ripped halfway through the Guard's neck, driven by her arm and the horse's speed. The hilt almost tore from Caina's fingers, but she kept her grip and wheeled the horse around. The second Guard came at her, sword raised, and Caina kicked the horse to another burst of speed. The animal plowed into the Guard, knocking him off balance, and Caina brought the rapier's pommel down onto the back of his neck. The Guard's sword tumbled from his fingers, the flames vanishing, and he rolled down the stairs.

Caina reached the first terrace, the horse's hooves clicking against the polished black marble. Her horse trembled, frightened by the smell of blood, but Caina kept the beast under control. She steered for the next flight of stairs and stopped.

A dozen more Magisterial Guards stood atop the stairs, their burning swords bright points in the sullen gloom. There were more men standing behind them, Caina saw, Sons of Corazain, even ragged Saddai peasants. They shared the Guards' blank, glassy expressions, and their short swords and daggers flickered with flames as well.

Kalastus must have enslaved them as he made his way from the Temple to the pyramid. It seemed that he had retained enough sanity to guard himself from interference during his final spell. Caina could not possibly fight them all, and nor could she hope to sneak around them. Overhead the clouds continued their mad revolution, the flames from Corazain's pyre clawing ever higher. The tingling against Caina's skin grew worse. She had to reach the top of the pyramid now. Could she try to simply ride through them? She might make it past a few, but sooner or later her horse would panic, or someone would land a lucky blow…

"Ghost!"

Caina wheeled around in surprise. Men in red cloaks and leather armor hurried up the stairs, pikes and swords in hand. Valgorix walked at their head, his face strained beneath his steel helm.

"What is happening?" said Valgorix. "The heavens themselves have gone mad. Lord Nicephorus has locked himself in the Basilica, refuses to come out. I went out to do…to do something. What is going on?"

"Our murderer is atop the pyramid, Decurion," said Caina in her disguised voice. "Master Kalastus of the Magisterium. He found a book of the Ashbringers' old teachings, and fell under their influence. He's going to murder Sister Tadaia and use her blood in a ritual to summon tremendous arcane power. It will probably destroy the city, unless he's stopped."

"Gods," said Valgorix. He pointed at the Guards and the Sons of Corazain, who watched them blankly. "And them?"

"Victims of his sorcery," said Caina. "He's enslaved their minds, stolen their wills. They will fight to the death."

Valgorix stared at them, his face gray with fear. For a moment Caina thought he would turn and flee, his men following after. Then he steeled himself and nodded. "What must be done?"

Caina smiled beneath her mask. Valgorix may not have been very bright, but he did not lack for valor.

"If I can get to Kalastus I might be able to stop him," said Caina. "But I can't, not with those fellows blocking the way."

Valgorix nodded. "We can clear them for you."

"Be careful," said Caina. "They don't feel pain, not even crippling blows, and the only way to stop them is to kill them. Don't let your men handle those burning weapons. I don't know what the sorcery might do if they touch one."

"What will happen if you fail?" said Valgorix.

"If I fail," said Caina, "we will all die. Now enough talk. There's no time. We will either succeed, or die as true men of the Empire." And women, but Valgorix didn't need to know that.

"At least it will be good to fight," muttered Valgorix, "instead of chasing shadows and trying to quell the Saddai. Men!" The militiamen formed up around him. "Drive these rebels from the pyramid. They have been cursed by sorcery, and feel neither pain nor fear, and we will have to kill them all. The curse resides in their weapons, so do not touch them after you have slain their bearers." He pointed at the stairs. "At them!"

His men yelled, and they surged up the stairs. Caina put her boots the horse and galloped with them, the rapier ready. The Guards and the Sons of Corazain rushed forward, burning weapons raised. Valgorix killed one and wounded another, and then the rest of his men crashed into the melee around him. Caina's half-panicked horse trampled one man, and she killed a Son of Corazain with a quick blow from the rapier as she galloped past. Kalastus's enslaved men rushed at the militia, and Caina broke free.

For a moment she hesitated. Valgorix was badly outnumbered. But, no, she had to go on. If she failed Valgorix and his men would die anyway. So would Ark, lying wounded in the ruined Temple, and her maids at the Inn, and Sairzan, and Sister Tadaia, and every last living soul in Rasadda.

Caina jerked the horse around, made for the next flight of stairs, and kicked the poor animal to a gallop.

CHAPTER 27
TO MAKE THE WORLD BURN

Her horse staggered to the twelfth terrace, wheezing and trembling. All of Rasadda lay spread out beneath Caina like a map, the wind howling and tugging at her cloak. Caina slid from the saddle and let the exhausted beast go. If she was to have any chance at all, she had to take Kalastus unawares, and she could not do so from the back of an exhausted horse.

Throwing knife in one hand, rapier in the other, Caina ran up the final flight of stairs.

A flat expanse of gleaming black marble topped the pyramid. In the center stood a block of stone the size of a house, wreathed in Corazain's everlasting funeral pyre. Even from a distance Caina felt the terrible heat, the fire covering everything with hellish light.

An altar stood halfway between the stairs and the pyre. Sister Tadaia lay bound on the stone slab, struggling against the ropes, face drawn and lined with fear. The massive book Caina had seen on Kalastus's desk lay open on the altar, its pages unruffled by the wind. Kalastus himself stood over the book, a dagger in hand, chanting and making intricate gestures, his black robes billowing around him.

Kalastus looked…Kalastus looked younger.

Thirty years had dropped from his face, the wrinkles and lines vanishing. His hair had even grown back. Power, awful power, covered him like a cloak, and Caina felt it howling through him like a storm. He looked strong, terribly strong. If his sorcery had reversed his aging, he would have the power to kill her with little more than a glance.

The storm overhead trembled in time to his words, and the flames danced and quivered with the rhythm of his incantation. This was sorcery of a level that would have made her mother flee shrieking in terror. Every

221

muscle and nerve in Caina's body screamed for her to run far away.

But Kalastus had his back towards her.

Caina crept forward, rapier angled for a stab. Then Kalastus raised his dagger and brought it down, and for an awful moment Caina thought that she had come too late. But he slashed the blade across Tadaia's left hand, drawing blood. He rubbed the dagger over her palm twice, thoroughly soaking the blade in her blood.

Blood. She had been right. The spell required blood.

Caina came closer.

Kalastus stooped. Lines of glowing flame had been written upon the black marble, she saw, forming three concentric, glowing circles. Strange sigils and symbols filled the spaces between the circles. Kalastus placed the bloody dagger at the exact center of the sorcerous symbol, and stood.

He saw her then.

There was no hint of sanity, of reason, in his eyes.

Caina stiffened, prepared to charge him in the vain hope that she could cut him down before he worked a spell.

But Kalastus only laughed.

"It took you long enough, my wispy little Ghost," he said. His sonorous voice boomed over the wind, and it sounded almost the same, yet Caina heard the power snarling just below his words.

"You were expecting me?" said Caina, inching closer. Just a few more feet, just a few more steps, and she would be close enough to throw the knife. If Kalastus had been too careless to guard himself with a steel-warding spell...

She tossed the rapier to her left hand and the knife to her right. Kalastus seemed not to care.

"I thought the Emperor would send someone to stop me," said Kalastus. "Especially after I butchered those Ghosts and devoured their lives." He smiled. "Their screams were like kisses to me."

"You murderous dog," said Caina. She flipped the knife and gripped the blade. Distract him, distract him, just a few more steps...

"Run!" screamed Tadaia. "Whoever you are, run, run now before he kills..."

"Do shut up," said Kalastus. He flicked a finger, and Tadaia fell silent.

"You'll pay for what you've done," said Caina. Another six steps closer, she judged.

"No I won't," said Kalastus. "I see that clearly now. When I was young I saw that there were no gods, that laws were only lies that men told to one another. The rankest hypocrisy. The strong did as they pleased, and the weak were there to be used by the strong. I was strong, but others were stronger."

"You still aren't strong enough," said Caina. Another step. Another.

"You finish this spell and you'll die along with everyone else in Rasadda."

"And I will laugh as they burn," said Kalastus. His voice rose to a scream. "I hate the Saddai! I hate their language, their customs, their rank superstitions. I hate the way they smell." His face twitched back into a jerky smile. "But in their superstitions I found the answer. The Ashbringers were fools, but they had power. They are dead but I have claimed their power for my own. For I learned the truth, you see, the final truth that explains the world."

"And that truth?" said Caina, gloved fingers tightening against the knife.

"That there are no gods," said Kalastus, "and those with power may do as they please. After tonight that power …"

Caina flung the knife. Despite the wind, it was a perfect throw. It flew end over end, making for Kalastus's unprotected throat.

Or it would have, had it not come to a sudden stop in midair.

The weapon hovered a foot from Kalastus's face, caught in the grip of his will. Caina snatched another blade from her belt and flung it. Against it stopped in midair, floating next to the other.

Kalastus smiled and made a fist, and Caina felt the surge of power.

The knives began to glow, shining brighter and brighter. They lost their shape, melting into writhing orbs of molten steel. Caina began backing away. Kalastus laughed and flung out his hand.

The molten metal flew towards Caina. She dove, rolled, and felt the heat as the arcs of liquid steel flew over her head. They splattered against the black marble, freezing into twisted shapes. Caina came back to her feet, rapier in hand.

"Is that the best you can do?" she said.

Kalastus laughed, high and wild. "No. It really isn't."

He thrust out his palm, and again Caina felt the surge of power. Flames swirled around Kalastus's fingers, drew into themselves, and erupted out. A white-hot bar of liquid flame erupted from Kalastus's palm and swept towards Caina's knees. She raced to the side, cloak snapping out behind. The ribbon of flame carved into the marble terrace like a knife slicing through butter. Kalastus whipped his hand towards her, and Caina flattened herself against the stone, the white-hot bar spinning over her head. Kalastus dipped his hand, and again the line of incandescent flame sliced into the terrace.

The floor shifted and groaned beneath Caina as part of the terrace began to fall away. Cracks splintered through the black marble, and Caina felt herself sliding. She sprinted for the glowing gash Kalastus's sorcery had left in the black marble and jumped over it. A minute later part of the terrace tore free from the pyramid, falling down its sides in an echoing, booming avalanche.

"Well done!" called Kalastus. "Your will is strong. Perhaps I shall burn you alive and devour your strength for my own." He hesitated. "No. No point, not when I'm about to devour all of Rasadda. Better just to kill you."

He gestured again, and another surge of power stabbed at Caina's skin. Flames erupted from the floor before him, twenty feet tall, thirty feet tall, fifty. The wall of billowing flame roared towards Caina like a tidal wave. There was no place to dodge, nowhere to duck. Caina ran for the edge of the terrace and rolled off the edge. She tumbled down the sloped side, and jammed the rapier into a gap between the stones. A heartbeat later the wall of flames roared over the edge. For a moment Caina thought the fire would pour down over her, searing the flesh from her bones, and she screamed.

Instead the flames leapt up into the night and vanished. Caina gritted her teeth, sweat pouring down her face, and began to claw her way back up. She had to think of something, had to think of something before Kalastus killed…

Kalastus appeared at the edge of the terrace, staring down at her. "Still alive?"

He gestured.

Invisible force seized Caina, caught her in an irresistible grip. Pinned in the force of Kalastus's will, she floated up the slope until he had drawn her back to the terrace. Just as Ephaeron had floated Gaidan towards him, until magus had shattered every bone in the priest's body.

Kalastus walked back towards the altar, Caina floating after him. Her arms and legs were free, and she yanked a dagger from her boot, but she could not break free, and he stayed just out of reach.

"It is indeed impressive that you are still alive," said Kalastus, "little wonder Ephaeron was so afraid of the Ghosts. But I'm afraid I have no more time for games. You're just stubborn enough to disrupt my spell, and I can't have that. So I will kill you quickly. But first, let's see who you really are."

He lifted his hand, pushing aside her cowl, and Caina felt his will hammer into her mind. She gasped in agony, and felt her concentration start to crumple as his sorcery reached inside her head. If she did not distract him now, he would crush her will as he had crushed the wills of the Magisterial Guard.

Her arms were still free. Caina reached up and tore away her mask.

Kalastus's eyes focused on her face, and his mouth fell open.

Caina had never seen anyone look so shocked.

"You?" said Kalastus.

For just an instant, Caina felt his mental grip upon her waver. It was enough. She surged forward, dagger in hand, and stabbed with all her strength.

And as it turned out, Kalastus had not warded himself against steel after all.

Her blade plunged into his neck, and Caina yanked it savagely from side to side, opening his throat. Kalastus stumbled back with a gurgling scream, and Caina stabbed him in the chest. Still he stumbled backwards, and she stabbed him again, and again, her dagger wet with his blood. She punched him hard in the face, intending to bring him to knees, and Kalastus fell backwards.

And kept falling.

They had reached the edge.

Kalastus tumbled the fifty feet to the next terrace. He hit the black marble with a bone-snapping crunch and lay still. Caina stared down at him, breathing hard.

His fingers twitched.

And again Caina felt a surge of power.

Kalastus flopped onto his back, and Caina saw the ghastly wound in his throat shrink. The wounds on his chest began to close. Caina stepped back in sudden panic. He must have stolen enough power to heal even fatal wounds. What would it take to kill him? Would she have to cut off his head and cut out his heart?

He would not let her get that close, not again.

Caina kept backing away, the bloody dagger hanging from her fist.

The bloody dagger.

Blood. The spell required blood. And Tadaia's blood covered the dagger lying within the glowing circle...

Caina turned and sprinted for the circle. Tadaia's head turned towards her.

"Countess?" she whispered. "Is that you?"

Caina knelt besides the glowing circles, felt the power throbbing within them. Reaching for the dagger with Tadaia's blood was like pushing her hand through boiling water. But she seized the dagger, flung it as far as she could, and placed the dagger with Kalastus's blood inside the circles.

"Countess, Countess, you have to run," rasped Tadaia. "He'll kill you. He'll do worse than kill you. You can't save me. Run!"

"It doesn't matter," said Caina. She stood. "I can't get away before..."

Kalastus's roar of fury echoed over the pyramid. Caina turned, saw him levitating over the top of the terrace, wrapped in an aura of snarling power. He thrust out his hand, and his will hammered into Caina with catastrophic force. She hurtled backwards through the air at terrifying speed, spinning end over end. She saw the city flying up to meet her, realized that he had blasted her off the top of the pyramid, that she was falling to her death...

Then his will seized her again, stopping her in mid-flight. She rushed back towards the pyramid, swooping over the terraces, and came to a stop before Kalastus. His will hardened about her, holding her arms and legs immobile. Blood soaked the front of his black robes, and his face was so twisted with insane fury that it looked scarcely human.

He did not try to reach into her mind. Perhaps she had taught him better.

"You stabbed me," he whispered, rubbing his throat. A faint pink scar was the only trace of his wound. "You dared to stab me!"

Don't look at the circle, she prayed. Don't look at the circle.

"You were spying on me," he muttered. "That's why you came to the chapterhouse. You were spying on me!"

Caina did not answer.

He leaned closer, until his face was inches from hers, his eyes blazing "Do you know what I was going to do to you, my pretty little Countess? Do you? I was going to reach into your mind, to wipe away your will and your memories, until you were left with the mind of an infant. Except for the knowledge of how to please a man, for when I wished to amuse myself with you. Though I would have left you just enough of your mind to realize what had happened, and to feel horror at it."

"Go to hell," whispered Caina.

Kalastus laughed in her face, his breath hot and dry against her skin. "Don't you understand? There is no hell. Except the one I will make for you. You see, I've just thought of something better to do to you. You wanted to save all those people, didn't you? All those pathetic, stupid, stinking Saddai, you wanted to save their useless lives." He gestured, and she floated a few feet away, so she could see Kalastus and the city spread out behind him. "You're going to watch as I finish the spell, as I burn away their meaningless lives and claim their strength. You'll hear all those starving little Saddai children scream as they burn alive. And then I will lock you within your own mind, so that you will never again see anything but the flames, never again hear anything but the screams."

Caina said nothing, straining with all her will not to look at the glowing circles behind Kalastus.

"There are no gods, Countess," said Kalastus. "So I'll just have to take their place, won't I?"

He braced himself, looked down at Corazain's book, and began to chant once more. Caina felt the colossal surge of power, so strong that it felt like knives were plunging into her skin, and she screamed. The wind roared, louder and louder, until Caina could no longer hear Kalastus's chant. The clouds raced overhead, faster than maddened horses, flashing with crimson lighting.

And as Kalastus chanted, the flames of the pyre grew ever taller. Soon they had transformed into a single pulsing pillar of hellish light, clawing higher and higher. Kalastus's chant rose to an exultant scream, and he flung up his hands.

And the pillar of flame touched the clouds themselves.

The sound seemed to tear the world in half. The sky lit up from horizon to horizon, alive with fire, as if the gates of the heavens had been thrown open to rain flame upon the world. The dagger within the glowing circles began to burn, the metal twisting and melting. Kalastus laughed with delight, and turned to face Rasadda, ready to devour the lives of the Saddai as they burned.

Nothing happened.

Kalastus frowned in confusion. He looked at Tadaia, who lay untouched upon the altar, and then back at Rasadda. Confusion became outright bafflement. He looked again at Tadaia, and back at Corazain's book.

Then the pillar of flame shuddered, began to snap back and forth like a broken cord. The wind grew more violent, but it changed direction. No longer did it whirl around the pyramid.

Instead it started blowing towards Kalastus.

Kalastus staggered in sudden alarm. He looked down at the glowing circles, at the burning dagger, and his brow creased.

And Caina saw comprehension strike him.

His scream of fury threatened to split her ears, and he pointed at her, and Caina saw her death in his eyes.

She felt the power surge...but directed not at her.

Smoke rose from Kalastus's skin. He stared down at his hands in panic, and his howl of wrath became a scream of terror. Kalastus's own power bent upon him, and Caina felt the crushing grip of his will begin to waver.

The pyramid shuddered around them.

And Kalastus burst into raging flames, burning as Ostros had burned.

He raced back and forth, shrieking, his robes dissolving into ash, his skin blackening and crackling. The invisible force holding Caina vanished, and she hit the floor, climbing unsteadily back to her feet. Kalastus kept running, still screaming, while the fires burned away his flesh. It should have killed him by now, but she realized the spell was burning him alive to feed his own strength. And the mighty forces he had summoned above were spinning out of control. In flash of insight, Caina realized that Kalastus had gotten his wish. The power was pouring into him, like water piling up behind a dam.

A dam that was about to break.

She raced to the altar, drew her last knife, and began sawing through Tadaia's ropes. Kalastus's inferno grew brighter, until Caina could not look at him through the glare, until she could not hear his wails over the roar of the flames. She hacked through the last of the ropes and dragged the old woman off the altar.

"What's happening?" said Tadaia.

"Nothing good," said Caina. "Get down behind the altar and don't move."

She ducked besides Tadaia and risked one last glance over the altar. She saw Kalastus, burning as Ostros had burned, stumble over the shattered terrace's edge. Yet still the light grew brighter, the storm howling above them. Caina crouched behind the altar, tucked her head between her knees, and Tadaia did the same.

A heartbeat later the explosion came.

The pyramid shook and heaved like a child's toy. The sound felt like a living thing. Walls of flame roared past the altar, and Caina could feel the power Kalastus had summoned raging through the air. The altar grew hot, so hot that Caina could scarce huddle against it. Still the flames billowed past them. Caina might have screamed. She could not hear herself over the conflagration.

The flames died away. The sound faded to nothing. The power tingling against Caina's skin drained away. At last she dared to look up.

Raindrops struck her face. The clouds had stopped swirling, had lost their hellish glow, and now rain fell. Corazain's funeral pyre had returned to its previous size, hissing and steaming when the rain struck it. Caina looked at Tadaia.

"Are you all right?"

Tadaia blinked. "I...yes, I am. Other than my hand."

Caina stood, walked past the altar, and looked down at the pyramid.

Kalastus's death had blasted away a good portion of the pyramid's southern face. It glowed red-hot, rivulets of lava running down the stairwells, the rain dissolving into plumes of white steam. She saw scattered fires throughout the city, but other than that Rasadda seemed unchanged.

Kalastus's final spell had failed.

"That was for the Ghosts of Rasadda," she whispered to the steaming air, "you murderous son of a bitch."

She touched her father's ring beneath her glove and walked back to the altar. The glowing circles had vanished, leaving only scorch marks against the black marble. Tadaia leaned against the altar, staring at her in wonder, rainwater streaming down her face.

"You're truly a Ghost, Countess?" said Tadaia.

"Yes," said Caina. "We met that morning at the Temple. And again when I broke into your room."

Tadaia shook her head. "When...when we first met, I was sure that you were a remarkable woman. I did not realize how remarkable." She clutched at Caina's gloved hands. "Thank you, Countess. For my life. And for the life of all my people. I know what he was trying to do. He would have killed us all. We can never repay you."

"If you want to repay me," said Caina, pulling up her mask and hood, "then never tell anyone of me. Never. For if the Ghosts are to do good, we must do so in secret."

"I swear it," said Tadaia. She took a step forward, and stumbled

"Wait here," said Caina. "I'll try to find something you can use as a cane." She started towards the broken, steaming terrace. Maybe Romarion's rapier had survived the explosion.

Something struck her boot.

Caina looked down.

Corazain's book lay against her foot, undamaged by the firestorm, untouched by the rain. Little hisses of steam rose where the water hit the pages. Caina stooped and picked up the book. It felt warm against her gloved hands, and the tingle was not unpleasant. The black characters on the pages drew her eyes.

She though of how Kalastus had healed the wounds she dealt him. Could not the same happen for her? Might not this book have the power to heal her scars? The thought of holding a child, her child, struck Caina, and brought tears to her eyes. What would that be like, to hold her own child in her arms? That could be hers. The book could teach her. She need only...

She remembered Ostros screaming that alley.

She remembered her mother, gloating over her father's comatose form.

She remembered Maglarion standing atop that tower, illumed by the light from the great bloodcrystal.

Caina slammed the book shut and tucked it under her arm, wrapping it in her cloak so that Tadaia would not see it.

"There's nothing," said Caina when she returned to Tadaia. "I'll just have to help you down. We'll take it slowly."

"Thank you, again," said Tadaia, hooking her arm around Caina's. She sighed. "It's over. It's finally over, thank the Living Flame."

"No," said Caina. "It's almost over."

There were two more things to do.

CHAPTER 28
IN THE SHADOWS

Caina returned to the Temple of Living Flame with Sister Tadaia. A crowd had gathered around the Temple, and the old woman took charge of them at once, directing them to tend to the fires and help those hurt in the explosions. Caina envied Tadaia her energy. The stitched wounds on Caina's hip and shoulder throbbed, the bruises and cuts ached, and her face still stung from the heat atop Corazain's pyramid. She wanted to collapse into bed and sleep for a week.

Not yet, though. There was still work to do.

With the help of Dio and the Black Wolves, she got Ark loaded into the wagon and back to the Inn of Mirrors just before sunrise. The maids, already terrified from the colossal explosion, almost went out of their minds with fright at the appearance of a half-dozen armed mercenaries and a hooded specter wrapped in black. Caina calmed them down and directed them to be quiet, lest they inadvertently wake the timid young countess sleeping in the next room. They set up a makeshift bed and laid Ark upon it. Caina paid the Black Wolves and sent them on their way.

Once they had left, she went outside, scrambled up her rope, and climbed back into the bedroom. She stripped off her black clothes and pulled on a robe. Corazain's book she wrapped in her cloak and hid at the bottom of her chest.

Then she unbarred the door and staggered into the sitting room, feigning confusion.

The maids stared at her in surprise.

"My lady!" said Julia. "What happened to you? You look dreadful!"

"A…a terrible noise woke me up," said Caina. "I went to the balcony to look and thought the sky was filled with fire. I fell and hit my head on the railing. I only just now woke up."

She saw Ark watching her, his eyes only half-open. He was nearing forty, she knew, but for the first he looked almost…old, lying there.

"What happened to Ark?" said Caina, cutting off the maids' questions. "He's been hurt!"

"I don't know, my lady," said Cornelia. "Some strange men brought him here. They said that he had been wounded fighting rebels in the street."

"Go bring him some food," said Caina. "At once."

The maids hurried out, shutting the door behind them. Caina knelt besides Ark's bed.

"I saw," he rasped, coughing. Caina gave him a goblet of watered wine to clear his throat. "I saw you pull that rock down on Ephaeron's head. The damnedest thing I ever saw. I never thought anyone could get the better of him like that."

"How are you feeling?"

Ark coughed again. "Like a piece of meat hung up in a butcher shop." He shook his head. "But I've been cut up worse. And I lived." He squinted at the windows. "Is it morning?"

"It is," said Caina. "You were out for most of the night."

"What happened?" said Ark. "Is Kalastus still alive?" He started to sit up. "Is…"

"Quiet," said Caina, giving him a gentle push back onto the bed. "I will tell you, but only if you do not move and do not talk."

Ark scowled, but said nothing. So Caina told him what had happened. The battle at the foot of the pyramid. The confrontation before Corazain's pyre. The colossal forces Kalastus had summoned into the sky over Rasadda, and what those forces had done to him at last.

She did not mention the book.

Ark started to make a wheezing, rasping noise, and for an awful moment Caina thought that he was choking.

He was laughing.

"What in the hell," said Caina, "is so funny?"

"Everything," said Ark. "You tricked him. You switched the daggers, and he didn't even think to look." He laughed, winced, and laughed against anyway. "All that power, and he didn't even think to look at the dagger. You tricked the bastard into blowing himself to hell with a bloody dagger. You are a madwoman, Countess. Gods!" Ark roared with laughter.

"Oh, stop," said Caina. "You're going to split your stitches."

Ark nodded. "Gods. It's still funny." He winced. "And you're right. That hurt."

"Just lie still," said Caina, rising. "I'll see if I can find something to help you sleep…"

His callused hand caught hers.

"Caina," said Ark.

She looked at him in surprise. It was only the second time he had ever called her by name.

"You did what I could not," said Ark. "You avenged the Ghosts. You were right from the beginning, when you blamed the magi. Forgive me. I thought you were a fool. Forgive…"

"Arcion. Enough," said Caina, kneeling besides the bed. "You give me too much credit. I would have been killed a dozen times, if not for your help." She smiled, placed his hand on his chest, and let go. "Now go to sleep. You're going to need your rest."

Ark nodded, closed his eyes. "Will we leave Rasadda soon?"

"Yes," said Caina. "Very soon. After I take care of a few things."

That night Valgorix walked into his room, helm tucked under his arm, his graying hair plastered with sweat.

Caina stepped out of the darkness, her cloak blurring with the shadows. "Decurion."

Valgorix flinched, reached for his sword, stopped himself. "So. You lived through that explosion. I was sure that you were dead."

"As did I, but here I am," said Caina. "I am pleased that you survived."

Valgorix shrugged, walked to his bed, sat down. "It was a close thing. Those…Magisterial Guards did not want to die. Then we saw the light burst from the pyramid, and fire fill the sky. The Guards collapsed. Like they were puppets whose strings had been cut."

Considering that their puppet master had been burning in his own sorcerous fires at that point, Caina was not surprised.

"Then the ground started to shake," said Valgorix, "and I was sure that you had failed. We ran for it, got away just before the explosion came. Good thing, too." He shook his head. "The side of the pyramid just…melted. Like lava. I thought it was the end of the world. But the flames went out…and it was over." He looked up at her. "Is it truly over, Ghost?"

"It is," said Caina. "Kalastus is dead. He summoned more power than he could control, and it consumed him. He burned, just as his victims burned."

"Good," said Valgorix, his voice hard.

"I require only one more service from you, Decurion," said Caina.

Valgorix sagged. "Oh."

"Are Lord Nicephorus's associates still with him in the Imperial Basilica?" said Caina.

Valgorix scowled. "Yes. The craven fools still haven't come out."

"Good. Your task will be all the easier, then," said Caina. "At first light you will take your best men to the Basilica and arrest every last one of those merchants. You will charge them with slave trading, embezzlement, and illegal seizure of land. Furthermore, you will announce that their illegal land purchases are null and void, and therefore the Saddai peasants can return to their homes without fear of reprisal."

Valgorix laughed. "I will, will I? And how will you keep Lord Nicephorus from taking my head?"

"The Lord Governor will be in no position to object."

Valgorix blinked, puzzled. "But why wouldn't Nicephorus object? Not unless he...unless he..."

Caina saw him get it.

His eyes got wide. "You're going to..."

"Nothing," said Caina. "I will do nothing. Furthermore, you have never met me, never spoken to me, and if anyone asks, the Ghosts are a legend, a peasants' fable. Am I understood?"

Valgorix swallowed, nodded. "Perfectly."

"You'll be a hero, Decurion," said Caina. "Think of how it will look to the Imperial Council. You, and you alone, had the courage to stand against the corruption and slave-trading in the Saddai province, to restore the lands to their proper owners. You might receive command of your own Legion when all is said and done, perhaps even adoption into a noble House. All this will be yours, if only you do as I have bidden...and you forget I ever existed."

Valgorix sighed. "Very well." He stood up, set his helm on his head. "I'll have to make preparations..."

When he turned his back, Caina whirled, dropped out the window, and braced herself on the ledge. A moment later Valgorix stuck his head out the window, looking back and forth. Once again he failed to look down.

"Damn it," Valgorix muttered. He disappeared back into the window.

Caina counted to a hundred, and vanished into the night.

###

Lord Governor Anatsius Nicephorus paced the balcony atop the Imperial Basilica, a skin of wine in his hand. He looked quite drunk, and glowered at the city with a sullen, fearful expression. He kept looking at the scarred, misshapen bulk of Corazain's pyramid, as if unable to believe his eyes.

Caina seized his hair with one hand and put her dagger against his throat. The skin of wine fell at their feet.

"I'm going to give you one chance, and one alone," hissed Caina.

"You have stolen the peasants' lands, driven them from their homes, sold their children into slavery, and done nothing as a pyromancer rampaged through your city. Your actions are a stench in the nostrils of the Emperor. For all that you have earned death a dozen times over, but despite my duty I am weary of killing. In the name of the Emperor, I command you to repent of your crimes, resign the rank of Lord Governor, and return with me to the Imperial capital for judgment."

Nicephorus twisted against her, growling. "I have done nothing wrong! It is my right to do with this province and its people as I see fit!"

"So be it," said Caina.

She slammed the hilt of the dagger into his nose, stunning him. As his hands flew to his broken nose, Caina seized his arm, twisted it behind him. Nicephorus doubled over with a strangled cry of pain.

And before he could recover, she grabbed the back of his belt, flipped him over the elaborate marble railing, and let him fall.

His scream just had time to start, and then it came to a sudden end. Caina looked over the railing, saw him lying motionless on the basalt pavement a hundred feet below. She picked up the wineskin and tossed it after him.

Lord Governor Nicephorus, it seemed, had fallen to his death in a drunken stupor.

Caina reached into the satchel slung over her shoulder, pulled out the bundle of letters and papers Maltaer had given her, and flung them over the railing as well. They landed besides Nicephorus's outstretched hand with a thump.

Let people draw their own conclusions.

Two weeks later, Ark seemed well enough to travel, so Caina decided to leave Rasadda.

Organized chaos had reigned in the plaza ever since Lord Nicephorus had been found dead in a pool of wine, a stack of incriminating documents besides him. At first Caina thought a riot would erupt, but Sister Tadaia had taken charge, calling upon the Saddai to swear only to reclaim the lands that had been rightfully theirs. Now clerks sat at tables, watched over by Valgorix's men, sifting through papers and competing claims. No one seemed too eager to display their flame tattoos. Popular rumor held that the Living Flame had descended in wrath upon both the pyramid and the Temple, throwing down Gaidan for his belief in the heretical Burning Flame and Nicephorus for his greed and cruelty.

Caina knew better.

The book hidden in her chest often intruded upon her thoughts.

She stood outside the Inn, watching the crowds before the Basilica. Nearby Sairzan's servants and her maids loaded the coach. Ark stood besides her, leaning on a crutch, and had insisted upon wearing his sword belt.

"Countess!"

Caina turned her head in surprise.

Septimus Romarion strode towards her, a new rapier at his belt.

"Master Romarion," said Caina. "It is good to see that you are well. I had feared you were caught up in these momentous events."

"You've been hurt," said Romarion, peering at her face. The bruise on her jaw from the Sons of Corazain was still visible, and her lips were still chapped and cracked from the heat atop the pyramid.

"Yes," said Caina. "Some rebels broke into my room and tried to kill me." She sighed. "I fear that I've had quite enough of this city. I am leaving for Mors Crisius, and will take ship from there to the Imperial capital. Will you be joining me?"

Romarion shook his head. "I fear not. The chaos in the city has hurt my business. I have no choice but to go to Alqaarin, to try and rebuild my fortunes there."

Wise of him.

"Alas," said Caina. "It seems that you will not be paying court to me after all."

"Though I do regret it sorely," said Romarion. "Countess, I hope you will not think me forward if I say that you are a very exceptional young woman."

"You flatter me, sir," said Caina.

"No," said Romarion. "Perhaps after I return to the Empire, we…"

He was staring at Ark's sheathed broadsword.

Caina frowned.

Romarion looked at her, at Ark, and then back to her.

She saw the horrified recognition flood into his eyes. For a moment no one said anything. Ark's hand curled around the hilt of his sword, and panic flooded into Romarion's face.

Very slowly, very carefully, Caina put a single finger to her lips.

Romarion gave a jerky nod, turned, and hurried out of the plaza as if all the hounds of hell were on his heels.

"Do you think we'll have to kill him?" said Ark after a while.

"No," said Caina. "He's too frightened. I don't think he'll ever return to the Empire."

Ark grunted and let go of his sword. "Wise of him."

###

A week after that, Caina and Ark sat in the common room of Halfdan's inn at Mors Crisius. Her circlemaster brought them goblets of wine, and sat down across from them. Caina told him everything that had happened.

Except for the book.

Halfdan digested it all for a moment.

"Did you really have to kill Nicephorus?" said Halfdan.

"Yes," said Caina. "He tolerated slavers. The Ghosts have killed governors for less."

"And if she had not, I would have," added Ark.

"True enough," said Halfdan. "It may please you to know that a message arrived yesterday. The Emperor approves of what you have done, and sends his thanks. He says you have averted a great threat to the peace of the Empire, and can retire in comfort for the rest of your days, if you wish."

"No," said Caina. She touched her father's ring where it hung against her skin. "No. Not while there are more men like Kalastus out there."

"That could take some time," said Halfdan.

"I know," said Caina.

Halfdan nodded. "You've done very well. Both of you."

"Thank you," said Caina, and Ark nodded.

"You'll be leaving tomorrow for Malarae, as Countess Marianna Nereide," said Halfdan. "There are some things happening there that I would like you to investigate." He looked at Ark. "You, my friend, will accompany her, since you two seem to work so well together."

They talked for some time more, and then Halfdan went to bed.

"Countess," said Ark. He hesitated. "In our travels. We will take the time to look for Tanya, will we not?"

"We will," said Caina. "I swear it. Good night, Ark."

He smiled and limped off to bed. Caina watched him go.

She had told neither of them about the book. It was clear that it had some sort of sorcerous effect upon its possessor. Even now she felt it in her thoughts, whispering to her, and she began to understand how Kalastus had been ensnared by it. If she told Ark and Halfdan about it, what would it whisper to them? Would it promise Ark his wife and child back? Would he have the strength to resist its call?

Caina did not know if she herself could resist, but she intended to find out.

###

Two days later Caina, Ark, and her maids lodged on a ship traveling westward across the Alqaarin Sea, making for the city of Arzaxia, and then the Imperial capital of Malarae.

Caina walked across the deck to the helm. "Captain?"

The captain bowed. He reminded her somewhat of Maltaer. "Yes, Countess?"

"Do you remember the chest I had you bring on board?"

The captain frowned. "Yes, my lady. Though for the life of me, I can't imagine why you wanted a chest full of bricks carried on board."

"That is my own concern," said Caina, her best Imperial hauteur in her voice, "and I am paying you well enough for it. Where is it?"

"In the hold, my lady," said the captain.

"Good. I wish to be alone with it for a few moments," said Caina. "Then send four of your strongest men to carry it on deck."

The captain bowed. "As you will."

Caina climbed down into the hold. The iron chest, filled with bricks, sat near the ladder. She opened the lid and busied herself removing the top layer of bricks. After that was done, she unwrapped the bundle hidden beneath her cloak.

Corazain's book rested in her hands, and again she felt the allure. It had the power to heal her. Halfdan had said she could retire in comfort, had he not? She could find a worthy husband, bear not one child but many, could watch her sons and daughters grow up around her.

All that could be hers. She need only read the book, to learn its secrets. She need only...

She need only do what Kalastus had done.

There were tears in her eyes when she dropped the book into the chest. One by one she restacked the bricks upon it. Then she closed the lid, locked it, and tucked the key into a pocket.

"My lady?" The captain stared down at her. "Are you ready?"

"I am," said Caina, her voice calm.

As it turned out, it took six strong men and three pulleys to get the chest up on deck.

"What should we do with it?" said the captain.

"Throw it over the side," said Caina.

He gave her a suspicious look. "What did you put inside?"

"Love letters," said Caina. "A rich merchant won my heart, and he betrayed me."

The captain and his men shared a knowing look. "Ah."

After a few more moments of struggle, they heaved the chest over the side. It struck with a mighty splash, and vanished at once beneath the waves. Caina watched as all of Corazain's murderous secrets vanished forever.

She flipped the key into the water, touched her father's ring, and smiled.

"Are you well, Countess?" said the captain.

"Yes," said Caina. "Very well."

So long as men like Kalastus blighted the world, they would need to fear the shadows.

For in the shadows waited the Ghosts.

THE END

Thank you for reading "Ghost in the Flames." Turn the page to read the first chapter of the next GHOSTS novel, GHOST IN THE BLOOD.

GHOST IN THE BLOOD BONUS CHAPTER

There was going to be trouble.

Caina realized it the moment she walked through the door.

She would have expected to see a liveried steward standing inside, waiting to greet the White Road Inn's wealthy guests, or perhaps a porter or two. But instead of a steward or porters, she saw a dozen rough-looking men sitting at the tables, drinking and playing cards. Some looked like sailors and others like mercenaries, but none of them looked like sort of men she expected to see at a place like the White Road Inn.

Every eye turned to look at her as she walked into the common room, examining her like a cut of meat on the butcher's block.

It was not a comfortable sensation.

One of the men rose. He looked like a sailor, with a thick mane of gray hair over a leathery face. A sword in a worn scabbard hung from his belt. Caina found her eyes drawn to the bracers covering his forearms. Black leather, with various odd sigils cut into their sides.

She had seen those sigils before.

"Aye, girl?" said the gray-haired man, speaking in Caerish with a thick Kyracian accent. "What's your business here?"

Caina drew herself up, tried to look authoritative, and answered him in the same language. "What is your name?"

"Name's Tigrane," said the man, smiling at her. "I suppose you could say that I'm the steward of this Inn."

One of the men chuckled.

"I shall have you know that I am Julia, a maid in the service of the Countess Marianna, of House Nereide," said Caina, clutching her saddlebags. "My mistress has sent me ahead to prepare her rooms for her."

Tigrane stared at her, a cold glint in his eye. "We've no rooms available."

"But…but that's impossible," said Caina. She let a little fear creep into her voice. "My mistress stays here every year at this time, when she makes the journey from the Imperial capital to Marsis. The arrangements have been made well in advance."

Tigrane gave an indifferent shrug. "Alas. Yet we've no rooms available."

Caina stared at him for a moment. "Very well. I shall go and inform my mistress. Know that she shall be wroth."

She turned to go.

Tigrane reacted exactly as she expected.

"Wait," he said, stepping towards her. "Perhaps I spoke hastily. All our rooms are booked, but we can make other arrangements. And I cannot let a pretty young thing like you walk alone into the night. There are robbers and slavers about, you know."

Another man chuckled.

"Yes," said Caina. "I am sure. Very well." She lifted her chin, glaring up at him. "Take me to my mistress's chambers."

Tigrane gave a mocking little bow. "As you will."

Caina adjusted one of the bags, hand curling about the dagger hidden within. Yet Tigrane made no move against her. He took a lantern and led her up two flights of stairs, to the Inn's top floor, and ushered her into a suite. The rooms were richly furnished, and the windows had a splendid view of the courtyard and the moon-lit sea beyond.

"Here you are," said Tigrane. "I'm sure your Countess will find these rooms most satisfactory."

"She will," said Caina, dropping the saddlebags on a table.

Tigrane lit a few of the oil lamps. "Some of my men will be along shortly, to make certain you are comfortable." He gave her another cold smile and left the room.

"Yes," said Caina to the closed door. "I'm sure that you will." She was sure that Tigrane and his men had plans for her. Plans that ended with her naked corpse in a shallow grave behind the Inn.

Fortunately, she had plans of her own.

She barred the door and walked to the table, shrugging out of her serving maid's dress. Her saddlebags held more useful clothing. She pulled on loose black pants, black boots, black gloves, and a heavy padded black jacket, lined with steel plates to deflect knives. A man's worn signet ring went on the first finger of her left hand, beneath the glove. Around her waist went a belt of throwing knives and other useful tools. Daggers went into concealed sheaths in her boots, and more throwing knives beneath her sleeves. A mask of loose black silk covered her face, concealing everything but her eyes.

Last came the cloak.

It was a wondrous thing, light as air and black as shadow. Halfdan had told her that the great wizards of old had created these cloaks, weaving shadows together with spider silk. The cloak was virtually weightless, and blended and merged with the shadows in the room. Caina shrugged on the cloak, pulling up the cowl to conceal her face.

She was a Ghost nightfighter, a sworn spy and servant of the Emperor. Tigrane and his gang of thugs no doubt expected to deal with a helpless serving woman. They were in for a surprise.

She hoped they enjoyed it.

Caina wrapped the empty saddlebags in her discarded dress and tossed them under the bed. She crossed to the windows and opened the shutters. Moonlight flooded into the room, along with the steady crash of surf breaking against the shore. A broad ledge stretched beneath the window, circling around the Inn. Caina dropped onto the ledge, her cloak flowing behind her, crossed three windows down, and popped the latch with a quick flick of a knife. Inside she found another empty bedroom, rather less opulent than the suite Tigrane had given her.

The hall outside the bedroom was empty. Caina had a great deal of experience moving quietly, much of it under dangerous conditions, and had no difficulty keeping silent as she crept down the halls. She glided down the stairs, settled into the shadows on the landing, and watched the common room.

Voices drifted to her ears.

"Claims she's a maid," said Tigrane, speaking to a man out of sight. "In the service of a Countess Marianna Nereide. Says her mistress is coming soon." He shook his head. "I told you this was a risk."

"It was necessary," answered another voice, deeper and commanding. The voice spoke Caerish with the cold accents of a Nighmarian lord. "Our employer required additional merchandise immediately, and this was the safest way to do it. Too many more people disappearing in the city might draw attention."

"What about the maid?" said Tigrane. "What do we do about her? Does she go into inventory?"

"Don't be foolish," said the second man. "Innkeepers and servants are one thing. A highborn Imperial noblewoman is quite another. Someone will notice if she goes missing. Even taking a member of her household might draw unwanted attention."

"I say we take the maid with the others," said Tigrane, walking around a table. Caina leaned forward, trying to see Tigrane's companion. "And then when this Countess arrives, we can do the same for her."

"No," said the second man. "Kill the maid. Bury her corpse and all her possessions in the cellar. Once she's dead, take our inventory and head for the ship. Burn the Inn after we leave. At dawn, we'll sail for Marsis. By the time the Countess and her entourage arrive, we'll be long gone, with no evidence left behind."

Tigrane grinned. "And the men can enjoy themselves before we finish off the maid."

Caina grimaced.

"No," said the second man. "No rapes."

"Why not?" said Tigrane. "It's not as if we're going to sell her. No sense keeping her undamaged if no one's going to buy her."

"Because," said the second man, "men with fun on their minds make mistakes. And there can be no mistakes here, Tigrane. If we leave behind evidence of our presence – any evidence at all – we'll have the Ghosts on our trail."

"The Ghosts?" said Tigrane, a note of fear in his voice. "Gods of the brine, not again. The last time was a disaster."

Caina smirked behind her mask.

"Then you see the necessity for caution," said the second man. She heard heavy footsteps. "Still. It's on your head. Do as you will with her…but only after you take her and all her possessions to the cellar. I don't want a shred of evidence left in that suite. A single mistake and I'll gut you. Or I'll turn you over to our client. You'll wish I had killed you then."

"Yes, my lord," said Tigrane as the second man came into sight.

The deep-voiced man looked nothing like Tigrane. This man was tall and pale, his hair black, his face gaunt, his lips framed in a trimmed beard. He wore fine clothes and jewelry, a broadsword at his belt, and the same sort of strange bracers as Tigrane. Caina recognized him at once and suppressed a hiss of excitement.

Lord Naelon Icaraeus.

Son of Haeron Icaraeus, the traitor lord who had supplied the necromancer Maglarion with slaves for his experiments. Naelon has followed in his father's steps. He was a rebel lord and traitor to the Emperor, and most wanted and elusive slave trader in the western Empire.

And he was here, within her grasp.

"You three," said Tigrane, pointing to some of the men. "You heard his lordship. Get ropes and a gag, and take that maid down to the cellar. Do whatever you want with her, but only after you get her downstairs. Kill her when you're done. Understand?"

"Aye," said one of the men. They rose and went in search of their weapons.

Caina headed up the stairs, moving as fast as she dared. She contemplated hiding and discarded the idea. If the men searched the suite and found no trace of her, they would report back to Tigrane, and Icaraeus would realize that something had gone amiss. Better to spread confusion. And fear.

She reached the third floor, went out the window, and climbed back into her suite. Dousing the lamps, she looked around for a suitable hiding place. The wardrobe seemed more than adequate, and she climbed atop it, her cloak mingling with the darkness. Her heart raced with fear and anticipation, and she slipped one of the daggers from her boots. She was fast, but most men were stronger than her, and she could not win a straight fight against three opponents.

So she would not fight fair.

A moment later someone knocked at the barred door.

"Miss?" came a man's rough voice. "Come out. We've got a surprise for you."

She heard the laughter through the door.

The door shuddered against the bar.

"The little whore barred it," snarled another man.

"Well, you've got that axe, haven't you? Use it!"

There was a crack, and an axe blade came through the door. Caina waited as they chopped through the thick wood. Finally the men crashed into the suite, weapons in hand.

"Come here," said the first man, lifting his axe. "We'll have ourselves a good time, won't we?" They laughed. "She's hiding somewhere. Find her."

Two of the men entered the bedroom. The man with the axe turned towards the wardrobe, frowning. He grinned, and reached for the wardrobe doors.

He never once looked up. People never looked up.

Caina shoved off the wardrobe and fell upon him, her boots smashing into his chest. The man hit the floor with a stunned grunt, the axe flying from his hand. Caina landed upon him, throwing her momentum into her shoulder and arm. She just had a chance to glimpse his eyes, shocked and terrified, before her dagger plunged into his throat. Hot blood splashed over her gloved hand, his boots drumming his death spasm against the floor.

Caina sprang to her feet, snatched up the fallen axe, and hurried across the room. She pressed herself to the wall besides the bedroom door.

Laughter came from the bedroom. "Eh? What's that? She's putting up a fight, is she?" The other two men walked back into the parlor, grinning.

The grins vanished as they saw the corpse upon the floor.

"What the devil…"

Caina pushed away from the wall, axe in both hands, and buried it in the nearest man's neck. He stumbled forward with a choking gurgle, blood pouring from his mouth. Caina shoved him, and he stumbled into the last man. Both went down in a heap. She dropped to one knee, right hand dipping into her boot, and came up holding another dagger.

The last man didn't even have time to scream.

Caina retrieved her blades and wiped them clean, trying to ignore the churning nausea. The men had been slave traders. They would have killed her, after torturing and raping her for sport. Surely they had deserved to die. Yet still she wanted to drop to her knees and throw up. She remembered the dead men lying upon the floor of Maglarion's lair...

Enough. Sooner or later Tigrane and Icaraeus would realize that something had gone wrong. She had to put that time to good use. Doubtless Icaraeus had letters with him, documents that could bring him down, and all his clients and allies as well. If Caina could escape with those documents, Icaraeus would pay. And if her path should cross Naelon Icaraeus's before the night was done...well, he had sold hundreds, perhaps thousands, into slavery in the lands beyond the Empire.

His death would not trouble her in the least.

Caina retrieved the axe from the dead man's neck and slipped out the window, marking her slow way along the ledge. She rounded a corner and stopped, peering into the courtyard. A man stood guard before a set of sunken stairs, no doubt leading into the Inn's cellar. He was clever enough not to hold a torch, keeping his night vision intact, and kept watch upon the road.

But he didn't look up. People never looked up.

Caina dropped the axe. It struck the back of the guard's skull with crack, and the man collapsed. She climbed down the wall as fast as she dared, hurried over, and gave him a quick look. The back of his head was wet with blood, and he would not be waking up anytime soon, if ever. She pulled a set of keys from his belt, hurried down the stairs, and unlocked the cellar door.

The smell of blood and excrement hit her in the face.

Wine casks stood against the walls, secure in their wooden racks. Fifteen men, women, and children sat chained wrist and ankle to the racks, gags stuffed into their mouths. The only light came from a pair of lanterns on a table against the far wall. Another set of stairs no doubt led to the common room.

The captives, Icaraeus's "inventory", looked at her with wide and terrified eyes.

"Do not speak," said Caina, disguising her voice. Her words rasped and snarled like something inhuman. The captives flinched away even further. "Obey my commands, and you may yet live through this night."

She knelt besides the nearest man, unlocked his shackles, and wrenched the gag from his mouth.

"Who...who are you?" whispered the man. He was fat, his clothes rank with sweat. "Are you a demon, come to drag us down to hell?"

"Your name?" said Caina.

"Oscar, keeper of the White Road Inn."

"Lord Naelon Icaraeus. The man who took you captive," said Caina. "He has some papers in his possession. Where are they?"

"I...I..."

Caina hissed, lowered her shadowed face closer to his. "Where are they?"

"In my room, under the stairs," said Oscar, "I saw him writing in there."

"Good," said Caina, handing him one of the keys. "Get to work. The rest of you, remain silent."

The innkeeper understood and started to work. Caina moved down the line of captives, loosing their chains.

"Who are you, sir?" said one of the women, rubbing her wrists. Oscar's daughter, to judge from the resemblance.

"That is not your concern," said Caina. "Depart this cellar, and take the road south to Marsis as quickly as you are able."

"What of the slavers?" demanded Oscar. "Won't they just recapture us?"

Caina shook her head. "They've a ship waiting in a cove a few miles north of here. You were to have been loaded aboard that ship at dawn. Instead the slavers will flee to it shortly."

"Why would they retreat to their ship?" said Oscar. "They have no reason to flee."

"No, no reason," said Caina. "Not until I burn the building down."

"My inn! You can't!"

"You can either run for your life," said Caina, "or you can spend the rest of your life tending some Istarish emir's harem. After they make a eunuch of you."

That got his attention.

Shouts of alarm came from above, followed by the stamp of running feet. Someone must have found the bodies.

"Go, now," said Caina.

Oscar herded the others towards the cellar door. Caina snatched up both of the lanterns from the table and followed them. The captives stumbled into the night, fleeing towards the southward road. Caina crossed to the nearest ground-floor window, kicked open the shutters, and flung the lantern inside.

It shattered against the wall, hot glass and burning oil falling onto the bed. The blankets caught fire, embers falling onto the rich carpet. Caina kicked open another window and flung in the second lantern. Again the blankets caught fire, the flames spreading to the carpet and the tapestries. Caina vaulted through the window, dodged around the flames, and pushed open the door.

The fire spread to the hallway, licking at the varnished wooden walls.

Caina had no time to watch its progress. She hurried to the common room and looked around. The men had vanished, no doubt in search of whoever had killed their fellows. Caina ripped a tapestry from the wall and threw half of it into the fireplace, leaving the other half to dangle upon the floorboards.

As the flames spread, she ran across the room and opened the door under the stairs. It opened into the innkeeper's richly furnished room, lit by a single lantern on the table. A writing desk sat near the door, covered with papers.

Icaraeus's papers.

Caina seized them. There was a ledger, and something that looked like a journal, and she took them both. A leather satchel lay against the wall, and she dropped the papers, books and all, into it. Men began shouting, and Caina heard the heavy thud of running footsteps on the stairs. No doubt someone had noticed the fires, and the slavers had come to the conclusion that they were under attack.

She ran back into the common room, surprised by how quickly the fire had spread. A pair of mercenaries ran down the stairs, taking no notice of her, and escaped into the night. Tigrane's angry bellow rang down the stairs, followed by Icaraeus's cold voice giving rapid orders. Caina hurried back into the hallway, ducking low to avoid the thick black smoke billowing from the bedrooms. She entered a room still untouched by the spreading flames and went out the window.

The drum of hooves came to her ears, galloping away to the north. The slavers were making a run for it. Caina slipped around the inn, saw the horsemen pounding towards the road.

And then, for just a moment, she saw Lord Naelon Icaraeus himself.

He sat atop a horse not twenty feet away, turning his head to shout something at Tigrane. His sword was in its sheath, his whole attention diverted away from Caina, and he wore no armor.

Perfect.

Her hand plunged to her belt, coming up with a throwing knife. She stepped towards him, arm and shoulder flung back, blade clenched between gloved flingers. Her whole body snapped like a bowstring and sent the knife hurtling towards Icaraeus.

The blade flew true and plunged into Icaraeus's exposed neck.

Or it would have, had it not bounced away with a green flash. For a moment the bracers on his arms flickered with the same eerie light, the strange sigils shining with a sickly emerald glow. Pins and needles erupted over Caina, her skin crawling. She knew that feeling.

Sorcery. Some sort of sorcery to turn aside steel had been laid upon those bracers.

Icaraeus turned in the saddle, face tight with anger, his eyes falling upon Caina.

"My lord!" shouted Tigrane, "we must go, they'll be upon us at any moment!"

Icaraeus jerked the reins and slammed his heels into the horse. The beast galloped into the night, Tigrane close behind. Caina stared after them for a moment, and stooped to retrieve her throwing knife. The blade had been warped, almost as if it had been thrust into a forge and left to melt.

So the rumors had been true.

She shoved the ruined weapon into the satchel.

It was time to go. She doubted Icaraeus and his gang would return. But the fire would be visible for miles, and sooner or later someone would come to investigate. Caina had no wish to be found. Besides, she had come here to seize Icaraeus's papers, and she had them.

Caina grinned.

Freeing the slaves had been a bonus.

One of Icaraeus's men had taken her horse, so Caina walked into the night, her cloak blending with the darkness.

ABOUT THE AUTHOR

Standing over six feet tall, Jonathan Moeller has the piercing blue eyes of a Conan of Cimmeria, the bronze-colored hair a Visigothic warrior-king, and the stern visage of a captain of men, none of which are useful in his career as a computer repairman, alas.He has written the DEMONSOULED series of sword-and-sorcery novels, the TOWER OF ENDLESS WORLDS urban fantasy series, THE GHOSTS series about assassin and spy Caina Amalas, the COMPUTER BEGINNER'S GUIDE sequence of computer books, and numerous other works. Visit his website at:
http://www.jonathanmoeller.com